THE CONSIGLIERE

REVELATION: PART ONE

THE VALENTINI FAMILY

SERENA AKEROYD

FOREWORD & TRIGGERS

LOVELIES,

Welcome back to the world of the Five Points' Mob Universe and, more specifically, to the many trials and tribulations of the Valentini Family!

Just a few things for you to note…

Please make sure to always check the chapter headings for references to dates and character POVs. :)

If you don't know what the Euro 2020 Final is, it's a European soccer competition. Soccer is Aurora and Hunter's sport poison of choice.

I've taken liberties with a couple of things—the CONCACAF Gold Cup Final game actually took place in Vegas on August 1st, 2021. In this book, it will happen at the end of August.

You should bear in mind that this world is a corrupt world, and some things regarding prison and visiting rights are *not* true to life.

This is the painting Aurora is interested in at The Met:

Young Mother Sewing:

https://www.metmuseum.org/art/collection/search/10425

And this is the cake Hunter buys for her birthday:

Delizia cake:

https://italian-traditions.com/delizia-cake-most-famous-sicilian-cake-desserts/

This is the mask I took inspiration from for Aurora's carnival mask: https://www.simplymasquerade.co.uk/masqueradeshop/prod_2818813-Flame-Venetian-Masquerade-Mask-Nero.html

If you'd like a recap of character names and organizations, click here. (The link takes you to a chapter within the book.)

Much love and happy reading,

Serena

xoxo

Triggers:

- BDSM,
- References to degradation/humiliation,
- References to sexual assault,
- Self-harm,
- General violence

The
VALENTINI
FAMILY

THE CROSSOVER READING ORDER WITH THE SINNERS & VALENTINIS

FILTHY
FILTHY SINNER
NYX
LINK
FILTHY RICH
SIN
STEEL
FILTHY DARK
CRUZ
MAVERICK
FILTHY SEX
HAWK
FILTHY HOT
STORM
THE DON
THE LADY
FILTHY SECRET
REX
RACHEL
FILTHY KING

REVELATION BOOK ONE
REVELATION BOOK TWO
FILTHY LIES
FILTHY TRUTH

RUSSIAN MAFIA
Adjacent to the universe, but can be read as a standalone
SILENCED

BON VINUTI A LA FAMIGGHIA!

Luciu - Loo-cee-you
Custanzu - Cust-an-zoo
Giovi - Gee-oh-vee
Buttana - whore/bitch
Vicchiareddu - old man
Bona sira - good evening
Figghiu ri buttana - son of a bitch
Porca troia - Goddammit
Pezz'i miedda - piece of shit
Miedda - shit
Famigghia - family (Sicilian spelling)
Grazii - Thank you
Se - Yes
Capisci? - Understand?
Russu - red
Tuttu boni? - everything okay?
Vinnitta - vendetta
Chista è da me - you're mine
Culu - ass
Matri - mother

Patri - father
Soru - sister
Frate - brother
All'asilo - in Kindergarten
Tesoro - treasure
Talè - What are you saying?
T'avissi a mettiri na màschira - You ought to be wearing a
   mask (phrase, meaning to hide one's embarrassment.)

PLAYLIST

If you'd like to hear a curated soundtrack, with songs that are featured
in the book, as well as songs that inspired it, then here's the link:

https://open.spotify.com/playlist/5cT02Widx3DOMLnVUYAxzV?si=
3fd6873696534061&pt=99fb89f981112e43ebc183c6431c301f

PART 1

PRESENT DAY

"To burn with desire and keep quiet about it is the greatest punishment we can bring on ourselves."
— Federico García Lorca

1

HUNTER
FEELINGS - JOHN NEWMAN

AUGUST

SOME PEOPLE WERE DESTINED to lead ordinary lives.

Once upon a time, I thought that would have been my fate had I not met Aurora Valentini *all'asilo*—in Kindergarten.

A nice boring life, I'd imagined for myself. College, a wife—the girlfriend I met at school. A house. Maybe a dog. Eventually, we'd have kids. Go on vacation once a year and bitch about not being able to travel more, visit family, and savor Sunday lunches with them.

Until I was twenty-three, I'd thought Aurora was the reason that seemed so trite.

I just didn't realize that, from birth, I was meant for more.

Not that more was always good.

Case in point...

"Brunu, what the fuck are you doing here?"

With my grandfather having recently been sent to prison, as his heir, that meant I'd inherited his business as well as his men. One of whom was Brunu, my new Capo.

"Boss, I told you back in Vegas, there ain't nowhere you can go that I don't. *Capisci?*"

Eyes narrowed, I stared at him as I finished off the glass of milk I'd poured myself earlier. "How long have you been standing on my doorstep?"

He grinned at me, revealing two front incisors that had been replaced with gold decades ago. "Since I got here."

"Which was when?"

"Twenty minutes after you arrived." Christ. "What's the hurry, anyway?"

"I'm attending the wedding reception downstairs."

Brunu whistled. "Bert'd be glad you're bridging the gap with the *Cosa Nostra*. He wanted to do it, but the Valentinis know how to hold a grudge."

Didn't I know it?

Hell, their ability to hold a grudge without business getting in the way of things was something I'd been dealing with for years without even realizing there was beef between our bloodlines.

On edge, I wiggled the signet ring my grandfather, Alberto 'Bert' De Laurentiis, had given me for my birthday last December. It wasn't much of a gift considering, with it, he'd practically announced his retirement too.

As if it were on cue, Brunu flashed a glance down at the ring and up to my face again.

This ring changed everything. Took me from the sidelines to front and center stage.

Looking back, I had to wonder if he'd known this was going to go down and just hadn't warned me. I put nothing past Bert.

"Your presence won't help the situation," I remarked, even though I knew it was pointless.

"Bert gave me my orders. The last ones he could give as Don. Now I serve you." That had his chest puffing out with pride.

These Camorrans were insane, and I'd somehow inherited all of their sorry asses when Bert had 'abdicated' his position as Don, leaving the role to me.

"There isn't much to serve," I muttered uneasily.

Brunu shrugged. "You'll figure shit out, boss. In the meantime, I'm here and so's the council. If you can get friendly with the Valentinis, that's a massive coup."

My brow puckered. "It is?"

"Sure is. You know they're obsessed with those rubies of theirs, right?"

I reached up and rubbed my temple. I wanted to get into bed with the Valentinis literally, not figuratively. That was the reason I was here. Not to break bread with them.

"Brunu, can we have story time later? I have a wedding reception to attend."

This—his presence, the stories, the posturing—was one of the reasons why I'd flown out here alone.

"Sure thing, Don." He reached out and tugged on my bow tie, straightening it with a grin that revealed another gleam of those gold teeth. "Looking real smart, boss. Real smart."

Some tension loosened in my shoulders. "Yeah?"

He presented me with a chef's kiss. "You gonna have some bridesmaids lifting their skirts for you, that's for sure."

Closing the door behind me, I sighed. "I wasn't aiming for that."

"You got someone specific in mind?" he queried as we stepped down the carpeted hall toward the elevator.

Rather than answer him, I kept my focus on my Oxfords.

Aurora Valentini.

It always boiled down to her.

Yesterday, when Custanzu Valentini had called to tell me his older sister was acting weird, I'd known that there couldn't be a worse time to leave the West Coast, but because I was a sap for Aurora, I'd come.

I'd even arrived in time for the wedding yet had delayed attending so I could catch some sleep before the reception because my exhaustion was at an all-time high without the air travel, never mind everything else.

I'd paid for my expenses on my personal account, had sneaked out of my hotel suite, had driven myself to the airport—all of which I'd done to fly under the radar.

I didn't appreciate Brunu's presence.

Didn't appreciate that he'd outsmarted me.

As much as I liked him, the fucker could barely conjugate verbs. How he'd gotten the drop on me, I didn't know, but I was thankful that there was more to him than met the eye. At least he wasn't boring.

I doubly appreciated the fact that he didn't prod me for conversation as we made it to the elevator, just kept up a constant stream of words that somehow didn't need my response.

Until, of course, he said something that caught my interest.

"I paid your fees, boss."

"My fees?" I questioned.

"Yeah. This is The Victoria." He wiggled his head. "You know what that means, don't you?"

"No? It's a five-star hotel. I know that much."

"Yeah, but it's *The Victoria.*"

"Still in the dark, Brunu."

"It's neutral territory."

"It is?"

"Sure. Has been for the last couple decades."

My eyes bugged. "So long?"

"Yup. Old man Victoria's on his last legs though. That's why things have been doubling down. Fuck knows what'll happen if the fam sells out to corporate goons."

It always amused me when my grandfather's men talked like that. As if being a whore for capitalism was worse than being a mafioso—a literal goon.

"What does it mean for the hotel to be neutral territory?"

"If you're in the life, you gotta pay a fee for entrance. Then if you fuck up, you get fined."

"What constitutes a fuckup?"

"Shooting someone, attacking someone. Killing someone. The usual."

"Interesting." I tugged on my ring again, aware that Brunu watched the move, then I straightened up as the elevator delivered us to the ballroom floor.

Stepping out, I grabbed his arm to hold him in place.

"'Sup, boss?"

"I want you to stick to the outer edges of the ballroom."

"What if there's food?"

I rolled my eyes. "It'll have been a sit-down meal, Brunu."

"Yeah, but at this time, there'll be a buffet. I've been on my feet all day, boss—"

"Fine. You can eat. But don't talk to anyone. *Capis*—You understand?" I quickly corrected.

Goddammit, I refused to start talking like them even if I headed a motley crew that spanned Vegas to L.A. and over a quarter of the West Coast now.

Brunu beamed at me. "I understand, Don."

Dipping my chin, I moved away from him as I headed toward the door. As it opened, there was little fanfare.

The party was in full swing, the bride and groom were dancing, tables were gathered around the dance floor, and they were overflowing with people, food, and drink.

It was a good time to slip inside.

A quick glance around the room had me pinpointing her in a matter of seconds.

"Fuck," I muttered under my breath.

As if years hadn't passed since the last time I'd seen her in person, I noticed she still looked like she was an angel.

Which was the ultimate of ironies to me.

Aurora was *not* an angel.

She was a sinner, quite content to live in a paradise of her own creation, and I adored that about her. Jennifer Valentini, née MacNeill, might be the new Queen of the Valentini dynasty, but to me, Aurora would always reign over them.

Her intelligence knew no bounds; her capacity to strategize was terrifying.

New York didn't know what had hit it now that she was Luciu's Consigliere.

As if she sensed my presence, her head whipped to the side, away from her brother Stan who was sitting next to her, and our gazes collided.

God, she was beautiful.

Almond eyes that saw *everything* were topped by naturally arched brows which led to a pert nose. Mouth painted in a gloss I wanted to feel around my cock, the bottom lip luscious, the Cupid's bow on the upper had my tongue begging to follow its curves.

Her cheekbones were sharp, making my fingers long to trace the angles, and it led to a chin that declared to the world exactly how stubborn she was—there was even the tiniest divot at the center.

Tumbled dark waves bobbed around her shoulders, spilling out of a loose bun: oddly neat, oddly messy. Like she'd just gotten out of bed.

There went my dick.

Her reaction was the opposite of mine—she froze. In horror. Everything about her tensed. Before, in a flurry of action that broke the collision of our eyes, she reached for her purse.

But what resonated most with me after clashing with the woman I hadn't seen for years?

The starburst earrings that dangled against her cheeks.

Earrings I recognized…

And that was when my cellphone vibrated in my pocket.

CHASTESUNLIGHT *enters chat*

ChasteSunlight: *D? Are you there?*

CHAPTER TWO

****CHASTESUNLIGHT** *enters chat***

    ChasteSunlight: *D? Are you there?*

    DDoSunlight enters chat

    DDoSunlight: *I am but I'm busy. Is everything okay?*

    ChasteSunlight: *Not really. I'm kind of overwhelmed.*

    DDoSunlight: *How can I help?*

    ChasteSunlight: *I don't know that you can, to be honest. Just... please, I know you love HER, but don't stop answering my messages?*

    DDoSunlight: *I won't. I love her, yes, but you're my friend, Sunny. That's how we started. Me, the rookie, and you, the old pro.*

    ChasteSunlight: *Less of the old.*

    DDoSunlight: *:P Trust you to focus on that and not the 'pro' part.*

    ChasteSunlight: *I'm not a prejudiced fool... Where are you? Not like you to be busy.*

    DDoSunlight: *I'm attending a family event.*

    ChasteSunlight: *Ugh. Me too. I hate those.*

    DDoSunlight: *Family or events or both? Lol.*

    ChasteSunlight: *Family drives me nuts, but I couldn't live without them.*

DDoSunlight: *You say you're at a family event, so you're someplace safe, Sunny?*

ChasteSunlight: *I am.*

DDoSunlight: *You're not going to punish yourself, are you?*

ChasteSunlight: *You're not my Dom anymore. You don't get to ask questions like that.*

DDoSunlight: *Is it so bad that I care about you? Are you so incapable of seeing that?*

ChasteSunlight: *Dammit, D, I don't always do that. Just sometimes.*

DDoSunlight: *'Sometimes' is too much. When was the last time?*

ChasteSunlight: *A month ago. I'm not in a situation where I want to do that right now. You know I don't do it for the normal reasons.*

DDoSunlight: *I think you're trying to justify your actions.*

ChasteSunlight: *I'm not. I do it because I like it. It feels good. Sigh. I need to not talk about this because I'll ask you to punish me and we can't do that, not when you're behaving like a monk.*

DDoSunlight: *I've always been like a monk. I didn't exactly sow my wild oats while we were together.*

ChasteSunlight: *Really?*

DDoSunlight: *I think I'm offended. Did I come across as a player?*

ChasteSunlight: *No. But there was no reason for you to stay celibate. That's my thing. Not yours. Although, I guess you weren't celibate for me. You were celibate for her.*

DDoSunlight: *I don't have time to get into this. I'm a faithful kind of guy. We were together. Ergo, I was faithful to you. Even if it wasn't what society would call an ordinary relationship, I was.*

DDoSunlight: *We're friends, Sunny. Before anything, we're friends. I gtg.*

DDoSunlight leaves chat

3

AURORA

DDOSUNLIGHT: *We're friends, Sunny. Before anything, we're friends. I gtg.*

DDoSunlight leaves chat

Before I tucked the device into my purse, I stared down at the screen of my phone, trying and failing not to be hurt about losing D, short for DDoSunlight, to a shadowy woman whom he'd loved since time began.

Desperation had me seeking D's presence in the wake of Hunter's arrival. An arrival that was my brother's fault.

It was instinct to study Hunter as he pocketed his own cell, to watch as he strolled out of the doorway and into the ballroom, then to immediately turn away from him.

I always looked away.

Always.

And that was before I had the memory of him covered in my husband's blood to contend with.

Sometimes, I thought back to that day when everything had changed. The irony being, of course, that if I asked Hunter which day that was, he'd give me a different one.

He'd tell me it was the day he'd killed my husband.

It wasn't.

That was why I'd picked up my damn phone.

Urges...

So many of them.

Every one of them wrong.

Depraved.

But that was me.

Depraved, depraved, *depraved*.

I shuddered at the thought of all the ways I was just plain *wrong* as Stan mumbled around a piece of strawberry shortcake that he stole off my plate, "What went down between you two?"

I ignored my brother Custanzu's question, didn't even tense up at it, because it was loaded with genuine curiosity and concern and not the usual shadowed criticism.

My family liked Hunter, and I couldn't blame them. He was eminently likable. It was impossible, in fact, to dislike him.

But I didn't dislike Hunter.

I never had.

Never would.

My radio silence had nothing to do with dislike and everything to do with shame.

From the corner of my eye, I studied him, taking his tall leanness that had been stacked with muscles in the years since I'd last seen him in the flesh. His hair, on the cusp of light brown and dark blond, flopped over his forehead until he swept it back with his hand. A heavy gold band took up real estate on his pinkie.

Since when did he wear a ring?

Hunter hated jewelry.

As I wondered what else had changed, I took in those hazel eyes that were sometimes blue and sometimes gray depending on his mood or the weather. The solid jaw, the nose that Stan had broken back when he was eighteen, and the lips that, even I had to admit, begged to be kissed.

The thought made everything inside me tense up, enough that I sniped at my baby brother, "Why do you never gain any weight?"

"Huh?"

I stared pointedly at his overflowing fork. "You eat like a horse, but you're stacked like a stunt double."

He smirked. "Good genes. Don't get jealous because you didn't get them."

Squinting at him, I drawled, "Did you just call me fat?"

"Nope. I told you not to get jealous."

"I'd only be jealous if I were fat, and I'm distinctly Rubenesque—"

He released a fake yawn. "You can't manufacture an argument to get out of this conversation. Seriously, Rory, what the fuck went down between you two?"

"Why does it matter? That was years ago."

"It still affects you," was his stubborn retort.

"Why do you and Luciu persist in thinking that I'm some kind of robot, hmm?" I shot him a disapproving look. "Am I not allowed to be affected? I should stab you in the thigh for inviting him here. Maybe I should stab Luc, too. Is he involved?"

"Are you kidding?" Stan jeered, glowering at our brother who was so happy in his connubial bliss that it was distasteful. "He's so up her pussy he can't see the bush for the wood."

"The forest for the trees," I absently corrected while accepting he was right about Luc.

I wouldn't say our eldest *frate* was pussywhipped; he just acted as if Jennifer MacNeill had *El Dorado* between her thighs.

The problem with Sicilians?

They didn't think emotions were anything to be ashamed of. They didn't mind displaying them to the world. Did, in truth, believe that made them stronger.

My twin wasn't a fool, but love had made one out of him.

"Still can't believe he's married her," I muttered, snagging my wine glass and taking a sip from it.

He leaned back against his seat. "She's carrying his heir. Speaking of, Air Force One is locked and loaded for their flight tomorrow. I got the notification a couple minutes ago."

My nose crinkled as I hid a laugh. "He *is* going over the top, isn't he?"

"He's making you look like a Type B personality," Stan mocked.

Luc wasn't as good with strategy as I was, but he was smart and controlled. Those smarts and that control were currently focused on making sure he didn't lose his wife to pregnancy.

I thought that was more than likely because her best friend had suffered a miscarriage this year. Otherwise, I doubted he'd have been so neurotic. Cautious, sure. This insane? No.

Jennifer had more doctors than the president, hence the fitting Air Force One joke.

Luc had chartered a plane with a team of medical staff on board and a fully-stocked operating/delivery room to make sure his very pregnant wife was safe on the long-haul trip to our homeland.

My inner romantic was at war with my inner cynic.

The romantic thought it was sweet that Jennifer was willing to shuffle across the pond to make sure their child had dual citizenship as a gift to Luc.

The cynic didn't trust her as far as I could throw her, and I couldn't throw her far enough away.

"Why did he have to knock her up?" I questioned wistfully.

"It was the only way we wouldn't give him shit for marrying her."

"You think he did it on purpose?"

"I think it's likely."

Luciu was far too old-fashioned for his own good. It was why the papers had taken to labeling him 'New York's Italian Darcy.'

Not that he *was* Italian, of course.

We were Sicilians.

And yes, there was a distinct difference. A Scotsman would never want to be called an Englishman. An Andorran would never wish to be described as Spanish either. Americans never understood such minutiae; they were perfectly willing to label themselves as being of German heritage even though the last ancestor born on German soil had died two hundred years ago.

"Fucker thinks he's wily," Stan muttered, snatching my glass this time to top it off and take a deep pull on it.

"So do you," I pointed out, my tone cold as Hunter started to force a path through the crowd.

Every instinct in my being told me to get away from him, but I wasn't simply Aurora Fitzwilliam née Valentini at this wedding, sister to the groom—I was Luc's Consigliere. Consiglieres didn't run away from a wedding reception because their once best friend had seen with their own eyes that said Consigliere had a pain kink.

My cheeks burned at the thought. I could feel the heat overtaking me like I'd been slammed into an oven.

"So do I, what?"

Distracted, I said, "Think you're wily."

"What the fuck's that supposed to mean?"

Stan, thankfully, was more interested in what I had to say than what I looked like and how badly I was blushing. My younger brother wasn't as cerebral as Luc and I.

Well, that wasn't entirely fair.

Not when his current project wasn't for idiots, but his intellectual strengths lay elsewhere—in a laboratory.

"It means I know about your little sideline," I told him coolly, pleased with myself for containing my anxiety.

Not by one drop of a note in my tone did I sound as if Hunter's presence here put me on edge. Which, to be frank, understated entirely how stressed I was that Hunter and I were sharing breathing space. There was definitely less oxygen in the ballroom now.

"What little sideline?" he groused, breaking through my distressed thoughts with a sledgehammer.

"I'm talking about Agatha? Which is a totally inappropriate name considering you're besmirching the memory of Saint Agatha. Rename it. I'm not having the patron saint of Sicily being linked to any drug." I cast him a glance and saw that he was pulling a face. "Did you think I wouldn't find out about it?"

He huffed. "I don't report to you, Rory. You're not my mommy."

"No? I clean up your messes as if I were your mother. Did you hear about what happened last night?"

"No. Where?"

"A client killed one of our girls. Strangled her then passed out in the bed because he had a weak heart."

Stan's shoulders hunched. "*Cristo,* really?"

"Yes, *really.* It's not something I'm going to lie about." I pursed my lips. "If I were your *matri,* you'd probably have better impulse control because I'd have spanked the disobedience out of you by now and slammed some sense between those ears."

"I have good enough impulse control, and I'll tell *Matri* you said that."

"Snitches get stitches," I taunted, snagging my glass back out of his hand and taking a deep sip, hoping that by the time Hunter showed up at our table, he'd attribute my flush to the red wine.

Stan gritted his teeth—I could almost hear the enamel on them cracking beneath the pressure. "You're a pain in my ass."

"This shouldn't be news to you."

"Oh, it isn't."

"I thought you were working on C-L-O."

"I am. Red was an accidental discovery. Agatha came as even more of a surprise."

"And you want to continue selling it? Even after what I just told you?"

"You think it's cheap coming up with new formulas?"

"No. But it's not like money is an issue."

"Luc has me on a leash as you well know," he rumbled. "My hobbies have to be profitable."

My brow furrowed. "That's simply not true, Stan."

"Of course it is. All aspects of our business have to be beneficial to the *Cosa Nostra.*"

"This is a passion project of yours," I pointed out. "Each of us has our own methods of escaping. You could putter around that lab of yours on the compound for the rest of your life and he wouldn't say anything. Neither would I. We're entitled to the things that bring us peace."

"Maybe this isn't a pastime. Maybe I have to prove myself."

His logic was illogical.

Not that that came as a surprise.

For a man who'd been reared in a scientific setting, who knew that every true conclusion came after observation, hypothesis, and experimentation, he was oddly shortsighted at times.

That was guilt for you though.

Guilt—better than cancer at eating through the soul.

Stan blamed himself for our father's passing, and while his actions as a teenager had contributed to the situation, there was no denying that our beloved *patri* had been marked for death the day he'd been born.

"*Patri* wouldn't want you to waste your talents on drugs," I murmured, tone warmer than earlier. "Why bother with C-L-O, Red, and Agatha when all they'll do is damage people's lives?"

"They're a stepping stone."

"To what? A Netflix show on you?"

His scowl would have felled a lesser man.

I wasn't lesser, nor was I a man.

"We're in the goddamn mafia, Aurora. Everything we do ruins someone's life. That's the deal."

I knew that. Of course, I did. He was right—I didn't have to like it.

Showing some intelligence for once, he changed tacks. "Did you know that the chemical compound in Viagra is beneficial to slowing heart disease, reduces the likelihood of a heart attack, and decreases pulmonary artery resistance?"

"Yes, I knew that."

"But what is Viagra?"

"An impotence drug."

"Not a drug prescribed for heart disease patients?"

"No. For men who can't get it up."

"Exactly."

I pursed my lips as I tracked Hunter's progress through the room. He'd already been stopped by the Irish who were talking to him about... well, I didn't know what. I'd like to know though. What business did he have with the Five Points? The Camorra were West Coast-based while the Irish held influence purely on the East Coast.

"What's your point, Stan?" I grouched, trying not to look as if I were stalking Hunter with my eyes. "That the American health system is broken? That pharmaceutical companies prefer to invest in vanity drugs rather than ones that'll make people's lives better? I already knew that. Life isn't fair, *frate*—"

"Shut up, Rory. Take that stick out of your ass and listen to what I'm actually saying."

Turning to him, gracing him with my full attention, I took note of the temper spitting in his eyes, the tension in his face, and I almost, *almost*, smiled.

So earnest.

So like our father sometimes that it hurt.

Luc had inherited more of the Valentini genes, his features aristocratic. Stan was like the bastard son of one of our royal ancestors and a chambermaid. He looked like what he was—a bruiser. Especially since he'd taken to inking up.

But what he lacked in noble Valentini looks, he made up for with his passion. That Sicilian passion. I'd eradicated it from my own nature, but my brothers hadn't. The fools.

"You're saying that you're starting an experimental drug lab?"

"Yes."

"And you're selling off the byproducts?"

"Yes."

"Interesting."

"It is, actually."

"I thought C-L-O was supposed to be the next MDMA?"

"Nah, just a pleasure drug."

"With the end goal of curing heart disease?"

He popped an olive into his mouth. "Among other things."

"What's Agatha's miracle property?"

A smirk creased his lips. "It works on women."

That smirk told me everything. "Fuck's sake."

He tapped his nose. "We'll make a fortune."

"You're going to cause a riot is what you'll do. Saint Agatha is the patron saint of rape victims, Stan. *Change*—" Before I could finish my rant, I spotted Hunter shaking hands with O'Donnelly, which prompted me to blurt out, "What do you think they're talking about?"

"What are who talking about?"

"Hunter. With the O'Donnellys."

The Irish Mob were allies. I didn't trust them. My family would say I trusted no one. They were wrong.

I trusted them.

That was more than enough.

"He's the head of the Camorra now, Rory. They're probably just making introductions."

My mouth tightened at the reminder of our failings. "How did we not know that?"

"We did?" Stan retorted.

"I don't mean about him becoming the head of the Camorra."

Though, what Hunter thought he could achieve as the new Don of Vegas and L.A. was beyond me. Hunter wasn't a rabid pit bull like Luc. He was a Golden Retriever.

I'd seen him kill, but that was different. He'd murdered to spare our mutual best friend, Rachel Laker, from my rapist fuck of an ex.

Defense was one thing. Hunter wasn't mercenary enough to survive this world. God, he was going to get his ass butchered—

"Then what the fuck are you talking about?" Stan was grousing, breaking into my panicked line of thoughts.

"I'm talking about the fact that we didn't know he had ties to the Camorra until he was literally made the new leader of it."

Stan shrugged. "I knew he'd joined."

"Why didn't you tell me? I only found out earlier this year."

"I didn't tell you because you're insane where he's concerned."

"Fuck off."

"Nowhere to fuck off to. This reception is only getting started."

Both of us heaved a sigh.

Tapping my nails against the table, I muttered, "We need to expand our knowledge base. It was only recently we learned what this hotel is."

Another failure, one I was working on rectifying.

Stan nodded. "Luc was pissed about that, let me tell you."

The Victoria was neutral ground in the city. 'Do no harm' was a basic tenet when you crossed the threshold. Even in my position as DA, I hadn't known this was a safe haven for the criminals of New York and further afield.

Disapproval filtered through me when Stan continued, "Imagine that we only found out because Jennifer is friends with the Irish."

"Not just friends," I remarked. "Blood."

"*Se*, but you know their dynamic isn't like our bond."

True.

Jennifer had only learned this year of her true heritage—her father was the brother of Aidan O'Donnelly Sr., the head of the Irish Mob.

While that made her Irish royalty in NYC, it didn't make her anything less than a gold digger who'd spent most of her life on the hunt for an easy ride, something she'd found in my dumbass brother.

As much as I loathed to admit it, Stan was right about her ties coming in useful. Even without the blood bond, she was best friends with the Irish money man's wife as well as the heir's bride, but...

"I still don't like her," I sniped.

"You and me both, but I'm adjusting. She grows on you—"

"So do genital warts."

"—and Luc has never been as happy."

I scoffed, "*Happy.* We're not in a position to be allowed to experience *happiness*."

"Jesus, Rory. Is that how you feel?"

"Don't pity me," I snapped, annoyed by his expression. "We're all in the same boat. We won the war and Luc sits on the throne, but that doesn't mean dick if we can't keep his ass glued to it."

"Who's going to come after it?"

"This is why we leave the strategy to me," I ground out, clenching my fingers around the glass in my hand. Exasperation for his short-sightedness filled me.

Luc was lucky. He didn't know it, but he was. He'd fallen for his bride, and that bride who should have been an albatross around his neck, was actually a boon. We weren't supposed to marry for happiness. We married to cement ties.

Before the truth of her parentage had been revealed, Luc's gold-digger wife brought nothing to the table; that was where his luck came in.

Jennifer was an O'Donnelly.

"Hunter's heading this way," Stan warned.

"I have eyes."

"You're such an ornery bitch."

"And you need to use your brain more."

We glowered at each other, and for long enough that I didn't even realize Hunter was there.

Standing *there.*

Right there.

Until he cleared his throat.

My head swiped to the left where I instinctively knew he was positioned. My gaze landed at hip height.

Where his hands were resting.

Where he was fiddling with that ring on his pinkie finger.

A signet ring that I—

I blinked.

No.

No.

Just… no.

My stunned bewilderment had me freezing in place, but Stan came in useful for once. He was on his feet, his arms sliding around Hunter like the long-lost brother I knew they were to each other.

While they'd put distance between one another partially for my sake and partially for business, I knew they'd been in constant contact over the years.

As, apparently, had I.

That signet ring…

December.

That was when D had started wearing it.

I remembered it distinctly. How couldn't I? His fingers had been wrapped around that anaconda between his legs and I'd been watching him get off.

Just the memory made my cheeks tinge pink.

No.

No.

Just… no.

I hadn't seen Hunter's hand… His dick.

I hadn't.

This couldn't be happening.

This *wasn't* happening.

I refused to think—

I'd worked so hard to keep my life compartmentalized. No way was this happening. No way. It couldn't be. He couldn't know the depravity to which I'd sunk—

It's just a ring, Aurora. It doesn't mean anything. Plenty of men wear signet rings.

And that was the truth.

Yes, it was.

Plenty of men wore them.

I knew Hunter was Camorra, knew he'd joined the ranks… but this ring was unique.

It was a status symbol.

An open eye sat in the center, a black stone, likely a black diamond, for a pupil, with channel-set clear diamond baguettes acting as the iris. Thick lines of gold rimmed the settings.

How hadn't I recognized it for what it was when I'd seen it over the webcam?

The O in the 'Camorra' tag was *always* an iris.

Goddammit, I knew D had turned me into a moron for him, but this took the cake.

Nausea churned in my gut, making me wonder if I was going to puke on his Ferragamo Oxfords. The panic was unreal. The terror was all-consuming.

He couldn't know.

He couldn't.

But he did.

He knew the worst about Sunny.

He knew about the pain kink and the need to be punished. He knew about the self-inflicted punishments and the darkest, deepest desires that I'd whispered to him in the middle of the night.

He'd held my chastity in his grip.

He'd made me do things, things that would shame another woman but that had made me fly.

Oh, God.

My house of cards was crumbling down around me.

How could DDoSunlight be Hunter?!

This couldn't be possible.

It couldn't be.

It *wasn't.*

But that eye…

That all-seeing, all-knowing eye of the Camorra.

My cell phone buzzed and I took full advantage of the distraction as it allowed me to duck out of my seat and to dash away from the table.

As I moved, however, a hand snagged mine. Strong, lean fingers with the faintest of calluses rubbed against my flesh, drawing sensations…

No.

Not just drawing them.

That was a trivialization.

It *stirred* them into being.

Into life.

Life whispered inside me.

Breathed into me by *him.*

D.

How many times had I wanted to stand before him? Have him at my back? How many times had I craved his touch? How many times had I fought the urge to ask him to come to New York—to be here, to hold me, to embrace me?

I just never imagined it would be *here*. Had never foreseen that it could be *him*.

Goddammit to hell.

"Aurora."

His voice. D's voice.

Fuck.

Fuck.

It *was* him.

It was—

Hunter *was* DDoSunlight.

Oh, shit!

The earrings.

Jesus.

The starburst diamond earrings that I'd worn out of nostalgia today because I was missing him—he'd given them to me.

He'd know—

He couldn't know.

He couldn't.

How the hell would I live that down?

The shame collided with the desperate need I felt to experience his touch.

For so long, I'd craved it. Craved him. Wanted more, wanted him. Now, here he was, but I couldn't—

Tears burned my eyes, making the lash lines feel like they were brimming with droplets of acid.

D's ability to ferret out information from me, to discern what others never spotted, was terrifying in this instance. It meant that the longer he looked at me, the more chances there were of him spotting the earrings. I'd never have said Hunter was so detail-oriented, but I'd never have said he was a Dom either!

I dragged my hand out of his grasp, not allowing him to restrain me, and darted into the crowd. It wasn't his MO to call out to me. At least, it hadn't been before, and as D, his discretion was absolute so I took immediate advantage and forged a path through the throngs of people.

As I did, someone grabbed my hand again. I almost slapped at them, but a quick twist of my head revealed it was Luc.

Fuck, he was beaming.

The joy in his eyes at being wed to this gold digger would have broken my heart had I not been freaking the fuck out.

His smile started to die, though, as Luc, whose ability to read between the lines was legendary, realized something was going on.

"Aurora, you look *amazing* in that dress," Jen declared. *Loudly.* Then, even goddamn louder, she drawled, "I'm so pleased you managed to fit into it."

My top lip almost quirked into a snarl but I didn't have the time to get pissy with her. I didn't like her and, unashamedly, I'd made it known. Hence the custom dress I was wearing that she'd commissioned for me with its too small sleeves and the skirt that made me look like I was wearing a sack of potatoes.

I'd have applauded her if I hadn't spent the last month carb-free because of her prank.

More fool me for not going to that final dress fitting because I didn't have time. I wouldn't underestimate her again.

"*Soru, tuttu boni?*" 'Everything okay, sister?'

I shot him a tight smile. "Fine. Are you enjoying yourselves?"

Luc didn't look convinced, but I frowned at him to shut him up, and he huffed but declared, "Eat! *Se?* That'll put you in a good mood."

If his wife hadn't stuck me in a cheese grater for a dress, then I would have. Instead, I just blindly nodded at him as I gave him a quick hug. It was probably a clue of how messed up I was over Hunter that I even pressed a kiss to Jennifer's cheek.

I didn't stick around to be grilled. Instead, I dashed into the crowd and ducked, with a wobbly breath of relief, into the ladies' restroom.

There, I practically tore out the earrings, and even though my panic made my fingers tremble, I handled them with care so that they wouldn't get tangled up in my purse.

With that done, I headed over to the small seating area and slumped down onto the sofa. Hands still shaking, I lifted them and pressed them to my face as years' worth of memories cascaded before me.

All the shit we'd done together, all the dirty, wicked things, the secrets I'd shared, the…

My brain screeched to a halt because if I didn't switch it off, I was pretty sure that I was going to hyperventilate.

Either that or faint.

Because the panic attack that loomed on the horizon wouldn't be pretty, I grabbed my cellphone, swiped away from the missed call notification from Giovi, a foot soldier, and quickly found Rachel's number.

Rachel had been my BFF through the trials and tribulations of life —of which there'd been many. The only downside? She was Hunter's close friend too, seeing as we'd met in college. But in this instance, that was a positive. Definitely not a negative.

With the ringing tone in my ear, I tried to think about what I'd tell her. How could I explain why I was on the brink of passing out from shock?

My secret Dom is the man I've been ignoring for years because he burst into my bedroom where he thought my husband—you know, the one who raped you—was beating the ever-loving shit out of me but was, in fact, working me over and getting me off.

How did I verbalize that?

How did I tell her that that was only the beginning?

I swallowed.

Shame was the best of motivators. It could make people do the damnedest things—like cut out a person they loved from their lives, a person they missed every day. Like be mean to that person over something that wasn't their fault, something they regretted every day.

The tears hit me again.

God, I was such a viper sometimes. My tongue had more blades than barbed wire. Apart from here, now. Where I was at my most vulnerable.

Where I was on a collision course with my innermost shameful secrets.

The risk of exposure had me sucking in a sharp breath, one that whooshed out of my lips when I heard a, "Rory?"

Then, "Aurora?"

One sounded in my ear, the other came from the doorway beyond the restroom.

Oh, fuck.

Fuck, fuck, fuck.

He was outside!

"Rachel," I whimpered, hating myself for sounding so weak, but I could no more stop that than I could stop myself from staggering over to the toilet stalls and locking myself inside one.

"Aurora? What's going on? Are you okay?" she screeched, which was a testament to how bad I sounded because Rachel and I were the same under pressure—neither of us showed emotions or weakness.

Ever.

Unless family was endangered, that is.

I wished that I could tell my heavily pregnant friend that I was fine, but I was the opposite of okay. My secrets were burning up in a fiery revelation that was biblical in proportion.

In fact, it was pretty much Old Testament—that was how bad this situation was.

"AURORA!" she shrieked. "Talk to me. Where are you? I'll come get you—"

That got me out of my catatonic state. Rachel did not need to be busting her baby belly across state lines to come and pick me up. "I'm not. Not okay, I mean. But physically, I'm safe. I promise."

"Rory, I need to speak with you." *Hunter.*

Or was he here as D?

Did he know who I was? Did he know I was Sunny?

The need to swallow down air almost overwhelmed me but I wheezed, "I need you to stay on the line with me, Rach, and I need you to text Hunter to tell him to give me some space."

"What?!" Rachel's confusion was clear. "I'm not a freakin' go-between, Aurora! Do it your damn self. You're both adults—"

Desperate times called for desperate measures.

"I'll tell you why I don't talk to him," I hissed.

She fell silent. But I heard something in the background, then a cell rang a few feet away.

The relief almost had me dropping to the floor.

"Hunter, Aurora's asked me to ask you to give her some space," I heard her say, letting me know that she'd called him on another line.

Hunter sighed. The sound was so loud that I knew he'd come into the restroom. My eyes widened as I plunked my ass on the toilet seat.

Would he kick down the door?

Or was that too much?

Hunter was D though.

Hunter was…

Hunter *had* broken down a door to get to me. *My bedroom door.* I'd been so into the scene, my mind so focused on what was happening, on the rug flogger that my then Master had been whipping me with, on the purest, bittersweet pain that rained agony down my nerve endings and that made me feel like I was on fire with ecstasy, that I hadn't even known what was happening until it was too late. Until he was there, a witness to my shame.

"I'm right here with her, Rachel," Hunter was saying. "This is ridiculous. You don't need to do this."

In my ear, I heard Rachel retort, "You're telling me. When the hell are you two going to grow up? I don't have time to always act as your referee. And when this kid comes along, I've got to be Mommy to that first, ya hear?"

She wasn't wrong.

This wasn't fair to her, especially not in her condition. Pregnancy wasn't a handicap, but her fear of being pregnant was.

Guilt over dumping this at her door had me bowing over in the stall, unable to drop my head between my knees because of the impossibly tight dress I was wearing and the Spanx beneath.

That, in itself, stirred up my panic.

I wanted out of my *skin.*

Hunter rumbled, "I never asked you to be the referee."

That tone—so deep, so dark, so husky.

I sucked in a breath as memories stirred to life.

Good ones.

That voice—he could talk me off better than some men could get me going with their fingers, mouth, and cock.

Now's not the time to be thinking about any of that, I snarled to myself.

"You don't have to ask," Rachel countered. "I just know being the referee is my role, and trust me, Hunt, I'm not into ménage."

"Even if you were, I don't think Rex is," he mocked.

Rachel laughed. "No, he definitely isn't."

Were they seriously about to do this?

I was about to die in a toilet stall like Elvis without the constipation, and they were talking about—

They were.

"How are you doing anyway? How's kiddo?" he teased, but his laugh, D's laugh, let me breathe a little deeper. A little easier.

"The baby's fine," Rachel was telling him. "I'm not but I'm getting there."

"You want me to send you some more of that ice cream you like?"

"I can buy it myself."

"I know, but gifted ice cream always tastes ten times better."

I heard his footsteps drift away.

The door closed as he left the restroom, prompting me to sag against the stall in relief, letting it take my weight, then, it opened again, the hinges squeaking and creaking faintly as I jerked upright.

"You can't run away from me forever, Sunny. This once… I'll allow it. *This once.* But there are consequences for everything. As you well know."

PART 2

THE PAST

"When you give someone your whole heart and he doesn't want it, you cannot take it back. It's gone forever."
— Sylvia Plath

4

———

HUNTER

I MISS U - JAX JONES AU/RA

THREE YEARS EARLIER

TIPPING my head to the side, I asked Sara Barranco, "You sure that doesn't hurt?"

The owner of Sugar & Spice & All Things Nasty snorted at me. "Yes, of course, it hurts. That's the point."

I pulled a face. She pulled one back.

"I don't get it."

"You don't have to get it. It's not your thing. You're allowed to not share a kink, but you do not demean it, debase it, or shame it. Understood?"

"I understand," I told her immediately, and not just because she was strong enough to knock me over the head and to take me down, but because she was right. "I wasn't demeaning, debasing, or shaming," I pointed out. "I, just... Why?"

"Some women like it. As do men."

"I don't want to do it."

She clucked her tongue. "Then don't shove your dick through the gloryhole, Hunter. I was showing you around the club. Nothing more."

I grinned at her waspish tone. "Regret offering to show me the ropes?"

"No. I don't. You got me out of a sticky situation, and I appreciate it."

She'd had her ID stolen. I'd stolen it back, as well as every lost penny that had been snatched from her.

Sara wasn't to know that I was the one behind the theft of her ID just so I could force a conversation between us about the sex club she owned...

Every New Year's, I told myself *this* would be the year I'd learn why Aurora—my childhood best friend, first crush, love of my life, and the future mother of my children (if she stopped friend-zoning me long enough to get her pregnant)—was into this, and I'd see if it was something I eventually could like.

I usually gave up before I began though.

Mostly out of fear.

Self-limiting fear.

I'd read *Fifty Shades of Grey* as a dare from Lauren, her mom. I knew that it seemed implausible for someone to learn submissiveness or dominance. Fear that I'd never be able to be enough for Aurora had kept me paralyzed.

This year, I'd acted on it purely by chance.

Flicking through porn, I'd been jacking off and had found a scene that had me shooting my wad faster than usual.

A woman, wrists tied and bound to a staircase, had a guy looming over her, making her beg for his dick. She'd lunge forward to try and suck it, but he'd back off and she'd plead with him... Then he'd plunge into her mouth, forcing his dick down her throat.

It was so easy to imagine Aurora in that position.

So easy to replace that porn star with her and have her begging for my cock.

Which was why I was here today.

And they said porn was a bad influence.

Shortsighted fools.

"Hunter?"

I rubbed my chin as I studied the women behind the gloryholes, distaste filling me at the sight.

Everything about the scene put me on edge.

Where was the respect for them?

The guys might as well have been screwing the wooden rim itself in the partition wall.

"Hunter, you need to think more about what you *do* like rather than what you don't." Before I could reply, she ticked off on her fingers: "You don't like duct tape as a binding tool, and you don't like golden showers. You don't like breast bondage, and you don't like—"

My nose crinkled. "I don't 'dislike' breast bondage, just not the… you know."

Her lips twitched. "I know what you mean. You don't like tit torture."

Having seen it in the flesh, with a woman I adored being treated to it, *no*, I didn't like it. "It's not my thing," I concurred.

"Tell me three 'things' you do like or I'm going to leave you to get some work done."

She meant her threat. We'd been here twice already and on each occasion, I'd uncovered more stuff I disliked than liked.

It wasn't helping my confidence.

But…

Tonight, before the gloryhole, I'd seen a woman on something called a Sybian.

Gaze drifting as I thought back to the woman's pleas, I murmured, "I like it when they beg for orgasms."

"Good. Okay."

"I like it when they have too many orgasms and beg for them to stop."

"Orgasm control with a mix of forced orgasms in there too—"

My brow furrowed. "No forcing."

She tapped my arm. "It's not like rape. It's good that you care about that though. What's the golden rule?"

"It has to be safe, sane, and consensual."

"Perfect. Go on, what else? Two more. Those two are entwined."

"Sounds like two distinct things to me."

"Who's the expert here?"

I eyed her. "You sure you're not a Domme?"

"I'm sure." She grinned at me as she shuffled closer to my side. Both of us stared through the two-way mirror and watched the glory-hole scene going down. Unlike me, I could tell that she liked what she saw. "Go on. Continue."

"I like to have rules, and I want to punish them if they don't follow them."

"Standard dominance. Good. Does that appertain to anything in particular?"

I thought about that a second. "Day-to-day things."

"Such as?"

"Jesus," I bit off, scraping a hand over my face. "I sound like a weirdo."

Sara smacked my arm again. "Shut up. You don't debase your own kinks, just like you don't debase someone else's. We do not shame here. We embrace who and what we are. Understood?"

"Understood."

"Tell me."

I pursed my lips. "Bedtimes, bathroom breaks, when they eat, what they dress in. Things like that."

"You want to control it all?"

"There'd be some reprieve, but to a certain extent, yes. Mostly, I think, for punishment."

"That's intense, but you prefer that type of discipline rather than corporal punishment. Interesting."

"Why?"

"Maybe you're a pleasure Dom more than a soft Dom." Before I could question her about either of those things, neither label I'd heard her use prior to this conversation, she queried, "You do know that if you control the bathroom breaks, it could lead to subs having *accidents*, don't you?"

I blinked. "Accidents?"

"Accidents," she confirmed, an amused gleam making an appearance in her eyes. I knew she liked shocking me. "You make a woman wait for nineteen hours to use the bathroom—"

"NINETEEN HOURS?"

"Jesus, Hunter, keep it down," she groused, tugging on her ear.

"Who the hell makes someone wait that long to use the restroom?"

"So, you're not as into the idea of controlling bathroom breaks as much as you thought you were."

Discomfort filled me. "Clearly."

Christ, maybe I was more in over my head than I thought?

"As a Dom, when you implement a practice, whether it's for pleasure or for punishment, you have to assess the worst-case scenario and think about the consequences.

"If you showed signs of being a Master, then the humiliation of a slave having an accident might be what turns you on—"

Before we could get deeper into this conversation, I muttered, "Worst-case scenario. Got it."

"Good. Third one?"

"Third one?"

She huffed, obviously back to being impatient again. "Third like."

"Oh."

My throat felt thick as I thought about what I wanted. I pictured Aurora in that position from the porn flick, thought about other rabbit holes I'd fallen down in the land of pornography, and I blew out a breath before admitting, "I want there to be complete trust between us—"

"Well, that's a standard."

"You didn't let me finish."

"Sorry. I'm just used to you waffling."

Unoffended, I grinned, which helped me relax so I didn't choke on the word: "Somnophilia."

Her brows rose as she looked at me. "It's always the quiet ones."

Ignoring her words, I nudged her with my elbow. "There. Three."

I didn't tell her that I'd only learned what somnophilia was after extensive 'research.' The idea of it turned me on, and I wasn't particularly comfortable with the fact that it did.

I'd read up on it, though, and liked the idea of non-verbal cues such as the sub—in this case the maddening, bewildering woman who'd bewitched me at thirteen, who happened to be smarter than Einstein, more capable than the Supreme Court, and more cunning than the entire cast of the MCU, aka Aurora—placing an object on the nightstand to indicate that she'd be okay with me doing my thing to her while she slept.

Aware that the idea of slipping my cock between her lips as she dreamed—preferably of me (a man could hope)—was giving me a boner, and not particularly appreciating that it did, I turned slightly so Sara wouldn't comment on my obvious erection.

She was more than capable of it.

"I think you just uncovered the tip of the iceberg," she drawled before, eyes twinkling, she teased, "You just needed pinning down."

Mind still on Aurora's mouth, I managed a laugh. "Is that what that was?"

"Sure." She nudged me again. "You can respect women and respect their kinks. They're two sides of the same coin."

Slowly, I nodded. "They are."

"You don't have to understand why they want something, and you can try to make sense of it, but mostly, it's a two-way street. They tell you their limits, and you tell them yours. Then, you work between the lines."

"Where do you start, though?" I rubbed my brow. "Sometimes, I'm not even sure if I'm into this."

"Then why are you here?"

Did I tell her the truth? Even though she'd probably tell me that you couldn't learn to crave these things?

That she *had* pinned me down and made me talk about what I liked settled something in my head.

"I once saw something between a Dom and a sub," I admitted gruffly. "He treated her like shit, and she loved it. He broke her. At least, it looked to me as if he had, and she still got off—"

"There are different types of Doms just as there are different types of subs. Take me; I don't want to be broken. I'm pretty much always going to get my ass spanked for topping from the bottom. I can't help it. A Dom like the one you mentioned would never work with me.

"I talked about soft Doms and pleasure Doms earlier. Do you know what they are?"

I raked a hand through my hair. "Is the clue in the title?"

"Pretty much." Her mouth twisted. "But there's nothing soft about them when they're whipping your tush with a paddle. Trust me."

Soft Dom.

Was that what I was?

"Where pleasure Doms are *all* up in their partners' orgasms."

That sounded more like me.

I thought about the partners I'd had, about how I was in bed, and I recognized a strange truth—I *was* focused on their pleasure. I focused on it to the degree that I couldn't get off unless they were screaming and their cunts were clutching at my cock.

I thought about how I enjoyed picking out their outfits and how it'd piss me off if they didn't wear them…

No, those memories weren't a flashing neon sign that screamed, 'Hunter Lachlan is a pleasure Dom,' but they were stepping stones.

Sara tapped my shoulder to gain my attention, making me realize it wasn't the first time she'd done so. "Have you tried KinkWorld?"

"No."

"Sign up for it. It's only a chat room, but they have threads on there, and you can ask for advice or you can read about what real subs truly want, not what subs in porn want. It might be enlightening."

I pondered that. "Thanks for your patience, Sara."

Her smile lit her eyes. "I just topped you from the bottom."

Chuckling, I joked, "Is that why my ass is sore?"

Business soon called her away, and because nothing that was going down tonight really lit my fire, I grabbed my cell and searched 'Kink-World' on Google.

I'd scoped it out as a guest before, but never as a member.

An odd surge of nervous anticipation flooded me as I navigated through the site and signed up.

When it asked for a username, I dismissed my usual one—

Actaeon. Another handle drifted immediately to the forefront of my mind.

DDoS - **Distributed Denial-of-Service**

I.e., what I did for a living.

And then, Aurora.

But Aurora wasn't mine yet.

Yet being the keyword.

DDoS. Aurora.

The two words tumbled around my mind as a woman screamed when a Dom lit these two sticks up and started tapping her on the ass with them.

Aurora.

DDoS.

Aurora was another word for dawn. Or… lights.

Sunlight.

DDoSunlight.

A smile curved my lips as I input the username, and it seemed like fate when it was available.

More intrigued by the sign-up than what was going on around me, I slunk over to a booth, ordered a beer from the waiter who was wearing some kind of pony gear that I didn't bat an eyelid at anymore, and I drifted through the myriad options the site wanted to figure out where on the kink spectrum you were based.

When my profile was complete, a sense of achievement filled me.

The club was great. I'd learned a lot here and, some day in the future, I might want to return, but I felt like I was in the Little League and was messing around with MVPs on the team.

All around me, there were Doms and Dommes who knew the ropes. Literally. I couldn't even tie a fucking knot.

No, I was out of my league here. Sara was right in that I needed a sub who wouldn't mind my inexperience. Who'd encourage me to learn. Who'd accept my stumbles…

Because I was an upfront kind of guy, I wrote on my wall:

New Dom looking for a sub who's willing to take a leap of faith on me.

If it was anything like regular dating sites, that wouldn't work, but for a first attempt, it was better than nothing.

Satisfied with this initial step, I put down my phone, drank my beer, looked around the dungeon, and tried not to gawk at a couple who were doing very interesting things with a violet wand—I had too much respect for AC current to piss around with stuff like that.

By the time my beer was finished, I was ready to go. Picking up my phone, out of habit I checked my notifications. There were a couple from my grandfather, a few work calls that could wait until morning, and…

KinkWorld - You have one notification from User: ChasteSunlight.

Tapping onto the notification, I sat back in my seat and dove into a whole new world…

CHAPTER FIVE

TWO YEARS LATER

DECEMBER

CHASTESUNLIGHT *enters chat**
    ChasteSunlight: *Sir?*
    DDoSunlight enters chat
    DDoSunlight: *Yes, baby?*
    ChasteSunlight: *I'm home.*
    DDoSunlight: *Were you a good girl for me today?*
    ChasteSunlight: *Yes, Sir. Can I take it off, please?*
    DDoSunlight: *You know the rules.*
    ChasteSunlight: *I do.*
    DDoSunlight: *So why are you asking when you already know?*
    ChasteSunlight: *But I was good!*
    DDoSunlight: *Does that make up for being bad? Three days with*
ZERO *contact, Sunny? Is that something I should easily forgive?*
    ChasteSunlight: *I said I was sorry, Sir.*
    DDoSunlight: *'Sorry' doesn't take away from what you did.*

DDoSunlight: *'Sorry' doesn't stop me from worrying, does it?*

ChasteSunlight: *No, Sir.*

DDoSunlight: *No. It doesn't. You'll wear the chastity belt until I say you can take it off. Are you ready for a call?*

ChasteSunlight: *Yes, Sir.*

DDoSunlight: *No pouting, Sunny. Or I'll make you wear the belt an extra day...*

ChasteSunlight starts video chat

6

HUNTER

LIKE A STONE - AUDIOSLAVE

LATER THAT NIGHT

THE DEEP GUTTURAL groan that drifted from me when I saw the woman crawling on the floor toward her Dom surprised even me.

I didn't think I'd like that, didn't think it'd get my dick hard, but it started throbbing when I thought about Aurora in that position.

On her hands and knees.

Naked.

Tits bouncing.

Ass jiggling.

Hips rocking as she crawled toward me.

I closed my eyes for a second, trying and failing to dismiss the image. I felt like a piece of shit because ChasteSunlight deserved better than for me to be thinking about Aurora at a time such as this one. I should be seeing *her* in that position. Should be getting inspiration for things I did with her…

My only consolation was that we knew the score with each other, having been candid right from the start.

She knew I was learning the ropes and that she was my first sub.

She also knew I was in love with another woman and that we could never be fully committed for that reason.

I knew that she couldn't handle an offline Dom, that privacy was beyond a concern for her—years later, and Sunny, my nickname for her, still wouldn't go on cam without a mask and a voice modulator—and that she had no desire for us to move from the online world into the real one.

At moments such as these, I took comfort in that.

I only came to Sugar & Spice & All Things Nasty when I was in a mood, and today had been a clusterfuck. I was pissed at Sunny because she'd been incommunicative which, in a dynamic like ours, was a fucking disaster, *and* it was my birthday.

I didn't have a thing against birthdays, but my grandfather had decided to give me a signet ring as a gift. Now, I didn't have a thing against signet rings either. But this one represented a whole hell of a lot more than a piece of jewelry.

If a ring could encompass power, this one did.

Plus, Aurora hadn't sent me an email or a text wishing me happy birthday.

Just last night, I'd seen her on a news report so I knew she was crazy busy at work, but that didn't lessen the sting.

More than anything, more than the ring or Sunny being MIA, her silence pissed me off.

Scraping my hand over my jaw, feeling the gold against my skin, I ignored it and watched the scene in front of me.

Sugar & Spice & All Things Nasty had viewing corridors. Clients in private rooms could choose to close the privacy screens or not, and if they didn't, it was a silent invitation for an audience.

The prospect of bringing Aurora here, of using one of these rooms with her, had me reaching down and unzipping my cock.

Around me, I knew others had the same idea. There was the distinct sound of a guy jacking off and another of a woman moaning.

It wasn't my scene, but tonight was different.

Tonight, I needed this.

I pressed one hand to the window as, with the other, I grabbed a hold of my shaft. Pre-cum had bubbled at the tip, proof that the scene ahead turned me the fuck on.

I was still learning what I liked and disliked, and apparently *crawling* went on the 'likes' list.

And if Aurora, a woman who crawled for no man, were to approach me on her hands and knees?

Fuck.

My vision blurred as I stared at the strangers ahead. The sub had crawled over to him and the Dom was feeding her his cock.

I wouldn't do that with Aurora.

No, I'd lounge there, like a king in his throne, and I'd have her crawl between my thighs and I'd make her kneel there, looking at my dick, watching it, making her wait for it.

Making her crave it.

Then, I'd give it to her.

But I wouldn't let her suck or lick or kiss it.

I'd make her warm it. I'd put my cock between her lips and I'd tell her that I'd spank her if she moved her mouth, if she tried to tease me. Then I'd sit there. And she'd sit there. And—

I could so easily imagine Aurora's eyes looking up at me, desperation in them. The need to do *something*. The urgency she'd feel to taste my cum on her tongue.

My hand sped up, moving over the heavy fullness so that my thumb rimmed the sensitive tip. I gripped all the way down to the base then broke off to twist my ball sac in my palm, just sharply enough that the bite made my abs clench before I went back to a quick pace.

I'd make Aurora stay there, dick stuffing her mouth, and every time she shuffled on her knees, I'd pull her hair.

Every time she swallowed, I'd stroke her face.

Goddammit, that was hot.

Before I'd learned what Aurora was into, if you'd asked me if I was kinky, I'd have laughed and said the only kinky thing about me was that I liked my partner to get off if I did, but Aurora had opened my eyes to this world.

She'd shown me this, revealed it to me, and once that door was open, you couldn't just close it, not if it was the reason why you couldn't have the woman you'd wanted your whole life.

Until Aurora, I'd never wanted a partner to crawl toward me, to sit with my cock in her mouth for a half hour, to pull her hair until it hurt and to promise punishments if she didn't obey. But Aurora craved that, and now, I did too.

What she wanted and needed, I wanted and needed to give to her.

Along the path of self-discovery, I'd learned my own preferences and was growing more at ease with them. What she'd begun, I was finishing.

Absently, I watched the sub deepthroat her Dom's dick, but there was no passion in it. He used her mouth like she was a hole. She didn't spread her legs either. She just rocked back and forth with the motion of his hips as he fucked her face.

I wouldn't do it that way.

I'd have her kneel and spread her legs so I could see her cunt.

Which, of course, would be fucking drenched.

I'd tell her that if she was a good girl, she could get off.

That if she managed to stay quiet, if she kept my dick between her lips for as long as I wanted, I'd let her touch her clit.

Shuddering at the thought, my head rocked back slightly as the pleasure sizzled through my veins.

I imagined Aurora struggling to take every inch of my long cock. In my mind's eye, I saw how her lips would be stretched around the shaft. I thought about rubbing a finger about the taut pull on her mouth, maybe shoving the digit in there to make it more uncomfortable.

Fuck.

Her eyes would be big and round and so eager to please.

So hungry for me.

So desperate for my cum.

For *my* pleasure.

Fuck.

Her breathing would be heavy, her tits moving with the motion.

Fuck.

My hand sped up, faster, faster. I grunted as the guy pulled back and jizzed all over his sub's face.

What a fucking waste.

He didn't get her to beg for it, didn't get her to stick her tongue out so he had somewhere to aim.

My heart pounded; my balls drew up. Sweat prickled on my brow—*I was close.*

I thought about what I'd do instead. Something that'd be so much fucking better than this asswipe who was beyond unimaginative.

I'd get her to whisper, "I need your cum in my mouth, Hunter. Please, please, can I have it?"

"Have you earned it?" I'd reply.

Aurora would whimper: "I've been so good today."

I'd laugh—Aurora was incapable of being good all the time. I'd tell her everything she'd done wrong, just so that I could see the fear in her eyes that she wouldn't get to swallow my cum, then I'd rumble, "Do you want to know how you can earn it?"

Her head would bob with how hard she nodded—*always so fucking eager for me.*

"Rub your clit," I'd tell her. "If you can get off before I do, you've earned it."

Then I'd watch her touch herself, fingers lightning fast, speeding up as she sought her pleasure. When the incoming tension would appear in her expression, one that spoke of the dam of ecstasy being on the brink of rupturing, that'd be when I'd let go, when she'd be deserving of my seed.

"Open your mouth like a good girl," I'd tell her.

Out her tongue would pop and I'd watch as my cum pooled there.

She'd hold it until I said, "Swallow it down now, baby girl."

And she'd obey.

And—

I came.

I came so hard that it hurt.

I didn't stop until I'd wrung out every last drop of seed.

Blood rushing in my ears, skin flushed, body heated, I opened my eyes and saw the Dom in the room lacklusterly spanking his sub.

I closed them again.

Aurora in my fantasy was better than anyone in real life.

That was a truth that had haunted me for decades.

Feeling oddly ashamed of what I'd just done, I tucked my cock away and started to turn from the scene ahead.

That was when my cell buzzed.

Aurora: *I didn't forget!! It's been crazy today. Happy birthday, Hunter. I hope you had cake!!*

A stupid grin creased my jaw as I ran my thumb over the screen of my cell.

She hadn't forgotten.

I blew out a breath.

Maybe there was hope for us yet.

7

AURORA

DADDY ISSUES - THE NEIGHBOURHOOD

THREE DAYS BEFORE CHRISTMAS

RELEASING A SHAKY BREATH, I logged onto our chat.

Whenever I did this, I wasn't sure if I was a fool or…

I sighed.

To be frank, the alternative wasn't much better.

I was NYC's most feared DA, for God's sake—the city's criminal underbelly trembled at the mention of my name—yet here I was, pining over someone whose face I hadn't even seen.

Ever.

For years, I'd been hiding my identity. It had started as escapism, and I'd continued to shield it because of my position, but now, the masks might as well have been shackles.

"There you are."

As always, his voice instantly soothed me. Low, deep, grumbly. I knew he was a Primal, even if he didn't, and while I hadn't been into that before, I knew I was now.

Because of him.

What his growls could do to me made him the equivalent of

chasing a Valium with a bottle of tequila. That sounded bad, but in my line of work, I'd take a relaxant however I could find one. At least this didn't result in a stint in the ER getting my stomach pumped.

Plus, nothing worked better for making me want to spread my legs. A few whispers from him and my problem was keeping them closed.

"Hey."

My greeting had him tilting his head to the side. "How's my sunshine?"

Hating how I reacted to his question, my insides shrinking as I contemplated how to answer him, I hitched a shoulder.

"Words," he drawled, not an ounce of bite to his tone, but I knew to respond to it anyway.

I'd once mistaken a gentle demeanor for someone who could be led around by his dick. That lesson had been *learned* a long ass time ago.

"Last couple days have been crazy."

I noticed the tension in his shoulders lessen some at my mutter. "Your uncle?"

"Uncle?"

"Your uncle. The sick one?"

I blinked. Oh. *Oh.* Fuck. I'd told him my great-uncle was my uncle. Jesus. He didn't know he was in a prison hospital either.

Even when you were smart, lies caught up with you eventually. Especially when you were too busy ogling someone on the screen in front of you.

"Yes, oh. Sorry. Damn. My brain is rattled."

"What's going on, Sunny?" His concern oozed off the screen.

Sometimes, on days like today, his emotions were rawer than mine. It somehow made it okay for me to *feel*. For the armor-plated wall around my heart to crack and for my own feelings to be allowed to splinter through.

As a result, speaking with him was as calming as it was exhilarating. I'd yet to figure out how he managed to combine the two, which were polar opposite, and considered it his personal brand of crack.

It was what kept me coming back for more.

Unsure of how to answer, I just said, "Rough couple days at the office."

The best lies were couched in the truth.

That meant he knew I was in some form of law enforcement. I'd told him I worked for a security company that specialized in private investigation.

So many lies, so much to juggle. Was it any wonder some days I felt like my head could explode?

"Watch your tone," he said calmly but didn't give me a chance to apologize as he questioned, "What happened at work?" His interest was genuine.

That was D.

While we were both cagey about certain parts of our lives, he gave a damn. He didn't pry, but his care shone through. Never feigned, never pushed aside so that we could focus on sex.

I was his priority.

"Another rape," I told him though I probably shouldn't. "Same MO —" I cleared my throat and quickly corrected, "Same MO as the one my client's daughter endured."

"Jesus. I'm sorry," he rasped.

"Yeah. Me too."

Rapists and the *Famiglia* were my weaknesses.

I took down the Italian mafia from a legal standpoint while, behind the scenes, my brothers and I undermined everything the *Famiglia* stood for. I'd made a reputation on ball-busting them and being tough on rapists.

There were some perks to my job.

"That's the fourth one now?"

"It is." I sucked in a breath. "No woman's safe in this country with the antiquated laws we have in place, and the NYPD is doing dick to help. It's only going to get worse. Just watch them double down their efforts to overturn Roe v. Wade."

"Surely not?"

I shrugged, though deep inside, my heart ached. My body. *My choice*. What was it with governments who didn't realize they didn't have a say about what went down in my uterus?

"As for this rapist," D was grating out, "I hope they catch the son of a bitch and make him burn for it."

"You're not talking about the electric chair, are you? Isn't that the most antiquated law of all?"

"More than one kind of justice."

"I can't disagree," I said gruffly. In this, I'd always be pro-*lex talionis*. With my past, how couldn't I be?

"Does it rake up what happened in college?"

Behind my mask, I pursed my lips. "You know I don't like talking about that."

"Doesn't mean you shouldn't," was his immediate answer before his tone turned winsome. "But you and I don't see eye to eye on that topic, and I don't feel like arguing tonight or punishing you for being hard-headed."

"You don't?" I arched a brow he couldn't see, but I didn't feel like arguing either. Arguing would have been smart, considering. Only I wasn't feeling smart. I was feeling needy. And horny. "What do you feel like doing—" I gave a lengthy pause, seeing his posture shift before I breathed, "—*sir?*"

Behind the Guy Fawkes mask I both loved and loathed, the wide grin that made him look as if he were leering, the thick brows, the painted moustache and goatee beard, all I could see were his eyes. At that moment, I saw his pupils dilate.

Whereas I preferred low lighting, D had no problem with bright lights.

Why would he?

He was stacked like a god.

A god with eyes that could make me feel things I hadn't felt in years. A single look could have me tumbling down toward the depths of hell, and I didn't mind. Didn't care. Because he always caught me before I landed in front of Lucifer's throne.

I clenched my thighs at the thought.

Knowing that I could look into those eyes *in person*, that I could have his arms around me, cushioning me from every blow that life dealt, was a sweet torment.

Knowing that he'd work me over in person in a heartbeat made every video call bittersweet.

If I told him I wanted to meet up, at long last, I knew he'd hop on a plane before the night was over. No waiting around or playing games. He wouldn't make me go to him but would come to me.

He was like that—the perfect gentleman.

On the outside.

Inside was a different matter entirely.

But that was why we fit, I thought. From the outside looking in, I was cool and calm and the lady my noble-born British mother had raised. Inside, I was a welter of rash emotions that I rarely knew how to control… until him.

Always him.

Was it possible to love someone without ever having seen their face?

Without knowing their true scent?

Without having felt their touch?

With so many lies between us?

I knew the answer; I was just afraid to admit it to myself.

"Sunny," he practically crooned, his voice low as always, deep and dark and unctuous like molten chocolate. "Take off the robe."

Biting my lip, I got to my feet.

We had a routine—one we never deviated from, so in truth, I guessed it was more of a ritual.

He always answered his video call wearing a light blue Oxford shirt and charcoal slacks. I always wore a matching blue silk robe with nothing beneath it, the starburst waterfall earrings he'd bought me for my birthday, and a set of heels that were impractical anywhere other than the bedroom.

On my face, I wore a full carnival mask that only revealed my eyes. It was a dark blue, tonal to the robe, and had bronze dusted over the features which had swirled ridges along the brow, cheeks, and jaw in a floral motif.

Before the call, I lit several candles and sprayed the aftershave he sent me.

Tonight, I found no comfort in our ritual, in his cologne—I was nervous. More nervous than I'd been the first time I'd bared myself to him.

"I need you, Sir," I whispered, the words torn from me because the truth often had to be dragged out of me.

It wasn't that I preferred lies; it was that it was easier to exist in this world with them.

The truth got a person nowhere.

"I know you do, baby girl," he rasped, but though my words were standard in a sensual situation, he knew me too well.

I whimpered.

He straightened up and leaned forward. "What's going on with you tonight?"

At some point, I'm going to have to say goodbye…

My mouth trembled as I slipped out of the robe, watching his focus drift to my tits. The nipple rings were new—a request of his. As was the clit hood piercing I had.

For years, we'd played this song and dance together.

Years.

I didn't want it to end.

Wanted more, if anything.

But there was no place in my life for this.

The time for fooling around was running out.

Luciu was about to ascend.

My twin brother would no longer just be some penny-ante criminal trying to cause the Italian mafia as much hassle as he possibly could.

He was about to become the Don of the *Sicilian* mafia itself.

Not wanting to answer him—unable to, in all honesty—I reached up and rubbed my nipple where the rings were still pinching.

"Sore?" he asked, his voice a low rumble I felt in my core.

I nodded. "A touch. Not as much as before."

He let loose a heavy sigh as if he were thinking about sucking on one, and the very notion made me feel delirious with want.

Unfortunately, that was a weakness, and I had no room for that in my life. D was a big, fat, Adonis-shaped, hung-like-a-horse weakness.

"May I touch myself, Sir?" I breathed.

"You didn't send me a picture last night," he murmured absently, his focus on my tits.

"It was a heavy day."

"And how do we end heavy days?"

By rote, I answered, "Touching base with those who matter most."

He hummed. "You didn't answer my text message this morning either."

I knew I'd regret radio silence. "I had an emergency phone call to handle."

"There wasn't a single point in the day where you could have replied to me?"

His tone had darkened.

Turned sterner.

Inside, I melted.

I loved his gentleness. I loved that he could and would treat me like glass, and that he'd make me feel like a princess.

But sometimes, the princess was a pain slut who needed to feel the burn when she sinned.

Sometimes a princess didn't need to sit on a pedestal—but a nice, fat, thick cock.

Or dildo, as the case might be.

"Sunny?" he demanded. "Words."

The bite was there.

I shivered at the cocktail of emotion that could only be described as terrified lust. "I could have replied."

"Why didn't you?"

"Because I—" I bowed my head, not wanting to look at him. "Because—"

"It's that time of the year, isn't it?"

I reared back. "What?"

"It's that time of the year where you try to pull away, right?"

"No!"

"It is." His eyes turned frosty. "Neither of us wanted this, Sunny. We were both very candid with each other at the start, and this level of… *commitment* that we have to one another is unprecedented.

"You know I'm in love with another woman, and I know you're married to your job, but that doesn't mean we can just walk away from each other.

"This isn't something we can walk away from."

The words should have choked me.

A part of them did.

'You know I'm in love with another woman.'

Jealousy had me spitting, "If you're so in love with her, then why don't you go to her?" Whoever *her* was.

"Jealousy," he purred. "So unlike you."

I turned my face away from the screen.

"Look. At. Me."

My shoulders straightened as I forced myself to stare at him.

His posture projected his displeasure. "Nothing about this is ideal, Sunny. *Nothing*. But we do not resort to ghosting—"

"It was one text message!" I cried. The instant I said it, I knew I'd fucked up.

His voice flatlined. "Get the cane."

"No! I didn't do anything."

"This morning's text isn't the first you've ignored in the last couple days. Nor is it the first time you've failed to send a picture. We have rules for this exact reason. I've been lenient because I know this case is rough on you, what with your past, but you don't need me to be lenient, do you, pet? You need me to be me.

"How would you feel if I didn't answer your texts, hmm? Your calls?"

Like I was dying.

And that was why this had to stop.

"Sunny, *words*," he growled, and the bite made my stomach flutter.

A soft moan escaped me, pain-filled, *anxious*, as I caught his gaze. Honest words spilled from me. "It would break me."

He dipped his chin. "Now, if you want to stop, we stop. We don't resort to childish shit where you hide from me, okay?"

It went without saying that he'd never hide from me.

"Okay."

"Do you want this to stop?"

I needed it to.

"No."

I didn't want *it to.*

"Fetch the cane."

Swallowing, I drifted back to the closet where I hid my stash.

Amid the toys that gave me pleasure, there were very few implements of punishment.

My first Master—my husband—had been more punishment-heavy than D was. I still didn't know what I preferred. Maybe it'd be different if D was *here*.

The notion sent a rush of sensation down my spine.

"Sunny? What's the hold up?"

"Sorry, Sir," I called out and returned to the camera. I jolted in surprise when I found him standing because I knew what that meant.

"Assume the position."

I obeyed without a second thought. Sinking to my knees, grateful for his command, my focus on him, I watched as he began to unbuckle his belt.

My eyes caught on the elaborate signet ring on his pinkie finger. D never wore jewelry, and this was definitely new.

Before I could ask about it, the leather was sliding out of the loops and he gathered it in his fist. I could easily imagine him using that on me. Whipping me with it, making me hurt.

I shuddered in response to my own thoughts.

I knew it was wrong to crave pain the way that I did, but he never made it seem wrong.

Not like my ex-husband.

He never taunted me for it. If anything, he nourished it. Like it was a hunger that needed feeding, he never begrudged it. Always celebrated my quirks.

God, why did this have to be so complicated?

Why couldn't I just have him in my life?

When he dragged down his zipper after unbuttoning his fly, I felt my heart start to race. I could hear the blood rushing in my ears as he pulled his cock out, and he maintained a loose grip on it as he gave it a single stroke.

I swore my mouth watered at the sight.

There was something forbidden about him.

The fact that we'd never touched but were so up in each other's lives… We knew so much about one another and yet so little.

I knew what his cock looked like, knew what made him hard, knew what got him off quickly, but I didn't know what his lips tasted of, or if he'd jackhammer my face as he made me deepthroat that long shaft. I didn't know if his cum was salty or bitter or both. I didn't know what sounds he made when he brushed his teeth—did he hum? Or was he silent?

I'd bet he hummed.

D was infinitely cheerful.

He reminded me of Hunter in that sense.

Pain slithered through me at the thought, the emotional kind, not the physical. Give me *physical* hurt any day of the week.

Shoving it and memories of Hunter aside, I focused on D when he rasped, "Spread your legs and show me your new piercing." Pointedly, he said, "I didn't get to see how it's healing last night."

It wasn't *new*. But it was new for us because it had been a no-go zone since I'd had it done.

Much like the nipple piercings, it had taken a while to heal.

"Do you want a picture, Sir?" I whispered.

He grunted. It wasn't a dismissive grunt. More of a 'I don't have the words for how much I want that' grunt.

A soft smile that he couldn't see curved my lips.

D was predictable in some things.

He liked having photos of me. It made sense—images were all we had of each other.

Still kneeling, I parted my legs to give him a better view, then I reared up to grab my phone from the console. At the same time, I switched on a light.

This area was my play area.

It was void of all things personal so that he could never work out who I was.

I used two VPNs to communicate with him, and though I didn't like Android phones and preferred iPhones, I always called him from an Android, one that I kept stored in a safe here with the laptop I used for video calls with him and him alone so that there'd never be a trace of our conversations. A voice modulator deepened my words by an octave so that everything I said could never be recorded and used to trace back to my identity.

Paranoid?

True that.

With the light puddled around me as I sank back down, I saw that his hand had sped up. Biting my lip, I turned my phone between my thighs and snapped a picture.

Sending it to him, I watched as he picked up his cell with his free hand and stared at the photo.

He gave another of those grunts. "Those marks are getting better. Take a close-up shot." When I didn't obey immediately, he rumbled, "Sunny."

We engaged in a visual tug of war and, quickly, I bowed my head in defeat.

"You're sassy tonight."

I knew what that word meant.

He used it when…

Fuck.

Distress filling me, twisting and morphing into the crudest of needs, I swallowed. "I'm not, Sir. I promise."

He didn't answer my plea, just stared at me in silence as I moved my legs wider open.

D's silence achieved more reaction out of me than a judge letting an Italian fucker loose when I'd forged an ironclad case against the bastard.

I'd have preferred for D to want a close up shot of my cunt. Instead, he wanted to see the marks on my inner thighs. My ex had originally given me the scars during knife play. I'd consented to the play, just not to bleeding. He hadn't listened.

Marcus never did.

By comparison, D listened to more than I actually said.

He hated when I made myself bleed during my self-punishments. I couldn't say that I even did it for the normal reasons—because it was easier to feel pain than it was to hurt emotionally. I wished I did it for that reason, but I didn't.

I just liked it.

He did not.

I'd stopped doing it so much since he'd become a fixture in my life, but some days… the call, the *pull* was too strong.

A bizarre anticipation sizzled inside me as I took the photo and showed him the mottled flesh that was bright red in some areas, purple in others, yellow in some parts. The whole area was overlaid with tiny scabs that I enjoyed picking. Not the prettiest sight, but fuck if it didn't feel good.

One thing I loathed was that he treated it as self-harm and didn't punish me for it.

It *wasn't* self-harming. It was my pain slut coming out, needing to play.

So, truly, I was committing the worst sin of all in our kind of dynamic—topping from the bottom—meaning that I *deserved* a punishment, but he never gave one to me.

I had specific toys for this. Inserts that went into my bras which were dotted with spikes that I felt throughout the day. I'd sharpened them so that they'd prick my nipples and make the little holes bleed.

Just thinking about it made the hairs at my nape stand on end.

The ones between my thighs were different, though. They were created by a vampire paddle. A strip of wood studded with more spikes. The impact play combined with the spikes often made a blotchy mess of my inner thighs.

I loved it.

Especially because using it over and over created tens of pinpricks that bled and oozed. Fuck, the instant release of endorphins would forever make me want to melt.

"Next time you want to…" D hesitated. This was where his inexperience as a Dom came into play. I didn't begrudge him it because he got me on so many other levels that I simply couldn't. "…you tell me, baby girl," he intoned starkly, much as he always did.

I nodded.

"You want to hurt, I'll make you hurt. But we do it together. Not when you're alone, do you hear me?"

Swallowing, I whispered, "Okay, Sir."

"Spread your pussy lips."

I obeyed.

"I want a ring on your labia next," he mused. "Two to keep those pretty lips open for me at all times."

Shuddering at the prospect, I nodded again, knowing not to speak out. I hated having another woman's hands on me during the piercing process, but the pain did feel good.

I almost wished my clit hood piercing wasn't healed.

"I want six slaps of the cane to those scars." I often wondered if he was punishing me there, or my old Master. "Each side," he directed. "Go as hard as you can. I want to hear you howl."

It was my turn to give one of those grunts—the 'I don't have the words for how much I want that' grunt.

I snagged the cane and hit the soft pink flesh.

My throat arched as the pain slammed into me.

Sharp and toxic, dull and bittersweet.

It had ruined everything—my most cherished friendship, every relationship with a man I'd ever had.

It was addictive.

I could actually taste it.

It tasted like poison.

It tasted like strawberries.

It tasted perfect.

"You're so beautiful, baby girl," D praised, his voice so low that it didn't jar me from what I was doing. It just augmented it.

His words were the salve I needed.

They grounded me.

I closed my eyes, uncaring if I hit my pussy—almost wishing it would—as I slashed the cane down again. This time, it hit a raw nerve and I gave him what he wanted.

A howl.

I reared up onto my knees as my muscles strove to work through the physical discomfort I'd given myself, and like always, I imagined it was him doing this. Him hitting me better than I could hit myself. Hurting me without having to direct me.

God, the pain. I needed it. I'd do anything for it. Anything.

"Give me four more, my pet," he rumbled, his voice ever deeper as he grew aroused at the sounds I released. "Hard ones. Like you mean it. Nice and quick."

I sucked in a breath as I obeyed. Going fast and hitting heavy. Enough that, for a moment, a wonderfully beautiful, delicious moment, I thought of nothing.

Nothing.

My mind was blank.

Free.

These were the moments I chased.

These were the moments he gave me.

I tried it by myself, but it never worked.

Not even with my ex-husband was it this strong.

It wasn't subspace, just a freedom from my thoughts. A brain that always raced, that never stopped working. That woke me at three AM when I had to be up at five because something occurred to me, something that just couldn't wait.

Free.

Until it started working again.

Until thoughts returned.

Until I heard the slap-slap of his fist around his cock.

My eyes popped open because that was something I didn't want to miss. Something worthy of having my brain refocus.

"Pinch those pretty nipples, Sunny, until they bleed white," he ground out. "So delicious, do you know that? Like cherries I want to suck and bite. Would you like that?"

I moaned. "Yes, Sir. I'd like that. I'd want you to bite them. They're yours to bite."

His fingers tightened around his shaft to the point where I knew it had to hurt.

I gave him what he wanted, cringing at the pinch where the piercings were healing but also enjoying it because I was sick like that.

My pussy pulsed in time to the beat of my heart, and I knew if I slipped a finger inside, I'd be so wet I'd make a river look dry.

Only he could do that to me.

Only D.

Men in my office were too scared to approach me, too submissive in the face of my domineering nature to even think of trying to ask me out.

They called me a bitch behind my back because they were too unimaginative to understand that I was a strong-minded woman who didn't accept their BS. Were I a man, they'd have aspired to be me. Because I was a woman, they were scared…

I was surrounded by wimps.

That was why D was special; only he could break down my walls.

Could make me kneel.

Like he knew what I was thinking, he bit off, "Keep those fingers on your nipples. You can only orgasm tonight by playing with them. You're not allowed to touch your pussy."

I swallowed down a protest.

"You think that's mean, my little one?"

His fist had sped up. I could see pre-cum beading on the glans. Saliva flooded my mouth as I imagined sucking on that, sucking him dry. God, I could almost taste him on the tip of my tongue. Or, a facsimile of him, at least.

"Sunny!" he barked. "Answer me."

"I-I do, Sir," I whimpered.

"Sassy, so sassy. Not answering me when I ask you a question. Ignoring my texts. My calls. Not sending me photos. You tell me why you deserve release?"

"The last week has been hard."

"So's my cock." He tutted, the sound breathy, which I knew was a precursor to his climax. Then: "Get the belt. It's time to graduate to size three."

He'd stopped thrusting his hips.

His cock looked like it could burst, but his control was so strong that he could stop himself.

I'd never known a man who could be that close to the edge but be able to rein it in so well.

I knew, in bed, he'd be an animal. I knew he wouldn't stop until his partner got off.

That could be you, Aurora. You fool. You fool.

Instead, he punished me with chastity because there were few angles of leverage the man had in my life.

Because you're a moron and you wouldn't let him visit you even if he asked.

Clambering to my feet, I headed to the closet again. I picked up the items he wanted, then I returned to the laptop.

Placing the items on the towel I'd laid to the side earlier, I grabbed the computer, positioned it on the floor, and I turned away from it, swinging back and around so that he had a perfect view of my ass and pussy.

"So wet," he groaned.

"For you, Sir. Only for you," I whispered.

I knew I could plead out of this punishment. Use work as an excuse. Tell him more. But why would I want that? D wasn't unreasonable. If he knew the pressure I was under, if I explained it, he'd relent.

But I didn't want him to.

I needed this.

Even if I hated the belt.

Even if I loathed it.

This way, I experienced his touch all day, every day.

"You're to keep that on for three days. You can take it off to use the restroom *but* for no longer than fifteen minutes each time."

I glowered at the carpet, knowing he wouldn't be able to see my expression.

"I think a dry insertion, don't you, pet?"

Though I winced, my inner pain slut preened.

He knew I'd take it. Knew I'd do it. And my body *would* obey. Not just his command, but my own.

He'd sent this to one of the private mail services I maintained in the city, and over the years, the collection had increased.

It was a metal rod with several attachments hooked onto it: one for the front, one for the back.

I'd never asked if he remained chaste for me, but I knew this was a means of ensuring *I* was for him. He only brought it out when he was pissed at me, which was becoming a more common occurrence lately.

I grabbed the anal plug and rubbed it against the pucker of my ass, bearing down and grimacing at the chalky sensation of the metal ball rubbing against the rosette.

It was even more uncomfortable when I took the whole thing inside, but the pain felt good.

Somehow, that made me feel even more alien.

How could I like this?

Releasing a soft breath, I grabbed the larger ball and slotted it into my cunt. That was easy because of how wet I was. It was such a dissatisfying shape, though. I didn't want a *ball*. It wasn't him. But I took it. It was better than nothing.

The rod slipped between the lips of my sex and between my ass cheeks. It wasn't particularly comfortable, like a metal G-string without a crotch, but I didn't mind that.

At either end, there was a loop. When both balls were inside me, I turned around and reached for the thin metal chain that coiled about my waist. It sat low and slotted through those end loops like an obscene pair of panties. A tiny padlock kept it attached. For ease, I wore the key on a necklace so I could use the restroom.

When I was 'dressed,' I faced him again.

God, his cock…

It was so dark, pulsing with blood. I wanted nothing more than to soothe that ache, but I just pleaded, "Can I have your cum, Sir?"

His head tipped back, rocking on his shoulders as he quickened his pace.

A small whimper escaped me and the noise had him tilting his head forward, eyes connected with mine as he released the deepest groan.

When he came, cum bursting forth, leaking onto the table in front of him, I breathed, "I wish I could swallow that, Sir."

Low, hissed breaths rattled from him as he rocked his hips, pumping his dick into his fist, getting every last bit of pleasure out of his orgasm.

His hand shook with how hard his release hit him, and the sight had my pussy and ass clenching around the balls inside me. The pain would see me through, not as delicious as an orgasm, but almost.

"Don't ignore me again," he warned, his darker tone a surprise, especially after he'd come. "Go and run the bath, pet."

Quick to obey, I grabbed my cell and switched to the app that would modulate my voice during a call, then I buzzed him through our chat.

"Hello, little one," he greeted, his tone gentle. Soothing. Different now that he'd given me his warning.

I placed the call on speaker then ended our video chat. "Hello, D."

Leaving my laptop to power down, I headed into the bathroom.

Aftercare over a distance wasn't easy, but we made it work. Ironically, I thought he needed it more than I did.

I set the water running, threw in the bath bombs he sent me every few weeks, and I went around the tub lighting the candles he also had shipped to me so I could switch off the insanely over-the-top chandelier that would have been better suited to a ballroom but which I'd fallen in love with in a vintage antique store years ago.

Once the bath was filled to an adequate level, I settled into the water and released a sigh.

The quietness in my brain had been disrupted by his earlier warning of, "Don't ignore me again," and now that my tasks were complete, I could think about his words properly.

I never wanted to ignore him, but I had to place distance between us or, when the time came for us to part—and that time *would* come— my heart would break.

The truth was that Luciu's time was near. His ascension to the position of Don was in the works… I couldn't risk associating with D when that happened. Not just because he was something that could be used against me, but because his safety could be in jeopardy.

And I'd have to marry.

I needed someone I could use as a puppet, who would be the face of the Consigliere position because my identity could never become a matter of public information, not with my past as DA.

In a perfect world, D could be my husband, but he wasn't malleable. So even if I wanted to take this to the next level, I couldn't.

My life was about to change forever, and he couldn't be in it when that happened.

But, time… I needed more of it.

"You're quiet, sweetheart."

I both hated and loved that endearment, especially when he uttered it in that gentle voice. I'd give my left ovary to have him in the bath with me, to have his arms around me, to cuddle into him—and trust me, I was *not* a cuddler—but instead, I had the water and his voice in my ears.

It wasn't enough, but it was perfect all the same.

"I was just thinking, D," I told him softly.

His chair creaked, and I imagined he was rocking back in it so he could rest his legs on his desk. "What about?"

I sucked in a breath and gave him a promise I wasn't sure how I'd uphold: "I won't ignore you again, Sir."

That was the best I could do, and it was technically more than I was capable of offering.

He hummed his pleasure at the promise, and then we just relaxed together; thousands of miles separated us, but his words and his breathing and the care from the candles he sent, which permeated the air with warmth and with the scent of lavender, and the still fizzing bath bomb made themselves known to me like the silent hug they were.

And if cracks started making an appearance on the heart my minions at the DA office said was stone cold, then I was the only one who knew about that weakness.

It would have to stay that way.

More than likely forever.

HUNTER
MEASURE OF A MAN - FKA TWIGS

LATE DECEMBER

"I FUCKING HATE YOU," I ground out as I slipped on the Guy Fawkes mask and slotted it into place. The plastic made me sweat, the edges dug into my jaw, and yes, I was being a fucking baby. Sue me.

Once I'd adjusted the damn thing in the mirror, I looked at my watch.

I was running late, but Sunny was running *later* than late. She'd been better about communicating this past week—communication was one of her weaknesses—and I was only forgiving her now because we were still in the swing of things in the run up to New Year's.

When my cell buzzed, I heaved a sigh when I saw my grandfather's name on the screen.

"Bert, I'm busy." Busy being goddamn DDoSunlight when I seriously wasn't in the mood for games. "I told you earlier not to call."

"Those *Reyes Dorados* are driving me crazy."

"What do you want me to do about it?"

"Can't you put one of those viral things on them?"

"It isn't like giving someone a cold, Bert," I chided, though my lips twitched. "And I mean, sure, we could put them on TikTok, but I don't see how them going viral will help matters."

He huffed in my ear. "I've heard of that before."

"Heard of what before?" Feeling like a moron because I was talking to him with the mask on, I tipped it higher on my head and stared at myself in the mirror.

I was too fucking old to be playing dress up, but it was Sunny's biggest hard limit—her identity had to be shielded at all costs.

"Hunt? You there?"

Blinking, I muttered, "Yeah, I'm here. Sorry. I have to go soon though. And sure, I can set them up with a virus, but to what end?"

"Can't you just annihilate them?"

I rolled my eyes. "Malware attacks computers, Bert. Not men."

"I know that," he scoffed, but he said it in a way that made me think he'd been watching movies from the eighties again because he didn't sound like he believed me a hundred percent.

"You sure? What do you want to hit?"

"Their bank accounts. Hit 'em where it hurts."

"You're just asking for retaliation."

"They're begging for it too."

"Is this what the Camorra has to resort to? Tit for tat with a fucking gang?"

Silence was my answer.

Then, "You're right. We need to hit them harder. Wipe 'em out."

"You need to think about this, is what you need. Come to me with a plan of action that won't trigger a war on L.A.'s streets."

"They're my streets," he said with a sniff. "I can do what I want with them."

"The *Reyes* and those Vitales share borders," I warned. "You need precision if you don't want to—"

"Don't want to, what? They're here because I allowed the Vitales to come running to L.A. with their tails tucked between their legs after the Valentinis got slaughtered. They're here on my say so."

"They've earned their patch. It's theirs."

"So? I don't want to hit them. I want to hit the *Reyes*."

"And you know it's not as simple as that." I rubbed my eyes—dealing with him was like trying to appease a homicidal toddler sometimes. "Bert, if you want me to fuck with their online presence, I will, but I want more of a plan than toss a hand grenade, duck, and run for cover."

He sniffed. "You're too up in that big brain of yours, Hunt. That's always been your problem."

My cell pinged with the notification that was set for my interactions with Sunny—it meant that she was in our chatroom.

Just that had my heart racing, blood surging through my being and pooling right at my dick.

Before I could leave the conversation with my grandfather behind, he grated out, "Those *Reyes* are getting too big for their own good. I told Paulu last year that they needed bringing down a couple pegs but he talked me out of it."

I clicked my tongue. "You know what I think about Paulu."

"Starting to think I should have listened."

"Brunu doesn't like him either, does he?" Brunu was Bert's Capo. Paulu was his Consigliere.

"Nah," he disregarded. "But you know Brunu, funny fucker. Doesn't like many people."

Another ping sounded—Sunny wasn't used to me being late.

"I'll help, Bert. You know I will. We have enough shit with the Macmillans right now. Don't act in haste."

"Sometimes that's the best way to wage a war."

"It's also the best way to get your ass handed to you."

"The only Macmillan who still has a problem with us is that moronic ADA."

"Understandable given the circumstances," I said uneasily.

"How is it understandable?" Bert argued. "No body, no crime."

"His brother's been missing for years." And I'd been the one to deliver him to the Reaper.

"The man should have been born in Sicily. We're the only ones who can usually hold grudges that long." Damn if Bert didn't sound impressed by the feat.

Scowling at my reflection, I muttered, "Macmillan's a problem."

"You give him too much credit. There's nothing on you, Hunter. Nothing at all. And if there was, what would you say? You found the eldest Macmillan, American aristocracy, raping some poor college girl and put a stop to it?"

"That doesn't mean he isn't dangerous. He's been climbing the ranks—"

"I know he has, but as I told you when you shared the truth of your history with the Macmillans, there's nothing to worry about. If there is, I'll handle it."

"I'm not afraid of the consequences of my actions, Bert," I said, my tone somewhat stiff. That was usually how it rolled, though, when I thought about Aurora's ex-husband, Marcus Macmillan.

"No? Then what's to worry about?"

"You're being obtuse on purpose." I heard the sound of a lighter flicking in the background. "And those things will kill you."

"Cigar a day keeps the doctor away."

I snorted. "If you say so. Now, I'm going—"

"Got a date?" he inquired before I could end the call, his question making me groan.

"Not this again."

"A man your age should have kids already," he retorted. "You're not getting any younger."

"A man my age knows what he wants to do with his life," I countered, "and doesn't need to be told by his grandfather what he should or shouldn't have at the grand old age of thirty-fucking-five."

Bert cackled in my ear. "Touché, kiddo. Okay, okay, I'm going, I'm going. Speak later."

While he was reckless, he'd put me in a better mood by the time he'd cut the line. Wearing a slight grin, I strode over to my computer and started a video call, only remembering at the last minute that I'd tipped up the damn mask.

As I dragged it down to cover my features, I heard a soft gasp. "Oh!"

I wasn't the one bothered about anonymity, but I still laughed. "Sorry, Sunny."

"I've never seen your lips before," she whispered. It was only when her tone was soft or sharp that I heard the faint notes from the voice modulator she used.

With the levels she took to shield her identity, I figured she was high up in politics so I never pushed it. It rattled my cage that women in power were deeply scrutinized. I'd only just finished reading an article about a teacher who had a side gig as a romance author who'd been fired once some troll had outed her pseudonym online.

People fucking sucked.

"You've never seen them before because we wear masks all the time," I pointed out with a chuckle. "Trust me when I tell you, you're missing out."

"I'm sure I am," she said, amused.

The midnight-blue mask she wore, reminiscent of the type worn at Mardi Gras, provided me with as many clues about her identity as my Guy Fawkes one gave her.

Sometimes, the secrecy felt like a vice grip.

Sometimes, I appreciated it.

Today, I vacillated somewhere between the two, and I knew that was because Aurora's Christmas card had arrived—a couple days late.

Her mixed messages drove me fucking insane.

Good enough to remember to send a card to, not important enough to make sure it arrived on time.

I'd been agitated ever since. It was probably why I'd given Bert shit, too, instead of just doing as he wanted. Dropping malware on the *Reyes* was easy as pie. Too easy for me to even care about his motives or end game. But that was Aurora—she always managed to fuck me off more than most.

Hands curling into fists, I murmured, "Show me your inner thighs, Sunny."

There wasn't much of a segue, but there didn't need to be with Sunny and me. Plus, I was interested to see how she'd coped over the holidays.

I got my answer a moment later when I caught sight of the mottled skin.

If I were there, I'd throw that goddamn vampire paddle out. But I wasn't. And that was the problem.

As much as Sunny liked to hide behind masks, she needed a full-time Dom. Not an online one. I tried but there was only so much I could do from a distance.

My hands just itched to spank the fuck out of her ass. To paddle those plump cheeks until they were bright red and leaching into purple and her pussy was glistening with juices.

"I told you not to use that paddle anymore." A soft gulp from her was the only answer I needed. "What happened, Sunny?"

"The holidays were stressful and I needed the release," she mumbled.

I tapped my fingers against the desk, uncertain—and not for the first time—on how to give her what she needed when she put so many barriers between us.

If we were in the same room, it'd be so much easier, but I knew she'd never allow that. Even if she needed it. Or, hell, maybe because she *did* need it. Sunny was a masochist through and through.

"Get a towel, the dried garbanzo beans, capsaicin gel, and the wand."

A hiss escaped her, but she complied. "Yes, D."

It didn't sound like the most terrifying punishment in the world, but I knew both could and would drive her crazy.

Smiling to myself, I watched as she smoothly straightened up, her hurried steps betraying her eagerness. I permitted her free sway with the lighting in her room as long as I could see three out of four walls. That meant I watched her head to her play closet and saw her pull out the items I'd requested.

She returned to the mat where she resituated herself.

"Lay the towel down and pour the beans onto it."

"Yes, Sir." I watched as she spread the full jar of dried beans on the towel. "Is that okay, D?"

"It's perfect," I told her cheerfully. "Assume the position. Robe off first."

The blue silk robe puddled around her, and she neatly folded it and moved it aside before she placed a hand on the floor and used that as leverage so she could kneel on the towel.

The second the dried beans collided with her skin and gravity did the rest of the work for us both, she groaned.

"Every time you wriggle," I informed her, "that's one more minute of the wand and no orgasm. You're going to stay there for fifteen minutes total and afterward, I expect an apology."

"Yes, Sir."

There was the slightest of movements as she tried to shuffle without showing me so I barked, "One minute."

"D! I need to—"

"I told you not to use that paddle." I took a seat and settled back, keeping an eye on the clock to monitor the time. "Why did you use it?"

"I was stressed, Sir," she whispered.

Because she was naked, I could see how her tits vibrated with the inherent need to fidget.

When I'd come up with methods of punishing her from a distance, I'd tried this out and could confirm that it *hurt* like a motherfucker. The beans were hard and like small stones and they dug into the flesh and made the muscles themselves sore.

The need to ease the discomfort by shifting one's weight was natural.

Stopping her from moving entirely wasn't exactly cruel, but it served a purpose.

"Stressed about what?"

"My family."

"What about them?"

"My brothers got into some trouble."

Behind my mask, I arched a brow. "What did they do?"

She cleared her throat. "They don't get along well with these people on our street."

Her street? "They got into a fight?"

"Of sorts, Sir."

What were they—twelve? "Did they get injured?"

"No." She sighed. "But we also lost a couple family members."

Eyes flaring wide, I demanded, "Jesus, Sunny, why didn't you tell me sooner?"

"They're not blood-related—"

"Doesn't mean they're not kin."

"No. They're sorely missed."

"What did you think about when you were striking yourself?"

"I wished that you were doing it for me," she admitted miserably. "I know you'd hit harder."

Sunny would push my limits, I knew. I leaned toward softer punishments, but they weren't enough for her so I'd graduated over the years.

I rubbed my chin, absently noting another wriggle. "Two minutes."

She released a sharp breath, one soaked with pain.

Another wriggle. Followed by two more.

"Four minutes."

"Fuck," she whispered.

Then, I hit home with a punishment I knew she'd hate. "I want you to tell me five things you like about yourself."

"Five?" she whined.

"For that, you can tell me ten."

She grunted.

"Sunny," I warned when no reply was forthcoming. "One…"

"I like my hair."

"Two."

"I like that I'm smart."

"Three."

"I like my family. Even if they drive me crazy."

"Four."

"I like that I have curves."

So did I.

"Five."

"I like that I'm good at making sugar cookies."

That made me laugh. "How do you know they're good?"

"My mom doesn't bake them anymore; she makes me do it."

"Ah, a compliment indeed. Six."

"I like you."

"That doesn't count. Six."

This time, when she wriggled, it wasn't because of the beans.

"And another minute added… You're going to be miserable when that wand is on your clit," I reprimanded, amused when her throat bobbed. "Five minutes."

She huffed. "I like that I can speak several languages."

"What's your favorite?"

"Italian."

Something about her answer made me wonder if she was lying, but then, I had to ask myself why she'd bother to lie about something as simple as that. Instead, I asked, "Why Italian?"

"My family hails from there," was her stiff reply. "How much longer?"

I cast a look at the clock. "Seven minutes."

"Fuck," she gritted out, then she wriggled.

"Six minutes with the wand."

"Fuck," she repeated.

"You swear again," I warned, "and I'll add two minutes to the total time."

Her head whipped to the side before she quickly bowed it.

"You told me you like pain, Sunny," I crooned. "Name something else you like about yourself."

"I-I like that I'm good with plants."

"You are?" I inquired, surprised.

"Yes, D."

"I didn't know that. Remember I sent you that yuzu tree the first year?"

She released a choked laugh. "It's in my greenhouse."

"The question is," I said lightly, "is it still alive in there?"

Another laugh. "Yes. It's flourishing. I love it. Thank you."

"Eight."

"I appreciate that I'm good with numbers."

"Like balancing a check book?"

"Yes, like that." Another hiss whistled between her teeth. "How long, Sir?"

"Four minutes."

Her head bowed. "Thank you, Sir."

I hummed. "Nine."

It saddened me that she found it so difficult to compliment herself. In all our years together, I'd never been able to help her with that.

"I like that I'm close with my mother."

"What do you do together?"

"Nothing in particular. But we talk every day."

"Really?"

She blew out a breath. "Yes, Sir."

I'd known she had a close relationship with her mom but I was still curious. "What do you talk about?"

"Um. Everything?"

"What did you talk about today?"

"How long, Sir?"

"Two minutes."

"Thank you, D. Um, so, today, she was complaining about how her gardener keeps overpruning her bushes."

"Is that a euphemism?"

She let loose a choked laugh. "No. At least, I hope not."

"What kind of bushes?"

"You know, um, topiary?"

"Ten."

"I like that I can beat my brothers in a fight."

"What kind of fight?"

"Play fight."

"Do you do that often?"

"Not anymore."

"Then how do you know you can beat them?"

"Because I know their weak spots."

I chuckled. "Vixen."

"That's me," she gasped.

After casting a look at the clock, I murmured, "You can stand and apologize now."

A deep groan escaped her as she leaped upward. It always amazed me how the woman could hit herself with a spiked paddle and she'd be fine, but things like this were so difficult.

Breathlessly, she whispered, "I'm sorry for disobeying you, Sir."

Knowing she'd use that damn paddle again, whether it broke the rules or not, I didn't accept the apology, simply instructed, "Rub down your shins," then watched her brush away the beans that were stuck in the indentations they'd made in her skin. "Apply the gel on that area."

She paused in her ministrations. "Sir?"

"Do as I say," I told her calmly then remained silent as she followed my requests.

When the gel was applied, I took note of the clock, well aware that it took a few moments to kick in. "I want you to go stand in the corner now. For a half hour. You're not to speak to me. No requests for the time. You're to stand there and not utter a single word, Sunny. Do you understand me?"

She bowed her head, shoulders hunching. Sunny, more than being a masochist, did *not* like being ignored. "I understand, D."

Unlike her hurried strides of before, she shuffled over to the corner. It was the only one that she kept free from furniture and for this express reason.

Setting a timer on my watch for thirty minutes, I split my screen in two, keeping her at the forefront while also running through some of my programs.

Seeing that Lodestar had messaged, I grunted and decided to deal with her later—the woman needed my full focus or God only knew what she'd wheedle out of me.

As the minutes ran down, it didn't surprise me when I heard sniffling. Introspection and Sunny didn't go well together. I cast a look at her, making sure she hadn't turned away from the wall, and monitored her to make sure she wasn't suffering an adverse reaction to the gel or something.

When her shoulders shook, the need to comfort her was strong, but she didn't require that from me. Truth was, if it wasn't one of her requirements that we remain purely online, I didn't think I'd be pushing for us to meet IRL anyway.

We both had reasons for needing one another, and as much as I was fond of her, moving this to the physical wasn't something I wanted.

The thought made me feel bad, like I was being deceptive, but Sunny and I were honest with each other. IDs aside, that is. She knew why I was here, as much as I knew that she needed a Dom but didn't trust anyone enough to play with them in real life.

Scraping a hand over my jaw, I found myself relieved that the half hour was almost up. I didn't like making her cry, even if it was cathartic for her sometimes.

With the clock still ticking, I checked my email and immediately regretted doing so.

A couple minutes before my session with Sunny started, Aurora had emailed me.

I didn't thank you for sending Matri those flowers.
  This time of the year is always tough for her.
  A

HER FATHER HAD BEEN MURDERED the week before Christmas. It amazed me that she sounded surprised that I remembered when it had been one of the darkest times of both our lives.

The alarm on my watch buzzed, but my brain wasn't on the scene anymore. It was on Aurora. Always fucking Aurora.

No one pissed me off like she did.

No one.

When was I going to change the status quo between us? Every

fucking year I made myself a vow that I'd force her to see *me*. To forgive me. To do something that would help us reconnect.

Instead, here I was, fucking around with Sunny.

What was the matter with me?

Where was my brain at when the only woman I wanted was Aurora goddamn Fitzwilliam née Valentini?

Cracking my knuckles, I urged myself to face facts.

Bert wasn't wrong about me not getting any younger. I was too fucking old to be dealing with unrequited love, and I knew that this milk-water dynamic with Sunny wasn't going anywhere either. I deserved more than empty shells of relationships. I deserved to be loved.

But what did that mean?

No more wasting time.

It was precious.

With that in mind, I set myself a time limit.

A year.

Twelve months to make Aurora see me.

Three-hundred-sixty-five days to make Aurora mine.

But before then, I had to clean things up here.

I wasn't cruel, so I knew I had to finish this scene properly, and then, I had to end things with Sunny.

No more dicking around.

It was time to turn Aurora Valentini into Aurora De Laurentiis.

Or… let her go completely.

CHAPTER NINE

DDOSUNLIGHT *enters chat*

    DDoSunlight: *Sunny?*

    ChasteSunlight enters chat

ChasteSunlight: *Yes, Sir.*

DDoSunlight: *I'm really sorry but I can't do this anymore.*

ChasteSunlight: *You mean... us?*

DDoSunlight: *Yes.*

ChasteSunlight: *Are you KIDDING ME?*

DDoSunlight: *No. I'm really sorry.*

ChasteSunlight: *May I ask why?*

DDoSunlight: *It's complicated.*

ChasteSunlight: *Is it because of HER?*

DDoSunlight: *In a way.*

ChasteSunlight: *She snaps her fingers and you come running?*

DDoSunlight: *She doesn't know I'm alive, Sunny. Doesn't mean I don't know SHE is.*

ChasteSunlight: *Well, it doesn't matter. I was going to break things off anyway.*

DDoSunlight: *There's no need for bitterness between us then, is there?*

ChasteSunlight: *I suppose not.*

DDoSunlight: ***sigh** That means you're going to hold a grudge. If you ever need me, Sunny, I'm at the other end of the line. Please, don't let this take you down a self-destructive path. I'm here. I'm not going anywhere. I just can't be sexually involved with you anymore.*

DDoSunlight: *I care about you, Sunny. That hasn't changed.*
ChasteSunlight leaves chat

AURORA

EARLY FEBRUARY

MY CHIN JUTTED out in annoyance as I took a seat on my regular bench at the Met. The ginger in my ass didn't make itself known as much as I'd like.

"Desperate times call for desperate fucking measures," I grouched under my breath as I grabbed my purse, retrieving a sketchpad and pencil from its cavernous interior.

If I purposely rocked my hips back to feel the thumb of ginger inside me, so be it.

But…

Goddammit, *nothing*.

It did nothing.

Where was the tingle? Hell, screw the tingle, it was supposed to fucking burn. I'd scoured the internet for options that'd help ease the craving that wouldn't quit, and this was one of them, but it was useless.

Was I so desensitized to pain that I didn't experience it anymore? That raw ginger against tender tissues like the anal cavity didn't spark even a smidgen of discomfort?

"Should have stuck with the capsaicin," I hissed to myself, well aware that I looked like a crazy person, but to be frank, I *was* going crazy.

And crazy didn't look good on someone like me.

I was the stern negotiator. The woman who didn't blink when faced with a man pleading for his life after he'd had his eyeball scooped out. The bitch who stomped on men's dicks in boardrooms for fun.

Such thoughts only added to my stress, and a soft breath escaped me as I forced myself to focus on the art up ahead.

It might be over one hundred and twenty years old, but Mary Cassatt's *Young Mother Sewing* never failed to make me feel like a failure.

A woman was seated in a conservatory of sorts, a garden at her back. A child, looking at the viewer, leaned against her mother, elbows on her knees while her parent was sewing.

Such a simple image yet so powerful too.

Once upon a time, that had been my mom and me. Once upon a time, that had likely been my grandmother and her mom. It was timeless. It was emotional. It was…

I reached up and rubbed my forehead.

I didn't crave that.

I didn't.

I had goals. Aspirations. I had a vendetta to avenge.

Huffing, I took a quick glance around the room, noting that it was quiet because it was midweek. I settled in to recreate a painting I'd recreated every week for only God knew how long.

It was always this one.

Always.

Just as my mind shifted focus, my cell buzzed.

The distraction annoyed me, but because it was Hunter's chime, I begrudgingly picked up my phone and stared at the message.

Hunter: *Is it true?*

Me: *Give me something specific to work with.*

Hunter: *Rachel's pregnant?*

I rolled my eyes.

Nice try, Hunter.

Me: *Don't make out like you don't already know. She told me you sent her ice cream. A ton of it. You never could do anything that wasn't in excess.*

Hunter: *You didn't complain last time.*

He had me there. Hunter was better than Willy Wonka for being equipped with candy and sweet treats.

Me: *No, I didn't.*

Hunter: *In fact, if memory serves… you LIKED my excess.*

Me: *Don't get ahead of yourself.*

Hunter: *:P Tell me you didn't enjoy that birthday cake.*

Me: *Why would I lie about cake?*

Hunter: *Four tiers of Delizia cake… There enough nut for you in that?*

Me: *No. I didn't share it with Luc or Stan either. It was all mine.*

Hunter: *That comes as no surprise. How about with your mom?*

Me: *I shared some. I take my cake seriously. Where do you think Stan gets it from? It started with me and now it runs in the family.*

Hunter: *Why do YOU think I bought it for your birthday? Anyway, how are things?*

I hesitated over my answer. We weren't close anymore. Hadn't spoken, *verbally,* in years, but it was still too easy to share things with him. Things that I didn't really want him to know.

Me: *They're fine.*

Hunter: *Saw you on the news.*

Me: *You did?*

Hunter: *Yup. You looked scary.*

Me: *Lol. That's me.*

Hunter: *Stan still call you Cruella?*

Me: *He does but hasn't for ages. I mustn't have been acting cruel enough.*

Hunter: *#LifeGoals*

Me: *Yup. I gtg.*

Hunter: *Yeah, no worries. Just, Rory, if you need me, you know where I am, right?*

I didn't answer.

Answering was beyond me.

I didn't have words to accept his kindness or to reject it.

Hunter's problem was that he knew too much and that would always push distance between us.

Because the thought made me want to cry, and New York's ball-busting DA did *not* cry in an art museum, I forced myself to refocus on my sketch.

Thankfully, the minutes drifted away, merging into a half hour as I used a soft 6B pencil to try to recreate the subtle bloom of the brush-strokes from Cassatt's portrait, allowing my mind to wander and not to work because that wasn't a concern right now.

Luciu, my twin, was. His new whore of a girlfriend too.

That plan had exploded in my face.

There I'd been, dancing in *Russu*, and I'd seen him bring that slut into the VIP room.

Who wore a dress that small in Manhattan in the winter?

Only a gold digger, that's who.

And the way she was all over him made my skin crawl.

In an effort to spare him, I'd lied to her. Demanded she get the hell away from Luc, told her I was his wife, and she'd ran, only to pop back up on New Year's Day.

In that time, Stan had done his investigations, merely proving that my instincts were right—Jennifer MacNeill was a seasoned pro in the ancient art of gold digging, only she kept failing and had yet to bag herself a keeper.

I'd had to eat brunch with the bitch while she sat on Luc's lap, and Luc had defended her!

He even attacked *me*.

The audacity.

Granted, he'd been pissed that I'd gotten him arrested on suspicion of desecrating a cemetery, defacing a casket, and committing arson, but still, here *I* was, protecting the family, trying to ensure that our goals were attained, and he had the nerve to wreck it all by bringing in a nobody!

What connections did she have?

Zero.

A soft grunt of annoyance drifted from my parted lips as I recreated the child's face, her features gently petulant, uncaring that she was disturbing her mother's work.

Then there was Stan to worry about and his preposterous idea for C-L-O—the wonder drug that was going to revolutionize the club scene in Manhattan.

Matri was probably going to have to go into her yearly stint at rehab because she was drinking too much again. Stan and Luc thought she went to a spa upstate, but only she and I knew where she really was.

Then, there was Currau Valentini, my great-uncle, who remained in prison after years of trying, and failing, to liberate him.

Was I destined to die with a full to-do list?

"That's pretty."

The words jarred me from my introspection.

A glower etched into my expression as I peered up at the intruder, only for it to be washed away when I took note of her amused smile.

Grainne Ledger—Manhattan's Divorce Maker.

An Irish madam who ran Queens of Heart over in Hell's Kitchen with a name so complicated that even after all this time, I still struggled to pronounce 'Grah-nya' properly.

New York's DA should *not* be seen fraternizing with a known criminal, but I wasn't just the NY DA—I had a business to run.

She took a seat at the other end of the bench and withdrew her own sketchpad. As she settled in, she murmured, "Why must it be this one every time?"

"I like it."

"I'd never have guessed," she muttered. "You should switch it up. We'll get caught because you 'like' this painting."

I knew humans registered patterns, and I knew my work had made me famous in the city. A photo on Facebook of the DA sitting beside Manhattan's Divorce Maker would go viral—I wasn't the one who'd be in danger if it did.

I didn't cut her a look because now that we'd made eye contact, it was imperative that we remained distant.

"Next week, I'll choose another painting."

Her sigh was loaded with her relief.

"Any news for me?" I asked after a couple moments of silence.

She hummed. "David Foundry visited Queens of Heart last Friday. Incognito. I recognized him, naturally."

"Naturally."

I'd already been aware of the Attorney General's preference for expensive hookers, but it seemed that particular need hadn't diminished any.

They never did.

That was why I was sitting here with ginger up my ass, trying to recreate what only D could give me. My thighs were ripped to shreds from the vampire paddle, and not in a good way. Hence the ginger.

Plus, the last time I'd used capsaicin, which felt like heaven and hell combined on my nipples, I'd almost given myself second-degree burns.

"Which girl did he use?"

"The Queen of Heart."

My lips twitched. "Who'd have thought he was into FemDom?"

"I would. The slimy toad."

We could agree on that one.

"I wouldn't mind, of course. To each their own. But his stance on women's reproductive rights makes me sick to my stomach."

"He belongs in the eighteen hundreds," I concurred. "Anything else for me this week?"

A USB drive made an appearance on the bench between us. Nonchalantly, she moved her hand away, and equally as nonchalantly, I retrieved it.

"Nothing out of the ordinary apart from Foundry." She cleared her throat. "How are my girls?"

I broke my self-imposed rule of ignoring her to shoot her a gentle glance. "They're fine."

I'd never met a madam like Grainne Ledger. She was probably

responsible for five percent of the city's divorce rate, but her girls were her family, which was why she was here, and it was a trait I took advantage of.

She provided me with tidbits of information about her clients, and I made sure her girls were in protective custody with some luxuries that only knowing the DA could provide.

Things like windows were worth their weight in gold when you were serving twenty-to-life for murdering a john because that john didn't realize that 'no' meant 'no' even if you were paying two-thousand bucks an hour.

In the eyes of the country, New York was a liberal state, but we still subsisted in a patriarchal society. That meant the rapist client had more rights than the prostitute.

She returned her sketchpad to her purse. "I'll see you next week unless, of course, I see you at Queens of Heart this weekend?"

My mouth tightened. "That was a mistake I won't be repeating." As was purchasing a membership at the known sex club.

"Sandrine, the floor manager, said you didn't even leave your booth." Grainne arched a brow at me. "That's probably why you're in such a sour mood. Bye for now."

With her words putting me on edge, I let her go, not bothering to watch her departure, and rather than focus on that disastrous visit to the sex club, I tore apart my schedule instead. I had to make sure that I could visit the Met twice in a week: once for my meeting with Grainne, and a second time so that I could recreate a painting that spoke to my soul.

You had to make time for the things that mattered in this life because before you knew it, those chances were gone for good.

Tears pricked my eyes as I whispered under my breath, "Just like D."

CHAPTER ELEVEN

AURORA: *Don't forget it's the FAST gala tonight. Rachel's really gone the extra mile this year.*

> **Hunter:** *I haven't forgotten.*
> **Aurora:** *Donated?*
> **Hunter:** *Yup. You?*
> **Aurora:** *Of course.*
> **Hunter:** *You going?*
> **Aurora:** *No. Luc is though.*
> **Aurora:** *GTG.*

12

———

HUNTER

"HUNTER, what's with the picture you sent me?" Rachel demanded.

"Weird, right?" I chuckled as I stared down at the world's weirdest gift bag. Not only was the bag itself bizarre with 'Sucks To Be You' embossed into the front, but its contents didn't bode well for me. "I think it's actually a death threat."

I didn't 'think.' I knew. That was why I'd called her.

My family was under enough strain with the impending court case that had been laid at our door recently; Bert did *not* need to learn that the life of the grandson he loved, *his heir,* was in danger while he was facing decades in prison after being Caponed by the ADA.

What Rachel didn't know about the underworld, she'd find out.

She made a bloodhound on the hunt for prime rib look lazy.

And as someone who ran the Ledger, who knew which hits were out and on whom, this was off the books. I had to think that meant it was a governmental hit. Which was why I'd gone to Rach and not my contacts.

"You do?" She probably thought she sounded calm, but I heard the concern in her tone. Hell, I shared that concern even though I did my best to modulate my voice. The last thing I wanted was to cause her undue stress when she was pregnant. Though, I wasn't sure how you could downplay what I'd been sent. Typical Rachel—she brought the conversation back to where it needed to be: "What have you done to deserve a death threat?"

"Recently, you mean?"

She sniffed. "Well, yes."

"I've done a lot of shitty things over the years," I pointed out, including murder our mutual best friend's husband. Not that I felt bad about that.

"I know. I was there for a few," she drawled, which made me chuckle.

Where my relationship with Aurora had faded after Marcus's death, it had only strengthened with Rachel.

It was only when I'd witnessed Marcus forcing himself on Rachel that a side of myself I'd never known leaped to the fore.

When it came down to flight or fight, I was a fighter.

Until that day, I hadn't known if that were the truth or not.

Then, in the aftermath, I hadn't failed her.

Neither had Rory, to be fair.

Rachel had broken down entirely, but we'd strived to keep her on track. In the end, she'd been institutionalized. After everything, Rach and the father, Rex, had given the baby up for adoption.

Sometimes, when I *did* feel guilty, it was more a case of wishing that I'd gotten there ten minutes earlier.

If I had, Rach would never have been raped, she and Rex would probably have had their happily-ever-after, and their kid would have been raised with her birth parents.

Not that I said any of that. I just agreed, "This is very true. Still, I don't think I've done anything to deserve death by assassin. That's usually above my pay grade."

Beyond above it.

Bert might have given me his signet ring, but that didn't mean dick in the grand scheme of things.

Her voice was tense as she asked, "What *is* your pay grade?"

"Do you really want to know?"

"If it's pertinent to whoever wants you dead, then yes." Her huff sounded in my ear.

"Add a couple of zeroes to whatever your top-paying client pays you and that's about right."

"The fuck?"

"Do you want into my pants now?" I teased, unable to stop myself as I picked up the Voodoo doll that I retrieved from the folds of tissue paper in the bag and squeezed it.

It was a stuffed toy with buttons for eyes, patches here and there, visible stitches, and a zipper that ran down the front of the body. I'd peeped inside—there was hair in it. That was the creepiest thing of all. Whose hair? That question would probably plague me for the rest of my life—hopefully that wasn't within the next two weeks.

"This isn't funny, Hunter!"

My lips twitched as I peered at the hair. "I think it's hilarious." Ridiculous too. Who sent a Voodoo doll stuffed with hair to a target?

Weird.

"You would," she sniped, her disapproval evident. "This is serious. Someone's threatened your life."

"Gah, someone's always doing that; this is just the first time it's been gift wrapped. I've heard rumors about an assassin who does this, of course, but I've never seen it before. Wonder who she gets to send the gifts—"

"Why? Do you want to use them for the next party you host?"

I chuckled. "You know I don't host parties. What's got your panties in a bunch, anyway? Rory told me you were full steam ahead with the FAST gala." Well, her text had surmised as much. As usual, she'd kept things short and sweet. I knew she'd only messaged because the FAST foundation was Rachel's 'baby' and she wanted to remind me to make a donation. Speaking of… "My donation is in the charity accounts, by the way."

"Thank you, Hunter."

"Very welcome, very welcome."

"I wish you'd come to one of the fundraisers though—"

I snorted. "We've discussed this."

We had. Many, many times.

I hated parties. Plus… "I don't see the point of fundraisers. Someone pays forty grand for a plate, right? But a lot of that money goes to waste on renting the hall, on the food, on the entertainment—"

"We get subsidized rates and we also get a lot of things donated—"

"I don't care. I just think it's dumb. But you did have a nice lot in one of the auctions. I bought it over the phone."

"Meaning you had someone come to the party you disapprove of?"

"I did."

"Who?"

"That's for me to know, and for you to not find out."

"Let's get back to the matter at hand."

I heard the smile in her voice.

"You mean the death threat?" I clicked into the Ledger, making sure my name wasn't there and I'd missed it. Hard thing to miss, but mistakes happened. "Yes, very intriguing."

"Not intriguing," she grumbled. "What are you going to do?"

"Not sure. I mean, ordinarily I'd go to my people, but I sometimes contract out without their knowledge, and if this is to do with that, then I'm screwed on two fronts."

"Do you make a habit of contracting out to other people?"

"No. Just the Valentini family."

"Should have known that without asking."

"You really should." I tsked. "You're slipping."

"Pregnancy makes me forgetful," she discounted.

"It might make you forgetful, but it doesn't make you stupid."

"That's harsh, isn't it?"

I smirked. "Should I say sorry?"

"Yes."

"Sorry, Rach," I declared at my most penitent, not that she swallowed my BS. We didn't have that type of relationship.

Disregarding my apology entirely, she demanded, "Does Rory know you help the Valentinis?"

"Nope. Only Custanzu." Luciu likely did as well.

She let loose a soft gasp. "Is that why you forced Lodestar onto them?"

Ah, Lodestar—hacker extraordinaire and my second favorite pain in the ass in the whole world.

After Aurora, of course.

"Sure is. My people were starting to get suspicious."

Plus, if I had to work with Rory full time and have her ignore me and only talk business, I'd want to blow out my brains.

"Could they have sent you the death threat?"

I chuckled. "No."

"Well, you're not as clever as you think, Hunter, because not only did someone send you that pretty package in the mail, they sent it somewhere that actually got delivered to you—"

"Shit, you're right," I groused, my amusement finally souring. "I need to move, don't I?"

"You don't. That's the last thing you need to do. You move and you'll get hit."

"Damn. This is an inconvenience," I complained. "I have a routine, you know? I go for—"

"I don't need to know if you still have a coffee and a Danish every morning after you go for a run. Rex told me that he knows someone who could, potentially, call the shooter off."

"And you rang me and not them?!" I spluttered.

"I wanted to check in with you first."

"Ah, you wanted to know I wasn't dead yet."

"That too." Sucking in a breath that whistled in my ear, she bit off, "It's been a busy night."

"I bet," was my sympathetic retort. "I'd really appreciate—"

"You don't have to ask. The hacker you introduced to Custanzu is the one who knows the assassin anyway, so…"

"Lodestar knows Dead To Me?"

I'd met Lodestar quite by accident almost five years ago, and it was safe to say that she'd brought nothing but trouble ever since. But she was phenomenal at what she did, and with Bert starting to offload more work onto my shoulders as he slowed down, I thought it was wise to bring in outside help for Stan, Luciu, and Rory.

In the new year, I'd told Rachel that this was my year. That I'd be claiming Aurora as my own. That plan was going to have to be put on hold if I had to stay glued to my home in Vegas.

"Dead To Me?"

Absently, I heard her question. "That's the assassin's name. To be honest, I thought she was an urban legend. I didn't realize there was a sniper batshit enough to go around giving her victims gift baskets, but you live and learn."

"Seems like she has style."

"I can't disagree." A creepy style. I glowered at the hair-stuffed doll. "I'll get in touch with Lodestar. Leave it with me."

"You sure?" She surprised me by chortling, which filled me with relief—the last thing I wanted was stress from this BS putting the baby at risk. "Will you call me to tell me you're not dead?"

"It'll take more than a sniper's bullet to kill me, Rach," was my droll assurance. "But if she comes at me with a flamethrower or a pitchfork then know that I love you?"

She heaved a sigh. "I love you too. Please, Hunter, stay safe."

"I will. I promise," I told her, tone more somber than before as I cut the call.

Zipping up the Voodoo doll, I frowned at the odd stitches and tossed it on my palm like it was a hacky sack.

What I really wanted to do was phone Rory, but seeing as she'd prefer to stick her face in a vat of sulfuric acid than deign to talk to me, I fell back on someone who actually wanted my company. Well, ordinarily. Before I'd broken things between us.

DDoSunlight enters chat

DDoSunlight: *Sunny? You there?*

When she didn't answer, I heaved another sigh, this one more miserable than the last, and dialed Lodestar.

"Yo."

While Rachel had told me she knew the sniper, I still asked, "You know someone called Dead To Me?"

It was best to be cagey with Lodestar.

Cagey… huh.

Me: *Rory, do you know someone called Dead To Me?*

I wasn't surprised when she didn't answer, but Lodestar, on the other hand, did. Well, sort of. "Sounds like someone Harley Quinn would bone."

"Do you never give a straight answer?" I queried though I knew the answer was a big, fat NO.

"Not if I can help it." She paused. "You get those files I sent you?"

"Yup." The sound of traffic roared in the background. "What the hell's going on? Are you near a road or something?"

"And they say you're smart. Jesus."

I grunted. "Where are you?"

"NYC."

"Thought you were in Jersey."

"They let me out for day trips."

"It's night," I pointed out.

"What the fuck are you? My father?"

"Why are you in the city?"

"Business." I heard a car door open. "Well?"

"Well, what?"

"The files."

An engine started. "You know the Ledger is unofficial." I knew it shouldn't bother me, but: "What the fuck are you doing in New York? You hate the city."

"So?" Before I could retort, she said, "Meaning that if a kill order comes from Uncle Sam, you wouldn't know about it?"

"Exactly."

"How does the Ledger work?"

I wished I could pinpoint a specific day when it had become my job to hold hitmen accountable, but there wasn't one in particular. It had just happened.

Much as Christmas had been stolen from the Pagans and Las Vegas was no longer just a barren desert. Although, with climate change and drought, maybe Mother Nature would swallow up Sin City again.

"You know how it works."

"Remind me."

I huffed out a breath. "Hits are sent to me, and I note them in the Ledger. If a hitman is requested, I pass that information on. It's to stop multiple hitmen being sent out on the same job. Plus, I act as escrow. I hold the funds from the petitioner and pay them out once I receive proof of death."

I made a cool fifteen percent on each hit for my pains too. Not that I said that aloud.

"How busy have you been recently?"

"Not particularly. Shit's up in the air right now, Star."

"Those Sparrows," she groused, and I couldn't argue.

The NWS, or New World Sparrows, had infiltrated every aspect of American society, creating a toxic web of contacts that spanned not only the country, but the globe.

"I can tell you that it's a free-for-all."

"What do you mean?"

"I mean that snipers are going down like they're two-buck whores. The exact opposite of what the Ledger is supposed to do," I grouched.

"There's a global kill order? On what? Snipers in general?"

"Yes. And it's outside my purview." I tapped my fingers on my desk as I thought about the similarities between the men and women who'd been silenced during this hunt. "They're targeting snipers who can kill over seven-hundred-fifty yards."

"That specific?"

"Yeah. They want to target the elite, and because there are a bunch of bottom feeders in the mix who'd like to take out said elite so their run-of-the-mill asses can graduate to the next level, the good ones are sinking like the *Titanic*."

"Wish you'd told me this yesterday," she complained.

"I told you when I had the answers you needed. The Ledger's been quiet. I had to find you answers elsewhere." Mostly because my clients were being killed off. "Why does it matter if I told you today or yesterday?"

"I wouldn't have had to come into the city."

"You were taking someone out?"

"Protecting someone."

"Since when do you protect people in the life?"

Not that she was in the life. Lodestar had her own subsection within the criminal underworld. It was why we got along so well— criminals didn't altogether trust her because of her past in the CIA, but I acted as a go-between and things sailed along nicely.

"This was personal."

"Personal?" Now, I was even more confused. "Since when do you mix business and pleasure?"

"Since recently, okay? Is this a game of twenty questions?"

Defensive. I hummed under my breath. *Interesting*.

Lodestar was never really on the back foot.

"What do you know about Dead To Me putting a hit out on me? Is it because of what you've got me researching?"

"You don't sound pissed by the notion," she drawled, her tone curious.

"Why would I be? I'm more pissed at the inconvenience."

"Inconvenience?"

"Yes. I'll have to barricade myself in the house."

A laugh escaped her. "Remember that time in Cleveland?"

"I do," I grumbled, though the need to smile made my lips twitch when I thought about her foster daughter who was obsessed with the singer Camden Daniels. "Two weeks in that house of yours with you and Kat and I was ready to die. I still have nightmares about Camden." I purposely drifted into a high falsetto that Kat used whenever she talked about her celebrity crush.

She chuckled. "She had that playlist on repeat for hours on end, didn't she?"

"She did. My nightmares come with a soundtrack of his songs now."

"So melodramatic. Worth it, though, wasn't it?"

"Was it? Showing the O'Donnellys we could rampage through their security systems didn't do much other than piss them off."

"You left before that happened."

"Don't make out like I was fleeing. I had to get back to Vegas. Some of us have responsibilities."

A harrumph sounded in my ear.

Tone nonchalant, I asked, "You're friendly with aCooooig now, aren't you?"

"I am."

I didn't think anyone truly *knew* Lodestar. She was like the witch's house in *Hansel and Gretel*. Good to look at, enough to drool over, but the second you took a bite, you regretted it and ended up face-first in a fire. Having worked with her off and on for years, though, I knew her silence was loaded.

"Business turning personal…" I blinked. "It's well documented that aCooooig's baby brother is The Whistler." My tone turned teasing. "You caught feelings for the Irish Mob, Lodestar?"

"Fuck off."

I smirked. "You have."

"Fuck. Off."

"How can I? You have info I want and I have info you want. If I fuck off, neither of us get the answers we need."

"Dead To Me is unstoppable. She can't be bought either."

"Everyone has a price." So, not only was the urban legend not an urban legend, but Dead To Me *was* a 'she.'

"Yes, and someone paid it to off you." She huffed. "I don't blame them."

"I'm wounded. Truly."

"You sound like you are. I'll ask her what's going on. But I make no promises."

"You should work with her to keep my ass safe. The info I have about this kill order is incomplete. You know me well enough by now to realize that I'm not blowing hot air up your ass. Shit like this takes time."

"What *do* you know?"

"The original order came from Moscow."

"Why does this have to be so complicated?"

"You're the one who decided a life in espionage was a smart career choice," I retorted.

"I didn't decide anything. You know I'm only here because that bastard, Dagda, killed my mom."

Dagda had been a ghost at one time. A sniper so renowned that there were urban legends about his abilities to get into impenetrable locations to take out targets.

He'd started out as a private in the British Army, then after the Troubles in Ireland, had essentially defected and turned to the Irish's side. Eventually, he'd become the head of the *Éire le chéile go deo*, an Irish organization dedicated to uniting Northern Ireland with the Republic, and he'd retained that position despite spending three decades in prison.

Though guilt hit me at the reminder, I muttered, "What do you want me to do, Lodestar?"

"Keep looking. When you say Moscow…"

"I mean Moscow. Not the Kremlin."

"Bratva?"

"Not sure yet. This group appears to have links to both but acts independently."

"How much are they willing to spend on it?"

"A million."

"Sterling or dollars?"

"Sterling. Per assassin."

"What?!"

"Yup."

"How do they claim?"

"From what I've heard, proof of death and proof of ID."

Her tone shifted. "I'll get in touch with Dead To Me."

I narrowed my eyes at the abrupt change of topic. "I appreciate that."

"Heard about your grandfather," she said unexpectedly.

"The ADA is jonesing after him and has been for a long time."

"Because of your little problem?"

"I regret telling you that."

She cackled. "You didn't mean to tell me. I got you drunk and you spilled the beans."

The reminder had me sniffing. "Just get Dead To Me off my back. I'll try to find out who's behind the sniper witch hunt. Deal?"

"Deal."

My phone pinged.

Rory: *I've heard of Dead To Me, sure. Why?*

A smile curved my lips. Two birds, one stone came to mind.

Me: *Doesn't matter.*

Rory: *Hunter, I'm too busy to be your personal search engine.*

Me: *You're always busy.*

Rory: *Yes. This I know. I forgot to ask you earlier but did you get those tickets I sent?*

Me: *Shit, didn't I tell you?*

Guilt hit me. Things had been kind of crazy lately but tickets to the Super Bowl in one of the lower-level suites had been a wicked, out-of-the-blue gift.

Rory: *You didn't. I was just making sure you'd received them. It doesn't matter.*

Me: *It DOES matter. I appreciate the thought.*

Rory: *I'm glad the Chiefs lost.*

My lips twitched because, of course, she had to spoil it.

Me: *Because I wanted them to win?*

Rory: *Of course. Anyway, gtg.*

Naturally.

I pressed my cell to my lips.

I wasn't making much headway with her, but some was better than nothing. And that was what last year had amounted to. I'd spoken to her more in the last few months than I had all last year, *and* she must have spent a couple hundred grand on that ticket to the game…

Faith.

Or as the Sicilians said, 'God made things straight, the devil came and twisted them.'

He'd definitely twisted Rory… but maybe, just maybe, he'd

twisted me too so that her edges and mine could sit together, God and the devil be damned.

The thought made me smile, and after a night like tonight, with the promise of death landing on my doorstep, I figured only Rory was capable of that feat.

13

AURORA

"ARE YOU KIDDING ME?" I screamed at Vicente who bowed his head at my fury. "I told you those blocks were where he picked his victims, and you didn't keep an eye on things like I told you to! Your job was to prevent another rape from happening. Goddammit to hell!"

"I'm sorry, Aurora."

"You really sound sorry," I snarled, my temper surging because his use of my first name was a way of diminishing what I was as Luc's second. "And it's Ms. Fitzwilliam to you."

We'd lost too many men when my brothers had stormed the Fieri compound to reclaim what was rightfully ours; those men had respected me. This fresh breed of imbeciles didn't.

It was really starting to wear on my patience.

"I didn't mean for it to happen," he mumbled, shoulders hunching higher around his ears.

"No? That stops a woman from having to have a rape kit today, does it? That stops her from being terrified she's caught some STD—" I raised a hand when he made to talk. "Shut your mouth, Vicente, before I get Stan to shut it for you."

His eyes flared wide; for the first time, real fear entered them, and fuck, that pissed me off.

He should be terrified of *me*, not just Stan. Not just Luciu.

"Get out," Stan intoned darkly, watching as I turned away to look out the window onto *Russu,* our nightclub, which was in the middle of being cleaned before it opened again this evening.

Another woman had been hurt on my watch. Someone else I'd failed.

I thought about the letter on my desk, its contents providing me with the confirmation that our great-uncle, a man who'd been framed for the murder of his brother, my grandfather, and had been left to rot in prison, was now in the process of being released.

Freedom didn't feel how I hoped it would for him.

He'd die in a hospital bed if we couldn't find him a kidney before he even had a chance to live a life.

I'd failed him too.

Luciu was intent on staying with his gold-digging girlfriend—I'd failed him by not freeing him from her clutches.

And while the announcement hadn't been made official that I was Luc's Consigliere, I knew that to gain any respect in that position, I was going to have to wind up with some lame-ass prick as a husband all so that I could take my rightful place in the *Cosa Nostra.*

I'd failed myself.

I reached up and rubbed my eyes.

D.

I missed D.

I missed his dominance, his caring. I missed his punishments and his ability to see *me*. Even with a mask shielding my identity, he saw me. Always had.

"You okay, *soru*?"

Stan's question had me tensing up. "No. Someone else got raped because our dipshit men think being a woman makes me weak."

"Rumor has it that the rapist died, if that helps."

I cut him a look. "What rumor?"

"They say O'Donnelly Sr. was involved."

The head of the Five Points' Mob had murdered some penny-ante rapist? Had I dived down the rabbit hole when I'd gotten drunk in the club last night?

"*What*? Was the rapist Irish?"

Was.

Past tense.

That lessened some of the tension in my shoulders.

The victim was still a victim but there'd be no more suffering at that bastard's hand.

"I don't think so. But if he really is dead, news will be breaking soon."

"True."

"Anyway, should you be at *Russu*? Weren't you here last night?"

I was on the brink of leaving the DA's office, merely tying up loose ends because I didn't know when to quit. Quitting meant I'd be accelerating the timeline toward wedding bells and I'd prefer to lead a double life rather than that.

Reaching for my phone, I texted Greg, my assistant at the DA's office.

Me: *The rapist who was killed last night… Was he Irish? Any affiliations to the Five Points?*

I didn't have to be in my office to know Greg's eyebrows would be so high on his forehead they'd be reaching another stratosphere.

My stance was notoriously anti-Italian. Not anti-Irish. I dipped my toes into those waters so I couldn't be accused of favoritism, but I didn't seek out cases.

Greg: *Not Irish. No affiliations. But the rapist wasn't murdered.*

Me: *What?*

Greg: *Accidental death.*

Me: *Huh?*

Greg: *After he was done raping his victim, apparently, he tripped and hit his head.*

Me: *Are you shitting me?*

Greg: *No? Why would I? It's what the files say.*

Greg was a robot, so he had a point.

When I didn't answer his question, Stan mumbled, "You're flying too close to the sun."

"I know when to descend before I get burned. My assistant just told me that the rapist tripped and hit his head."

"What?" Stan reached up and rubbed his jaw. "Sounds shady as hell to me."

"Me too." I tapped my phone against my lips.

"You're going to leave it alone, aren't you?"

"One rapist is dead. I don't care how."

While I was curious, with old habits dying hard, I didn't go looking for trouble, not when I had enough of my own to keep corralled.

I'd been leading this double life for so long that it had become second nature. I was naturally overcautious, naturally wary about the battles I fought, because that level of self-preservation was what had gotten us here today—the Valentinis reigning over our own slice of hell in Manhattan.

Thanks to me.

My strategies.

My plans.

My organizational capacities.

Not Luc. Not Stan.

Me.

Unable to stop myself, I grabbed the first thing I could snatch off the desk and hurled it at the wall.

The glass paperweight shattered into a million pieces.

Stan, who'd picked up a banana from somewhere, peeled it and started eating it, his attention never shifting from me.

He was growing accustomed to my outbursts.

"You need to get a husband before you're announced as Consigliere, Rory."

My mouth snagged into a snarl. "Fuck off."

"I can't keep standing around here like I'm your babysitter when you officially take your place."

"I shouldn't need one!" I howled, my outrage complete.

"Not saying you do. We both know you're the brains behind this whole operation, but *they* don't know that."

My hands tightened into fists. "This is ridiculous."

"Pick a man. Marry him. Use him as your beard."

"None of that sounds appealing." I shuddered. "The prospect of marrying a man who'd let me lead him around like that—"

He shrugged. "That's what affairs are for."

"Not helping."

"You don't have to like the man."

"No, but I have to trust him." My spine turned ramrod straight. "You don't know what that entails, Stan. You've never been in a position where—"

His expression softened and, for once, he dropped his half-eaten banana in the trash then moved over to me. "You'll never be in a position of weakness like that again."

"I know I have to marry, but I can't yet. I just can't."

His hand moved to my shoulder. "Hunter would help."

I stiffened. "There's helping and then there's marrying someone. No. I'll figure things out. I always do."

"Why do you have to make things so difficult for yourself, Rory?"

"I'm sorry I'm not pliable, Custanzu," I snapped. "You can go if you're so busy that you can't help me with the foot soldiers."

His brow puckered, but his mouth twisted into a grimace that told me he knew he'd fucked up. "If you need me, I'm here."

That was about as much of an apology as I'd get out of him.

Watching one of the housekeepers fish a pair of panties out of *Russu's* infamous red fountains, I dipped my chin. "How did the FAST gala go last night?"

"Luciu bought a ridiculously expensive purse at the auction. I swear it just looks like a fishing basket."

I cut him a glance. "Why did the gold digger want a fishing basket?"

Although, if it was ludicrously expensive then at least it was going to a good cause.

Rachel ran FAST, a charity that gave pregnant women options and helped them gain an education after they'd given birth. The foundation needed every dollar they could get.

Making a mental note to check in with her, my mind screeched to a halt as Stan stated, "Fuck knows. Met her mother today."

"*You* did?" I frowned at him. "I thought you and Luciu were quiet earlier. What happened?"

"It doesn't matter—"

My frown morphed into a scowl. "Stan."

"You know you're not *Matri,* don't you?"

"I do. I also know I'm scarier than she is. What. Happened. Today?"

"It was messed up. Jen—"

"Jen?" I shrieked.

He winced. "*Jennifer* got a call from her mother. Luc didn't want her to go by herself, so we ended up heading there together. When we arrived, the mother was waiting. So were two gangbangers."

I rubbed my forehead. "What the fuck?"

"The mother had debts."

"And she was going to use her daughter to pay them off?"

"Yeah. Luc didn't appreciate that—"

"We just went to war with a gang and neither of you thought to keep me informed?!" I shouted, the edges of my vision started to pulsate black as I had confirmation, physical fucking confirmation, that Jennifer MacNeill was going to be the death of our family.

"We didn't go to war with a gang," he grouched. "Calm down, Rory. You look like you're going to have a heart attack."

"And you'd be fucked if that happened, wouldn't you?" I took a calming breath, well aware that getting angry with Stan would get me nowhere.

If he grinned at me, so help me fucking God I'd smack him.

"We would," he appeased.

"Which gang?"

"Honestly, *soru,* we handled it."

"Which. Gang?" I spat.

He sighed. "The *Chorros.*"

Brain shifting gears, I rifled through the information I had on them.

"We have the leader by the balls. The gangbangers are dealt with. Her mother isn't allowed back in the city, not unless she wants to rent someplace at the bottom of the Hudson. There's no need to worry. Although, telling you not to worry is like telling me not to eat."

My lips *almost* twitched. "Don't try to make light of this. She'll be the death of us."

"That's coming on strong, Rory."

"She already killed that fucker associated with the Bratva."

He grimaced. "Luc mentioned he met with the Pakhan last night. He knew about the prick's death. There'll be no repercussions from it."

So we had a mole.

Great.

I made a note to start weeding through the ranks for anyone with ties to the Bratva, just as Stan sighed. "I don't like her, and I don't think she's right for Luc, but hell, she comes with benefits too. You don't deal with Luc on a daily basis like I do. Trust me, she cheers him up better than antidepressants."

"That's because both of you think with your second, *smaller* brains."

"No, it's because she makes him happy," he corrected.

"Happiness isn't for the likes of us."

"You've said that before—"

"And I'll say it again until it's rammed home."

"Is it so wrong to want to be happy?" he asked wistfully.

"Happiness is a myth. It's a con they try to sell you to make you marketable for those antidepressants you mentioned earlier. You shouldn't seek happiness. You should seek peace."

A single brow quirked. "Since when did you turn into Gandhi?"

"I didn't. Happiness is fleeting. Peace isn't."

"Have you ever felt at peace, Rory?"

My mouth tightened. "Don't start. Go, but before you do, make sure Luc hasn't started a turf war with someone else over his gold-digging girlfriend, hmm?"

Without a word of farewell, Stan tipped his chin in agreement and retreated.

For a man so heavyset, he didn't clomp around like a bull in a china shop, and when he left me to the silence of the office, I reached up and rubbed my eyes, not liking the look in his as he departed.

Stan saw too much. Which was ironic because my major problem right now was that being seen and heard by everyone else was harder than I'd like.

I felt as if I were being dragged back to the sixties themselves and women's rights were wrongs in the eyes of the made men who acted as our foot soldiers.

We were only in the early days of Luc's reign, and until the Five Families' council was restored and the first meeting between the heads of the major factions—a Summit—was held in the city, I wouldn't feel secure enough in our position to start making waves.

And a woman underboss was practically the Hudson River's tidal bore turning into a tsunami on this patriarchal culture.

Annoyed, I returned to my seat and slumped behind the desk.

When my cell vibrated, I didn't even huff because Hunter had been texting me more than usual and he always seemed to know when I was pissed off.

Hunter: *Got a ticket to the Biennale in Venice.*

Me: *So?*

Hunter: *So, do you want to go?*

Me: *No.*

Hunter: *Geez, try to spare my feelings, would you?*

Me: *We don't work that way.*

Hunter: *We weren't always like this.*

No, he wasn't wrong, and God, I missed the old days.

Me: *We do now. Enjoy the trip to Venice.*

Hunter: *When was the last time you went?*

Me: *Haven't been back to Europe in a long time.*

Hunter: *The ticket is for you. I can't leave the States at the moment.*

Me: *I don't have time.*

Hunter: *Let me guess, you don't have time.*

Our messages came simultaneously.

My cheeks burned with heat but I refused to apologize for my work schedule. My double life was helping us make history. You didn't make history by going on vacation every week.

Me: *You got it in one.*

Hunter: *When was the last time you had a break?*

Me: *What are you? Matri?*

Hunter: *No, just someone who gives a damn.*

Me: *I didn't ask you to give a damn.*

Hunter: *No, you didn't. You make it really fucking hard sometimes, Rory. Do you know that?*

Me: *Hard to what? Do you expect Luc or Stan to be 'NICE' to you? No. Why would you expect anything different from me?*

Hunter: *I'm here if you need to talk.*

I could have said something cutting, but I really didn't want to be a bitch. It wasn't his fault that he brought it out in me sometimes.

Goddamn men. Why did they always have to push?

I was busy. I was the youngest DA in New York's history, and I was also my brother's second-in-command. What about that made it seem like I had time to just waltz off to Venice at the drop of a hat?

Though he'd pissed me off, our interaction left me feeling guilty.

I hated feeling guilty.

In my head, I heard *Matri* chiding me. 'He's only trying to be kind. He cares about you, child. Lord knows why when you always push him away.'

Gritting my teeth, I forced myself to type out:

Me: *Thank you for caring even when I'm at my most vicious.*

I didn't expect an answer, and it was a good thing seeing as I didn't get one. Of course, when I didn't, that made me wonder *why* he hadn't replied, but before I could grow more agitated, a knock sounded at the door.

"What?" I snarled.

Giovi, a (wisely) wary foot soldier, popped his head into the office. His shoulders were hunched so I knew *he* knew I wasn't in the best of moods. "Your car's waiting around the back like you asked, ma'am."

Jesus, was it eight o'clock already?

I blinked at Giovi. He blinked back, but that wariness was still there.

He was scared of me.

But he wasn't repulsive.

And his smile was pleasant enough.

Giovi was trusted by Luciu, and he'd yet to let us down. Plus, I didn't hate his guts. That was an advantage few men had.

Could he be an option as a future husband?

He'd be a smart choice. Someone I could mold. Someone who had never expected to be more than a foot soldier.

Smart…

I only made smart moves.

But, God, I just couldn't imagine allowing him to touch me. I couldn't imagine him allowing me to hold sway over my position either. He wasn't sexist, but was he forward-thinking enough to allow his wife to hold a higher rank than him?

I didn't think so.

"Ma'am?"

I blinked at him again. "Yes?"

"Your car's ready?" he prompted, his confused frown making an appearance as he studied me. "You wanted to get out of here by eight-fifteen."

I did. He was right. Efficient, a good memory, punctual… all good traits. But our marriage would be Catholic. That would be it for us—no divorce, only death. I couldn't fuck him. He wasn't ugly but he just…

He wasn't D.

"I'll be there in two minutes," I rasped, watching as he nodded and started to make his retreat. "Giovi?"

He paused. "*Se?*"

"Did you make sure the guys outside were fed?"

The foot soldier winced. "I did. There are more and more every day, ma'am. We're not a soup kitchen."

I pursed my lips. "You're what I tell you we are."

He grew tense, not because I'd gotten his back up, but because he remembered *who* I was. *What* I was.

That shouldn't have sent arousal sparking through my veins but it did.

No, he definitely wasn't D.

"Do you want me to bring caterers in?"

"To feed the homeless outside? No, Giovi, I don't want you to bring in caterers." Annoyed, I tapped my pen against the desk. "What do you think this is? A society wedding? Just... hire a kitchen. Get people in to man the stoves. Hunger is the best sauce," I quoted in Sicilian at him as I wafted my hand. "Just make sure they're fed."

"Does Luciu know about this?" The question was carefully posed.

Temper sparking, I leaned forward. "I don't have to ask my brother for permission, Giovi." There was another old Sicilian saying I had no problem in quoting, "There's honor amongst thieves." His cheeks flushed at the reference. "We can't rely on the government to help those people out there, so we'll do it ourselves. They're on our turf, therefore they're our people, *capisci?*"

It wasn't often I brought out the Sicilian, but when I did, it always rammed things home neatly.

His shoulders still hunched, Giovi disappeared, leaving me with the knowledge that he'd do as I requested after putting up a fight.

Not so smart a move, perhaps?

My mind drifted to what Stan had said earlier about Hunter... Luc had told me last night that he was in the Camorra, which was a problem, but it wasn't insurmountable. He *would* help. I knew he had feelings for me, though, and it felt wrong to exploit those feelings. Plus, for all that he appeared easy-going, he was no one's puppet.

"Jesus," I muttered to myself. "Maybe you do need to take a break if you think Hunter's an option."

As I gathered my things together, slipping on the scarf I used to hide my hair and slotting on the oversized tinted frames that took up half my face, the thought made me chuckle uneasily to myself.

When I slipped into the car, my mind drifted somewhat as I headed across town to my apartment.

No, Hunter wasn't an option even if he was the only potential husband who wouldn't try to strangle me after being married to me for an extended period of time.

14

———

AURORA

MARCH

"I'M BORED."

Rubbing my eyes, I grumbled, "Since when am I your court jester, *Matri*?"

"You're the one who insists I come here."

"I think it's good for you."

"You think I'm an alcoholic."

"I think you're too dependent on alcohol, yes, but I also know you agree. Otherwise you'd kick up a stink when I made the suggestion you head upstate to your 'spa.'"

Her 'spa' vacation was our little secret.

My mother huffed in my ear. "Thank God it's only for two weeks this time."

"You've been better since Luc took power."

"*You* haven't."

I winced but didn't bother lying. Lauren Valentini knew her children too well not to spot a lie from twenty yards.

"What happened, sweetheart?" she prodded. "I thought taking charge of things would make you happier."

What was it with my family and happiness?

"I don't want to be happy. I want to be at peace."

Matri snorted. "Yes, yes. We've all heard your repeated diatribes on the subject."

My lips twisted. "Have I been a broken record?"

"You have," she said glumly, then she perked up and my warning signals flashed. "Have you heard from Hunter recently? Such a good boy. He sent me some lilies before you dumped me in this place. They came with a card; 'Thinking of you.'"

I rolled my eyes as I waited for it…

"He'll make some woman a very loving husband one day."

"Yes, he will," I agreed blandly.

Sensing that I wasn't about to get into that conversation, she sniffed but, sadly, didn't change the subject. "I called him."

"Have a good talk?"

"He was sick. Had a bug or something."

I tensed. "Really?"

"Uh huh. Did you know they don't allow Netflix here?"

"Probably because they don't want you to watch shows that could trigger you." Keeping my tone light, I said, "We both know how you get when you watch *Goodfellas*."

Unable to stop myself, I switched screens on my cell and tapped:

Me: *Matri said you're sick.*

Hunter: *Better now.*

Me: *What was wrong?*

"I get angry when I watch *Goodfellas*," she confirmed.

"And you reach for a glass of red."

Despite being obsessed with them, *Matri* couldn't watch mafia movies without getting drunk. Understandable considering the mafia had taken out her husband. Not so understandable considering her children were the head of the *Cosa Nostra* now.

She groaned. "I'd kill to watch the Food Network even."

"I'm sure you would," I teased, my lips twitching. "When you're back, we'll have a marathon, hmm?"

"What kind of marathon? I don't do running, child."

Hunter: *Food poisoning.*
Me: *That sucks.*
Hunter: *Trust me, you've no idea.*
Me: *You're better now?*
Hunter: *Yeah.*
Me: *Do you need anything?*
Hunter: *I'm good. Thanks for asking. :)*

"Dear? What kind of marathon are you talking about?"

Shifting my focus back onto the conversation, still uneasy with the idea of Hunter being sick enough to share that info with *Matri*, I answered, "I mean a movie marathon."

"I wanted to clarify. It's always best to check my bases with you, Aurora."

I grinned. "Remember in January when you fell for the charity hike?"

"I do. So does my bum. 'We'll go for a hike,' you said. Within minutes, I realized it was a run."

"You were slow on the uptake. Who hikes in Central Park anyway?"

"I know to never trust you where exercise is concerned again. I'm not sure what I did to produce such active children. I can't decide if it's a blessing or a curse.

"Of course, it makes you happier when we do these things so I can't complain. You even smiled when we hit the finish line. I couldn't move for two days but it was worth it for that. You never could handle breakups, dear, could you?"

"I haven't been dating anyone to break up with," I drawled, though my nerves kicked in.

"No one you brought around, certainly," she said dismissively. "I thought it was one of those online things at the time. What do you call it? An LBD?"

Patience, where are you, my old friend? "That's a little black dress."

"Oh. LDR?"

"Long distance relationship," I choked. "No, *Matri*. I haven't—"

She tutted. "No lying, Aurora." For a second, silence settled between us. "You don't have to talk about it. Although, I suppose we should discuss marriage prospects—"

"No!" I croaked.

"You're the one who told me to look out for options," she grumbled. "I still don't understand why you want to do this."

"I don't."

"It won't stop you, though, will it? You'll marry for business, and…" She sighed. "That's not what your father or I would want for you, darling."

"We can't all have love matches." I knew I sounded bitter but I couldn't help it.

"You can't if you just marry a man because you need a husband to consolidate your power," she argued. "Your grandparents tried to do that to me, Rory, and I ran to Sicily and met your father—"

"We're not all as lucky as you either."

"I need wine for this conversation," she muttered glumly before, her tone falsely cheerful now, stating, "By the way, you're welcome."

"For what?"

"When I was in your room last month, I found your sketch pad."

"You found it?" I questioned sweetly, though the idea of her looking through the sketch pad mortified me. "Underneath my mattress?"

"Yes. Quite by accident."

"I'm sure," I mocked. "You do know I'm past the point where you have to worry about me sneaking out and doing drugs at night?"

"You were never the one I had to worry about that with, dear. That was Stan. It was by accident this time, I promise. Maria and I had to flip your mattress."

"Why were you doing that? Why didn't Maria get another housekeeper to help?"

Another hum. "I like to keep active in my own ways."

Rolling my eyes at the BS, I ground out, "You didn't look in the sketch pad, did you?"

"Yes, of course. I didn't even know you were still drawing. You were wasted as an attorney," she said, her tone bleak. "Your father would be so sad to know that he's one of the reasons why you didn't take up art full time."

"*Matri*," I warned. "I don't want to get into this."

"No, I know."

"Then why do I need to thank you? And why are you bringing this up?" If I was sweating with relief that I'd kept that journal at the family home in Brooklyn relatively PG, that was between my skin and me.

"Because I sent one of the sketches off to a competition, dear. It's gone to the next round—"

"You did what?" I shrieked. "How could—"

Before I could finish, I heard someone in the background: "Now, Lauren, you know you're not supposed to have a cellphone! Give that to me, please."

"Damn," *Matri* muttered. "I'll see you in a few days, Rory. You can tell me off then. I love you, sweetheart."

She didn't wait for a reply. Instead, she just left me wanting to gouge my eyes out as I stared at the wall opposite me.

She'd sent one of my sketches in for a competition? What kind of competition? The ones on the back of a cereal box?

Jesus Christ.

Mortification and agitation swirled around inside my gut, making me want to puke.

Then, the faintest sound trickled forward.

A scream.

I sucked in a breath then released it.

That conversation had hit closer to home than I'd have liked.

Not only with the sketch—which one had she sent off? The last time I'd drawn in that pad was around the holidays—but in regard to the LDR she thought I was in…

D.

God.

D.

The one man I'd wanted in years and he didn't want me back. That was irony at play. I sank back in the desk chair and reached into the bottom drawer of the desk where I knew Luc kept a bottle of Armagnac.

While this was technically his office at *Russu,* now that I was working full time for the family, I was spending more hours in the day here than he was.

The plantation desk that had once belonged to a pirate and had ended up in my grandfather's office was my mantel of power, the labyrinth-like back offices that were of Luciu's design for easy escape from the cops during raids were my kingdom, and the faint hum from the club that not even the best soundproofing in the world could drown out entirely was starting to be my home.

I should have been happy about that.

I'd been working for so long to reach this point in my life, but everything was going to shit.

At last, I'd resigned from the DA's office, and we'd implemented a new council: four of the old families who'd reigned alongside my grandfather before his murder had been reinstated as checks and balances.

The only trouble was that at least two of the families consisted of sexist asswipes and only saw a woman sitting where one of *them* should.

Annoyed, I reached for the decanter and didn't bother to pour myself a glass. I tugged the crystal topper off, grabbed the bottle, and placed it to my lips.

After I took a deep sip, I cut a look at the door when another faint scream made itself known to me.

That it was audible at all told me how much pain the man must be in.

Curious, I lifted my laptop lid and switched onto the screens and watched the back rooms where men were currently under question.

When Luciu had officially taken his seat at the head of the *Cosa Nostra,* the Carusos, Puglisis, Brunos, and Messinas had eagerly returned to the fold.

A foot soldier from each house was represented in the back rooms where Italians, men who'd been loyal to the old leaders, the Fieris, were being questioned.

Jennifer MacNeill had killed her mother's pimp. The news had somehow reached the ears of the Bratva Pakhan, Maxim Lyanov, which meant we had a mole.

Mouth tight as I flicked through each interrogation, I started to watch the Carusos at work.

The head of that family, Gianni, was one of the few men on the new council that I actually didn't hate. He, along with the Bruno head, weren't sexist pigs.

Gianni would be a good choice for a husband. I didn't like consolidating power or giving his line more influence in the council, but it would piss off the Puglisis and I was starting to live for that shit.

My cell buzzed, breaking into my line of thoughts as I watched Gianni get to work on one of the potential moles. There was a reason there were so many—we were looking for *one* specific traitor today, but that didn't mean I didn't think there were more out there.

This was a purge.

I tilted my screen and grimaced when I saw Hunter's message pop up.

Hunter: *Belle or Sleeping Beauty? Which is your current favorite?*

Me: *Hunter, I'm not seven anymore.*

Hunter: *That didn't answer the question.*

Me: *It did.*

Hunter: *Are you going to sit there and tell me you haven't watched either at least three times this year already?*

My cheeks burned with heat.

Me: *Go away.*

Hunter: *Ha! So, I'm right. Knew it. Which one?*

Me: *I haven't watched Beauty and the Beast since last year, and if you tell Rachel that I still watch cartoons, I will eviscerate you.*

Hunter: *How are you going to do that from a distance?*

Me: *I'll find a way. Trust me, I will.*

Hunter: *Ooh, scary.*

Me: *Why do you want to know?*

Hunter: *Watch out for a gift in the mail.*
Me: *I don't need a gift.*
Hunter: *Maybe you don't, but I need to send you one.*

Growling under my breath, I almost slammed my laptop lid down again, but this time, my brother's name popped up on the screen. Huh. Not only Luc, but he'd started a group call with Stan too.

A fizz of anticipation sang through my veins, dispersing the heavier thoughts of before.

Luciu had flown to Monaco—against my better judgment—to retrieve a ring that was alleged to be one of the Anjou rubies that had been stolen from us in the sixties.

With six pieces to the collection in total, one of which had been returned to us—the tiara—the rubies were tied to a blood curse: '*When the Valentini queen drips in the blood of the earth, only then will the family's star continue to rise.*' They were also more trouble than they were worth, but like any self-respecting Sicilian, I was striving, as much as my brothers were, to return the jewels to our possession.

Did it irk me that that queen would more than likely be Jennifer MacNeill?

Yes.

But some things were just beyond my control.

Despite my bad mood, hope filled me as I accepted the request and found them waiting for me to join the call.

Stan was sitting in his new laboratory like a Sicilian Walter White, while Luciu was clearly in a hotel suite, and in his hand, there was a ruby ring.

The momentousness of this moment resonated deep in my being.

The urge to share this with D, the one man who mattered, hit me hard.

I choked on the words, though, and staring blindly at the ring, rasped the first thing that came to mind:

"Let our dynasty be reborn."

15

HUNTER

"SHE MESSAGED to ask me if I was okay," I muttered under my breath, a dopey smile curving my lips.

My plan was working.

The year of Rory and Hunter was totally happening.

Now I just had to find her a gift that would ram that message home.

CHAPTER SIXTEEN

CHASTESUNLIGHT *enters chat***

    ChasteSunlight: *D?*

    DDoSunlight enters chat

    DDoSunlight: *Hey, stranger.*

    ChasteSunlight: *It's really bad today.*

    DDoSunlight: *What's happening? Want to talk about it?*

    ChasteSunlight: *No. I just needed to touch base with someone who knows the worst parts of me.*

    DDoSunlight: *They're not the worst parts of you, Sunny. That's insane. It's very normal for someone to have a pain kink.*

    ChasteSunlight: *You call this normal? I want to hurt myself, D. I like it when I hurt. That's abnormal.*

    DDoSunlight: *It's actually a very interesting phenomenon. Did you know YOUR brain associates pleasure with pain because of a type of endorphin confusion?*

    ChasteSunlight: *That doesn't make me feel better. But you geeking out does, lol.*

    DDoSunlight: *You know what serotonin and dopamine are, right?*

    ChasteSunlight: *The neurotransmitters responsible for increasing and decreasing pain and pleasure.*

DDoSunlight: *Yeah. When you experience pain, your body gets flooded with endorphins and it creates a pleasure response. So when YOU experience pain, you get flooded with endorphins and you get off on it. Your brain mistakes pain for pleasure and you get off either way.*

ChasteSunlight: *You've been watching TikToks again, haven't you?*

DDoSunlight: *I've been stuck at home, lol. So, yes. BUT I researched it too, and it's based in fact. (Of course, knowing you, you'll ignore what I say.)*

ChasteSunlight: *Why? Have you been sick?*

DDoSunlight: *Yeah, stomach problems. Stress hasn't been helping. Lot of shit going down atm. (See? Knew you'd ignore me.)*

ChasteSunlight: *Oh. I hope everything's okay?*

DDoSunlight: *It isn't, but it will be. My grandfather was arrested.*

ChasteSunlight: *HUH? On what charge?*

DDoSunlight: *You don't want to know, lol. I didn't tell you to get you involved or anything. He got out on bail.*

ChasteSunlight: *How could I get involved? I don't even know your home address.*

DDoSunlight: *Like that would stop you if I asked for help.*

ChasteSunlight: *:P Seriously though, if there's anything I can do to help, just tell me?*

DDoSunlight: *I will.*

ChasteSunlight: *I'm really sorry.*

DDoSunlight: *Don't be. He probably deserves to rot in prison.*

ChasteSunlight: *Probably? You're not protesting his guilt?*

DDoSunlight: *He's many things, but I don't think he was innocent even in the cradle. Doesn't mean I don't love him.*

DDoSunlight: *Anyway, what's going on with you? You didn't start a chat after months of radio silence to talk about family.*

ChasteSunlight: *I messaged to talk to you. I'll take anything. I need the distraction.*

DDoSunlight: *I can't do that, honey.*

ChasteSunlight: *You can. It doesn't have to be sexual. Want to hear a funny story?*

DDoSunlight: *I'm all ears.*

ChasteSunlight: *It starts off sounding sexual, but mostly, it's...*

DDoSunlight: *Hit me with it.*

ChasteSunlight: *I made my own capsaicin tincture.*

DDoSunlight: *Jesus! Was that smart?*

ChasteSunlight: *Yeah, that was me, dropping to my knees in prayer when I put it on my nipples. Lol. And, no, it wasn't smart.*

DDoSunlight: *You're using less now, right?*

ChasteSunlight: *No. Why would I? That's the point of it, isn't it?*

DDoSunlight: *Did you get off?*

ChasteSunlight: *Isn't that a sexual question?*

DDoSunlight: *Yes. Did you?*

ChasteSunlight: *I did. Not the same as it is with you, but it's getting me through. I miss you.*

ChasteSunlight: *You said it yourself that she doesn't know you love her. I don't see why this has to be over.*

DDoSunlight: *Like you weren't already pulling away. You forget how well I know you, Sunny.*

DDoSunlight: *I miss you too, but we can be friends... That's an option. And I want you to be safe. I'll listen to anything you have to tell me if it means you're safe.*

ChasteSunlight: *You're such a gentleman.*

DDoSunlight: *A gentleman Dom. That's me. Lol. Anyway, I'm supposed to be distracting you. How's the fam?*

ChasteSunlight: *My brother's gotten engaged and I HATE her.*

ChasteSunlight: *She's a gold digger.*

DDoSunlight: *And she wants a piece of the action?*

ChasteSunlight: *She got it. She's not only wearing his ring but she's pregnant. ALREADY.*

DDoSunlight: *Does your brother like her?*

ChasteSunlight: *I'd hope so. Seeing as he's intending on marrying her and having a kid with her.*

DDoSunlight: *Then what's the problem?*

ChasteSunlight: *She's a slut.*

DDoSunlight: *Oooooooooffffffffffff. You do know that if I'd said that you'd have threatened my balls, don't you? Slut shaming isn't like you.*

ChasteSunlight: *No. It isn't. But she is. She's self-proclaimed. That's different, right?*

DDoSunlight: *Lol, I don't know. Maybe? How can you be a self-proclaimed slut?*

ChasteSunlight: *She just is. She's totally unapologetic about it.*

DDoSunlight: *Well, it's the new millennium. What do you want her to do? Be ashamed of her past?*

ChasteSunlight: *No. Just marry someone else.*

DDoSunlight: *Hahahaha.*

ChasteSunlight: *Shit. I gtg. Did I tell you that people annoy me?*

DDoSunlight: *No. But I can believe it.*

DDoSunlight: *Hey, before you go. Please don't punish yourself today. For me?*

ChasteSunlight: *I'll try.*

DDoSunlight: *Stay in touch.*

ChasteSunlight: *I will.*

ChasteSunlight leaves chat

17

AURORA

JUNE

"YOU'LL NEVER GUESS what I found out today, *Prozio*," I said chattily as I sorted out his blankets so that they covered his horrifically thin form.

As usual, he ignored me; his head faced the window as he peered onto the hall.

When I'd told him we were getting him out of prison, he hadn't been happy about it, but I thought he'd get over it.

It seemed like obstinacy was in the Valentini blood.

Dismissing the fact that he was freezing me out, I continued, "I went to Rachel's baby shower today. You remember I told you about Rachel, don't you? I don't know if I told you she's pregnant though. If I didn't," I teased, "*surprise.*

"Anyway, it was interesting. Her partner is the head of an MC. The Satan's Sinners—they're based in New Jersey—and she proved her worth today." I whistled. "This woman came along and brought trouble with her and she and Rach got into a damn catfight.

"It was hilarious, and she did so good. I was really proud of her. Especially because the *buttana* tried to kick her in the belly." Heaving a sigh, I poured him some water. "She's terrified of being pregnant but it looks so good on her.

"I met her daughter too. The last time I saw her, she was a tiny little thing. All wrinkles and a mop of hair. How the hell has so much time passed?

"It's sad, really. Rach ended up putting her up for adoption, but they've reconnected. I'm glad. Rach deserves to be surrounded by family."

I moved over to his nightstand and started sorting out his magazines. I brought them every week and the only proof I got that he read them was the dog-eared pages and the folds that acted as a bookmark.

While I chatted about what I ate at the party as I continued with my tidying, I kept it light even though my mind was on the conversation Rach and I had had at the baby shower.

At the start of the year, my brother had sent a laptop to the hacker we used. The laptop came from my future sister-in-law's ex.

From the files on the hard drive, we'd helped the Dragon Head of the Triads rescue a son who'd been kidnapped, as well as liberate a Canadian hockey player in the NHL.

Rachel had just informed me that there was more information on that laptop than we'd initially known—there were videos. Damian Headley had been a rapist. He plied his victims with drugs and recorded what he did to them.

A recording of Jennifer had been found among the files.

If Luc found out the same thing that had happened to his sister had happened to his fiancée, it would break his heart.

The magazine in my hand crinkled as I clutched it in my fist.

Rachel had the source files, but what if Headley had released the videos online? I had to protect Luciu and Jennifer from that fate; I just didn't know how.

I knew D was an ethical hacker. Could he help?

Hunter would do anything for the family, but I didn't want this information spreading. Loose lips sunk ships, after all.

Rachel's intel had spoiled the day for me, and coming here wasn't exactly improving my mood, but that didn't mean Currau didn't need visitors. Whether he liked it or not, he was free and Valentinis stuck together.

Oddly exhausted by everything I'd learned, I plunked my ass on the comfortable seat and tried to relax.

Currau had gone from a prison ward to the best suite in the hospital, and I appreciated that because it made for a much more pleasant visit.

Settling back, I started to shuffle through the pages of an art magazine. I didn't know what he liked to read so I brought him a variety of topics. Art was my thing so I started reading an article about Jane Kaufman who'd recently died and her membership in the Guerrilla Girls.

After, I flipped a couple pages and that was when my heart stopped.

It was a simple pencil sketch of a kitchen table. A mother sat at the head with a paring knife as she peeled apples while four children were busy with their homework.

I almost choked when I saw the title and name.

A Fall Afternoon by A. Fitzwilliam.

Unable to stop myself, I went to write *Matri* a text, but before I could hit send, I remembered she was back in rehab and her cell phone had been confiscated by the staff again.

Goddammit.

Stan would laugh if he saw, and Luc would ask me what my problem was—*it was good enough to be featured in a magazine, wasn't it?*

I snarled at the thought.

Taking a photo, I sucked in a breath and vented to the only person who'd be willing to listen to me rant.

Hunter: *Very nice. You did that?*

Me: *I did. It's in a fucking magazine. Matri told me she sent it in, but she didn't tell me it would be featured in a magazine if it 'won.'*

Hunter: *I'm surprised you're not dosing her wine with Alka Seltzer.*

Me: *Promise you won't tell anyone?*

Hunter: *Tell anyone what? Whatever IT is, I promise that it'll stay between you and me.*

Me: *She's in rehab.*

Hunter: *Oh, shit. Why?*

Me: *She drinks too much.*

Me: *I was hoping she'd gotten better but it ebbs and flows.*

Hunter: *I'm sorry.*

Me: *That means I can't argue with her, though, because they confiscated her damn phone.*

Hunter: *So you're venting to me? Lol. I think I remember that day. Didn't she make strudel?*

Me: *Yeah, and she burned it.*

Hunter: *Haha. She never could bake.*

A soft smile curved my lips.

Me: *No, but it didn't stop her from trying.*

Hunter: *Did you draw that from memory?*

Me: *Yeah.*

Hunter: *Impressive. I know you're pissed but... your talent should be showcased. I can see why she sent it in. Happier times, no?*

Me: *She didn't ask me. You know I don't like people to see my drawings.*

Hunter: *Okay, let's assess the situation. How popular's the magazine?*

I thought about that then Googled the circulation.

Me: *Two-hundred thousand copies are printed every month.*

Hunter: *So, that's the damage.*

Me: *It's a LOT of damage. Goddammit, doesn't she know I want to stay under the radar?*

Hunter: *She's probably tired of you not showing off your work. I can empathize. That's really beautiful, Aurora.*

Me: *Thank you, I guess.*

Hunter: *I'm always here, you know? If you want to vent, I mean. It doesn't just have to be if your mom is in rehab or whatever.*

Me: *It's hardly fair, is it?*

Hunter: *Life rarely is.*

I didn't know why, but that had me staring down at the photo. Back to a time when things *had* been easier. When we'd been close. Before everything had gotten so complicated. When *Patri* was alive and we were happy. Really, genuinely happy.

Me: *It was idyllic, wasn't it?*

Hunter: *Our childhood?*

Me: *Yes.*

Hunter: *It was. We were lucky.*

Me: *We really were. I'd better go.*

Hunter: *Okay. Take care.*

Me: *You too.*

My rant had turned maudlin.

I cleared my throat and tore out the drawing from the magazine. Getting to my feet, I placed it on Currau's table, snagged one of the pens he did crosswords with, and wrote in the background of the drawing:

Valentini Estate,

Catania

1999

Lauren Valentini (head of table,) Luciu and Custanzu (on the right side), Aurora and Hunter Lachlan (on the left side).

We picked apples from the orchard and Matri made them into a strudel which she burned. :)

And with that, I replaced the pen from where I'd found it, left the drawing for him to look at or throw away, whichever he wanted, picked up my purse, then walked out.

CHAPTER EIGHTEEN

JULY

****CHASTESUNLIGHT** *enters chat***

    ChasteSunlight: *D?*

    DDoSunlight enters chat

    DDoSunlight: *Hey!*

    ChasteSunlight: *Always so cheerful. I wish I had your outlook on life, lol.*

    DDoSunlight: *It's a blessing and a curse. I figure that I live up to my nickname, at least. How are you doing?*

    ChasteSunlight: *I got my labia pierced like you wanted.*

    DDoSunlight: *Sunny.*

    ChasteSunlight: *Sorry. Couldn't help it.*

    ChasteSunlight: *Do you want to see?*

    DDoSunlight: *No. I told you already that side of our relationship has to be over.*

    DDoSunlight: *How's life?*

    ChasteSunlight: *It's okay. My brother's getting married next month. Did I tell you I quit to help out with the family firm?*

    DDoSunlight: *You did? Am I allowed to ask what the family* *firm is?*

ChasteSunlight: *No.*

DDoSunlight: *Simple and to the point. LOL.*

ChasteSunlight: *You're not my Dom anymore. Apparently, I don't have to be polite when you piss me off now.*

DDoSunlight: *I didn't mean to hurt you. Mostly, I think you're pissed that I'm the one who pulled back when I know you'd been on the verge of saying goodbye for at least eighteen months.*

ChasteSunlight: *You might be right.*

ChasteSunlight: *You could also be wrong.*

DDoSunlight: *50/50 split?*

ChasteSunlight: *Yup.*

DDoSunlight: *Life's just a 50/50 split, I guess.*

ChasteSunlight: *Speaking of... I know you're in computers.*

DDoSunlight: *In a big way.*

ChasteSunlight: *Did you ever look me up? Or try to find me?*

DDoSunlight: *No. Why do you ask?*

ChasteSunlight: *Why didn't you?*

DDoSunlight: *Because privacy was a big deal to you.*

ChasteSunlight: *And you respected my boundaries just like that?*

DDoSunlight: *Of course. You never said it was a hard limit but you didn't have to. We wore masks with each other for years, Sunny. Never let it be said that I can't read between the lines.*

DDoSunlight: *TBH, I thought you might be famous.*

ChasteSunlight: *If you wanted to investigate me, find where I live, could you?*

DDoSunlight: *I wouldn't.*

ChasteSunlight: *No, I know. I'm trying to figure out what kind of computer guy you are. Do you tell people to just switch their computers off and on again or do you hack?*

DDoSunlight: *You know there are plenty of jobs in between?*

ChasteSunlight: *Not for my purposes.*

DDoSunlight: *I'd consider myself an ethical hacker.*

ChasteSunlight: *Sounds like BS to me.*

DDoSunlight: *It would.*

ChasteSunlight: *Aren't ethics subjective?*

DDoSunlight: *Do you really want to get into that argument?*

ChasteSunlight: *Fair point.*

DDoSunlight: *Where are you going with this?*

ChasteSunlight: *I just found something out about my soon-to-be sister-in-law.*

DDoSunlight: *What?*

ChasteSunlight: *She was date-raped and footage was recorded of her while she was unconscious. I know the original file will be deleted, but I'm concerned about there being other files online.*

DDoSunlight: *Jesus.*

ChasteSunlight: *Yeah.*

DDoSunlight: *I wouldn't be able to go hunting without you giving me some information that could lead to me figuring out your identity, Sunny.*

DDoSunlight: *I will always respect your privacy, but if I know your future SIL's ID then it won't take much to figure out who her fiancé is and, as a result, who YOU are. Are you ready for that?*

ChasteSunlight: *In all honesty, no.*

DDoSunlight: *You know where I am when you are. And if you never are, then that's okay too.*

ChasteSunlight: *Is it? Someone could use it against her. I hate the idea of that.*

DDoSunlight: *I sense a but.*

ChasteSunlight: *I feel like a bitch by not doing everything I can to help.*

DDoSunlight: *Thought you didn't like her? Why do you even care if it has been leaked?*

ChasteSunlight: *I can hate her guts and not want her to have to endure knowing something so heinous happened to her and was recorded. No woman should have to see herself like that.*

DDoSunlight: *I get it. But I also get that you're protective of your privacy. That isn't a crime. When you're ready, I'm sure you'll come to me, and I'm not going anywhere...*

ChasteSunlight: *I'll think about it.*

DDoSunlight: *Do that.*

ChasteSunlight: *Any news on your grandfather?*

DDoSunlight: *It's not looking good.*

ChasteSunlight: *I'm sorry.*

DDoSunlight: *Don't be. Like I told you before, he deserves to be in the position he is, but that doesn't mean I'm happy about it. Speak soon?*

ChasteSunlight: *Yeah.*

ChasteSunlight leaves chat

CHAPTER NINETEEN

JULY

RACHEL: *You're still looking for the Anjou ruby necklace, aren't you?*

Aurora: *Yes. Why?*

Rachel: *The new Prez of the Sinners' Ohio Chapter told Rex about some necklace that's apparently tucked away in a hidden safe on the MC's compound.*

Aurora: *Sounds like a Disney story for MC bikers.*

Rachel: *LOL. It does kind of. Anyway, I contacted Storm (new Prez) for more details because, to be honest, I was curious, and he said that this necklace belonged to a crime family in New York. Those were his words. That this MC in Canada stole it a decade or so ago from a rich tycoon.*

Aurora: *You caught my attention.*

Rachel: *Hmm. Thought I might have. Well, there's no dice yet. Storm said the guy who 'told' him about the necklace mentioned it could be pearls AND these safes are so damn secret that they've nearly torn the place apart trying to find them so don't get your hopes up.*

Aurora: *I won't but thank you for keeping me in the loop.*

Rachel: *Always.*
Aurora: *Ha. Lies.*
Rachel: *:P*
Aurora: *TTYL, babe. GTG. xo*
Rachel: *Same xo*

CHAPTER TWENTY

JULY

HUNTER: *I may or may not have tickets to the Euro 2020 FINAL.*

Aurora: *The FINAL? As in... Italy vs. England?!!!!!*

Hunter: *Yeah. Scored them last night. Great seats. A box. Not as fancy as what you got me for the Super Bowl but still pretty nice, huh?*

Aurora: *Very!!*

Hunter: *Do you want to come with me?*

Aurora: *Don't ask me that because I'll have to cry when I say no.*

Hunter: *Why do you have to say no? Is it just on principle?*

Aurora: *Because I don't have time to go.*

Hunter: *When do you live, Aurora? That's a serious question too. I'm not being facetious. WHEN do you get a chance to do anything other than work?*

Aurora: *I don't. And I don't need a lecture either. Someone has to keep this ship from sinking.*

Hunter: *It isn't sinking.*

Aurora: *Because I'm at the helm.*

Hunter: *You have Stan and Luc. You're not doing this alone.*

Aurora: *What do you mean by 'on principle?'*

Hunter: *I mean, are you saying no to spite me?*

Aurora: *Why would I do that?*

Hunter: *Because that's how we work, isn't it?*

Aurora: *No?*

Hunter: *No? I'd ask if you were for real but you clearly aren't.*

Hunter: *Nvm.*

Hunter: *Say yes, Aurora. You know you want to come.*

Hunter: *I shouldn't even be leaving the country but I'll make an exception for THIS.*

Hunter: *Italy vs. England?! How can you turn that down? It's not Sicily but for this, we'll be Italian, no?*

Aurora: *I really can't, Hunter. I wish I could. You know how much I love soccer, especially when it IS Italy, but I just can't. Things are heating up here.*

Hunter: *What do you mean?*

Aurora: *Stan's up to his old tricks.*

Hunter: *Drugs? He's taking them?!*

Aurora: *No. He's making them. FML.*

Hunter: *Oh. I heard about Red.*

Aurora: *Yeah. It's a pain in my ass.*

Hunter: *Aren't both of them that anyway?*

Aurora: *True. Which is why I can't go. I really hope you have a good time though.*

Hunter: *It'd be better if you were there.*

<u>TWENTY MINUTES later</u>

HUNTER: *Do you ever get tired of being Aurora Valentini?*

Aurora: *What kind of question is that?*

Hunter: *A genuine one. Isn't it lonely in that ivory tower of yours?*

Aurora: *Very.*

Hunter: *Then change it. Move towers.*

Aurora: *You can't change what's inside you. The location doesn't matter. It never does.*

Hunter: *You're being obstreperous.*

Aurora: *And that comes as a surprise, why?*

CHAPTER TWENTY-ONE

JULY

AURORA: *Holy SHIT. DID YOU SEE THAT GOAL?!*

Hunter: *I did!! The crowd was so pissed. Hahaha. They thought they had it!!*

Aurora: *:O They almost did. Two mins in and Italy took so fucking long to score.*

Hunter: *Are you watching the game?*

Aurora: *Lol, of course.*

Hunter: *You'd have had more fun here. IRL.*

Aurora: *I'm working and watching at the same time. Here, I can multitask. There, not so much.*

Hunter: *You could have multitasked here. I'm at home.*

Aurora: *What?! You didn't go?*

Hunter: *No. It was an impulse buy because I knew you'd want to go. Shit's rough here at the moment; it wouldn't have been wise to leave. But I bet I have a bigger TV than you... Just saying. :P*

Aurora: *Are you okay?*

Hunter: *Aren't I always?*

Aurora: *What's going on there?*

Hunter: *Just the usual. :) Wanna make a bet?*

Aurora: *Sure. I bet it goes to penalties.*

Hunter: *That's easy. Of course it will. Italy isn't blowing me away, and England's on the defense. Though we ARE picking up momentum after that last goal, we shouldn't need defense to score. Jesus.*

Hunter: *3-2 England. That's my prediction.*

Aurora: *Really? You're betting against the Azzuri?*

Hunter: *Yeah. I think England wants it. Plus, they're on home turf.*

Aurora: *And Italy doesn't want it? Lol. They're undefeated in their last 33 matches!!*

Hunter: *I got a feeling.*

Aurora: *Willing to stake 200 bucks on it?*

Hunter: *Make it 500. I'm feeling confident.*

Aurora: *Shit! Shaw almost had that!*

Hunter: *Fuck. That was too close.*

10 MINUTES *later*

AURORA: *Insigne deserved that yellow card.*

Hunter: *Asshole. Three yellow-carded Italians so far this game. Dumbasses.*

Aurora: *Bet you there are five Italians yellow-carded by the end of the game.*

Hunter: *You're on. Another 500?*

Aurora: *Yup.*

Hunter: *Penalties.*

Aurora: *Had to be.*

TWENTY MINUTES *later*

HUNTER: *Goddamn. Another yellow card!*

Aurora: *:P*
Aurora: *Maguire deserved that. Bitch of a foul against Belotti.*

TEN MINUTES *later*

HUNTER: *Shit.*
    Aurora: *You owe me a grand.*
    Hunter: *I did the math, lol. Will you take a check?*
    Aurora: *Will it bounce? ;)*
    Hunter: *I could hand deliver it…*

22

HUNTER

AUGUST

I HAD no idea what woke me up, but I blinked bleary eyes at the ceiling, yawning when a light flashed from the nightstand—my phone.

Reaching for it, a surprised, but pleased, smile graced my chops.

Aurora had taken to messaging me at different times of the day and night, and I anticipated each text like she was sending me a photo of her tits.

Aurora: *Do you know what I could just eat?*

I knew what *I* could just eat.

Her pussy.

Fuck, it was too early for morning wood.

Hunter: *What could you just eat?*

There, that wasn't weird. At all.

Aurora: *Torroncini.*

Hunter: *It's been years since I ate that.*

Aurora: *Yeah, because you hated it.*

Hunter: *It's nougat. It's gross.*

Aurora: *Sacrilege.*

Hunter: *Want me to send some to you?*

Aurora: *I can buy it myself, lol. It was just an early morning craving.*

Hunter: *You still working?*

Aurora: *Sadly.*

So… she was reaching out to me 'just because?'

Bombing Aurora with my presence was working.

Thank God.

Hunter: *You should get some sleep.*

Aurora: *I'll sleep when I'm dead.*

If I were her Dom, I'd spank her for that blasé comment.

Aurora: *Anyway, gtg. Work calls :)*

Hunter: *Night.*

Aurora: *<3*

A fucking heart emoji?

Okay, what the hell was going on? Had she been abducted by goddamn aliens?

That was by no means a complaint… but it was odd. Odd enough that I reached out to Stan.

Hunter: *Is your sister okay?*

Stan: *Yup. Why?*

Hunter: *Nvm. She's working?*

Stan: *When isn't she?*

Stan: *You coming to the wedding?*

Hunter: *Nah.*

Stan: *Luc'll be pissed.*

Hunter: *Luc's always pissed.*

Stan: *Lol. You haven't seen him with Jennifer. He's happy. It's fucking creepy.*

Hunter: *LMAO.*

My fingers froze as a scream ricocheted through the house.

What the fuck was that? Had I drifted back to sleep without realizing it?

Hunter: *Gotta go. Night, bud.*

Stan: *Yup, night.*

Dumping my cell on the sheets, I grabbed the baseball bat I kept under my bed then leaped out from under the covers and carefully drifted into the hall.

Peering in all the rooms for whoever had made that goddamn sound, I made it through the house without coming across anyone.

Was that why I woke up? Were nightmares a thing when you were half-awake?

I didn't suffer with bad dreams much, but I'd had a couple these past few weeks.

Everything was going to shit.

My grandfather was bearing the brunt of a family vendetta that only existed because of me, and was likely going to rot in jail as a result, and I had a sniper still hunting me down.

Well, sort of.

Rachel was acting as my go-between for interactions with Dead To Me and, thus far, to stop her from painting my bedroom wall with my skull, she'd had me on a treasure hunt for information.

Some of it was interesting—I'd learned the real ID of the guy who'd murdered Lodestar's mother, for example. Most of it was just random.

Another scream echoed through the house, making me jolt.

"No way *that's* in a dream," I muttered to myself. "Not unless I'm sleepwalking *and* sleeptexting."

It was definitely the year for it, but at least I knew where the screaming was coming from now.

Had a pretty good idea who was behind it too.

Storming over to the door that connected the kitchen to the garage, I opened it up and found my grandfather sitting on the bench there, a bottle of brandy I knew cost as much as some people's houses plunked on the armrest, a Cuban between his lips that he continued puffing as he greeted me, "Hunter, my boy! Take a seat, take a seat."

"So kind, Bert," I grumbled. "Inviting me to take a seat in my own damn house."

Peering around the rest of the garage, I nodded at Brunu, his Capo, who waved at me. Paulu, Bert's Consigliere, was watching the situation with a weather eye too, his back to the wall, arms folded against his chest, but he didn't turn his head to look at me. That was fair—I thought he was a prick too.

Wet work wasn't my strong suit. Ergo, I didn't know the other guys my grandfather depended on for these stunts.

A kid I knew was a Lombardo started punching their 'victim' in the gut. Strung up how he was, the fucker swayed back and forth like a dead cow on a meat hook.

I didn't have much pity in me for whoever the schmuck was.

The Camorra didn't beat the shit out of just any random person, and it wasn't like they *asked* people to take out loans or to build up debts in their casinos.

After a couple minutes of watching the dude have the shit kicked out of him, I realized that, while I didn't know the names of the foot soldiers in here, I knew which *house* they belonged to.

Each family on my grandfather's council had someone in attendance.

A coincidence? Not likely with Bert.

As the stranger got a beating, I asked, "Who's the stiff?"

Bert took a big puff of his cigar. "He's a gift."

"For whom?"

"You."

I yawned. "A gift. You mean a punishment? I'm going to have to cleanse this place of DNA."

"The boys will sort that out." He wafted a hand. "You'll be grateful once you know who it is."

"You're not going to tell me?"

"All in good time, son. All in good time."

"Should you be doing this the night before closing arguments?"

He snorted. "You and I both know that's going to be the shortest jury deliberation in history. Everything will be handled tomorrow apart from sentencing so there's no time like the present for loose ends." Another puff of cigar smoke surrounded us. "Get him between the legs, Rickie."

Rickie, the Lombardo grunt, did as he asked, punching the guy's dick repeatedly until even I was grimacing at the howls the poor bastard was letting off.

I scratched my jaw. "Who is he?"

"Rapist."

"Since when do you care about vigilante justice?"

"I don't normally. I never said I was a saint."

Snagging his cigar, I took a puff. "No shit."

Tilting my head back, I blew out a smoke ring, a move I'd perfected after college when I'd smoked too much pot and had partied too hard. Bert cackled as I returned the Cuban to him.

"Got a call from Ramirez about this guy. DNA tests pinged a bunch of matching results from attacks on coeds around the country."

My brow furrowed. "And?"

"Do you recognize him? He was at Brown with you."

I peered at the guy. "Even if I did, you fucked up his face."

"Reilly Green."

"Huh. I know that name. He was on the football team with me, I think."

Bert nodded and passed me the cigar again. As I inhaled, he rumbled, "Bastard's MO hasn't changed any over the years. He doses a girl's drink, rapes her. Leaves."

I swore my blood turned to ice as I processed his words. "No."

Knowing exactly where my mind had taken me, he arched a brow. "Yes."

My jaw clenched to the point where I was surprised my teeth didn't break as I managed to grate out, "He's the guy who date-raped Aurora Valentini?"

Bert gave me a slow nod. "As a favor to me, the LVPD let him loose on a technicality so I could collect him.

"It's the first time he's ever screwed up. He only got caught because the victim's girlfriend came home early and she pepper sprayed him. It's fate that he's here." He tipped his chin at Rickie, calling out, "Take a break, kid."

Rickie, sweating from the workout, staggered back and leaned against the wall. Brunu was watching Bert and me, so were Paulu and the rest of the gang.

"You know what's going to happen tomorrow, son," Bert intoned, soft enough that the others wouldn't be able to hear. "I ain't coming home."

The shock of his revelation, combined with his words, had me blinking at him in a daze. I was sharing oxygen with the fucker who'd raped Aurora and he wanted to discuss his court case?

He grabbed my shoulder. "Tomorrow, you're going to be the Don. I've spent the last six months trying to prepare you, get you ready for the job, but if your heart's not in it, son, then they'll scent weakness and will attack."

I didn't need to ask who 'they' were.

His council.

The guys he trusted.

These fuckers' families.

"Brunu's the one I want at your side. He likes you but he doesn't know if you've got what it takes, Hunter. This gift is multifaceted."

My tongue felt thick in my mouth. "You could run the Camorra with your eyes closed. You don't need to stop being the leader just because you've been sent up—"

"It's your turn. The world's changing, son. I'm too old for this shit. Maybe prison will be a nice break, huh?" He chuckled at that, sounding genuinely amused.

I, on the other hand, wasn't.

Even if my blood was starting to boil with every pain-soaked cry Green released as he wriggled like the worm he was, even as I longed to shut the fucker up permanently, glaring at Bert, I bit off, "We couldn't have spent your last night as a free man in a nice restaurant? I'd have taken a strip joint over this."

"Naw. This is a solid way to end my reign and start yours. I like the symmetry, Hunter. Now, Green has recordings of every victim he's assaulted." I jerked up at that, on my feet without even realizing it. He grabbed my hand and dragged me back. "We got your girl's. No one will see it."

My throat felt thick. "You did? Did you—"

"'Course I didn't fucking watch it." He scowled. "When you pull your fucking finger out, she'll be my granddaughter-in-law." A huff escaped him. "None of these bastards know *why* I'm doing this. Except for Brunu."

Head whipping around to stare at the fucker, I rasped, "Where's the recording now?"

"It was a DVD. I burned it." Something touched my hand, making me peer down to see what it was. He had the baseball bat I'd been carrying in his grip, and he nudged me with it. "Go on, son."

Violence wasn't my MO. He knew that. But he also knew what I was capable of.

The only reason he'd been Caponed was because the ADA believed I'd conspired to kill his brother. There'd been no conspiracy. I'd just walked in on the fucker raping Rachel.

I killed to protect.

Not for fun.

But this was both, wasn't it?

Trust Bert to mess with this technicality and to use it to his own advantage.

I palmed the bat, not even seeing Brunu's curiosity or the other men's watchful expressions as I morphed from the guy they knew, the not-always-so-ethical hacker, into a killer.

Green, seeing me, garbled something behind his gag, and whatever he read in my expression had him twisting and writhing like that would set him free.

I raised the bat, swinging it like I was stepping up to the plate and facing a pitcher, and I hit hard.

Enough for Bert to cackle.

For Brunu to guffaw.

Cheers burst up around me as I was accepted into the boys' club I'd never wanted to be a member of, but for Aurora, I'd do this.

I'd erase this piece of shit from the earth.

It had nothing to do with earning the men's respect and everything to do with bringing her justice.

No one understood *vinnittas* like Aurora Valentini.

So I hit Green again.

And again.

And again.

Until her rapist was like a *piñata* that'd exploded on my garage floor.

When a hand cupped my shoulder, I realized I'd gone into a zone I only uncovered when I was hacking. Blinking at Bert, unaware that I was dotted in blood, brain matter, and gore, he declared proudly, "My heir."

Brunu clapped me on the back. "Don, I'll get rid of the body, *se?*"

Bert didn't reply, just squeezed my shoulder again. "He's talking to you, Hunter."

I gritted my teeth. *Don*. A role I'd never wanted. A job that was mine no matter my preference.

For the first time, I probably saw eye to eye with my old man, who'd run to Sicily with my mom to escape this life.

And he and I couldn't even agree on whether the best pizza was from Naples or Rome.

(Of course, after spending most of my adulthood in the States, I now knew the answer to that argument was Chicago.)

Exhaling, I muttered, "*Se*, get rid of the piece of trash."

Brunu clicked his fingers at Rickie and another kid, and the three of them got to work once they'd slammed their fists against their chests, right above their hearts.

Humming his approval at their declaration of loyalty, Bert guided me back to the bench. "They'll clean the place up for you. Probably a good thing if you stay at the Gallinaro for a couple weeks anyway."

The Gallinaro was our flagship casino.

"Why?"

"Center of command. Smart move to be in the thick of things for a while."

My mouth tightened as I watched the body being cut down.

The corpse—Aurora's rapist.

Fuck.

Custanzu and Luciu would probably give me one of their precious Anjou rubies in thanks for what I'd done tonight.

As for me, the relief was surprising. Closure. I just had to figure out how to give that to Aurora too.

"You don't have to get your hands dirty often. That's what Brunu and your Stidda are for. But, a guy like him needs to know who's top dog. You did that tonight, Hunter." Pride leached into his voice. "He'll have your back, and not only because he's loyal to me. You did good, kid. Nice gift, huh?"

I didn't bother scowling at him, just reached down and fiddled with the signet ring he'd given me for my birthday. "I'm sorry, Grandfather."

"For?"

"Being the reason the Macmillans have a grudge against us."

He scoffed. "Better for me to go to prison than you, son. It ain't like I didn't do everything they're accusing me of. Anyway, don't you worry. It'll all turn out fine in the end." Before I could argue with that bizarre statement, he got to his feet with a grunt. "Old bones'll be the death of me." Not seeming to care that I was covered in gore, he leaned down and, as was the Sicilian way, kissed my forehead. "Been proud of you since the first day we met, Hunter, but tonight, you just rammed home to those who matter that you are a *true* De Laurentiis. Get a shower, *se?*"

With a chuckle, he wandered off, bottle of brandy in one hand, cigar in the other, barking orders at the men, who, as one, appeared in front of me and slammed their balled fists above their hearts too…

23

AURORA

THE FOLLOWING DAY

NEW YORK CITY

"WHERE'S YOUR HUSBAND, Valentini? I thought you were going to get hitched soon?"

From the other end of the conference table in the council room at the family compound, Puglisi, my arch nemesis among the Five Families, sneered at me. So, me being me, I sneered straight back at him, but because he didn't deserve an answer, I didn't bother giving him one.

Luc's hand moved to my shoulder. "What business is it of yours, Puglisi?"

"It's not right, a woman being so high up the ranks—"

"She's the reason the Uruguayans are cutting their ties with the Albanians and are selling us their product instead," Luc sniped on my behalf.

We always presented a united front or I'd have told him to shut up.

I didn't need to justify why I'd earned my position. I didn't need to do dick.

Actions spoke louder than words and I was born noisy.

Taking a bite out of an apple, Stan chuckled around the mouthful. "Or how about the fact that the Valentinis gained back territory from the Triads that had been lost since the fifties…"

That wasn't technically down to me. This year, we'd helped the Triads when the leader's son had been kidnapped. Luciu hadn't done so with a fee in mind, but that wasn't how the Chinese worked—their system was honor bound.

So, I'd dealt with them.

As a result, we had a block of territory that the Chinese and Italians had been squabbling over for decades.

I didn't correct or confirm my brothers' words, and I was pleased that I didn't as Puglisi groused, "Anyone could have done that."

"Not just *anyone* could have," Luciu corrected. "There are hundreds of things that Aurora does on a daily basis that keeps us in a position of strength. Are your pockets not overflowing with dollars, gentlemen?"

The families around the table nodded their agreement, but Puglisi was an old-fashioned asswipe.

I knew he'd be the one to bring up the problem that was my lack of a wedding ring.

Well aware that he was hoping, once I was wed, I'd be focused on having babies and that Luciu would promote Stan to the Consigliere position which, in turn, would leave the role of Capo up for grabs— undoubtedly, he had someone from his line earmarked for the job—I tipped up my chin and unwittingly sought comfort in the last place I should be looking for it—the pink diamond locket with white diamonds encrusting the solitaire that Hunter had gifted me.

I stroked it once. "I agreed to marry for the sake of appearances, but I didn't say when, and—"

"It should be soon. We look weak taking orders from women." I wasn't at all surprised that came from Messina.

I shot him a cold look. "Did it seem like I was done talking?"

"We look weak," Messina insisted, interrupting me. Again.

"You look weak without my help," I retorted, watching with a cat-like smile as he jumped to his feet, hands slamming against the table in outrage.

That, of course, was when things took a turn for the worst.

The sound of a gun being cocked ricocheted around the room and Stan ground out, "Nothing about my family is weak, Messina. Do you understand me?

"Your pussy ass line has been whining about what you've lost when our grandfather was murdered. But you didn't fight for him, did you? Even though he was burned to death.

"None of you weak-as-shit dickheads did anything in the aftermath. You just rolled over when Fieri told you to and took his dick up your ass and came on command. Or should that be, *left* on command—"

"Custanzu," Luc warned.

"No, Luciu. *No.* Fuck this shit. These bastards are crying about having Aurora on the council when she's the only reason we're here. Without her, you pieces of pond life would still be back where your grandfathers and fathers tucked tail and ran to.

"My sister said she'll get married, which is decent as fuck of her. At least do her the courtesy of letting her pick who she binds herself to for the rest of her life."

His continued defense of me didn't come as a surprise. Stan believed in me, supported me, and, in all things, had my back. Much as Luc did.

"My son's of marrying age—"

"Here we go," Stan sniped. "This is why you're bitching about Aurora not being wed, isn't it, Puglisi? You want to worm your house up the ranks with a wedding. Well, it won't happen."

"No, it won't," Luciu intoned darkly, his expression just as fierce. "Aurora and Custanzu, when they eventually marry, will do so outside of the Five Families in the interests of neutrality."

Though Messina and Puglisi shared a bitter look, Caruso and Bruno just shrugged their understanding.

This wouldn't be the last I heard of this bullshit, I knew. Every time we held a council, it was creeping up.

Since I'd agreed to this antiquated measure, I'd felt as if they'd placed a noose around my neck. With each subsequent mention of my nuptials, it was like they were tightening it, choking the life out of me, and no one choked me unless I gave my explicit goddamn consent.

As we finally shifted gears and started talking about important things, like business, Caruso stated, "Chatter's kicking into gear about Red. Starting to spread past our borders."

Luciu pulled a face. "In a good way?"

"The best." Caruso cackled. "That shit's potent, Custanzu. I had a boner for eight hours last night."

Stan snorted. "You should have gone to the ER."

Caruso winked. "Oh, I went somewhere."

Luc rapped his knuckles against the table. "Keep the price high."

"That'll drive up demand," Caruso pointed out.

"I know," he confirmed, "but supply's limited right now."

And he didn't want Stan to increase his production.

Stan's lab work wasn't dangerous but the byproduct was, and neither of us approved of Red, but unfortunately, it was like gold. I knew there'd come a time when we'd have issues with laundering the cash we earned from it.

"I'm concerned about its effects too," I admitted.

Puglisi's chuckle was nasty. "Only a woman would be."

I ignored him. "The stables are reporting aggression from users."

"I'm working on countering the aggression. This fresh batch should neutralize those symptoms." Stan gripped the back of his neck. "Are you sure you want to handle the prostitution ring, Aurora?"

Annoyed he'd bring that up now, I arched a brow at him. "How else can I make sure there's no corruption if I don't manage it? Can you say you wouldn't sample the goods?"

Though my retort earned me a couple grimaces and some chuckles, Puglisi's scowl turned nasty.

I scowled right back at him. "If you have a problem with my fastidious accounting process on our stable of hookers, Puglisi, now's the time to tell me."

Grainne Ledger had given me tips in managing the myriad brothels the *Cosa Nostra* ran, and ever since, we'd been doubling our profits even after wage increases for the girls.

Puglisi's top lip hitched up, his displeasure evident as he grouched, "No problem on this end."

"Probably a good thing seeing as someone less discreet than me might mention your penchant for—" On this occasion, I didn't mind being interrupted.

Eyes flashing with both a warning and distress, he bit off, "I said I don't have a problem."

"Good to know," was my response, well aware that I'd just made a worse enemy out of him, but this time, he could be controlled.

In my position, I wasn't going to kink shame, but neither was I averse to good old-fashioned blackmail material to ram my point home and to get him off my back.

An hour later, when I was alone with my siblings again, Luc warned me, "You made an enemy there, Rory."

Now that the others were gone, I was back to being Rory. Just as Custanzu was back to being Stan.

"Please," Stan scoffed. "Like he wasn't already. Sure, his *son* is the right age for you. More like he wants you for himself."

Revolted by the notion, I shuddered. "No, thank you."

Luc, shaking his head, muttered, "What have you got on him?"

I smiled. "You picked up on that?"

"Like a hammer to the head," he mocked. "You and your black-mail, Rory. It'll bite us in the ass one day."

My cell buzzed.

Hunter: *Did you see the Yankees lost?*

Christ, I didn't have time for this.

Me: *I did. As did most of New York.*

Hunter: *You underestimate their popularity. :P I think the country saw their defeat.*

Me: *Not now, Hunter.*

Why was he texting me so much this year anyway?

Hiding a huff as I tried to avoid my team's crippling loss to the Red Sox, Hunter's poison of choice, I answered Luciu, "Maybe my predilection for blackmail will bite us in the ass. Maybe it won't."

With my position precarious, extortion was a double-edged sword. The businesswoman in me thought it was a brilliant way to step ahead. The submissive, the pain slut, knew I was tempting fate when I had secrets of my own in need of protection. But until that day, and because I was *only* a woman to these assholes in the *Cosa Nostra*, I had to fight fire by dousing it in gas.

How was it that Italian men were so fucking scared of their moms but forgot that, before they gave birth to their sorry asses, they were just as strong? Just as capable?

Did they think that it was the act of labor that gave them the super-power to corral a family? To keep it in line? To send fear shuddering through the hearts of their offspring?

I'd bet that every single man on the council pissed himself when his *matri* called him out on his BS. I knew my brothers did, and our mother wasn't even freakin' Italian!

Getting to my feet, agitated as usual after one of these meetings, I gathered my things together and asked, "Did you see that proposal I sent you about the casino for sale in Vegas?"

Luc nodded. "I'll look into it more after the wedding."

I didn't bother hiding my irritation as I informed them both, "I'm heading to *Russu*."

"Don't be late for the wedding rehearsal," Luc warned, making me glower at him.

"When am I ever late?"

They probably knew they'd lose their eyeballs if they rolled them, so neither commented as I departed the council room.

When I found Puglisi there, waiting for me, I straightened my shoulders. "What do you want?"

"You ever heard that phrase 'you catch more flies with honey than vinegar?'"

While there was no arguing that I had the same effect on people as an unripe lemon, I wasn't about to take any crap from him.

"Bees don't waste their time explaining to flies that honey is better than shit. So I'll dismiss that just like I dismiss it when men, i.e., *you*, tell me I should smile more.

"You seem to forget, Puglisi, that it isn't my job to be sweet. It's my job to be smart. You should think about picking up a book sometime—"

His hand snapped out to grab my arm. The bite to his grip would probably make another woman cry out. For me, it was child's play.

I sneered at the fingers that were digging into the soft flesh of my bicep. "I'd reconsider your stance if I were you, Puglisi."

"I've seen those fucking *pezz'i miedda* following me around the city—"

I didn't wait for him to reply. I merely shifted my weight and slammed him between the legs with my shin.

As he yowled, I went to kick him again, this time with the pointy toe of my stiletto, which was when he released a scream that had Luc and Stan racing out of the council room behind me.

"*Porca troia!*" Luc roared as the prick dropped to his knees then wobbled backward with a keening wail. "What in the hell's going on here?"

"Puglisi thought he could get handsy with me." I gave a dismissive sniff. "So I showed him that every action has an equal and opposite reaction."

Stan cupped my shoulder and drew me into him. "Are you okay, *soru*?"

I sneered, "Takes more than a *vicchiareddu*—" An old man. "—to bring me to my knees. I just didn't like where this conversation was leading."

Amusement gleamed in Luc's eyes as he scanned me over, checking me for injuries. His focus was on me as he demanded of the creep, "What did you want that couldn't be discussed in the council meeting, Puglisi?"

"You're a scary piece of work, Rory," Stan mumbled in my ear as the old fuck carried on sobbing, but I could hear his amusement too.

We might snipe at each other but we always had one another's backs.

Always.

"S-She kicked me in the balls, Don," Puglisi garbled out.

"There's a saying for that but I doubt you remember your Sicilian all that well. 'Who looks for a quarrel, finds a quarrel.'" When he hissed in pain, I shrugged. "You shouldn't have touched me."

"Where did he touch you?" Luc demanded.

"My arm. But he tried to restrain me." I sniffed again. "I really grind your gears, don't I, *vicchiareddu?*"

"Women have no place being on the council," he spat the same old broken record, his hands still between his legs as he cradled his limp dick.

"Aurora has *earned* her place on the council," Luc intoned. "You haven't, Puglisi. I invited you back into the Five Families because I wanted a return of the old ways. Checks and balances. But this isn't how it works. You sit on the council at *my* pleasure, *capisci?* I put you on it, and I can easily throw your sorry *culu* off it."

Finally.

Finally.

Luc was standing up to these pricks. *We* brought them on board. *We* were the ones in power. Not them. Jesus, it had only taken a couple months for him to figure that out as well.

It was a good thing I was the intelligent one in the family.

Feeling flushed with success, I straightened up. "Puglisi was, yet again, complaining about how I do my work."

"She's got those fucking freaks following me around. You think I don't know what your game is, *buttana?*"

My brothers stiffened around me. Luc even started to loom over him, his intention clearly to pick the fucker up to deal with him, but I didn't need them handling *my* business.

I grabbed his arm and held him back. "You're being paranoid."

"Paranoid?" he shrieked, finally rolling onto his knees before staggering upright. "I know they come to *Russu*. I've seen them. You've got that soup kitchen—"

Stan shot me a sharp look that I ignored. "Just being charitable. But I think we both know what neither of us is willing to say, and I also think it's telling that you're standing here, alone, without your lapdogs barking around, nipping our heels." Knowledge gleamed in my eyes. "You don't piss off someone who knows the very worst about you, Puglisi."

His nostrils flared. "Is that a threat?"

"More a piece of advice. I'm not the one who tried to get you alone and who tried and failed to intimidate you, am I?"

"*Talè?* I approached you to ask you a question and you attacked *me.*"

"If you say so," was my dismissive retort.

"I do," he snarled, finally straightening up, groaning as he did so. "You'll regret this—"

Again, my brothers snapped to attention, but I merely quirked a brow at him. "I'll regret nothing. I'm not the one whose son has that little problem… You think I'd want to marry *him*?"

When he blanched, I knew I had him. "They *are* spies."

I neither confirmed nor denied that. "Says a lot that you know exactly what he is but tried to marry him off to me anyway. Run along, *vicchiareddu,* and be grateful for the power you have before you talk yourself out of your seat and into a body bag."

Rage flashed in his eyes, swiftly followed by a loathing that would have slashed at my flesh if I gave a damn about the man. That look spoke louder than words when he shuffled backward, gaze locked on mine until the very last moment when he knocked into the wall.

Bright red now, he staggered off, leaving me with my brothers.

"He'll make a powerful enemy," Luc said tonelessly.

"He's too chicken shit to retaliate," Stan argued before, changing the subject, he queried, "You've weaponized the homeless by *Russu*?"

"*Porca troia*, Aurora, this is the kind of thing I need to know," Luc griped.

"You don't need to know how I do what I do, my darling brothers."

Twisting around, I patted each of them on the cheek and shot them a teasing smile. "You can just appreciate it and me for being smarter than either of you."

Stan snorted where Luc grunted out his exasperation.

"Two months in Sicily will do you the world of good, *frate*," I informed Luc. "You're looking stressed."

"Gee, I wonder why." He scrubbed a hand over his face. "How the hell are you two going to manage the council when I'm gone?"

"Why do you think I upped my game?" I sniped. "I'm sick of being undermined in that goddamn room. No more. I'm sick of it being about my reproductive organs instead of my brain, and I'm even more tired of it being about a wedding ring.

"We're a patriarchal society—I get it. Boy, do I. And I agreed that I'll marry, but not only because it's more palatable for the foot soldiers, but so that my identity remains under wraps.

"With my past, that's imperative. But in that room, I demand respect. I won't accept their bullshit anymore, Luc," I warned.

"Surprised you've taken it as long as you have."

"Well, I didn't have enough information on them," I said grouchily, annoyed that he wasn't annoyed. *Yes*, I knew I was being contrary.

"And now you do?" Stan questioned. "What kind of information?"

"The best kind," I told him promptly. At his arched brow, I continued, "Their dirty secrets. I have them all and I'm not afraid to use them." Though concern was etched into their expressions, I merely smiled. "Don't worry. In this pissing contest, *frates*, I can piss longer, harder, and faster than that *vicchiareddu* can."

I was tired of this BS, tired of playing, and tired of the infighting.

Puglisi could bring it and he'd soon find out what it meant to go head-to-head with Aurora Valentini.

As would Hunter.

Me: *The next time the Sox meet the Yankees, prepare to get your asses whooped.*

Hunter: *You poor soul. I guess you have to live in hope…*
Hunter: *How about the next game we watch it together?*
Me: *Maybe…*

24

HUNTER

THE FOLLOWING DAY

"RACH, TODAY'S NOT A GOOD DAY." I stared around my bedroom in Suite No. 1 of the Gallinaro and tried to figure out where the maid had packed my shaving kit. It'd make sense if it was in the bathroom, but *no*. It wasn't fucking there. "My grandfather's in court. It's the closing arguments for the prosecution; the jury's about to go into deliberation."

"I'm sorry, Hunter, but it's Dead To Me. She made a call and you know we have to get her some answers."

"For fuck's sake," I grated out, scraping a hand over my face as I thought about the assassin who, instead of killing me, wanted information instead. "What does she need now?"

"She wants some info on a guy called Warren Kieran Winchester. He's based in New Jersey."

Annoyed, I headed over to the dresser that held a phone to call down to reception. There, I spotted a pen and notepad. I jotted down the name, muttering, "I'll get something back to you by the end of the day."

"Thanks, Hunter."

I cut the call, finally found my shaving kit, wished like fuck I could use my main rig back home, but instead, I took my laptop into the living room and hooked it up to the TV.

Because of goddamn Dead To Me, I couldn't be in the courtroom, but I could still watch and work at the same time as the lawyers made their closing statements.

Four hours later, when the jury had been sent to deliberate, I hit Rach up and she answered immediately, "That was fast."

"Yeah, it was easy." Ish. I'd looked in all the wrong places so it had taken longer than I'd have liked. "He's interred at Windy Ocean Pet Cemetery."

"Huh?"

I understood and shared her confusion. "You heard me right."

There I was, breaking into secured governmental databases, and Warren Kieran Winchester was a fucking dog. A dead one at that. Dead To Me had to be playing us for fools. Why the hell would she want to know where a dead dog was buried?

"Windy Ocean Pet Cemetery?"

"You got a pen? I'll give you the address if you want."

"The fuck is she asking us about dead pets for?"

"Who the hell knows? At least this time it was an easy task," I groused, rubbing the back of my neck as I yawned.

Last night's escapades had been followed up with an early morning drive to the Gallinaro to settle myself here for the next couple weeks. I'd barely gotten any sleep after I'd killed Green.

"What a weird name for a pet," she mused.

"Heard of weirder. Do you want the address?" I asked hurriedly when, just as grandfather predicted, news of the jury's return filtered through the courthouse.

A mere thirty minutes after they'd called recess.

It wouldn't break records but it was a close won thing.

"Best of luck today with your grandfather, Hunter."

We didn't need it because he was fucked. I didn't tell her that though, just said, "I appreciate it, Rach. Thanks for everything."

LATER THAT SAME DAY

Rachel: *Fantastic news. Dead To Me says that's the last time she'll contact us.*

Somehow, out of everything that had happened over the last couple days, that made less sense than any-fucking-thing else.

Over the past six months, as Dead To Me dangled me on a string, making me her very own personal search engine, she'd asked for the most irrelevant information imaginable.

I'd heard great things about her, but after our interactions, I was underwhelmed.

Which was saying something when I was the one who'd die if I fucked up.

Though I was on the phone with Custanzu who was trying to get me to go to his brother's wedding in New York City tomorrow, I tapped out:

Me: *You're sure you can trust her assurances?*

Rachel: *YES.*

I'd ask her later why Dead To Me wanted to know where a pet dog was interred. As of right now, I had bigger fish to fry. Bigger even than the sniper who'd wanted me dead until five minutes ago.

Me: *Thank you for being the go-between on this, Rach.*

Rachel: *I love you, Hunter. I'll do anything to keep you safe.*

I released a breath at her text.

Why couldn't we have fallen in love with each other?

I knew what we felt was fraternal. An incredibly strong bond, but nothing romantic.

Not like what I felt for Aurora.

Fuck, she consumed me and I hadn't seen her in years.

Me: *Love you too, Rach.*

"Hunter?" Stan queried.

I was such a fucking sucker for his sister, but without Dead To Me watching me through a set of crosshairs, and with Grandfather in jail now that his case was over, I could go to New York. Not for long. A week, tops.

"I'll catch a flight tonight."

"You sure? Tomorrow's—"

"It doesn't matter." I'd read in the papers about the society wedding of the decade taking place at The Victoria hotel tomorrow. I could easily pack for a black-tie event. "I'll be there."

CHAPTER TWENTY-FIVE

AURORA: *I'm really sorry about your grandfather. </3*
Hunter: *Yeah, me too. Thank you for giving a shit.*

26

AURORA

THE NEXT DAY

"WHAT IS IT?" I ground out as I dragged on the too-small dress that my sister-in-law was using to torture me.

Huffing, cheeks bright pink from the exertion, I stared at myself in the mirror and conceded defeat—I needed shapewear. Maybe even two sets.

That was going to be comfortable.

As I dragged off the torture device masquerading as a dress, Giovi mumbled, "Ma'am, I'm really sorry but I think you're going to have to come down to The Night Lounge."

Pulling drawers open on the hunt for Spanx, I frowned. "What on earth for, Giovi? Today's Luc's wedding, for God's sake. I can't be late." Even if I had no desire whatsoever to attend.

Giovi hadn't ended up on my *Famigghia* version of the Bachelor, but I'd quickly scooped him up as an assistant. He was a great help with the stable of hookers we ran. Being gay made him the perfect candidate for the task of running the girls' side of the operation. It had improved his chances of being my husband too, but he got on my nerves.

If push came to shove, he was at the top of my shortlist.

He cleared his throat. "We have a situation."

"Spit it out," I snapped.

"The police commissioner is passed out in one of the beds."

"So?"

He sighed. "He hired Klara for the night."

A grunt barked from my lips as I squeezed into shapewear that promised to compress everything—organs included. The effort meant that it took me a while to remember who Klara was.

Sweating once the panties were in place, I dabbed at my face with a tissue from my vanity so I didn't wreck the makeup that had taken an hour to apply. "Klara… Is she the pony? No, wait, she's the, erm, Domme, right?"

"Neither." His gulp was audible. "She's just a sub."

I grimaced at that phrasing.

Just a sub. Like me.

"Why are you contacting me about this, Giovi? Even if today weren't important, this is something you can deal with. Just get him out of bed, for God's sake." I had enough blackmail material on Commissioner Kingston to last a lifetime anyway.

"He strangled her to death, ma'am," Giovi choked out.

My shoulders straightened. "What?!"

"He's…" Another gulp sounded in my ear. "Carmela—" *The madam.* "—she said he was high on Red."

Staggering backward, I slumped on the bed. My lungs protested the move because of the Spanx, but I ignored that discomfort as the most excruciating guilt hit me.

A girl had died on my watch and because of my brother's drug.

Tears pricked my eyes as I stared down at the little rolls of fat that had tunneled out on my legs because of the taut compression. If my vision blurred, so be it. Klara deserved no less.

When I cleared my throat, I recognized that was why Giovi did too —he'd been crying as well. It was sweet. Just not in a foot soldier.

"How long has she—" Death was a routine part of my life. *Cosa Nostra* aside, as DA, I'd put more murderers away than I'd had hot dinners on a job that had a crippling workload. There was no reason for my voice to be choked as I asked, "How long has she been dead?"

"Carmela found them forty minutes ago. She called me—"

"That isn't what I asked."

"I think about two or three hours. Her face is starting to go stiff and her arms are too."

I knew rigor spread throughout the body over the span of eight or so hours, starting in the face around two hours in.

"When did he hire her?"

"He came in late. Three AM."

"Have you heard of Red making men pass out?"

"No. But if his heart is weak, maybe that's why?"

No longer caring about my makeup, I rubbed my brow. "Have a car waiting for me. I'll be down in twenty minutes."

Cutting the call, I straightened up, wincing again with the discomfort from my underwear.

Checking the time, I saw I had less than three hours before I needed to be at the chapel. I was supposed to meet up with my family at *Matri's* house first, but that'd have to wait. They'd probably have a better time without me anyway.

I refused to accept that that thought stung.

On the verge of heading into my closet to gather my things together, my cell buzzed again.

This time it was Hunter.

Relief hit me that it wasn't more work, until I read his message. What in the what?

Hunter: *Have you seen the price of milk?*

This had to be a joke.

Me: *Milk? Is that a euphemism?*

Hunter: *No, it's not a euphemism. What would it be a euphemism for?*

Me: *I don't know.*

Hunter: *I'm talking about cow udder juice.*

Me: *Ugh. Why the fuck are you buying milk?*

Hunter: *Are you seriously asking me that? What's wrong with milk? It's not like I'm blowing a million on a Bugatti.*

Me: *How expensive is the milk?*

Hunter: *Four dollars a gallon.*

Me: *That seems cheap.*

Hunter: *The last time I bought it, it was like two bucks or something.*

Me: *When was this? 1988? When you were a fetus? Are you going to bitch at me about the price of gas as well? I have shit to do, Hunter.*

Hunter: *I'm not stopping you.*

Me: *Yeah, you are. You're distracting me. With MILK! You don't even like milk.*

Hunter: *How do you know?*

Me: *Because you never take it in your coffee. And I have never, EVER, seen you drink a glass that your mom didn't force you to drink with all those vitamins she used to make you swallow.*

Hunter: *Bad times. Thanks for the memories. NOT. Anyway, maybe I'm eating Cheerios.*

Me: *You don't like Cheerios either.*

Hunter: *No? What cereal do I like then? o.O*

Me: *I don't have time for this.*

Hunter: *If you don't know… then just say so.*

Was he for real?

Oh, who was I kidding?

Of course he was!

Annoyed enough to answer, I tapped out:

Me: *Corn Flakes. With enough sugar you can stand your spoon in the bowl.*

Hunter: *I like milk now.*

Exasperated because that meant I was right about the Corn Flakes, I sent him the bird emoji, shut off my cell, and, with a sniff, got to my feet and started on the important shit I had to do today—like deal with a killer police commissioner and his victim.

A track record of using hookers and of snorting blow as he fucked his lady of the night was one thing. Murder? That was a whole other ball of wax.

My stomach churned at the thought because, while I loved having people in my power, it saddened me that Klara had had to die for me to gain the ultimate checkmate against the head of the NYPD.

Once I was in my closet, I pulled on a pair of jeans and a tee then slipped into some sandals. Not exactly officewear but this wasn't a regular day at the office.

An hour later, wedding attire in hand so I could finish getting ready at The Night Lounge, I walked into the establishment to find that Giovi was waiting for me in the entrance, hands fussing in front of him as if he didn't know what to do with himself.

He'd seen worse, *done* worse. His nerves had me arching a brow at him. "Are you going to be okay?"

His tension transmitted itself to me. "Of course."

"Did you know her well?" I inquired, keeping my tone distant.

"We used to go out for drinks together. A bunch of the girls and me, we party every Saturday."

I filed that information away. "I'm sorry you lost a friend."

His Adam's apple bobbed. "Me too."

Now that I understood his grief, I left him in peace, letting him trail beside me without asking anything of him, knowing that he'd lead me wherever I needed to be.

When I made it to the room, I saw the commissioner was still passed out even though someone—I assumed Giovi—had cuffed him to the bed.

Withdrawing my phone from my pocket, I took a couple snaps of them.

Taking note of, and dismissing, Giovi's disapproval, I asked, "Is he sick? His pallor doesn't look too good."

"I had one of our doctors come in and check him over. He's on heart meds. They say he should go to the hospital once he wakes up."

"They didn't suggest an ambulance?"

He shook his head. "I don't think they thought that was an option."

Well, they weren't wrong.

"How long do they think he'll be out?"

"They said an hour or so, but it's guesswork without them taking blood and investigating further."

The rigidity of Klara's body caught my attention, but the frozen horror on her features, the bruises around her throat, how her arms and legs were posed, spoke of someone who'd died a painful death.

Bitterness turned to ash in my mouth as the commissioner stirred.

Lucky for my schedule, but not lucky for me.

Giovi and I watched as a confused frown flashed on his face, then came the rattle of his hand as he realized he was cuffed, and then, his eyes popped open and he saw Klara.

The horror in his expression matched hers, but it was too late for that.

Too late for both of them.

Right now, it didn't matter that I felt sorry for Klara, that the needless waste of a life made my stomach upset and my heart ache.

It didn't matter that he'd recognize me, that he'd be able to ID me as the once DA of this fine city—business, as always, came first.

In this instance, it was the kind that would plague my dreams, but I was too pragmatic to let that stop me.

I had his balls in my hand and I wasn't afraid to squeeze them.

"Commissioner Kingston," I purred, ignoring Giovi's censorious stare at my tone, "we meet again."

PART 3

PRESENT DAY

"Love can be found in unexpected places. Sometimes we go out searching for what we think we want and we end up with what we're supposed to have."
  - Kate McGahan

27

AURORA

11 MINUTES - YUNGBLUD, HALSEY, TRAVIS BARKER

"YOU CAN'T RUN AWAY from me forever, Sunny. This once... I'll allow it. *This once*. But there are consequences for everything. As you well know."

Frozen solid in the restroom stall, Hunter's words a death knell in my ears, I barely heard Rachel as she groused, "You promised you'd tell me what made you two fall out."

Blinking, dazed, still fighting the need to puke, still struggling with the act of breathing, I whispered, "I did. I know. But I'm in a toilet stall at my brother's wedding, Rachel. This is really bad. Like really, really bad." I swallowed down some bile then garbled, "Beyond private, Rach. So private. I've never told anyone who mattered this."

D, at the time of our meeting, hadn't mattered.

Now, he did.

Fuck.

And D was Hunter. Hunter was D.

Hunter was a Dom, my once online Dom, and I was a pain slut and this was crazy and I was going to lose my mind—

"Are you rambling?!"

I bit my lip. "I think I might be."

"There's no 'think' about it. I didn't hear you this stressed out when you thought you were going to get a B in Torts."

I hissed. "Don't bring that up."

Her chuckle was warmer than I'd like. "The one and only time Aurora Fitzwilliam ever got an A and not an A+."

I sniffed. "Like you're not as bad as I am."

"That's why we get along so well," she disregarded, her tone dismissive. Rachel wasn't ashamed to admit that she was a know-it-all. "Okay, if you're rambling and getting defensive about a class we took in our early twenties, I know you're stressed as fuck. I'll let you get away with putting this conversation off for a short while."

"How short is short? A decade?"

Rachel scoffed, "A day."

"Fair," I said with a grumble.

"Aurora?"

"Yes?"

"A part of me always thought you were angry at Hunter for killing Marcus after h-he raped me."

My chin tipped up. "Rachel Laker, I never thought you were a fool."

A shaky breath sounded in my ear. "So it wasn't that?"

"Of course not. He could have strung him up by his ball sac and I wouldn't have thought the punishment was strong enough to fit the crime."

Back in college, when Torts had heavily featured in my nightmares, Rachel, Hunter, my ex-husband, and I all shared a townhouse in Providence.

Hunter had walked into the kitchen and had found Rachel being raped by Marcus.

To which, like any sensible man, he'd rid the earth of someone who should have understood the nature of consent.

The thought, as always, made me sick to my stomach.

If he could rape Rachel, what fate, down the line, did he have in store for me? By that point, I had already learned safe words weren't something he abided by...

"I'd hate to think that I was the reason you two fell out," she admitted sadly.

"I swear to you it isn't. H-He—" A shuddery breath rattled from my lips.

"It's okay. You can tell me tomorrow."

"Thank you," I whispered. Desperate to change the subject, desperate for her not to leave me just yet, desperate to escape my train of thought, I quickly asked, "Did you know about Hunter being in the Camorra?"

"Not until recently… You didn't know either?" she asked carefully.

"No. I didn't until earlier this year. Things have been so chaotic here that I guess I've let go of my handle on the bigger picture."

"You can't control everything at all times."

I could.

And did.

And had.

For years.

But…

I rubbed my temple. "I'm having issues with the transition and I shouldn't be talking about this in a bathroom stall either."

"Call me later? We can talk then."

"If I don't pass out from how tight this shapewear is first, I will." I wouldn't renege. I didn't want to discuss the past, but Rachel… Maybe if I could talk to her about this then, when Hunter forced a dialogue between us—because he would… I knew D too well now not to know that was coming—I might be able to talk to him without wanting to vomit first. "Are you sure you're doing okay?"

"The baby's fine. I'm fine. Physically."

"Emotionally is another matter?"

She whistled in my ear. "You got that right."

Rach had only just gotten back together with Rex, her fiancé and the love of her life. She'd also recently come to know the daughter she had given up for adoption back when we were in college.

The kid who had only been put up for adoption because my bastard husband had done what he had to her.

Who had only raped her because, after Hunter had seen what he had, I'd stopped putting out.

Guilt had me swallowing down more bile before I choked out, "You must be ready to pop. I should head over for a visit before you have a squalling brat glued to your side."

She sniffed. "You say the nicest shit, Rory."

"It's a talent."

I didn't have to look at her to know she'd be rolling her eyes at me. "How about you? I was only teasing about the B in Torts. I don't think I've ever heard you so… manic."

"I thought I was going to lose my shit, Rach," I admitted, still feeling the storm clouds whirring into being deep in my soul.

"Just because he showed up at Luciu's wedding?" she queried, her surprise evident. "He's friends with him. Has been for as long as you, so why wouldn't you think he'd attend?"

"I don't know." I rubbed the bridge of my nose. "I just thought he'd bypass it like he bypassed everything else. He's never pushed the situation before." When she didn't have a cocky answer, I knew she was withholding something from me. "Rachel? What do you know?"

"Nothing."

"Nothing?"

"Nothing," she confirmed before she cleared her throat.

"What aren't you telling me?"

"Plenty of things," she said with a sniff. "One being… Did you know Alberto De Laurentiis was sent up yesterday?"

"Of course I did. Just because I didn't know about Hunter's ties with the Camorra until recently doesn't mean I didn't have *them* on my radar." I thought about that signet ring and what it represented. "Hunter's the new Don. I didn't…" I shook my head. "He doesn't have it in him."

"I disagree."

"You would," I groused while I stared at the ridiculously ornate toilet paper holder in front of me.

"What did he say to upset you?"

"Nothing."

"Nothing?" She whistled. "He just showed up and you freaked out?"

I swallowed. "Pretty much."

"Why? That's not like you."

It wasn't.

"When was the last time you even spoke?"

"Years ago." Technically. That was when Hunter and Aurora had last spoken, anyway. But we'd been texting more this year. Not a lot, but keeping in touch. The thought made me uneasy, enough that I changed the subject. "They've cut the cake. How much longer do you think I have to stick around here before I can leave?" A notion occurred to me. "In fact, how the hell did you get out of not attending?"

"Society weddings are *not* my thing, and your brother is a pushover for a pregnant woman."

Thinking about his wife who definitely shouldn't be wearing white, I rolled my eyes. "Don't I know it."

"You need to get over your snit," Rachel murmured. "Before you push Luciu away."

"She's not right for him."

"I'm sure there are plenty of people who'd say I wasn't right for Rex."

"That's bullshit."

"I'm also sure that Jen's friends would say the same about you not liking her…"

"Stop with the logic."

"Ha. That's my money maker."

I grunted as I rubbed my eyes. "Stan's pretty much broken bread with her, but even he thinks Luciu is insane."

"Aren't we all insane when it comes to love?"

I thought about D—about the grief I'd felt when he'd cut ties with me, about the feelings that had surged to the forefront the moment I wasn't allowed to have him like that again. I thought about how he gave me what I needed without making me feel as if I were a freak.

Then I thought about Hunter—I'd loved him since I was a child. Not in a happily-ever-after kind of way, but love was love.

Swallowing, I rasped, "I guess we are. Luciu's gone totally insane with a private charter and a full medical center on board the plane just in case she pops out the sprog over the Atlantic."

"Why didn't they just stay in New York?"

"So the kid can be born in Sicily."

"That's kind of sweet," she pointed out.

"Yes, I know," was my grouchy retort.

She snorted at my grouchiness. "What are you going to do? Sneak out?"

Somehow, her shifting the topic spoke louder than any words—she thought I should cut my new sister-in-law some slack.

"Aurora?" she prompted. "What's the plan?"

"I think sneaking out is a smart move."

"How?"

I pulled up the specs of the building in my mind's eye. I knew where the emergency exits were for a reason—not that I imagined that reason would be to escape my one-time BFF who was somehow the Dom who'd dumped me for…

I closed my eyes.

Her.

Only, *I* was her.

She was me.

The woman he loved—the woman I'd been jealous of for years— that was me.

I knew it like the moon followed the sun every night and would continue to do so for eternity.

I pinched the bridge of my nose. "I know of an exit."

"You can't avoid him forever," she said gently. "If I know Luciu *and* Hunter, then I know that now they're leaders, the Camorra and the *Cosa Nostra* are about to get real friendly in a business setting."

"You don't have to know Luciu to know that. Hell, I don't let personal matters get in the way of business either. Only yesterday I was telling him about a casino that was for sale on the Vegas strip that we should dip our fingers in."

"I know. He sent me the proposal. So… if you run away, aren't you just trying to outrun the inevitable?"

"Yes," I agreed, "but I need some room to breathe. To… come to terms with things."

"With Hunter being Don?"

"No. With everything between us."

Her silence was pensive. "Why?" she asked eventually.

"When I tell you my story, you'll know why."

"Do I need to bring popcorn?"

"No. You need to bring a blanket. You're about to hide under that blanket with me and cringe like crazy over what—" I sucked in a breath. "Please don't hate me, Rachel. I-I can't help—"

Rach, seeming to read between the lines, drawled, "Aurora, as long as it's between consenting adults, there's nothing you can or could do that would make me think you were a disgusting piece of shit. Calm down. I can hear your breathing. It's accelerating again.

"Jesus, whatever the fuck this is, it's doing a number on you. I don't think I've seen you be anything other than hard as nails for years."

The description didn't hurt. Not from her. She'd seen me before, after all. Before everything had changed.

"Is Hunter *why* you're hard as nails?" Her voice had roughened, but none of this was Hunter's fault.

"No. Marcus isn't either. It's on me."

"Okay. Well, look, you need to get going if you intend to escape, and if you want to call me later when you get a second, I'm all ears."

"Curiosity killed the cat."

"Only the answer brought it back," she sniped. "Speak soon, Rory. Don't be a dumbass forever, okay?"

She didn't let me reply to that, and reply I ordinarily would.

I was many things but a dumbass wasn't one of them.

My scores at Brown were legendary. I collected *summa cum laude* degrees like they were shoes and had worked in several states on my meteoric ascension to NYC's youngest DA as I gathered Bar certifications like they were a collection of expensive perfumes. All while running a criminal empire with my brothers behind the scenes...

I wasn't a fool in anything other than my personal life. Unfortunately, that was where everything was shot to hell. Because the only personal life I had revolved around my family and D.

Somehow, Hunter was both.

Fuck.

My.

Life.

28

———

HUNTER

SUNNY WAS... Aurora.

Aurora was Sunny.

And I needed her to know that I was fully aware of who she was.

"You can't run away from me forever, Sunny. This once… I'll allow it. This once. But there are consequences for everything. As you well know."

I felt like Solomon laying down a judgment on Delilah, but for the first time in my life, I was well aware that I was in a position of power with her.

She was so domineering in most things that it was easy to let her lay waste to everything around her. I'd allowed her to steamroll over most of my future plans, had traipsed after her like a puppy for the majority of my adolescence so this new power shift was interesting.

Heady, in all honesty.

I wasn't that kid who'd gone to college with her, who'd followed her from Sicily to the States. I wasn't that kid who'd stood up as a witness at her wedding to that psychopath when the act alone had killed something inside me—watching her marry another guy had been slow torture.

I was Hunter Lachlan De Laurentiis.

I wasn't the man she'd once known.

I was her DDoSunlight. Her D.

For the first time in too long, lightness put a spring in my step as I finished chatting with Rachel, well aware that she'd be returning to her conversation with Aurora.

I made a mental note to try to visit her in Jersey before I returned to Vegas, but I switched gears as soon as I left Sunny, well, Aurora, in the restroom—that was going to take some getting used to.

Veering toward Stan who watched me from the same table as earlier, I avoided the dance floor.

"Nothing changes with you, does it?" I muttered once I arrived at his side, having watched him chow down a massive slice of cake from a distance.

"Why is everyone so interested in what I eat?" he groused before slipping another defiant bite between his lips.

"Because you pack away more than five people combined? It's an impressive feat."

"Spare me the compliments." He jabbed the air with his fork. "You make shit right with Rory?"

"She hid in the restroom."

"You went in after her?"

I scoffed, "Of course I did."

He beamed at me. "It's about time you stop listening to her press."

"I never listened to it."

"Tell that to someone who didn't see your moon eyes firsthand, Hunt. Jesus. She used to lead you around by your dick something fierce."

My scowl darkened. "I can shove that cake down your throat, you know? It'll get to your stomach faster than it would with a spoon."

He smirked. "You know I'm right."

I did.

And knowing Aurora as I did now, knowing what she needed, what shamed her, what made her tick… I was well aware that was probably why she'd never seen me how I wanted her to see me.

Her kinks were why she'd friend-zoned me.

Her kinks were what had made me explore that world further.

Funny how things had turned out, wasn't it?

I plunked my ass down on the seat beside him, snagged an open bottle of red on the table, and poured myself a large glass. Taking a deep pull because I needed it after this evening's revelations, I asked, "She doing okay? When you invited me up here, you said she was being weird."

"She's Aurora. Of course she's being weird," he said unapologetically. "You got the invite from Luc, didn't you?"

"I did. I wasn't going to come though."

"I know. That's why I called you. You should be here. You're family, Hunter. Just wait until *Matri* sobers up. She'll be pissed you weren't at the ceremony."

My eyes widened. "Lauren's drunk?"

"She's practically fizzing with how much champagne she's knocked back." He shrugged. "She's happy."

"Should she be drinking?"

"It's a party. Why wouldn't she?"

Okay, so clearly he wasn't in the know about her stints in rehab. When Aurora had asked me to keep that between us, I didn't realize she meant from her brothers too.

In Lauren's situation, I'd probably have turned to drink as well. Losing Stan's father, Custantinu, had been rough on the whole family, but Lauren had lost her soulmate.

The bond between their parents was one of the reasons Stan, Luciu, and Rory were so strong. They came from a unified clan. They'd been reared in love. Their ties and the bond between them were unbreakable as a result.

That was when the memory from one of my conversations with Sunny hit me square between the eyes again.

Sunny had mentioned how much she loathed her future sister-in-law, how she thought the woman had trapped Luc into marriage with a pregnancy.

She'd also told me that her brother's bride had been date-raped and the act had been recorded...

With that information skewed toward the Valentinis and not just Sunny's unknown family, the realization settled hard inside me.

I cast the beaming bride a glance, saw the possessiveness in Luciu's hands as he held her tight in his embrace, whirling her around the dance floor like the queen she was to him, and two distinct emotions flared to being inside me—pity for what she'd endured and jealousy for their love.

"I'm not sure why you love her."

I blinked. "Huh?"

"Aurora. She's a bitch." He ignored my ever-darkening scowl. "I mean, I have to love her. She's my sister. I'd kill for her, but sometimes, I just want to kill *her*."

Though he was pissing me off, I murmured, "What's she done now?"

He huffed. "Nothing."

"Bullshit." For some reason, I felt like I was a kid again. If Rachel was the go-between for Aurora and me, then I was the Valentini siblings' referee.

At least, I used to be.

He scratched his chin. "She's getting a bee in her bonnet for the prostitution rackets we're running."

"You didn't think, with her past, she would?" As DA, she'd taken a tough stance on the pimps but not the prostitutes.

"No, but she's already raised their wages."

A grin curved my lips. "She said she'd do that."

"I know she did, and I'm glad, but now she's bitching about—" He pulled a face. "Never mind. It's just that I'm the one who has to deal with the ground level uprisings."

"Isn't that what your Stidda are for?"

As Capo, Stan had his own men who worked directly under him. They were a smaller, more focused version of a council.

"It goes deeper than that. She faces trouble every day on the council just for being a woman. This isn't a hill she should be willing to die on."

"She was raped, Stan. Our best friend was raped too. Sex work is the most vulnerable employment a woman can be in. Of course it matters to her."

It was his turn for his scowl to darken. "Remind me why you didn't kill her rapist?"

I didn't mention Reilly Green. "I killed her husband. Wasn't that enough?"

"I guess it has to be. Your first and only kill?"

I gave him a dismissive grunt. "Think that'll be changing now I'm wearing this."

His gaze drifted to my pinkie finger. "Heavy is the hand that wears the ring."

I snorted. "Fuck off."

Though he was smirking, Stan just told me, "We're here when you're ready to do business."

"That easy?"

"'Course. You're family."

"There are mutterings in the ranks so I could probably use your assistance," I admitted. "Not sure that I blame them."

"About your suitability for the job?"

"That obvious?"

"Well, I mean, I know you, Hunt. You're not exactly mobster material."

"And you and Luc and Aurora were?"

"No, but we had a vendetta to make right. There's a difference."

"I have a grudge against a certain ADA," I countered grimly, cracking my knuckles as I thought about Robert Macmillan—Aurora's ex-brother-in-law.

"That fucker's been fixated on taking your family down for years," he concurred with that particular understatement. "You gonna delete him?"

"Can't. Not yet. Will eventually. When he least suspects it."

I sensed that my words surprised him. "You sure you're ready for this world, Hunt? You sure you don't want to jump back behind your computers?"

"Of course I do. But I can't. If I try to run from this, I'm practically begging for a bullet to the temple."

"We could protect you."

"Thanks for the offer, man, but I don't think you'd be able to protect me forever."

Before he could reply, my cell buzzed.

Half-expecting to see a text from Sunny—well, Aurora—I was disappointed when I saw it was one of my Stidda instead.

Adrianu's photo message had me tipping my screen down so that passersby wouldn't have to see the grisly scene looking back at me with 4K precision.

Stan, of course, unable to keep his nose out, ignored the attempt at privacy and whistled.

The picture showed men and women and children strewn around a patch of sand in the Vegas desert. They were clearly immigrants trying to make a new life in the Land of the Free.

That same old Land of the Free where the Supreme Court had only recently been headed by one of those secret society fuckers from the New World Sparrows...

"Hunt?" Stan prompted when, shuddering, I stared at the carnage in front of me.

That he was used to seeing worse sights over dessert didn't come as a shock. For me, this was a brutal learning curve.

God, the youngest had to be a toddler—

"Hunt?" Stan repeated.

"We must have a coyote problem," I mumbled, just wishing it were of the animal variety—coyotes were the peddlers who helped get immigrants across the border for an exorbitant fee.

"Hunt, death is a part of this life. You know that, right?"

Anyone else might have been talking about the circle of life itself, but Stan wasn't. He was talking about *this* life. This horrible world that I'd never really wanted to be a part of but in which I found myself integral to regardless.

And that was before Bert had formally made me his heir.

I ran the Ledger, after all. Still did.

"There are kids amid that pile of corpses, Stan."

He hitched a shoulder. "I know. Crime touches them too."

"That's so wrong."

"Tell me about it. Not many people were as lucky to have been raised how we were. My mom might have liked Amaro Averna too much and your dad didn't believe in sparing the rod to spoil the child, but in the grand scheme of things, we were fortunate."

"Tell that to my ass back then."

He chuckled. "You usually deserved it."

I scoffed, "I didn't. I only ever got into trouble because of you three hellions."

That, of course, was when I realized what he'd done. *Broken my train of thought.* I shot him a glance, saw his arched brow that was begging me to tell him to shut the fuck up, so I heaved a sigh.

"You can't be emotional about this shit, Hunter. You have to suck it up and suck it in. I know that'll give you an ulcer—"

"Is that where all your food goes?"

He patted his gut. "I have to keep it well fed."

"Freak."

"You know it." His lips twitched. "You need help with anything, Luc and I are here, okay?"

"You going to give me Mobster 101 classes?"

He tutted. "*Mafioso* 101 classes."

"Do you wipe your asses on toilet paper with the Sicilian flag on them?"

"Why would we desecrate the flag like that? Now, the Italian flag? Sure." He winked. "But our bedsheets *are* red and gold."

"Stylish," I mocked before I nudged him with my elbow. "Thanks, Stan. I appreciate the offer."

"You'd have done the same back in the day for us," he said simply.

"You're right. I would have. But this is definitely outside of my expertise." Brow puckering, I stared at the message that had just come in. I tilted the screen so that Stan could see it.

Adrianu: *We got the coyote, boss.*

"Who's Adrianu?"

"One of my grandfather's Stidda. Well, he's my Stidda now."

"You guys work differently than us. Only the Capo has that here."

I shrugged. "The Don, Consigliere, and Capo have them in the Camorra."

Bert's Stidda was a lot more populated than his Consigliere, Capo, and council knew, though.

"Sounds like how the Irish run their shit. Each of the O'Donnelly brothers has their own crew. Interesting. That's probably smart, to be honest." He narrowed his eyes at nothing in particular. "Saw you getting cozy with them. What did they want?"

"Meet and greet."

He nodded his understanding. "Aurora could use a crew. She takes on too much. You remember Giovi? She's got him acting as an assistant of all things. God love my sister," he joked.

The news came as no surprise to me, but it had my free hand balling into a fist. I wanted to have the right to say, "I'll convince her to get one," but I had no rights to her. And Stan would rip me a new one for even making the damn suggestion.

Among the siblings, chromosomes were disregarded. It was one of the trio's more endearing qualities. Only, this had nothing to do with Aurora being a woman and everything to do with the fact that she was *mine*.

I knew she was overworked. That was Aurora. She was dedicated and steadfast. But from the insights I'd gleaned from Sunny? Prior to her—

The clues had been there all along.

Had my subconscious suppressed it or something?

I knew Aurora was into kink—that was the reason I'd taken classes on 'how to be a Dom,' for Christ's sake.

Even on the outer edges of her life, I kept abreast of all things Aurora so I knew that she'd accomplished her goals and was working as DA in New York. I also knew the city was where Sunny was based —it was the reason that we wore masks on the camera. She wanted to secure her privacy... Made sense now.

I knew Luc had gotten engaged. Sunny had been bitching about her future sister-in-law.

She'd said she loved her family and was close with her mom—facts I was well aware of. And her sugar cookie recipe was to. Die. For.

Rubbing my temples at how dumb I'd been, I almost missed it when Stan said, "You need to kill the coyote."

"Okay," I mumbled, beginning to tap out the message for Adrianu.

But Stan, shaking his head, grabbed my wrist and stilled my hand. "No, Hunter. *You* need to kill the coyote. The fucker's working on your patch, right? The Camorra run all trade lines in and out of Vegas, no?"

"Yeah. There's no other faction in Vegas. L.A. is a different matter."

"You got troubles?"

I nodded. "*Reyes Dorados* are a pain in the Camorra's ass."

"No, Hunt. They're not a pain in the Camorra's ass. They're a pain in *your* ass. You are the Camorra now, buddy. You."

He was right. Shit.

"If your heart's not in it, then it'll get you killed," he warned. "You need to take a stand. Delete the coyote."

"How?"

He took another bite of cake, chewed it slowly, then afterward, mused, "Doesn't matter. You're not like that fucker O'Donnelly Sr. who likes a show with a side of murder. You just need to get your hands dirty." Hadn't Bert uttered those same words to me a couple nights ago? "That's part of Luc's strength. Even though he's Don, he still walks into the fray and he leaves a lasting memory."

I thought about my childhood friend's habit of gifting his enemies with one-sided Cheshire Cat grins and blew out a breath. "Do I need that?" I motioned to my mouth. "To leave a lasting memory?"

"It depends."

"On?"

"Your intentions."

I thought about my grandfather rotting away in a jail cell. I thought about my family, living peacefully in Sicily, but only as long as I picked up the mantel Bert had left me. Then I thought about Aurora, a woman who only respected strength in a man...

"I don't want it but," I rasped, then my tone morphed, turned ashamed. "I don't want to die either."

Stan grunted. "None of us do. It's not like this was any of our choice, Hunter. You wanted to be a freelance software engineer, commuting between Catania and Silicon Valley, and I wanted to putter around a lab for the rest of my life—"

"That was when we were kids. We're making the choice now to be *this*, aren't we? To do *this*?"

"Kill or be killed. People are naive if they think we've grown past that point."

"Are you always so gloomy?" I complained.

"You're the one talking about not wanting to die," he grumbled back.

A flash of color in the distance caught my eye. Maybe it was that, or maybe it was just how she affected me, but I saw Aurora slipping out of the bathroom at the same time as I noticed Brunu heading toward me.

Torn.

I figured that was the story of my life.

If some brave soul ever decided to write my biography, it should be called that.

Brunu was striding toward me, mouth taut and shoulders high like a bristling tomcat, while Aurora, in a slip dress of scarlet silk that cupped her ass and revealed every inch of her form to my covetous eyes, was trying to escape me.

Not following her was a battle.

Keying me into the fact he was just as aware as I was of Aurora's retreat, Stan muttered again, "How is it the man who loves her the most is the only man she'll run from? Never let it be said she's not contrary.

"She'll stand up to mobsters, Bratva foot soldiers, and serial rapists in court, but you're the one she flees from." He scratched his jaw. "I'll never understand my sister."

"Isn't that what makes her special?"

Stan let loose a hoot. "Maybe if you're a masochist."

Funnily enough, through Aurora, I'd realized my leanings veered in the opposite direction.

Not that I told *him* I was more of a sadist, of course. I liked my nose where it was and I'd already experienced a knuckle sandwich delivered via Stan years ago when, even as a teen, he'd outweighed me by fifty pounds.

"You see this, boss?"

I nodded at Brunu when he waggled his phone at me. "I saw it. Can you arrange for flights back to Vegas?"

His brows arched. "Thought I'd have to drag you back."

"Why?" I asked crossly.

"You know what you're going to have to do, don't you?"

I shot him a dour glance. "Just arrange the damn flights."

He raised his hands in surrender then backed off, but I saw the pleased gleam in his eye.

Bert had told me I wouldn't have to do this often—what else had he fucking lied to me about?

"Mind if I come with?"

Turning to Stan, I asked, "Why? Want to save me from getting my ass killed? Brunu won't let anything happen to me. He's my grandfather's man through and through and Bert loves me."

"I'm bored. Weddings were never my thing. This one is worse than most. Jen grows on you like athlete's foot, and because of who she is, she's not the worst match politically for that *culu* I call brother, but I can only take so much of this lovey dovey shit before I toss my cake."

We shared a glance.

I dipped my chin, appreciating his attempt at appeasing my pride. "You're more than welcome to come along for the ride."

That was when I got a notification on my phone. Only, this time it wasn't Adrianu. Nor was it another of Bert's men.

ChasteSunlight enters chat**

ChasteSunlight: *Did you know who I was? Was this a ploy to get closer to me?*

Jesus Christ, I was so tired of being the bad guy in her eyes.

Why did I even bother?

DDoSunlight enters chat

DDoSunlight: *No.*

DDoSunlight leaves chat

29

AURORA

LUCIU: *Where the fuck did you and Stan disappear to last night?*

I scowled at the screen as I peered up at the ceiling in the hotel room I'd booked after my flight from the reception.

My scowl deepened.

Talk about a wimp.

I'd reserved a hotel room when I had a beautiful apartment on the Upper East Side so that Hunter wouldn't be able to show up at my door.

Out of habit, I checked the app we used to communicate as Sunny and D and saw that he was radio silent.

I'd admit that I was surprised, but I shouldn't have been.

Hunter had always chased me.

D didn't though.

Which was the real man?

Was D a more mature Hunter? The one I'd known had been a student the last time we'd properly spoken. I was a different woman from the girl I'd been back then. Why wouldn't he be too?

I was half-tempted to scroll through our *many*, many, *many* chats, trying to pick apart the information that would have given me clues about his real identity, but rereading the secrets I'd shared with him would make me feel like an even bigger fool, and after yesterday, I'd already made an ass out of myself, fleeing like I was a runaway bride.

Annoyed at myself, at the world, at D and Hunter and my brother, I switched screens back to our text chat.

Me: *I made an appearance. I didn't have to stay all night long, Luc.*

I'd have probably had more fun if I had.

Staring at the city skyline from one of The Victoria's most expensive suites had been about as much fun as watching paint dry. I hadn't even had it in me to work… That was when I knew I was fucked.

Work was as much a pleasure for me as being whipped was.

If I didn't want one, I usually wanted the other.

Last night, I'd wanted D.

Me: *Let me know when you arrive in Sicily.*

Luciu: *Se, I will. Do you think she'll like it?*

Jennifer was probably going to be calculating how much every antique she came across was worth, I thought on a huff.

Me: *How could she not? Enjoy your time there, frate. <3*

Luciu: *Thank you, soru.*

His text was a reminder that I didn't have all day to lounge around in bed. His absence put me in charge, and after yesterday morning's debacle with one of our hookers being murdered on the job, I had work to do.

Thoughts of my responsibilities faded, however, once I flung back the covers.

I froze on the path to the shower and stared down at my semi-nakedness.

I wore one of the hotel bathrobes, but at some point in the evening, the two parts had split open, revealing my nudity.

I didn't hate my body. Far from it. I was curvier than was probably fashionable, but things like that didn't bother me.

Fashion was fickle.

For a lot longer than was the current preference, society had preferred rounder curves on women because it represented wealth and affluence.

Proof, in my opinion, that society (and its opinions) was incompetent.

My body was the softest thing about me. I didn't even hate the mottled flesh on my inner thighs that was evidence of the lashes I'd given myself last weekend.

The thought made my lips curve as I traced one of the lines that was lingering longer than the others.

Deep on my inner thigh, this one curved toward my pussy. It was bare, as always, and when I spread my legs, I could see the glint of my piercings and my labia part.

Absently, I reached down and touched myself.

The move was clinical. Borderline *bored*.

Then an urge hit me.

An urge so strong…

Fuck.

It was illogical.

Without reason.

Nonsensical.

But I thought about Hunter. Then I stripped D of his mask. Those eyes that haunted me, the lips I'd seen one time and that had stalked my fantasies for months. Eyes that I'd dreamed of staring into as those lips sucked my clit…

I shivered at the idea, then shivered again when I thought about Hunter being the one doing the sucking.

Hunter.

Hunter was D.

Hunter was the one who'd chided me for self-punishing. Who'd told me to whip myself. Who'd sent me very unique butt and pussy plugs. Who'd owned my chastity.

What world was this?

Hunter was a Dom.

A Dom who bordered the lines of a pleasure Dom, a sadist, and a Primal.

A variation that, until him, I hadn't realized was my favorite kind.

Having always preferred the sadists, D's brand of domination had come as a delicious surprise.

Those eyes, that mouth… Fuck.

Hunter had never been my type. Not as a partner. As a best friend, sure. But a partner, no. He was too suggestible. Too…

I winced at the adjective that sprung to mind.

Soft.

I'd always known that, in a relationship, I'd end up hurting him with my abrasiveness.

Yet D wasn't soft.

At all.

So, how were D and Hunter the same man?

It made zero sense, but he was.

They were one and the same.

With those eyes of his at the forefront of my mind, seeing into my soul as if it were an open book for him alone, I rubbed my clit, gentle when I was never gentle with myself, and I thought about D/Hunter. I thought about him doing this to me, about finally experiencing his touch.

I thought about how I'd craved D for years. How I'd missed him and the things he made me do. I thought about the last time he'd made me wear his chastity device.

I'd acted like a moron yesterday: running out on him the way I had. But a strange slither of *something* rushed through me, powerful enough to overshadow any lingering embarrassment. It made my heart quicken. My pulse throb. It made my skin feel heated and tight, and it made arousal burn like a low hum in my core.

Rebellion.

I was mortified. So beyond mortified over what he'd learned about me when he was playing the role of D, but it couldn't be helped. Hunter wouldn't lie to me. He hadn't known that I was Sunny. Just as I hadn't known he was Hunter.

It was… fate?

Or bad luck?

How I was feeling right now, though, the mortification and the rebelliousness were swirling together, combining to create a weird Molotov cocktail in my being that I didn't know how to catapult away from me so that I wasn't caught in the blast.

With my fingers still rubbing my clit, I reached down and felt the slick juices beginning to gather at my core, and I flopped back against the sheets as I used that to lube up my fingertips.

A groan escaped me as I shimmied my hips, feeling flushed and overheated and oddly turned on even though nothing had gone right this past week and I should be feeling stressed instead.

I thought about that mask D always wore.

I thought about his hand curving around his cock.

I thought about how badly I'd wanted to suck that dick. How deeply I'd wanted to swallow his length until I was gagging, eyes watering, spit everywhere like a filthy whore. Only for him.

And finally, I thought about how I'd wished to be able to reach out, to make more of our relationship—

It was that that did it.

It was what had me reaching for the phone I'd dropped onto my stomach, and it was why I switched onto the camera app. It was why I spread my legs wider, and it was why I buried my fingers inside my pussy as I took a picture.

Need slalomed into me when I looked at the image, and before I could chicken out, I uploaded it to our chat.

It was reckless. Foolish. Stupid. I immediately regretted it the moment it sent, and then, I shuddered.

DDoSunlight enters chat

DDoSunlight: *Did I give you permission to touch yourself?*

What the fuck are you doing?

The question reverberated around my skull like a bullet to the brain, but God damn me for a fool, I could no more stop myself from shuddering at his response than I could stop my fingers from sliding back out of my pussy and retreating to my clit.

"Fuck," I cried out as the slippery tips worked me over better than before.

What that hint of authority did to me should be illegal. Especially as Hunter was D and D was Hunter—

My cell rang.

Siri announced, "Hunter Lachlan is calling."

It was like a bucket of ice water being poured over my head.

I wasn't a masochist for nothing.

So, of course, *that* felt good too.

I shivered as my fingers sped up, then when he didn't stop calling, I grabbed my cell and pressed the vibrating device to my clit. The call didn't last long enough for the vibrations to do much, but the symbolism of it got me off faster than my fingers could. No longer was I on the precipice of climax—I was there.

Back arching as the pleasure rattled around my body, I savored the moment for the few seconds I was graced where the world didn't exist.

The only trouble was that self-induced orgasms were about as satisfying as scratching a mosquito bite.

About as satisfying as self-punishments and self-enforced chastity too.

Bleugh.

Distressingly fast, I came down from my meager high which was when I noticed my phone had stopped ringing and started again. As Siri informed me it was Hunter, I sucked in a breath, moved it away, then jumped when it buzzed, the corner of my cell just glancing over the bump of my clit.

Quickly shifting it aside, I stared at the device with a grimace, regretting the foolish impulse to do that as I questioned how I'd clean it.

Then, I wondered what the hell was wrong with me.

I was worrying about sanitizing my phone when I'd just sent Hunter a picture of my pussy.

Hunter.

Not D.

His name was there.

Right. There.

He called me on my birthdays and at Christmas—I rarely answered.

Usually, I texted him back.

This year, he'd been messaging me more and I guessed we'd started to rebuild a rapport.

With the gaping hole that was D's absence in my life, I'd come to appreciate Hunter's ability to send me an inappropriate message at the worst possible moment.

I'd never been more isolated than this year, but he'd breached that isolation in ways only he was capable of.

But, could I answer him now?

Did I dare?

The thought had my brain screeching to a halt.

The trouble with being the only girl in a family of boys?

Dares were ample motivation to pull ridiculous stunts.

That was, I recognized, the only reason why I didn't hit the 'disconnect' button.

A dare.

Maybe I was as much of a moron as my brothers were…

30

HUNTER

"AURORA."

I wasn't sure what game she was playing, but when I put two and two together, merging what I knew of both Sunny and Aurora, I registered that she'd be regretting this in a short while.

As much of a gentleman as I was, I wasn't *that* kind. No way in hell was I going to let her worm out of this. Not when it was forcing a confrontation that I'd been certain she'd avoid like the plague.

"Hunter."

Fuck, her saying my name in that breathy whisper, not even from arousal but worry, made my dick ache.

Considering my current location, I had no business getting an erection.

I'd heard Aurora say 'Hunter' in every intonation under the sun—angry, amused, agitated, anxious—but never aroused.

The most important 'A' of them all.

"What game are you playing, little dove?" I crooned, turning away from the guy who was bleeding out in the warehouse, his head lolling on his neck as he sang what sounded like a Spanish hymn to himself. Delirious wasn't the word.

She swallowed. "We can't do this."

"You made the first move."

"I didn't mean to."

I narrowed my eyes. "Sure you did. Since when does the great Aurora Fitzwilliam not foreshadow every move she makes?"

"This isn't a game of chess," she spat on a hiss. "This is—"

"This is what?" I prompted when her voice fell silent before I mused out loud, "Those new piercings look beautiful."

She released a choking sound just as Stan questioned, "Is that Rory?"

I twisted back to look at Stan who, *naturally*, was eating. A honey bun this time. "Yeah, it's Rory," I answered, rubbing my tired eyes when Brunu slammed his brass knuckles-covered fist into the coyote's face.

"Is Stan there?" Aurora questioned, her confusion clear. "And is that—is someone being beaten in the background?" I heard the sound of fabric rustling, and the notion that she was in bed, *Aurora was in bed*, and that she'd been touching herself and had thought of me was enough to make me regret accepting the signet ring I hadn't even wanted.

I'd give my left nut to be sliding between those sheets with her.

"Yes to both questions."

"Fuck! I dropped a call yesterday, after… well, everything… Put him on the line. I need to know what's going on—"

"This isn't *Cosa Nostra* business. It's Camorra-related."

"Camorra-related in New York?" she asked carefully.

"No. We had to fly to Vegas."

"Stan's in Vegas?" she shrieked.

"Jesus, tell her that her voice makes bats come out of hiding," Stan groused. "Even I heard that."

My lips twitched as he rubbed an ear like it was hurting. Me? I was used to worse noises coming from that sinful mouth of hers.

Better noises too.

I didn't need to be thinking about this but it wasn't as easy as switching it off. I'd left New York under the storm cloud of believing that I'd managed to scupper my plans of ever winning

Aurora over, and yet, here she was—sending me pictures of her pussy.

"Tell him to go fuck himself," she sniped.

"I'm not your referee anymore." I knew how Rachel felt.

She fell silent at that. "No, I guess you're not."

It was on the tip of my tongue to tell her that I'd be that again in an instant, but I didn't think it would get me anywhere with her.

Not when she'd liked D.

She'd fallen for *him*.

She'd been jealous of *his* feelings for another woman.

She'd wanted to get back with D after *he'd* ended things.

DDoSunlight wasn't a role I played. It was me. I was D. But I was different around Aurora.

Not weaker, just...

Hell, I figured it was because I loved her, and love made me kinder to her than I was usually with other women.

My feelings for her made me more aware and triggered a welter of patience and calmness in me that only she'd ever inspired.

Ironically, they were traits she didn't seem to appreciate because she'd fallen for D, not Hunter.

Was it weird to resent my alter ego?

Why did she like *him* but not me?

Anger had me biting out, "What game are you playing—" I wasn't sure why I did it, but I tagged on, "Sunny?"

Her gulp was audible.

As was her breathing.

Fuck.

Trying to control a hard-on shouldn't have been at the top of my priorities but the sound—

When you did everything long distance, stuff that most couples would never begin to appreciate resonated more—sounds, sights. When touch, taste, and scent were absent, the last two senses became turbocharged.

That tiny hitch in her breathing registered next, which keyed me into the fact that her masochistic side was surging to the forefront, and now was not the time for that part of her to be let loose on society.

"Sunny, where are you?"

"The Victoria."

I frowned, pulled out my arm so that my cuff would shift and I could see the time on my watch. "It's eight AM there. Why are you still at the hotel?" Her silence had my scowl deepening. "Aurora."

There it was again—that soft hitch.

"Aurora," I repeated, aware that her name had turned into a rumble.

"What the fuck's wrong with her now?"

I cast Stan a glance. "She's at The Victoria."

"Why?"

"That's what I'm trying to find out." I rolled my eyes at him. "You really need to learn patience."

"I can learn it when I haven't been awake for forty hours. Luc was dead sure Jennifer would do a *Pretty Woman* and wouldn't show up—"

"What?" I pulled a face. "Wasn't it *Runaway Bride*? *Pretty Woman* was where she was the hooker."

"That you know Julia Roberts's movies is both disturbing and sweet," Aurora whispered in my ear.

"Stan's the one who brought it up."

"Stan's tastes are eclectic." She cleared her throat. "If you came to my apartment, I didn't want to be there when you knocked on the door."

I tried not to be hurt by that. "You could have saved yourself the reservation fee."

"Well, I didn't know you'd be flying west to Vegas, did I? What are you doing there anyway? And why's Stan with you?"

As much as I disliked that her tone was turning into the regular shrewish version that was her comfort blanket, it made it easier on my dick as I dealt with her.

"A coyote got a caravan of immigrants killed then dumped them in my desert—"

"Your desert?"

Her interruption had me pausing. "Well, isn't it?"

"*Se*. I guess it is."

That slight reversion to Sicilian had me arching a brow.

What the hell was going on with her?

I hadn't heard her speak Sicilian in years—and that was before she'd given me the close-to-two-decades' long cold shoulder.

Since her move to the States, she'd focused on becoming the All-American Girl.

It had worked, too.

Unlike Stan and Luciu, whose accents were neutral but could have British notes, hers was purely American.

"What happened with the coyote?"

"He's still alive."

"Why?"

"Is she asking you why he's still alive?"

I glowered at Stan. "Shut up."

"You can't let him live," Aurora said calmly, much as if she were telling me I couldn't drink milk because I was lactose intolerant.

"It's not as simple as that. Brunu, he's my version of Stan, worked him over. He's with the faction in L.A. who is trying to take over Camorra turf."

"The *Reyes Dorados*?"

"You've heard of them?"

"When I learned you were in the Camorra, I made sure to know who your enemies were," she admitted.

"So you could give them pointers on how to end me?"

"No, Hunter," she snarled.

"I might as well have been dead to you," I retorted. "Why would you care if my grandfather's enemies got to me first?"

"Is now really the time for this conversation?" Stan mumbled, making me realize that he'd ambled over.

"No," I conceded, but I motioned to him.

Together, we left the open space of the warehouse floor and shuffled into a small office.

The warehouse stocked most of the coke we'd received in a shipment late last month.

Thanks to Bert's court dates and the verdict, I'd had his Stidda keep the stock in storage until things weren't as chaotic out on the streets.

The LVPD was in our pocket, but with the old Don so newly imprisoned, it'd be nonsensical to push the limits of their abilities.

The council didn't agree, but I wasn't a moron and I had no intention of ending up dying in prison like Bert.

"I'm switching this over to a video call," I told her the second the door clicked to a close behind me. My tone brooked no argument. "Accept it, Aurora. After you make yourself acceptable for company, of course."

A soft hiss escaped her, but a couple seconds later, she was there, looking ruffled and rumpled and so goddamn gorgeous that I wanted to fuck her and kiss her and everything in between all at the same time.

Maybe she saw that in my expression. Maybe she saw my need for her, my hunger, because her nostrils flared and her eyes refused to tangle with mine. Instead, she asked the bed, "What are you doing in Vegas, Stan?"

"Felt like a change of scenery."

"A change of scenery? What is it with my brothers? Since when do you think you have a choice about these things? You can't just go on vacation because you feel like it." She harrumphed. "Am I the only one who understands duty?"

"Yes, Rory, you're the only one in the family who has *ever* made sacrifices," was Stan's droll reply.

A huff sounded down the line.

My lips curved. "He's here to make sure that I kill the coyote."

Stan hunched his shoulders. "Just keeping an eye on things."

"Why wouldn't you kill the coyote?" was Aurora's question.

"It seems a drastic move to make."

"He dumped a bunch of bodies on your turf, Hunter. I get why you might have questioned it before, but after Brunu beat the ever-loving fuck out of him, why wouldn't you want to retaliate when he confirmed the *Reyes Dorados* are involved and are trying to piss on your parade?"

"Why dump the bodies in Vegas?" Aurora asked next. "It's not like there's a crossing from Mexico to Nevada."

Stan smirked at me. "You sure about that, Aurora? Wasn't geography always your weakest subject?"

"Har-har-har," she sniped.

"They traveled through their turf in L.A. and then headed into Nevada," I explained before they could start bickering.

These two, I swore, pains in my ass.

Had I really missed this?

Yeah.

Dumb fuck that I was, I had.

"Nevada's a big place, Hunt. They were making a statement."

"He said he was taking the I-15—"

Aurora snorted. "Because that's the only road out of Nevada?"

I grimaced because she wasn't wrong. "Why kill him when he isn't the boss? Isn't it like cutting your nose off to spite your face? Why wouldn't you just maul the face?"

Silence fell at my questions.

Then, Stan whistled beneath his breath. "Maybe you're not as big a pussy as I feared, Hunt."

Aurora's voice was husky. "That's a fair point, Hunter." Ah, fuck. I recognized that tone. Before I could dwell on it, she continued, "But you can't get to the head of the *Reyes* yet, can you? You're sending a message to him."

"This idiot is a nobody," I pointed out. "Just a worker bee. He won't care."

"It's a matter of respect," Stan reasoned.

Maybe it was to them. But just because it was how they worked, didn't mean it was how *I* worked.

Sure, they'd made it to the top of the New York tree, but this was different. The West Coast was like the Wild West in comparison to the East.

There, factions ruled over territory. Lines and borders were the demarcation zones, not blocks.

The West Coast was less rigid. More fluid. Apart from Vegas.

The *Reyes* had fucked up by entering that turf, and a message *did* need to be rammed home—I wasn't arguing about that. I just didn't think killing some punk ass nobody would achieve anything.

Pondering the situation, I pursed my lips. "Wouldn't it make more sense to do what Luciu does?"

"You can't steal his signature move, dude. He's practically trade-marked it."

I had to grin. "No, Stan. I wasn't going to go through the whole Cheshire Cat rigmarole. I just mean, you know, send a message that doesn't end in the death of someone the *Reyes* probably don't give a fuck about. Wouldn't that be more powerful?"

"What do you consider to be more powerful?" Aurora's voice was fractious enough that even Stan started frowning in concern.

"You okay, sis?"

"Too much red wine yesterday," she lied, her cheeks flushing when I studied her with a measured glance.

There was something inherently liberating in knowing this was Sunny. It was a horrible reason—but what was the point in hiding from the truth?—it put her at a disadvantage.

Our whole lives, Aurora had been a step ahead.

But in this, there was no ahead.

Only confusion.

Neither of us had realized how the fates would fuck with us by pairing us off together, and I was well aware that of the two of us, I was the only one ecstatic about this situation.

I shot her a knowing look. "Red wine never agreed with you, did it?"

Her mouth tightened at my mockery. "No."

"What kind of message do you want to send?" Stan questioned, withdrawing another honey bun from his pocket.

I raised a hand and showed off my signet ring. Personally, I thought it was ugly, but my grandfather set a lot of stock in it as it had been passed down from father to son for the past three hundred years.

Eyeballing it, Stan queried, "Is it true that it used to be a brand?"

"I heard that too," Aurora stated. "Do you know why they stopped that practice?"

"Grandfather tried to go white collar in the nineties. It's why we're having issues now with territory. Ex-*Cosa Nostra* included," was my pointed retort, and the flash in her eyes told me she knew exactly who I was talking about.

"The Vitales refused our invitation to sit on our council," she said stiffly in what, I assumed, was a half-assed apology.

"Instead, they're pains in our ass in L.A. Anyway, it's not like Bert decided to go straight. He just stopped with this drama."

Stan chuckled. "Drama?"

"Yeah. That's what I said. Jesus, everything's about ceremony with you mafia fuckers. In the real world, someone offends you, you just take it and move on." I smirked. "Or you key their car and slash their tires."

"Nah, that ain't drama. That's the only decent part of this life," Stan joked. "We get to tear their throats out for the insult."

I grunted. "Messy."

Rory ignored Stan's cackle to say, "Luc's started to slice a 'V' into our enemies' cheeks. It means they're no longer allowed on our territory."

"They die if they're found on your turf?"

Stan nodded. "It's hilarious actually—"

"What is?"

"He's only ever done it to his mother-in-law."

I laughed. "Well, that's one method of dealing with family."

Stan grinned, but Rory sniffed. "She was a hooker who got what was coming to her."

That had me arching a brow. "Really?"

"I told you I didn't like Jennifer for a reason."

"When did you tell him that?" Stan inquired, his curiosity piqued as he finished up the honey bun.

"We talk. Sometimes," was her stiff reply.

"You holding out on me, Hunt?"

I could tell he wasn't upset, more confused. He and Luc, after all, had been trying to set the pair of us up since they realized I had feelings for her.

Unlike most brothers, they didn't threaten to slice my throat if I hurt her. They'd offered me condolences, because they knew that if I did fuck up, Rory would be the one slicing my throat.

That I still wanted her despite the threat—or because of that threat depending on your viewpoint—had cemented me in their minds as the man for their sister.

"No," was my simple answer.

"Ooookay," he drawled. "Do you two need a moment or something?"

"Yeah—"

"No!"

Stan's brows lowered. "What's going on with you, Rory? You've been acting weird since Hunter showed up at the reception."

"You had to know he'd come, for Christ's sake. He's family. He should have been there for the ceremony—"

Her nostrils flared. "Leave it, Stan."

I grabbed his shoulder. "Do me a favor? Ask Brunu if he knows where Bert kept the master brand?"

"Master brand?"

"They used this but it's impractical to keep tossing a priceless heirloom into the fire," I mocked. "Plus, it doesn't exactly leave much of a mark."

His gaze darted between the pair of us, but while Rory had asked him not to leave, when he shot her a questioning look, this time, she didn't make a response.

Stan, still confused but clearly sensing that we needed some privacy, withdrew, leaving me alone with her.

The silence between us throbbed. It had a heartbeat of its own as I looked at her and she tried to deny me eye contact but—

My mouth twitched into a smile.

Her focus switched to my lips before she dove into my eyes. It wasn't the same as eye contact though. She seemed to fall into the look, her cheeks turning pink as she did so.

"When two worlds collide, it's bound to cause shockwaves," I told her softly, trying to soothe her.

"Shockwaves?" she choked out, her hand clutching at the lapels of her bathrobe. "You call this 'shockwaves?'"

"No, I call this good news," I told her honestly. "But I know you won't."

Her brow puckered. "Do you know what I've never understood about you, Hunter?"

"What?"

"Why you love me. And I know you do. Doesn't take a genius to figure out I'm the woman you stopped speaking to Sunny for—a woman who had genuine feelings for you… What is it about me that has you on the hook when I'm not the most loving and warm person out there? You should have someone like that. Someone better than me."

Fuck, she meant that.

Did she think herself unworthy of love?

Annoyed, I told her, "You're lucky that I'm not like Stan."

"What? Melodramatic?"

"Yes. Do you think any man would appreciate being asked that question?"

"No, but you're not just any man, are you? You're Hunter."

I choked out a laugh. "And what pigeonhole does 'Hunter' come under in your mind?"

"I-I don't know anymore."

"Before yesterday, what was it?"

She released a breath. "Guilt. Shame."

Stung, I staggered back and took a seat on the edge of the desk. "That's all you feel for me?"

"No," she snarled. "You've always been family too. More than a friend. But—"

"But what?"

"You know what," she cried, her voice breaking. "YOU SAW!"

She screamed those two words at me, her panic real, her terror and distress and disgust combining into a bitter cocktail that I had to, somehow, swallow to make sense out of.

That scream channeled nine-year-old Rory when she'd gotten her period early and had learned that her brothers—and me—wouldn't have to go through the ordeal.

"What did I see?" I asked, keeping calm because I'd—

Jesus, I'd never seen her like this as an adult. Not Rory. Sunny, yes. But not Rory.

D and Hunter went to war inside me.

Hunter was used to backing off with Rory, because she was a Molotov cocktail just waiting to blow. A Molotov cocktail Hunter really enjoyed watching explode in his face.

D was used to dealing with her like the naughty dove she was, punishments at the ready to get her out of her own head. D, in turn, enjoyed the benefits of watching her plead for pleasure in the aftermath…

Nothing about this was enjoyable, though.

She sniffed as she swiped her knuckles over her cheeks.

She was crying.

Dear God.

I hadn't seen her cry since her father's funeral.

Staggered by the sight, I felt myself mentally hover. Both sides of me wanted to make shit better, but as always, Hunter didn't dare, and D couldn't offer physical comfort when there was the entirety of middle America between us.

"You saw me. You saw what he was—" She swallowed, and her breathing turned frantic. I could see the panic in her eyes blossoming like droplets of blood diffusing into water, and it prompted me to bark:

"Aurora, take a breath. Slowly. Suck it down, count to five, then release it." I put action behind the words, showing her how to breathe, and when she followed me, much as Sunny had, it registered that I had to merge the two halves of me that she knew together.

It was the only way to get past whatever was happening here.

I just wished that weren't the mental equivalent of me stepping on a minefield.

As she worked on calming down her breathing, I murmured, "You started to pull away when I killed Marcus. At the time, I understood. I guess I let you pull away…"

"It's got nothing to do with that bastard's death," she stunned me by grating out. "You think I mourned that rapist fuck? After what he did to Rachel? After how broken she was because of him?"

"Not the man, but the idea of him, I guess."

Her head swiped to the side in denial, but it went deeper than that —it allowed her to keep her gaze averted from me. "No. There was nothing to mourn. There was a reason to hate. You, and you alone, know who I am. What I am." She swallowed. "I trusted him with me. With all of me. I let him… I allowed…"

"You trusted him to uphold your limits."

Except, from her expression, I didn't think the fucker had.

Her nod was brisk. "And you, better than anyone, know I don't have many."

She wasn't wrong. Her limits were different than most in that there were too few. It'd be easy to go too far with her. She'd take everything her man wanted to give. Hadn't I seen that for myself?

Wasn't that why we were even here?

Because seeing what her husband had done to her, I'd known that I wouldn't be enough for her. Not like this. Not me. I'd taken classes, trying to understand the lifestyle, the mindset, totally willing to learn just so I could mold myself into what she wanted, but inadvertently, I'd found my place.

Around Aurora, I wasn't necessarily a weak man; I was, I guessed, more aware of who and what she was.

Some people were born with power.

She was that kind of person.

So was Luciu.

They had charisma.

It was like they'd gathered it around them in the womb.

That was what I reacted to. Before her, I was a pauper bowing to a princess.

Maybe it presented as weakness. Maybe that was why she didn't see me how I wanted her to.

With Sunny, on the other hand, I was myself.

Exacting.

Demanding.

I appreciated perfection and order in my work, and I required that from her at all times.

My tolerance and patience ran deep, but my expectations were many and detailed.

Reaching up, I rubbed my brow and, swiftly, came to a decision. "Aurora, are you scared of me?"

Her hair whipped around her cheeks as she shook her head. "I'm scared of what you know."

"What I know?" I repeated, confused.

Her bark of laughter sounded in my ear. "I knew you wouldn't know—"

"Then what, dammit?" I snarled.

And that changed everything.

That snarl.

A softness replaced the tension in her shoulders. Her eyes turned big before they dropped down to something in her lap, I assumed. Her back straightened and—

"Aurora," I warned, but she mistook the warning.

I already knew she was confused. I'd figured that out when she sent me a photo of her pussy. By the look of that heightened flush on her cheeks when she'd picked up the phone, she'd gotten off. Then, she proved her confusion even more by seeking the safe space between us.

A place where there was no judgment.

Only acceptance.

She tugged on the lapels and drew the robe off her shoulders.

For a second, I was faced with the momentousness of the situation.

I'd seen Sunny's tits almost every day for at least three years.

But I'd never seen *Aurora's*.

Even that day when I'd burst into her and Marcus's bedroom, they'd been bound by duct tape, revealing flesh so purple it had scarred me mentally because they'd looked like they could drop off any fucking minute.

God, I'd never be like Marcus.

This conversation was a reminder of that. I'd never do that to her. I had my methods and my quirks, and I could be twisted and exacting, but that level of sadism was beyond my limits.

I preferred things cerebral to physical.

Then, the years we'd spent together online poured like a torrent through my memory banks.

I was the one who'd ended things. Not her.

Whatever I was, she'd liked it. She hadn't wanted it to end.

She didn't need me to be Marcus.

Had *he* scared her?

What he'd been doing to her had frightened me back then. Now, after visiting BDSM clubs, it wasn't as shocking, but that perspective also gave me another slice of information—Master and slave, not Dom and sub.

Another thought occurred to me—how he'd bound her was probably why I hadn't recognized her body. He'd distorted it with the tape to the point where it had been unrecognizable.

My free hand furled into a fist as the need to touch her taunted me, to soothe away aches that hadn't been aches for her as I knew she'd enjoyed it.

No wonder she was confused. I was, and I wasn't the one who was running scared with shame about my kinks.

"Did I ask you to take off the robe?"

Her throat bobbed. "Don't you—"

"I always want you, Aurora," I snapped then sucked in a breath at the burst in my temper. She didn't need anger. She needed careful handling. Though it made no sense to me, I queried, "Does it make you feel better to be exposed?"

Her nod was shaken.

I'd never understand this woman.

That didn't mean I'd ever stop trying to.

"You never have to be scared of me," I rasped.

Her eyelashes fluttered. "You know the worst things about me."

I wished I knew what the hell she was talking about—

"Are you ashamed of your kinks, Aur—" I stopped. "Sunny."

"They're disgusting."

I frowned. "Nothing about you is disgusting. Nothing. Your kinks are you and they're beautiful, just as you are."

"You can't say that when you know what I let him do to me," she shouted, tits heaving, face and chest flushing as she glowered at me, the two sides of her nature going to war.

I thought back to that day.

I'd admit that it had been a surprise. I'd walked through the front door and had heard sounds that had sent chills down my spine because I was certain he was beating her. Then, when I'd burst inside the bedroom, wanting to save her from the fucker, I'd seen… her.

The real her.

The 'her' that no one else was allowed to see.

The controlled, detail-oriented, domineering witch had been in subspace.

Her ass had been so purple it was almost gray from the beating, and I knew he'd pissed on her because her skin was drenched and it wasn't sweat nor was it water as there'd been no bottle or bowl in the vicinity.

There was more duct tape around her waist, taut to the point where it had to constrict her breathing. Even her legs hadn't escaped the silver binding.

At first, I'd thought he was raping her. Torturing her with that rug flogger that he used on her with no regard to the delicacy of her skin. Etching the swirling loops of the wicker into her flesh as he fucked her.

She'd been sobbing and moaning around the ball gag that deformed her jawline it was so big, and that was when her eyes and mine had collided.

And she'd climaxed.

That was why she hadn't talked to me for years?

That was why she'd shoved miles of space between us?

I wasn't sure whether I should be furious, upset, or happy that it was something so trite that had pushed her away from me.

Mind racing for a solution, I tried to figure out how to break her shame. This was a first step. I could sense it, and I knew that if I trod carefully, acceptance would be our end destination.

It'd take time, but time was something we had plenty of.

"Do you want to know what I saw that day?"

"I know what you saw—"

"You don't see through my eyes, do you?"

"No," she conceded softly.

Then, my tone a silken lash, I drawled, "Don't interrupt me again."

"Sorry, Sir."

I scrubbed a hand over my face, unsure if it was wise for her to call me that...

Coming to a decision, I corrected, "Sorry, Hunter."

Her gaze darted to mine, flaring so that those cocoa-brown orbs were wide enough to drown in. "Sorry, Hunter," she repeated.

"That day, I saw why you never looked at me how I looked at you. I realized what was wrong and I realized what I needed to do to make you see me as anything other than Hunter, the third brother. As Hunter, the friend.

"What I saw that day was my 'eureka' moment. It explained so much and it gave me a fighting chance. It took me a while to work up to it, but that day was why I took classes. It was how we met as D and Sunny, for Christ's sake.

"I will never do to you what Marcus did. It's not in me. By now, you know my preferences. My tastes..." I waited for her nod. "But those needs aren't feigned. They're not a lie. You awoke something in me that I didn't know existed."

"You can't learn dominance," she said uneasily.

"I dare you to tell D that," I snarled. "Stop looking at me as Hunter. Stop judging me when, even though you believe I saw you at your worst, I never judged you for that day. Ever."

She sucked her bottom lip in between her teeth. "How couldn't you? You saw the state of me. Y-You saw me climax."

"I did," I confirmed, watching her eyelashes sink down as I dotted the Is and crossed the Ts on her shame. It made me bark, "Stop it. There's nothing to be ashamed of. What you do with your partner, so long as it's safe, sane, and consensual, can never be wrong."

"I trusted him with me. Every part of me, Hunter. What kind of twisted judgment do I have if I didn't see that in him? Didn't predict what he'd do to Rachel?"

"How could you? You're not a psychic. Would you have said, with all your knowledge of me, that I'd be the kind of man who'd kill another?"

"No," she ceded.

"That's your problem. You think you know me, Aurora. We grew up together, but I didn't know you were a sub," I pointed out. "We never know everything unless we choose to share it with the right person.

"I think, at least, I can glean, that for you, D is that person. I know Sunny is for me when she comes with a side of Aurora." I didn't let her reply, just continued, "I want you to head into the shower and I want you to clean yourself. I want a photo of you clothed. Then, I want you to order room service and I want a photo of what you're eating too."

She swallowed. "I-I, w-we—"

"I always knew we were twin souls, Aurora. This merely confirms it. Now, be a good girl and do as I ask. I want a text when you arrive home as well. Do you understand?"

At her shaken nod, I cut the call and immediately blew out a breath.

Rome wasn't built in a day, but had I just laid the first building block to something more between us?

I guessed I wouldn't know until/if she fulfilled my requests.

Excitement buzzed through my veins much as if I'd snorted some blow. But this was better. The feeling was indescribable.

It was pure Aurora.

She was a direct shot of heroin to the heart. Only, she wasn't toxic. Well, maybe she was. She just wouldn't kill me.

Okay, not yet.

My lips twitched into a grin and, pocketing my phone, I moved swiftly out of the office.

An hour ago, I'd dreaded what I had to do tonight. Now, I accepted it for what it was—a move of dominance.

It was clear that Aurora wasn't the only one who had to accept the two halves of their nature.

When I headed into the main warehouse, I saw Stan was pacing, ear to his cell as he talked with someone in Sicilian.

The coyote was still singing a song I didn't want to understand, head lolling from side to side as he tried to downplay what was happening.

The scent of smoke came to me next, and I saw Brunu had set up a metal drum at the back. It gleamed orange from the fire, and sticking out of it was a pole.

Spying me, his grin beamed brighter than the sun. "Knew Bert wasn't losing it when he picked you, Hunter."

Great—approval from a criminal. Exactly what I'd aimed for when I was at Brown.

Heaving a sigh, I muttered, "How long until it's ready?"

"Five more minutes. You were gone a long while. Business?"

Not entirely.

Something far more vital to my sanity.

I arched a brow at him. "Of course."

He grinned at me again then called out to the bastard tied to the wooden chair, "You're about to regret the day you were born, *figghiu ri buttana*."

"No, he's about to learn that if he comes onto Camorra land again, he'll die," I corrected, seeing, for the first time, the man's concern as he let his gaze dance between the drum and me.

I didn't revel in his fear, but it satisfied a need in me that I hadn't known I possessed.

Ten minutes later, when I pressed the brand to the side of his throat, letting the glowing metal seep into his skin, ignoring his screams and how his face looked like it was going to explode under the pressure and intense heat, my senses clamoring at the scent of burning flesh, Brunu's words were confirmed.

The coyote, message branded into his flesh, passed out from the pain.

As for me, it was a lesson learned too—I could be the Don. I had what it took. As always, and like the beacon of light she'd forever been to me, Aurora had shown me the way…

31

AURORA

I WISHED I could say that I didn't know why I obeyed him.

But that would have been a lie.

I wanted to obey.

Obeying was easy.

Giving up control was easy.

Submitting was easy.

Nothing else in my life was that unless he was involved.

Hunter/D.

My DDoSunlight.

The childhood friend who, even before this revelation, knew more about me than anyone in the world.

For whatever reason, that thought sent shivers down my spine.

I didn't know why.

It wasn't acceptance. It wasn't rejection.

I couldn't put a word on it, and because I felt more exhausted now than I did last night when I'd eventually slept, I showered as he requested, dressed, and took a picture which I sent to him. I ordered room service, messaged him the photo of the half-eaten dish, then I called a car to take me to my apartment.

Simple.

Orders I needed to obey.

They gave me something to focus on without freaking out.

As if she knew I was awake, Rachel called. I let it ring. Though I knew I owed her a favor, at that moment, I couldn't deal with talking anymore.

Couldn't handle thinking anymore.

The ravaging effect of yesterday, of the cocktail of terror and shame I'd deepthroated, and this morning were endless, prompting me to rest against the town car door to prop me up as I stared out onto the city streets, chaotic as always. Just like my head.

Unsettled, my mind drifted to Catania. To the family estate. Not unreasonable considering that was where Luciu had taken Jennifer for their honeymoon and the last few days all he'd been talking about were the quirky parts he was going to show her.

Everything from the fresco Da Vinci had painted and which was half-peeling off despite our ongoing conservation efforts to the carved marble fountain that was Nicola Salvi's finest work, finer even than the *Fontana di Trevi* in Rome, and the special terraces that were like balconies to the ocean.

It had been too long since I'd been there last. Too long.

The urge for my home was strong.

To return to my roots. Back to the days when everything had been simple. Before I'd uncovered the plot to steal my family's heritage out from under us, before I'd even known what it meant to be a Valentini.

More exhausted than before with my instructions completed, my thoughts tiring me even more because there wasn't a cat in hell's chance I'd be able to travel to Sicily for months, I thanked the driver once we reached my building, quickly shooting Hunter a text as he'd requested.

Me: *I'm home.*

Three dots chased after themselves on my screen.

Hunter: *Good girl.*

My thumb drifted over the words that made butterflies flutter around my insides.

When no further orders were offered, a touch disappointed, I got out of the car.

The doorman greeted me, but I only shot him a wan smile. I didn't realize he was calling for me until his hand stopped the elevator doors from closing and he puffed out, "Ms. Valentini, there's mail for you."

Surprised by the urgency in his tone, I stared at the envelopes in his hand.

Hope surged to the surface, shrinking my exhaustion. "My great-uncle?"

"No, ma'am. Both are from a correctional facility in Las Vegas."

Though my heart sank, curiosity had me snatching the letter from his grasp.

I only knew one man serving time in Vegas—Alberto De Laurentiis. But why he'd want to send me a letter, I had no idea.

I ripped open the first envelope and had my suspicions over the sender confirmed.

Dear Ms. Fitzwilliam,

I hope this letter finds you well.

I've gone to the trouble of fast-tracking the background check on you so that the Department of Corrections here in Nevada could add you to my visitation list.

I'd very much appreciate speaking with you today at three PM.

I apologize for the short notice. In my situation, every moment counts.

Kind regards,

Alberto De Laurentiis.

In his situation? He was going to die in a cell. Time was a commodity he had in abundance.

After I opened the next envelope and scanned the letter of approval that was inside, as well as the copy of the Nevada DOC Visiting Rules and Regulations, I pursed my lips at the hour he'd requested, well aware that all of this had been perfectly coordinated.

No state Department of Corrections ran at this level of precision—*it takes a mobster to make the government work this efficiently*, I thought wryly. And I'd know, seeing as I'd been dealing with bureaucracy that was so slow it was crippling for years now.

Only just realizing the doorman was still standing there, I sought out his gaze. "Can you get me a car to the airport?"

"Of course, ma'am." His brow puckered. "Immediately?"

"I'll just go upstairs and pack a couple things, but I'll be back down ASAP."

"Okay, ma'am."

He hit the button on the elevator for the top floor. While I shuttled upward, I thought about my options.

Luciu wasn't using our private jet to fly to Sicily, so, because the jet was free, that was a possibility, but incognito might be best by traveling commercial.

Quickly scanning the outgoing flights from JFK, I managed to find one that would get me into Vegas early enough for the meeting.

Grateful for the time zone difference, I mentally planned what I needed for a short stay, totally hiding from the fact that the only reason I was interested in going to Vegas was for another De Laurentiis.

One who wasn't in prison.

I shouldn't leave. I knew that. I had yesterday's situation to handle, and the measures I'd implemented as a result would enrage the council. Plus, there was a body to be dealt with on the downlow.

Leaders didn't abandon their duties on a whim, but this wasn't a whim. Not wholly. This was also business. Important business. The ex-Camorra Don wanted to talk with me about *something*. My heading over to Sin City wasn't me slacking. Wasn't me abandoning ship.

Business.

Just business.

The thought enabled me to book the flight, something that took less than five minutes, and another five were spent picking up what I thought I'd need for the short trip.

When I was back downstairs, the car waiting for me, the moment I was seated, it registered there was one advantage to not being Luc's *official* Consigliere—no guards apart from the driver.

Knowing that the silence of the journey would drive me insane, I called Rachel.

Her greeting was charming: "Bitch, don't think you can hold out on me—"

Fingers nervously toying with the pink diamond-encrusted locket I'd put on in my apartment, the one that Hunter had gifted me, I had to laugh. "I'm not holding out on you. I'm heading to Vegas."

"Vegas?" Rachel fell quiet. "What on earth for? You're running to Vegas because Hunter's in New York? Oh, where in the world is Carmen Sandiego? You want him to follow you, is that it? No, wait. You don't want to speak with him at all. So... why Vegas?"

Rolling my eyes, I sniped, "Someone's a grouch this morning."

"Bet your ass I am. I'm making a human and I'm so tired of peeing; you've no idea. Then there's the hunger. I wasn't this starving with Wynter, I swear. I could eat Rex—"

"Please do."

My nose crinkled at the interruption in the background. "Didn't realize you two were into cannibalism."

Rachel mocked, "New kink unlocked. Anyway, enough of that. Why are you going to Vegas?"

"Hunter's grandfather sent me a visitation order."

"How odd." She wasn't wrong. "Do you know him?"

"Never met him in my life."

"Why so eager to go then? You didn't mention it yesterday."

"I didn't mention anything yesterday," I deadpanned. "I was too busy panicking."

"Yeah, you were." Rachel hummed. "I've never heard you like that before, Rory. I was scared for you."

"You didn't have to be. I don't want to stress you out with my shit. It's not important anyway."

"Not important?" she shrieked. "You and Hunter are my best

friends. Plus, it's annoying being your referee. I want to know everything. Everything isn't enough, in fact."

"You'll have to wait. I'm not telling you when I'm in the car to the airport."

She harrumphed. "If you renege, I'll seek payback."

My lips curved. "When have you ever known me to renege? You have to admit these are extenuating circumstances."

"I wouldn't put it past you to be visiting him only because you want to procrastinate over having this conversation."

"A part of me is glad that I don't have to discuss this yet, but no, I've already spoken with Hunter."

Rach fell silent then, eventually, said, "That's unexpected."

"Hmm." My gaze fell upon a homeless man who was dumpster diving. "I can't blame you. One minute." I opened the privacy partition and stated, "Pull over." Digging in my purse, I leaned forward once I had some bills in my hand and said, "Give that to the guy."

"Ma'am?" He frowned at me in the rearview mirror. "Which guy?"

"That one." I gestured out the window.

In my ear, Rachel confirmed she knew me too well by murmuring, "See a homeless guy?"

I handed the money to the driver who, thoroughly displeased, clambered out of the vehicle.

Watching him pass the vagabond the money, I retorted, "There are too many on these streets. You should start a foundation for the homeless too. I swear you get more done than City Hall."

The driver made his retreat while the guy stood staring at the couple hundred bucks in his hand before he shoved them into a pocket and returned to his treasure hunt in the dumpster.

"How long's it been since you actually talked?" Rachel asked, prompting me to turn my attention back to our conversation.

Quickly, I raised the partition. "To Hunter?" I cleared my throat. I.e., *not* D. "Years before the wedding. We've texted and emailed, but talking? No."

"How are you doing?"

"Been better, been worse. Mostly, I'm curious."

"About what?"

"Why Alberto De Laurentiis wants to see me."

"Do you think it's about business?"

"No." I tilted my head to look out of the car window. "I don't."

"Hunter?"

"Maybe."

"You're really informative today, aren't you?"

My lips twitched. "I'm not trying to be evasive. Very few people know about my role in the business. I'm not sure why he'd come to me and not go to Luc if it were about that though.

"If it's about Hunter, then there's nothing to say because we haven't had a relationship in years…"

My words waned as I thought about these past six months.

No, we hadn't talked, but we'd definitely started texting more, hadn't we? Our relationship wasn't what it used to be, but it was more than it had been these past fifteen or so years.

"You still there, babe?"

I jolted as her words broke my train of thought. "Yeah, I'm still here. Sorry, Rach.

"Anyway, I don't know. Is it likely it's about Hunter? Yes. But I won't know for sure until I get there."

"Did you just state the obvious several times?"

"I did. It tasted mighty fine too."

"Rex is making me pancakes."

"He is? I didn't know he cooked."

She laughed. "He doesn't. It's sweet he's trying."

"The big ol' Prez making his Old Lady breakfast gets you going, huh?"

"Ha. That shouldn't come as a surprise." A sigh escaped her. "You're allowed to be happy, Rory. You know that, don't you?"

"Where did that come from?" I questioned. "Of course I know I'm *allowed* to be happy." Not that I believed in happiness. I just didn't feel like a philosophical debate this morning. "What does that even mean?" Okay, maybe I did feel up to a debate.

"It means that you've been so focused on getting to where you are now, that though you've made it and have accomplished almost every-thing you set out to do, you're allowed to just take a step back and smell the roses."

"You know how many men would piss on those roses if I took a step back?"

"Lovely imagery there."

I grunted. "Am I wrong?"

"No. But you also know what I'm talking about."

"I actually don't," I sniped.

"When you fight something so hard, you have to question what it is you're fighting. I know you miss him."

Neither of us had to name names.

"Of course I miss him. I was closer to him than I am to Luc and Stan. He knows things about me that no one else, not even you, does —" And I wasn't talking sexually. "Being without his friendship has been like losing my right arm.

"People wonder why I'm such a bitch, and that's because the one person who could actually temper me—" I broke off, suddenly aware that I was crying and that I hadn't even realized it.

"Go on, Aurora. Get it out," she said softly.

"I don't like this touchy-feely side of you." I swiped at my cheeks. "Getting with Rex has changed you."

"It's made me happy. You think I didn't feel the exact same way about him? You and me, Aurora, we're too much alike. We both pushed away the people who matter the most to us, and for what?

"I know you don't have the same feelings as I do for Rex. I know your love for Hunter is as a friend, but there's no reason you can't have *that* again with him."

Her words had me biting my lip.

She was both wrong and right.

I'd never thought of him as anything other than a friend. Not ever. I didn't have my head in the sand, but those feelings weren't something I'd believed could be mutual.

We were Rory and Hunter.

I was the forest fire and he was the water that'd put out the flames.

The water just had a non-reciprocal thing for the forest fire.

But D… I could admit to myself, now, that I'd loved him.

I really had.

Rubbing my tired eyes, I jolted in surprise when my phone buzzed.

Hunter: *Thank you for the photos.*

There were a million things I could have said. Hell, I could even have ignored him.

Instead…

Me: *Do you have any other requirements?*

"Aurora?"

"Hmm?" I asked absentmindedly, watching the three dots dance on the screen as he formulated an answer.

To be honest, knowing how early it was there after such a late night, I was surprised he'd taken the time to look through them.

Skimming through my other messages, I arched a brow when I saw Stan had texted me too, which made me think both of them had just gotten in from wherever they'd been holding the coyote.

Stan: *He did us proud.*

Me: *Killed him?*

I didn't move from the screen because I knew Stan took a long time to come down after a beating. The adrenaline whacked him up, and I knew he craved drugs. That was why he ate and worked out so much. They were other forms of addictions, but hell, we all had to get ourselves to sleep at night.

Mostly, I was just jealous about how much he packed away. I certainly hadn't inherited the same metabolism.

Stan: *Nope. Fucker's got a nice big brand on his throat. Thought his head was going to explode in the process.*

Me: *There could be internal damage.*

Stan: *Bahahaha. No shit.*

"Aurora, Jesus. Are you even listening?"

"Just give me a couple minutes, Rach," I muttered.

A huff sounded in my ear. "Call me later. My pancakes are ready anyway. Love you, Rory. I'm always here for you. Being with Rex doesn't change that."

Appreciation for her, for our friendship, filled me. While we were close, we weren't in each other's faces regularly, but that never seemed to matter. We always had each other's backs.

"Love you, Rach."

"Fuck, is the world ending and nobody told me?"

"Maybe."

She sniffed. "Love you too. Now, go on. Fuck off to Vegas and remember that you owe me an explanation. I also want to know why De Laurentiis requested a visit with you."

"You do know that I'm not like the Satan's Sinners' MC and think your word is the word of God, right?"

A chuckle sounded in my ear. "It'd be a lot easier if you did. Speak later."

I hummed. "Later."

Disconnecting the call, I replied to Stan:

Me: *Did Hunter puke?*

Stan: *Nah. The stench was bad though.*

Me: *I'm surprised. Thought he'd have vomited.*

Stan: *When I told you he did us proud, I meant it.*

Me: *Clearly. What's he doing with the coyote?*

Stan: *Brunu's having him dumped outside one of the nightclubs the Reyes Dorados own.*

Me: *Popular place?*

Stan: *Yeah.*

Me: *Loud message. Good. You coming back home tonight?*

Stan: *Yeah. I just didn't want Hunter to fuck this up. It's the early days of his reign. I remember how Luciu took a while to adjust. Didn't want to leave Hunt on his own.*

Me: *You're a good friend.*

Stan: *He's family, Rory. You've forgotten that, but I haven't. I'm just lucky that I was there with him when he got the news, and that I had some time to hold his hand through it all. Lol. Somehow, it's easy to underestimate Hunter, but we shouldn't. He just does shit his own way.*

I hadn't forgotten dick. But I refused to get into this with him.

Especially after the night I'd had and knowing he'd do anything to get us together—I'd never been blind to his and Luc's matchmaking attempts.

Me: *Get some rest.*

I switched screens and saw that Hunter had finally messaged me.

A part of me wanted him to acknowledge the fact that I was acting out of character. Another part just wanted D to dominate me. The thought alone had me fidgeting and feeling grateful for the privacy screen between the driver and me.

Hunter: *Are you alone?*

Well, that was both disappointing and promising.

Me: *I'm with a driver.*

Hunter: *Privacy screen is up?*

Me: *Yes.*

Hunter: *Where are you going? You said you'd arrived home.*

Why did that question make me want to squirm? Because I was going to lie? And I knew that lies came with consequences?

I blew out a breath and then I did the unthinkable—I hit the 'connect' button.

He didn't answer immediately. My first thought should have been something different than what it was. It should have been, 'Maybe he's with Stan,' or 'Maybe he's still working?'

Instead, it was, 'Is he with another woman?'

Which was ridiculous.

Not that Hunter wasn't a gorgeous man and could have had any woman he wanted, but—

Jesus.

I told myself, "Aurora, you need to turn your brain off."

In my defense, that was what I was trying to do by calling him.

I groused, "If he'd only answer the phone."

Naturally, he had to pick up the moment I sniped at him.

"Sass? Already?"

I grimaced, and from our interactions as Sunny and D, I knew he'd only accept the truth: "Jealousy."

His silence had my heart pounding.

"Who are you jealous of, Aurora?"

"I thought you might have been with someone."

"Someone, who?"

My throat felt thick with emotions I didn't want to name. "Another woman."

"Another woman or another sub?"

Ouch. I pressed a hand to my chest where it felt as if his words had morphed into a bullet that had a homing signal on my heart.

"Woman," I choked out. "I didn't—I didn't think you'd… I thought I was the only sub—"

He took pity on me. "You *are* the only sub I've had. I left you for you, Aurora."

His tone wasn't warm. In fact, it was the opposite of gushing. It didn't stop the relief from overcoming me like I was taking a shower in Horseshoe Falls.

I sagged into the seat. "I shouldn't care."

"But you do."

While it wasn't a question, I still answered it, "Yes, I do."

For a moment, all I could hear was his breathing down the line. Then, he rumbled words that went to my head faster than if he'd sucked on my clit, "That was the correct answer."

Which was the exact moment I felt the shift in the dynamic.

This wasn't Hunter. The man who smiled and who was perennially cheerful. Who took my bullshit and doled it back at me with a grin.

This was D, and that meant my words came with repercussions and my actions could be construed as disobedience.

Immediately, my body responded to the change. Like goosebumps popping up on my skin when I was cold, it was intrinsic. Instinctive.

"I'm not going to call you Sunny anymore, Aurora."

I swallowed. "Okay."

"You're going to stop calling me D as well."

The fatigue in his voice was audible, and though guilt made itself known to me, I pushed it aside.

I knew he'd probably traveled to New York and back to attend the reception in thirty-six hours, but I didn't want him to go yet.

I needed something from him.

Something to tide me over.

I just didn't know what.

"Aurora?"

Shaking myself, I whispered, "Yes, Hunter. No more D."

His soft chuckle rumbled in my ear. "Well, there'll be D. Just not that type of D." When I didn't reply, his tone deepened. "Have your hard limits changed now that you know who I am?"

I thought about the things I'd done to myself under his command, and I sucked in a breath at the prospect of no longer being the one holding the tools and toys that were an extension of him in my life.

God, did his question mean what I thought it did?

Hope churned inside me. "I-I don't think so."

"We'll have to reestablish your boundaries now that things will be happening in person. We can do that another time."

I didn't know why but my face crumpled at his easy statement.

Why was everything so simple with him? And why was it so complicated with me?

Shoving my fist against my mouth, I sucked in a noisy breath because the relief that he *did* want me was overwhelming.

I knew he wanted Aurora, but I was Sunny too. Sunny had depraved desires and liked to make herself come while her nipples burned from homemade capsaicin tincture.

Sunny was dirty, and Aurora was someone he'd always placed on a pedestal.

"Aurora?"

"Yes?" I managed to choke out.

"Are you scared of me?"

He'd asked me that earlier. Somehow, though it was the same question, the answer was different.

I knew I had to lay myself on the line here. Because if I didn't, I wouldn't be able to see him anymore and I couldn't bear that. I'd missed D's presence in my life so much that it was an ache in my being.

"I'm scared of myself," I eventually admitted, aware that he'd remained silent to force me to talk.

He released a soft sigh that made my ears tingle. "Why?"

I heard rustling sheets and knew he was getting into bed. The urge, the *craving* to climb in beside him was real and raw.

It wasn't Hunter, though, that I wanted to sleep beside—it was D. Or was it? The lines were blurring too much for me to see straight. My exhaustion probably wasn't helping either.

"I'm scared of what I'll let you do so that I can have access to D."

"I *am* D," he pointed out.

"Trust doesn't function like that."

"No, I guess it's something we have to work on. *If* you want to work on it. You don't have to, Aurora. You can walk away now. We can go back to how it was two days ago."

Panic hit me. "You'd want that?"

"Honestly? No. I've wanted you since I was thirteen years old and I watched you punch Vicenzu Garbo because he whacked me over the head with his book bag and told me I was a *pezz'i miedda* for loving computers."

The memory did the impossible—it made me smile. "Since then?"

"Since then," he confirmed. "You've never been afraid of people, have you? Now that I think back, I can always see you've frightened yourself."

"This is too deep a conversation for this time in the morning," I tried to dismiss.

"'Sunny' told me that you knew you liked pain when you were sixteen."

My chin tipped up. "That Swiss kid in our class, you remember him?" At his grunt of assent, I continued, "He pulled my hair when I went down on him. It got snagged in his zipper, and when *Matri* almost caught us, he closed the fastener too fast and got a chunk caught in the tines. Pulled some out by the roots."

"You liked that it hurt."

It wasn't a question. "I did."

"And you were fearful of getting caught?"

"I was sixteen, Hunter," I drawled. "Of course, I was. Can you imagine what *Patri* would have done if we'd been discovered?"

He chuckled. "He'd have killed him. I wish he had. Jerk off. I never did like him and didn't understand what you saw in him."

I stared out the window again. "He went on to swim at the Olympics. I think you can guess what I liked about him."

His grunt told me he didn't like my answer, but fuck, though it was twisted because *I was talking to Hunter*, I liked his jealousy too much to freak out. Mutual jealousy felt good. This wasn't one-sided anymore.

Even if this was nearly two-decade-old jealousy.

"Every boyfriend, it grew. Worsened. A hair pull here, a spanking there." My gaze turned distant, *inward*. "You remember Giovanni Kammler?"

"I remember his dad got arrested for embezzlement and they moved back to Germany so they could visit him in prison."

Nodding, I said, "We were at his house, in his pool, and there was CCTV. We had sex, he took the footage, and then he said that he'd show people if I didn't do everything he said."

"That bastard," he seethed.

My lips kicked up in a smile. "I was terrified at the time but I grew to like it. I was almost disappointed when his dad got arrested." *Not enough to regret engineering said arrest, of course.* "Then…" I paused. "Are you sure you want to hear this?"

"I'm sure." His words said one thing, but his tone said another.

"After Giovanni," I continued, "you know there was Ricardo Bellini. He was a good guy, liked spanking, but that ended when we left for the States which was when the date rape happened, and I met Marcus soon after. He tied a bow on what Giovanni had started. They weren't all bad though. This isn't a sob story."

"I don't think I've ever known anyone as tough on themselves as you." He sounded testy. "When did you start with the self-punishments?"

"You know this already."

"You told me tidbits, and now that we have a personal timeline, I want details."

"That started with Giovanni."

"Before… you said how it started was an accident?"

"It did. I never lied to you about what makes me tick, Hunter. My motives were pure. My untruths about my identity were something else entirely."

"I'm glad to hear it."

There was that growl again. It went to my head faster than ice-cold champagne.

"He tied me to the bed and couldn't get the knot loose," I mused, thinking back to that day. At the time, the part of me I now called my inner pain slut had enjoyed being coerced. It let me explore things I'd never have dared experience without the threat of exposure. "He cut the bindings and cut me at the same time. I liked it."

Understatement.

It was only now I was older that I recognized my sexuality, my *tastes*, hadn't been a pretty discovery. They were surrounded in shame and embarrassment. Marcus had only upped that. Had only confirmed that what I liked *seemed* perverted.

"I understand if you think…" I gulped. "I understand if you don't want me anymore. If I disgust you—"

"Stop it."

I blinked at his bark. "Stop what, Hunter?"

"Stop thinking that you're a pervert. You're not. You like what you like. There's nothing wrong with that.

"Do you also accept that I like what I like and that, as D and Sunny, we found a balance that suited us both?"

"I do," I admitted softly. "I want you to know that, after Marcus, I never went that far again. When you found us… that was the last time he and I had sex."

"Really?"

"Yes." Eyes watering, I confessed my worst sin: "It's why he raped Rachel."

"Jesus, Rory, that isn't *why* he raped Rachel. *He* was the pervert.

Did Rachel never tell you how he'd been sniffing around her for months? The bigger she got, the more he liked it.

"That had nothing to do with you or with you not putting out. It had everything to do with him being a monster who got used to treating you however he wanted, you not saying no and probably being grateful when he tossed out a handful of praise, ignoring safe words and the like, then him blurring the lines between you and every other woman out there—"

Ouch.

That hit too close to home.

"That is not on you," he continued, unaware he'd cut close to the bone. Then, I heard his rough exhalation. "Aurora, between now and when I wake up, I expect you to send me a photo of a handwritten document."

"A handwritten document?" I questioned warily.

"Yes. I want you to write two-hundred-fifty times, 'I am not a pervert.'"

"Hunter—"

"We'll learn the boundaries together, little dove. One step at a time. That first step is you accepting that what you want is not a deviance. As long as you are in a situation that is safe, sane, and consensual, you're doing nothing wrong."

"I don't have access to pen and paper but I have my tablet." It was too easy to try to accommodate his request. My mind hummed at the prospect of obeying such a simple order. "I can write on there?"

"I'll accept that. Two-hundred-and-fifty times, Aurora. No copy and pasting or duplicating an image. When I wake up, I want the email sitting in my inbox."

I squirmed. "It will be there waiting for you."

His hum made me squirm some more. "Say goodnight to me."

"Goodnight... Hunter."

Another hum. "I've missed the sound of my name on your lips."

Oh, fuck.

Unbidden, I rocked my ass on the seat and felt the pressure on my pussy.

As if he knew, he drawled, "No touching your pussy or your tits. No getting off. If you decide to masturbate, and I *will* know, just like I know you got off earlier in the hotel, I'll take that as confirmation that you do not want to continue this relationship with me. Have a great day, Aurora."

And with that, he cut the call.

My mind, still slow to process the last twenty-four hours, tried to assimilate when Hunter had gained that authoritative tone of voice.

But I'd been there for that, hadn't I?

His first and only sub.

I'd seen it with my own eyes, had watched his development, his growth, I just hadn't realized the friend I missed was the man I'd come to crave and, eventually, love.

32

———

AURORA

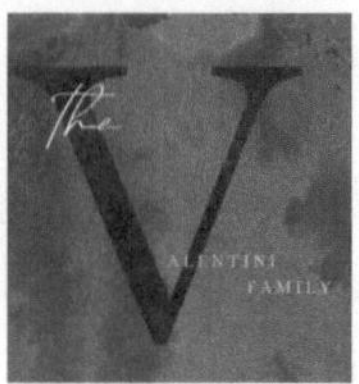

BY THE TIME I landed in Vegas, my curiosity had only increased.

Knowing the protocol for visiting high security prisons where cars could routinely be stopped and searched, I didn't bother getting a driver, just rented a car at Harry Reid and headed to the facility where Alberto De Laurentiis was being held.

Of course, my curiosity was stymied yet again when, at the gates, an officer flagged down my vehicle. "Visits have been canceled."

Aggravated, I peered over the top of my shades. "May I ask why?"

"Lockdown, ma'am. Have a good day." With that, he dipped his chin and, effectively, dismissed me.

Was I annoyed about flying across the freakin' country for this visit only to be turned away at the gates?

I should have been.

I knew that.

And maybe I was a smidgen, but mostly, I wasn't. I was too self-aware not to recognize that I'd only made the trek because Hunter was in the same state, otherwise I'd never have traveled here period. I owed the Camorra no loyalty after they'd failed my family back in the sixties.

Hunter, on the other hand, I owed a lot to.

Not just because he was my D, either.

I bit my lip at the thought, then as I drove away from the gates where the guard was starting to eye me suspiciously, I headed down the road that led to the highway, stopping only when I found somewhere safe to park on the curb. There, I texted Stan.

Me: *Where are you staying?*

When he didn't answer, I buzzed his cell. Cutting it after three rings, I did it again (and again) until I saw the ticks.

Stan: *I went to sleep at nine AM.*

Me: *So?*

Stan: *SO. Leave me alone. I'm tired.*

Me: *Where are you staying?*

Stan: *With Hunter.*

Me: *Which is where?*

Stan: *Why do you want to know?*

Me: *Do you want to get back to sleep or not?*

Stan: *I want to know why you want to know.*

Me: *Do you know that you were always a pain? Even as a toddler? You're lucky I didn't try to drown you at birth.*

Stan: *Shit like this is why you make a good Cruella De Vil.*

Me: *Yeah, yeah. I know. Anyway, where are you staying?*

Stan: *Before you give me crap, I kept away from the blackjack tables.*

He sent me a live location that had me frowning as well as a suite number—No. 1 at the Gallinaro.

Me: *Why are you at a casino?*

Stan: *Because that's where Hunter's living at the moment.*

Me: *Hunter doesn't gamble.*

Stan: *Nah, but he sure likes room service, lol, and his suite is fucking awesome. Even I'm impressed. They do shit differently in Vegas.*

Me: *Are you jealous?*

Stan: *Yes. I am. Considering I've been living with my brother for years.*

Me: *You literally have an entire compound to yourself. Two generations used to live on the Fieri estate. It's all yours now.*

Stan: *True.*

Me: *Spoiled brat.*

Stan: *:P*

Me: *Go to sleep.*

Stan: *Yes, Cruella.*

My lips twitched as I set the GPS to take me to the Gallinaro.

Hunter wasn't the type of guy to live in a hotel, so it surprised me that he was staying there to be honest. I figured he'd either have his own place or that he'd have rooms in his grandfather's infamous *palazzo* in the Nine Hills.

Everyone knew about the *palazzo*.

De Laurentiis had even had the audacity to be featured in architectural magazines back in the eighties when he'd had the damn thing built before Nine Hills had become the area synonymous with the wealthy in Vegas.

With a disapproving hum, I set off.

The hour-long journey sped by, and when I drove onto the casino grounds, pulling up behind a couple limos on the driveway, I turned to peer at the famous fountains which shot up into the air every hour.

As the water danced and tourists took pictures, I silently wished that things like that had the power to still impress me. I'd long since become jaded by life, but it was worse *knowing* what you were missing out on.

My apathy was borderline dangerous some days, and I was never more aware of it than in moments such as these when I felt dead inside at a sight that caused others joy.

Shoving the thought away, I headed toward the valet, tipped him, and told him that I was staying in suite No. 1. His eyes flashed in surprise, but he didn't argue even though he had to know that a woman wasn't staying in Hunter's suite.

Unless...

My throat choked at the notion he had hookers in there every night or something.

Hell, he was young, hot, and single. Why wouldn't he? This was Vegas. Sin City. And it wasn't like D and I had been together since January.

But… not Hunter. No, he wasn't like that.

He'd said it himself—he'd left me for *me*.

That was the man I knew.

Not so worried about the hookers now, and more worried about everything else, I stroked a hand over my hair as I strode into the reception area, unsurprised when my arrival, evidently triggered by the valet, had a man sweeping forward to greet me.

"Ma'am? You're staying in Suite No. 1?"

I arched a brow at him. "Yes. I'm Aurora…" My legal name was Aurora Fitzwilliam. I girded my loins as it were, electing to embrace who I was at that moment—in more ways than one. "I'm Aurora Valentini."

Recognition flashed in his eyes. "Mr. Valentini is currently staying with Mr. Lachlan. You're also a guest?"

"Yes. I am." Sometimes, you just had to fake it until you made it.

Uneasily, he said, "I didn't receive a notification of this…"

"Does Mr. Lachlan often inform his staff about who his guests are?" Embarrassment made his cheeks turn pink, and I winced—*way to go, Aurora; talk about living up to that Cruella title.* Annoyed at myself, I muttered, "I apologize. You're only doing your job, but it's been a *long* day of traveling, and I really would like to clean up. Call Hunter or do whatever you need to verify I have the right to access his suite."

The blank expression that spoke of his dislike after my sarcasm was replaced with confusion. "All right, Ms. Valentini. Thank you. I'll just be a moment."

When he retreated to the desk, I pushed my hands in my pockets and turned around to stare at the foyer.

Gold covered everything. From the walls to the floors to the decorations. It was like Midas had rolled around in here and had gotten it everywhere.

It was distasteful. Gaudy. Impressive, though, for all that. Especially when I saw a Picasso standing pride of place between a couple of marble columns.

The De Laurentiis art collection was said to be worth hundreds of millions of dollars…

It was clear that the rumors weren't total BS.

It was interesting, though, that the painting De Laurentiis had hung in pride of place in this palace of sin was *Portrait of Paulo*. I recognized it easily.

Paulo, Picasso's son, was only an infant in the painting. Considering what I now knew of the family, that Hunter's father had changed his name after fleeing the US to raise his son in his ancestral country, I had to wonder if De Laurentiis regretted his only child's self-imposed exile.

Still studying the unusual choice of art—even if it was the only classy object in the foyer—I didn't turn toward the concierge who'd popped up to murmur, "Mr. Lachlan says he'll be down immediately."

That had me moving. Head whipping to the side at the news, I felt the nerves in my body start to do a jig as horror hit me.

"He's coming down?" I squeaked, nervously tugging on my locket.

As in, he wasn't letting me come up…

What in the what?

Twisting away after the concierge merely nodded at me, I reached up and tried to pat my face. I'd expected to just…

God, what had I expected?

To waltz in as if the last fifteen years hadn't happened?

I'd obeyed him.

Aside from the whole hopping on a plane to Vegas in between thing.

He'd said that a failure to comply with his requests was akin to terminating our relationship, but I'd sent him the fucking lines on the plane, and I'd done as he damn well asked with his other orders too.

Before I could start to panic, lungs already burning with agitation, I tried to force myself to calm down.

My brother likened me to Cruella De Vil, yet here I was, about to have a fucking anxiety attack over a man. But I didn't have it in me to feel like a failure to womanhood, mostly because I was on the cusp of something vital. Of something I didn't think I'd ever experience in my life.

Acceptance.

The tears didn't just burn my eyes now, they flooded them.

Acceptance *and* love.

It was too much to ask for, but—

A hand settled on my shoulder and I literally jumped. Pathetic. So pathetic.

Huffing in irritation at myself, I twisted around to make sure it wasn't the concierge, but before relief could set in that a complete stranger wasn't seeing my meltdown, my gaze collided with the one man I never thought to see again.

Robert Macmillan.

My ex-brother-in-law.

He sent shivers of disgust rolling through me because Robert was like a miniature Marcus. The chin was weaker, his mouth smaller, he wasn't as tall, but the whole Macmillan effect was there for anyone to see.

"I thought it was you."

What a greeting.

I felt the adolescent stirrings that had urged me to seek Hunter out fading in the light of the hatred in Robert's eyes. He'd never outright said it, the police had done it for him, but I knew he and the rest of his family blamed me for Marcus's disappearance.

Because I was more accustomed to wearing my armor than being without it, muscle memory enabled me to snap into my usual comported self.

"Robert, what a pleasure. I didn't expect to see you here."

His top lip quirked into a snarl. "Scoping out the enemy."

"Enemy? It's a little late for that, isn't it?" I questioned dryly. "Seeing as you managed to put De Laurentiis away for life."

"There are more De Laurentiises in need of jail time," was his ominous retort. "Are you staying in town for long?"

His knowing I was out of New York wasn't ideal, but I simply answered, "An overnight trip."

Distaste flickered over his expression as he looked me up and down. I felt like a two-buck whore being told she was worth only fifty cents. "I hope I don't see you again," was all he said though.

"Me too," I told him, my tone contrasting his. He sounded bitter; I sounded congenial.

As he stepped away, taking his hatred with him, a hatred that hadn't died with time, I twisted back to face the Picasso.

The second my eyes collided with Paulo, however, the armor started to sink away.

The Macmillans had been a complication for years—Marcus's family had never approved of our match, and after his disappearance, they'd been angry when, seven years later, I sought to have him officially declared as deceased so our marriage was nullified.

To them, he hadn't disappeared.

To them, it had been a plot between Hunter and me.

Their belief had given us some grief with the investigating officers at the time, but they'd been repeatedly told by everyone who knew us that I'd friend-zoned Hunter years ago.

Who knew that friend-zoning could spare someone from a murder one charge?

Bad blood… *Vinnittas.* They were our stock-in-trade. Robert had looked at me as if Marcus had only disappeared yesterday. That level of hatred didn't fade. I'd know. My very normal family had turned into a crime *famigghia* to avenge my father's murder.

Uneasily, I wondered if I should have brought a guard with me. I'd left the driver back in New York, but maybe I shouldn't have.

Seeing me here, in the hotel of the man who he believed I'd conspired with to kill his brother… Was that enough to tip Robert over the edge? His focus was clearly on Hunter, but who knew what he was working on behind the scenes?

A hand reached for me. Because of the last time, and because of my thoughts, I almost slapped it away, but those nascent hopes began stirring into being again when I turned around and saw Hunter.

He looked exhausted. And confused. And beautiful.

God, so beautiful.

His hair was scruffy and he had stubble and he wore a T-shirt that he'd probably dragged from his bedroom floor—perfect.

Perfect.

That was how he looked to me.

"Aurora?" he rasped, his voice husky from sleep, his gaze etched with bewilderment.

Before discovering he was D, I might have mistaken that for hesitancy… What else had I misread over the years?

I swallowed. "Hunter." My lip trembled before I choked out, "Surprise."

Brow furrowing, he studied me. In fact, he studied me for so long that I thought the clock had stopped ticking. That the world had frozen. That the universe had glitched. Then, right when I thought all hope might be lost, he did the damnedest thing—he reached for my hand, cupped it with his as he tilted it slightly, then he pressed his lips to the inside of my wrist.

My knees almost caved in at that old-fashioned caress. When he locked his eyes on mine, and his tongue fluttered out to trace the vein that he could probably feel pulsing against it, I shuddered.

Hand still cupped in his, he lowered it to waist height and continued studying me in that steady silence that was starting to make me feel nauseated; his gaze darting between my eyes and the locket I wore. The kiss to the wrist was a greeting. But the silence, the stare, and how he held my hand—impersonally—didn't feel welcoming.

When he dropped his hold on me, I nearly burst into tears.

Then, when I didn't know which way was up and which way was down, he opened his arms.

A shaken sob escaped me as my entire being crumpled into him, as I tunneled into his embrace. Not only did he smell perfect, like home, he took my weight, absorbed the momentum of me flinging myself at him, and kept me upright.

At that moment, I didn't care about status or dynamics or family or anything.

I just cared about the things I'd been living without for years.

Acceptance.

Love.

Him.

33

HUNTER

PLACES - MARTIN SOLVEIG, INA WROLDSEN

CONFUSED DIDN'T CUT IT.

I was jet-lagged, a little world-weary after last night's adventures with a branding iron—words I didn't think I'd ever have in my brain—and in all honesty, I was hungry, proof that Stan must have been rubbing off on me.

But whatever I was, there weren't words to describe the epicness that was having Aurora Valentini in my arms.

My fucking arms.

For a moment, I just embraced her. I stood there and I held her and I let the ramifications hit home.

She was here.

In my city.

She'd come to *me*.

I fully accepted that I was a goner where she was concerned. That I usually did the running and I'd have gone to Antarctica if she'd have said, "Hunter, if you fly into Williams Field, I'll kiss you and give you a hug," I'd have hired a plane and would have been there the next day.

But she'd come to me.

This was… My brain blue-screened.

So, I defaulted. I simply held her.

And I held her.

And I fucking held her.

And it was heaven.

Better than cracking the firewalls of the NSA. Better than scoring a touchdown against Brown's archnemesis Cornell.

Everything I hadn't expected and so much more.

She was all curves and softness, so unlike her personality which was brash and domineering, caustic and hard. Well, that wasn't altogether true. I'd met Sunny, after all, and it was fitting that I'd seen that 'mask.' I had no idea how many she wore in her daily life, but I intended to find out.

Because I could, and because I never thought I'd be able to, I pressed a kiss to the crown of her head. That was when I realized I'd been making a soft humming sound as she sobbed against my chest.

Again, my brain shorted.

She was crying over me?

This was so fucking bizarre, and yet, from a woman I'd been chasing my whole life, it was kind of nice.

I figured I was allowed to think like a jerk so long as I didn't act like one.

"Aurora?" I rasped, my voice still husky from sleep. "What are you doing here?"

She tensed, her arms beginning to slip away from my waist, arms that had been clutching at me like a koala bear clung to a eucalyptus tree, as she made to step back. But I didn't let her. I stepped forward, right into her space, and I held her in place.

"Do *not* let go," I warned, inadvertently using a tone that I guessed was my 'D' voice.

Unsurprisingly, she reacted. Aurora froze but her hands moved back around my waist. I cupped her nape and drew her into my chest once more.

"Why are you here?"

"Do you want the truth or a lie?"

"What kind of question is that?" I scoffed. "We might have seen behind the mask, but that doesn't mean the basic tenets of our relationship have changed. The truth. Always. *Now*."

"Your grandfather sent me a letter," she admitted quietly.

Disappointment flooded me. As well as more confusion. "Why?"

"He wanted me to visit him in High Desert State."

"What the hell for?"

"I don't know. When I got there, there was a lockdown so no visitors were allowed in."

Concern hit me, but it was a concern I was going to have to adapt to. A concern I'd have to embrace because it wasn't going anywhere. Just like Bert. We were both stuck with him having to live in prison now. That meant lockdowns and the dangerous triggers for them were a part of our lives.

But she didn't stop there, "I-I only came because I wanted to see you though. He was an excuse I allowed myself to have."

"Why do you need an excuse to visit me? I've always been here, Aurora. I'm not the one who pulled away."

Her head darted back so she could peer up at me. "The blinders are off now. They weren't before."

God, it was too fucking early for this conversation. Well, not for the rest of the city, but four-thirty was too early for me after the last few days of traveling and torturing.

Though I frowned as I looked into her eyes, I asked, "Do you still like pancakes?"

"Do people fall out of love with their favorite foods?"

I arched a brow at her. "Is that an answer?"

She huffed. "No. And yes. I still like them."

"With Nutella?"

"Yes." This time, her cheeks turned pink at her admission.

Jesus Christ, that was cute.

And I'd done that.

Me.

"What's with the blush?"

Her shoulder hitched up. "Not the most elegant of breakfasts, is it?"

I snorted. "Who said breakfast had to be elegant?"

"I should probably have told you I like Eggs Benedict now." Something flashed in her eyes. Uncertainty. *Discomfort*. "You're a man. It's different for you."

Wanting to erase *any* insecurity, I took the leap of faith for both of us. "I'm your man. That means things are different for you too."

That had taken guts but it was worth it for the slight widening of her eyes and the gentle parting of her lips. I watched her pupils dilate then shrink into pinpricks, and one of her hands clutched at my waist, the fingers pinching me, while the other slid to my chest where she dug her nails into my pec.

"Do you mean that?" she breathed.

"I always mean what I say. That's why I think before I speak," I teased.

Her throat worked and, like her head was a heavy burden, she rocked it forward on her neck and rested it on my chest again. Her words were muffled: "That easy?"

"Nothing about you and me has ever been easy. But then, nothing worth fighting for is. And it's too early for me to be talking about philosophical stances on our relationship. Do you want Nutella pancakes or not?"

"With banana slices?"

My lips twitched. "With banana slices."

"And raspberry coulis?"

"That's a new one."

"Tastes good together," she muttered.

"And raspberry coulis too," I confirmed, hearing as well as feeling the whoosh of her breath against my shirt.

"Okay. Breakfast for dinner. Sounds good."

I squeezed her again, but she didn't let go. I already knew I'd fallen down the best rabbit hole ever, but I didn't think it'd feel this good. Or smell this good either.

I could scent soap, shampoo, and a faintly floral perfume that I was sure was jasmine but could have been lily or rose for all I knew. She smelled great though. I wanted to breathe her in for, oh, the next thousand years.

Which, if I had my way, was how long I'd have with her.

"You ready to come up to my suite?"

"Why didn't you let me come up earlier?" she asked, her face still hidden from me.

A part of me knew I should force her to look at me, just so I could read her expressions, but goddamn, it was too delicious holding her. I could chastise later. Reprimand *after* we'd talked things through. Now, both of us were reeling as our pasts clashed with the present and began its slalom into *our* future.

"I didn't let you come up because it was highly unlikely that the real Aurora Valentini would show her face at my hotel," I said dryly.

Congress should make today a national holiday—a miracle had really fucking happened.

"Oh."

She didn't deny I was right.

Hiding a smile, I rested a hand between her shoulders. "Stan's up there too."

"I know. He's the one who told me where you were. I-I guess I wanted to surprise you."

"If I'd seen you sitting in the living room of my suite, I'd have probably had a heart attack," I teased her.

"Don't joke about that," she whispered, finally pulling back so I could see her features. Her expression was loaded with misery and concern and... God help me. I wasn't ready to put a word to that yet. "Please."

"I won't," I retorted, my smile turning apologetic as I cupped her chin. Studying her, seeing the shadows under her eyes, I traced my thumb over the curve of her cheek. Was it just my imagination or was she gaunter than usual? "How much breakfast did you eat this morning?"

Her gaze darted away from mine. "Enough."

Reading that as the evasion it was, I scowled at her as I thought back to the photo she'd sent. "How much?"

"Enough to give me energy," she grouched. "I felt sick, Hunter. Until our phone call before you went to bed, I felt as if the ground had been dragged out from under me. What about that would make me hungry?"

I could concede that, especially after the conversation where she'd shouted at me like the Aurora I'd known as a little girl and not the formidable businesswoman she was today. In fact… huh. *This* Aurora was the kid I'd known. As well as a mixture of Sunny. But none of the businesswoman.

More masks, it seemed.

"When did you eat before then?"

She sucked her bottom lip between her teeth. "I've been dieting."

I gaped at her. "Why would you starve perfection?"

Her soft smile made an appearance. It was followed by a chuckle. "I think that's overstating things, don't you?"

"I've seen what's beneath the clothes, so no," I told her grimly. "I don't. Why would you diet?"

"That dress—" She sniffed. "Jennifer picked it. I wasn't a part of the bridal party on her side, but I still stood up with Luc at the ceremony."

"So?"

"She chose the dress. I didn't have time to go to the final fitting. But I refused to give her the satisfaction of altering it."

My brows surged. "So you dieted rather than have it altered? Couldn't you have done that without her knowing?"

"It was the principle of the matter."

"Why didn't you just buy a new one?"

"It wasn't off the rack." Another sniff. "It was *haute couture*."

I whistled. "Poor Luc."

She gaped at me. "Excuse me?"

"He's clearly stuck in the middle between two crazy women." I grabbed her chin, my thumb slotting into the center where there was a slight divot. "If we'd been together and I knew you were dieting over a ridiculous reason such as that one, you wouldn't be able to sit down for a month."

Rory gasped, her knees seeming to buckle as she tipped into me, then, her voice fervent, she rasped, "God, I want that. I want that so much."

There went my erection.

Her hips rocked as they felt it too, prompting me to rumble, "Don't start something you can't finish yet. Breakfast first, then we'll talk. Okay?"

Another shaky breath heated up my chest, but this time, the connotations were very different.

This was shaky with need.

Want.

Not fear.

I never wanted her fear. Ever. Her submission, yes. Her willingness, of course. But her fear? Never.

My heart sped up in response to her. She was better than cardio for getting my blood pumping, and that was *without* her presence in my arms. With? I was pretty much running a marathon all while standing still in the lobby of my hotel.

I stared down at her mouth, the desire to rub that pouty bottom lip with my thumb too tempting to ignore. Tugging it down so that I could see her pearly white teeth, I repeated, more to myself than her, "Breakfast first, then we'll talk."

Her eyelashes fluttered and the sweetest flash of *something* appeared in her expression.

Vulnerability.

Want.

Need.

Confusion.

Lust.

Hope.

A cocktail of emotions, and I just couldn't stop myself from taking a sip.

We were in the middle of a hotel lobby. It was *busy*. Crazy busy. People swarmed around us. Staff and guests alike. But in that moment, all I could see was her. That look. Those feelings. And I had to taste them.

I had to taste her.

Angling my chin down, I let my lips hover above hers for a second. I knew she was in a fragile headspace right now and I had no desire to fuck with that, but when she recognized my intent, the softest, gentlest whimper escaped her.

I had my green light.

Letting my mouth collide with hers, I just savored her. Like a fine wine. Like an old scotch. Like a vintage champagne. She was all three and more, and from the punch she packed to my bloodstream, that one taste of her had me intoxicated.

I swept my tongue along that pouty bottom lip, encouraging her to part them, and she did, so I rewarded her by thrusting it inside where I found myself immediately welcomed.

Her arms clung to my upper back as she burrowed deeper into my hold, and her hands clutched at my shirt, nails digging into my shoulders in a way that I wanted to experience every fucking day for the rest of my life.

That broken whimper escaped her again as she clung to me, and I gave her my focus and stopped thinking about how long I'd been waiting to do this. How many years that had been wasted without me knowing how she tasted.

I let loose a groan, deep and hungry and just as desperate as hers, and I let her swallow it as I thrust into her mouth, dragging my tongue against hers, enjoying the lack of hesitance as she fought back. Her kiss wasn't submissive. Her kiss was like mine— exploratory.

She shivered in my hold as I supped from her, savored her, drowned in her, and my own fingers rose of their own accord and dove into her hair. They didn't stop until they were taut and were digging into her silken locks as I pulled, hard enough for me to feel her guttural moan in response.

Like a marionette doll whose strings had been tugged, her head fell back on her neck and she acceded to me.

She submitted.

In the hotel lobby.

A part of me knew this was crazy. Knew that I should take this upstairs, but I couldn't.

I didn't want this to end.

It could *never* end, in fact.

Ever.

I wanted this for the rest of my fucking life and I'd fight dirty to keep it. To keep her.

As I fucked her mouth, the world stuttered to a halt. The universe itself registered the rightness of this moment, and the only thing that stopped me was a snappish, "There are *children* present."

It was spoken snootily enough that I got the feeling it wasn't the first time the woman had tried to reprimand me in my own fucking hotel.

Ignoring her, I gave Aurora one final kiss, enjoying the pressure of her nails against my shoulder muscles, delighting in how her tongue tangled with mine still, reveling in the gentle thrust of her hips against my abdomen as the pleasure deepened.

Only when *I* was ready did I pull back.

Both of us were panting, our mouths bright pink, eyelids heavy with a surfeit of pleasure that was more powerful than molly.

As I stared into her eyes and she stared into mine, the world kicked into gear again. I didn't know if the bitch who'd interrupted us was still gawking—neither did I care.

She was all I saw.

All I felt.

All I wanted.

And from how she was looking at me, I knew Aurora felt the same.

"Hi," she breathed, making my lips quirk into a grin.

"Hi." I let go of the tight hold on her hair, watching for any signs of discomfort, but none were forthcoming. If anything, as I let go, her hips rocked into me again.

How could I have forgotten?

My little masochist.

"Breakfast first, then talk," I ordered, the reminder for myself more than for her.

Before she could answer, I hustled her along with me.

When I dragged her into the elevator, though, I saw I had the full attention of every single receptionist on staff. Which, for a five-star hotel, was *not* where it should be. I arched a brow at them, the stony glance enough to make them jump back to work as the doors whirred to a close.

"I never imagined you being a boss."

The words had me studying her. "What did you imagine me as?"

"A beach bum."

Snickering, I squeezed her fingers. "I fail to see an insult there."

"You would," she drawled, but she squeezed back.

I reached forward and typed in the code for Suite No. 1 which triggered the elevator into action. As we shuttled toward the top floor, she shuffled nearer to me, not stopping until her side was rubbing against mine. When her other hand clutched at my arm and she pivoted so that her face was pressed up against my bicep, I frowned.

"Aurora?"

"Just ignore me," she muttered, even as her nails dug into me.

French manicure.

My lips curved.

She'd never been the kind of woman who went for jeweled tips or bright colors. That was Aurora. Old money to the point of belonging in a magazine spread for Ralph Lauren.

Some things were reassuringly constant, it seemed. Some things didn't change, even if the world was shifting around us.

When she took a couple deep breaths, a truth registered, prompting me to ask, my tone calm, "I didn't know you suffered with anxiety attacks."

"I don't," she choked.

"Just around me?"

"Yes."

Ouch. "You know how to hit beneath the belt."

"I'm sorry," she said miserably, but her lips brushed up against my bicep. Softly, at first. Almost in an apology. Then her tongue popped out.

As it slid across the muscle, I didn't have the strength to chide her for it.

Neither did I have the time.

The elevator arrived on my floor, and I tightened my hold on her hand to encourage her to move with me.

With the doors closing behind us and delivering us directly into my suite, I expected her to pull away.

She didn't so I prompted, "Do you want to wake Stan for breakfast? He's still asleep."

Her eyes were huge as she looked up at me, finally tugging free of my grip. Before I had a chance to miss her fingers tucked in mine, they were on the hem of her shirt and she was dragging it overhead.

I didn't even manage to grind out, "Aurora," because those supple digits were already on the front clasp of her bra and she was unfastening it, freeing her breasts from the bright-blue silk.

The same bright blue as the robe she wore as Sunny.

Intentional? I thought so.

She pushed her jeans and panties down, toeing off her shoes, whispering, "I need you to see me, Hunter. *Me*."

I was more than seeing her. She'd just stolen the oxygen in the room because all she wore now was my necklace. The necklace I hadn't even been sure if she'd keep or donate to one of Rachel's charities.

My voice was a deep, dark rumble as I warned, "Aurora," but I was only a man.

A man who was looking at the woman he'd worshiped since he was a kid.

A woman who he'd never imagined seeing like this…

Which was when I saw them—the translucent disks, like pasties on her nipples.

"What the hell are they?" I demanded, reaching for her as if I had the right to when I didn't, but she didn't shift away as I pulled on one of the plastic circles. She hissed as the disk didn't part from her easily, and that was when I saw why.

Tiny plastic spikes dug into the softness of her nipples.

Nipples that she'd pierced at my command.

There were small holes dotted all over the tender flesh; each one had a red pinprick at the center as if they'd been on the cusp of drawing blood.

"Did I tell you you could wear one of these today?" I grumbled, my voice darkening with displeasure.

"You didn't tell me I couldn't," she rasped.

Only because I hadn't goddamn known—

I sucked in a breath, trying to rein in my impatience. Something glittered in her eyes as she stood there, naked, unashamed as always, even of her flaws. Not that there were many. That was why her dieting came as a surprise; she'd never been lacking confidence. Either as Aurora or Sunny.

Reaching forward, I moved a finger along a darker spot just above the areola as a memory hit me. "The capsaicin gel?" I'd never seen it make that kind of burn before, though.

"Yes. I made a kind of, well, I guess it was a tincture. I think I told you about it at the time." She hitched a shoulder. "I did too good a job. It burned like a motherfucker."

The simple words had me barely withholding a snarl.

She'd given herself a chemical burn, for Christ's sake.

The urge to haul her over my shoulder was strong, to take her into my room and to paddle her ass for being so fucking reckless with her safety—

I couldn't.

Not yet.

Not until we discussed limits.

Sara Barranco's voice echoed in my skull, "Consent is king."

And while I'd had it as Sunny and D, it was different in person. Everything had changed in less than twenty-four hours. At least, in Vegas time it had.

Still, I grabbed the other disk and tugged that free of her skin. "No more of these," I snapped, tucking them into my pocket.

"Yes, Hunter," she said breathily.

Even as my ears were delighting in that tone of voice, it was a surreal moment having Aurora Valentini talk to me like that. Having her standing there *like that*.

She didn't touch herself.

Didn't try to entice.

Sunny had rarely topped from the bottom aside from when it came to self-punishments, and I always gave her leeway because I knew she wanted me to be more of a disciplinarian but, from a distance, I didn't know how to bridge the gap.

We weren't at a distance now, though.

Grinding my teeth, I balled my hands into fists. The silence between us was deafening, louder than a stadium.

One of my hands unclenched.

Like it didn't belong to me, I reached forward. The tip of my pointer finger smoothed around her nipple. Displeasure at the little holes the device had made turned my lips down at the corners, but I couldn't stop myself from flipping the nipple ring. Left to right. I watched the motion. Up and down.

My other hand tightened as I pulled on the ring, twisting it sharply until she jerked forward, closer to me. A mewl escaped her as her fingers settled on my abdomen, while mine twisted that poor abused nipple. When I tugged the ring, she arched onto tiptoe. When I pinched it, the soft tissue flattened and her head fell back.

My breathing turned erratic at the sight of what she was offering me.

Jaw working, I carefully moved my hand away and pressed it to her chin, forcing her to hold her head up, to look me in the eye.

"Are you on birth control?"

Her lips parted. "Yes."

Thank fuck for that. No way did I want anything between us.

"I'm clean."

"I am too."

"Green is go. Red is stop." Basic rules.

Knowing what that meant, she shuddered before she repeated, "Green is go. Red is stop."

I pinched her nipple again. "Green, Aurora? Or red?"

"Green, green," she groaned, desperation leaking into the words. Desperation for me.

That got to me more than anything else could.

Her tits were beautiful. She was gorgeous. Those eyes of hers were pleading with me. Her body language declared her need. But her desperation was what sent all my good intentions flying.

My mind whirred. The need to punish warred with the need to fuck her. To stake a claim. But I'd told her breakfast first, then a talk. Not sex. Not yet.

Jesus Christ, I was already fucking this up.

Yet those goddamn disks. The scar…

My temper trickled into being, making me push aside the lessons Sara had imparted, making me forget things I shouldn't forget. Things that should be intrinsic by now.

I stopped touching her. "Turn around. I want to see all of you."

She leaped to fulfill the order.

Perfection. Utter perfection.

"Show me how wet you are," I growled, watching as she dipped her hand between her legs and twisted her wrist so she could offer it palm side up to me.

I snatched her wrist in my grip and raised it to my mouth. She moaned as I sucked her fingers clean.

Sliding first one digit between my lips, I curled my tongue around it before gracing the other with the same treatment.

Another moan stuttered from her lips as I bit down on each tip, enough that each bite would sting.

Pulling back, I rasped, "Delicious. Better than Nutella pancakes."

Her smile was a complex combination of shy, amused, and aroused. "Nothing's better than that."

"You're wrong," I chided her before I pointed behind me at the glass wall. "We're going onto the terrace."

She stiffened. "What?"

"No one can see us. The Gallinaro is the tallest building in the city and we're on the top floor."

Her shoulders still rattled with tension but I waved my hand behind me, indicating that she should go first.

As she moved, her discomfort clear, I watched her ass. That ridiculous diet hadn't gotten rid of many of her curves, just some. I was going to spank her anyway for trying to deny me those inches she didn't need to lose in the first place.

Head angled to the side, I watched the jiggle before I shot a look at the door to the left that led to the wing where Stan was sleeping. The suite was a massive apartment, so I wasn't altogether concerned about him intruding. Especially since, earlier, he'd downed a bottle of tequila at a bar in the casino once we made it back from dealing with the coyote.

Her hand reached for the door handle and she peered over her shoulder at me, checking in with me. Almost as if…

"Aurora, I'm not going to lock you out there without any clothes."

"I probably deserve it."

"Deserve what?"

"The prank." She swallowed. "I've not exactly been nice to you, Hunter."

"And? You think that means I'm going to treat you like shit?" I folded my arms over my chest. "You think so little of me?"

"No. I think so little of myself." She blew out a breath. "And I'm not used to that. I don't normally care."

"But with me you do?"

She angled her chin up. "Apparently."

The non-answer had me arching a brow at her. "But with me you do?" I repeated.

"Yes," she hissed.

Pleased by the easy capitulation, I shot her a smile. "Get that fine ass of yours outside."

She blinked, evidently surprised by my lack of a rebuttal, but she huffed and did as I requested.

It was bright and hot, but once I watched her move onto the terrace, satisfaction laced through me.

I wanted her bare.

I wanted her exposed.

Aurora had been hiding away for too long.

She might not see the symbolism behind this, but I sure as hell did.

Or maybe that was why she'd stripped off in the hallway?

Whatever her reason, I was in total accord about not wanting anything between us.

Not even a fucking condom.

Moving toward her, I snagged her hand as she hovered in the center of the terrace, uncertain of where to go.

There was an infinity pool with a glass floor that revealed the Vegas strip below, then there was a hot tub, a chill out area, a bar, a canopy bed that was basically an outdoor four-poster for sunbathing, and a smaller dipping pool.

Her hand in mine, I raised it high and encouraged her to twirl around again. She graced me with a smile I'd never forget.

"I'd sing *Sleeping Beauty* songs to you, but we both know I can't sing." When her nose crinkled, I asked, "What's with the nose crinkle?"

She hitched a shoulder but laughed when I encouraged her to twirl once more on her tiptoes. "Hunter's allowed to know those things. I kind of wish D didn't."

"Why?"

"It's ridiculous that I still watch Disney movies."

"Why is it ridiculous?" I shook my head. "You're too tough on yourself, Aurora. We're going to work on that. What harm does it do to watch movies that made you happy as a kid?"

"I'm way past childhood."

"I. Don't. Care," I told her sternly. "If they make you happy, they make you happy. I mean, I love *Call of Duty* but that doesn't stop me from playing *The Sims* too."

At my wink, she nibbled her lip but, ultimately, nodded.

"I'm D. D wants to know these things. D wished he knew more about you as Sunny. D knew that being an online Dom wasn't enough for Sunny—"

"That's not true!"

"We both know I'm not as hardcore as…" I didn't say his name, but my mouth tightened. "You need more discipline than I could give you online."

When she shuddered, I knew it wasn't in disgust.

"Speaking of," I drawled, laughing when she shrieked as I scooped her up and onto my shoulder.

"Hunter!" she screeched, her hands scrabbling at the small of my back for stability—as if I'd drop her. Ha.

"Yes, Aurora?" I crooned, turning my face to her ass and taking a bite that had her squealing.

Her yelp mingled with a laugh. "You're insane."

"Maybe." *Over her.* I shrugged, which jostled her and had her hands tugging on my belt. "Maybe I'm just the right amount of crazy." When she snorted, I nipped her again.

"I'm too heavy for this," she grouched which, of course, prompted our very first physical spank.

I slapped her ass hard. Enough to sting. She didn't wriggle but I noticed she hooked one foot behind the other ankle and her legs tensed in reaction.

Before I bit her again, I rumbled, "You feel just fine to me."

When she harrumphed, I strode over to the bed and slung her onto the mattress, watching as all those curves jiggled in response.

Her tits were going to be the death of me.

"Elbows on the bed, palms flat, stick that ass out, legs spread wide."

She didn't even think to argue but immediately complied with an eagerness that told me more than she knew.

The two halves of my nature were entities in their own right at that moment.

Hunter wanted to make love to her.

D wanted to punish her and fuck her.

At the same time.

Instead, I squatted in front of her once she'd assumed the position and, in the searing hot light of the afternoon, I studied her form.

Her inner thighs were wretched from that goddamn paddle she still used. How there wasn't any severe scarring I didn't know. I could see silvery lines that were stretch marks on her ass, but also deeper tissue scars around the entire area.

Marcus.

My top lip curled into a sneer as I slipped my hands along her calves, tracing upward with the tips until her stomach clenched, rocking her hips farther back. She released a harsh breath, tension vibrating through her as my fingers moved ever nearer to her pussy.

Maybe a part of her wanted to focus more on the sex than the discipline too…?

That buoyed me. Gave me hope.

Of course, I didn't give her what she wanted.

No, I kept the tracing of my fingers nice and light, enough to make her squirm with the tickle as I shifted from a crouch to a standing position. When she was wriggling even more, I pulled a hand back and slapped her ass.

Once. Twice. Three times.

She yelped, but it morphed into a groan.

"No more dieting."

"No more dieting," she quickly agreed.

I stared at her inner thighs with displeasure.

I spanked her again.

Once. Twice. Three times.

"You're never going to use the vampire paddle again."

"Yes, S—Hunter."

The quick correction had me rubbing where I'd spanked.

"Good girl for remembering."

I saw the goosebumps rush down her spine at that. It prompted me to lean over her and whisper, "Do you care that I'm Hunter? Would you prefer D to be a stranger?"

Her mouth wobbled as she tilted her head to look at me. "A part of me does. It would be easier. But…" She swallowed. "I'd never have told D about Nutella pancakes."

She had no idea how much that pleased me. I let my fingers ghost over the outer lips of her pussy as a reward. It encouraged her to say:

"I-I think I just need to acclimate to the idea of you being one and the same man."

"And I have to do that too," I concurred, patting her cunt with the flat of my hand. "You're not always going to like what I tell you, Aurora. You're going to think we can revert to old habits. But we won't. Not where discipline is concerned. Do you understand me?"

She nodded. "I understand, Hunter. I-I don't want to top from the bottom."

"You do it so naturally as Aurora though," I mocked.

"Maybe I don't want to have to," she whispered back, turning to face the head of the canopy bed again. "Maybe I know I haven't been living. Maybe I know that…"

"What do you know?" I prompted softly when her words waned.

"I'd never have trusted D with my history. I didn't trust him with my present. So I could never have gifted him my future." She gulped. "I don't have to trust you. You've always been there. You've always had my back. There's no need to trust you. Trust isn't…" Her brow puckered. "The ties that bind us go deeper than that." She growled under her breath. "Damn, I'm not saying this right, especially when I've spent the past fifteen years pushing you away—"

I tapped her pussy again, making her yelp. "Remember what your nanna used to say?"

"She said a lot of shit over the years. Plus, do we have to talk about the old witch now?"

My lips twitched—Nanna had made her preference for her grandsons evident over the years. But the bitch had had some good sayings.

"We don't, but she used to say, 'If we want things to stay as they are, things will have to change.'"

Peering over her shoulder at me, she scoffed. "That wasn't her. That was di Lampedusa's *Gattopardo*."

I had a moment of revelation as her eyes clashed with mine. As the truth hit home that this was Aurora and Aurora was Sunny and that I could have the woman I'd worshiped from afar for decades.

Dumbly, I asked, "It was?"

"Yes," she said with a long-suffering sigh. "Nanna was a plagiarist."

Though my grin made an appearance, the wake-up call of this conversation had me shifting course again, encouraging her to take a seat beside me.

My erection hadn't deflated, but this conversation was vital, and it was stronger than my need to fuck—truly, that was saying something. But only once we'd set this aside could we let loose, and I really fucking needed that.

I needed no barriers between us.

"So," I mused, "what you're saying is that D can know this side of you, but nothing else, while Hunter can know about the past but not this? And, if you'd had your way, the two would never collide."

"Yes," she rasped.

Sadly, I shook my head. "Do you want to live a half-life, Aurora? Never fully opening up to the people who matter the most? *T'avissi a mettiri na màschira*," I told her. Mostly because it was fitting. 'You ought to be wearing a mask.' To the Sicilians, that meant covering up someone's shame or embarrassment. In this case, hers.

There was a bleakness in her gaze that I didn't like. "I've been on that path for as long as I've known about my family and what happened to them."

"Then it's time we changed that."

34

AURORA

THEN IT'S *time we changed that.*

Could it be as easy as that?

In life, I'd noticed that both of us had completely contrasting habits.

He tended to make light of things.

I tended to approach even simple problems as if they were a trigonometrical equation.

Opposites attract? Or just two people who'd grown up so closely that they naturally complimented one another?

"You were mentored in the BDSM lifestyle because of me."

His expression didn't change. "Yes, and before you ask, I didn't stick around because of you."

"I didn't need to ask that. At first glance, maybe my mind veered there, but I've seen you get off on the stuff you make me do for you too often to really question it."

"Good. If anything, what I saw that day was enough to put me off for life. I walked in thinking he was beating you, Aurora. I didn't—" He shook his head and something darkened in his eyes.

'Something' I knew was him thinking back to that scene with Marcus.

I didn't hurry to take his mind off that day even though the idea of him referencing that memory made my skin crawl.

He raked a hand through his hair. "It was still a 'eureka' moment for me. It opened my eyes to your true nature."

I tipped up my chin and, deciding to be brave, told him, "We both know that I have fewer limits than you. I trust you. As Hunter. And as D. I don't trust myself," was my shaky admission.

"Oh, sweetheart, that's something we need to work on."

My bottom lip trembled at the endearment. Something I'd never known I needed to hear from Hunter, something he'd so freely given as D.

"Marcus was the only one to truly degrade me. He took me so low—"

"Did you intend on tapping out that day?" He reached for my hand when I tensed. "It's okay if you didn't."

"It was the first time he'd pissed on me. I tapped out then." Head bowed, I didn't look at him as I admitted, "He didn't listen."

"That piece of shit." Somehow, it was even more powerful because he didn't snarl the words. They were measured and all the more vitriolic for it.

"Yes." I studied our joined hands. "After that, and coming to realize that the Master I'd trusted enough to marry was capable of rape, it messed with my head. How could I trust in my judgment? I didn't feel confident enough *or* comfortable enough to venture into that world again, not until I went onto KinkWorld and met you."

God, fate really could fuck with you.

Who the hell would have known that it would bring us to this point in the here and now?

He was quiet for a moment, then he surprised me by saying, "See? You do have a limit."

I blinked. "I do?"

"Watersports." He beamed a smile at me, looking more like a proud papa than a horny guy who'd been chasing after me for decades. "But you're right. I'm not that kind of Dom, and I never will be. I get my kicks in other ways."

How his voice bottomed out had me squirming.

God, I loved those 'kicks' of his.

He'd managed to keep me under his control for years as D, and the only thing that had been missing was the bite of punishments that weren't delivered by my own hand.

The prospect of what we could do now that we were together made me lightheaded.

"Remember: red for stop, green for go. You have an issue, you tap out. We can find out what your real limits are together, agreed?"

Nodding, feeling breathless, for the first time in my life feeling less like a freak and *hopeful*, I rasped, "Agreed."

35

HUNTER

SHE LOOKED at me as if I had the answers to the world in my skull.

I didn't.

But fuck if it didn't feel delicious for her to look at *me* like that. To see something in me that she never had before.

I kind of understood how a nobody musician felt after going viral on social media—one day a zero; the next day a hero.

Rolling with it, I reached over and cupped her chin, sliding my fingers around and back so that I could grip her nape.

Without asking, I dragged her over to me, not stopping until I was rearranging her totally and she had to scrabble onto my lap.

When she was straddling me, I reached down and grabbed one of her ass cheeks then, savoring the feel of her, savoring what I'd always craved, I drew her forehead against mine.

For a moment, I just soaked in her scent, but the urges I'd been fighting hit me.

I wasn't a teenage boy who'd have been happy with a quick kiss and maybe second base.

I was a man who'd been waiting for this woman for a lifetime and who finally had the chance to taste her.

My fingers dug into her nape and, leaning forward, I snagged her bottom lip between my teeth. The urge to mark her was strong, and it was offset only with the knowledge that Stan was here.

Stan would see.

Stan had also been trying to matchmake us as if he were Patti Stanger, but as much as he might be happy about how things were shaping up, I didn't think that happiness would extend to being slapped in the face with all the hickies I'd marked his sister with.

She released a shaky breath, annihilating my thoughts as she pulled away to whisper on an exhalation, "I need you to fill me, Hunter. I'm so empty."

When she combined it with a soft flutter of her eyelashes, I realized she'd basically declared my own personal 'open sesame.'

Darting forward, I snagged her bottom lip once again and bit down.

Hard enough that she groaned, ass squirming on my lap.

I didn't let go, tugged on her lip until it pulled away from her teeth, until the soft flesh would bruise. Until it would hurt every time she licked it, until the indentations would take a good twenty minutes to disappear.

If I could, I'd have broken the skin. Not because I was a vampire but because I wasn't about to let her continue with these goddamn self-punishments of hers.

She wanted to feel pain—I'd make her feel pain. But *my* way. No more of this vampire paddle bullshit. No more of these weird chemical burns she was accidentally giving herself in her reckless chase for pain-soaked ecstasy.

For the most intelligent woman I'd ever known, she was really fucking dumb when it came to her needs.

But it was my job to teach her a different path.

I'd make her *pass out* from pleasure; I'd make her hurt from how good she felt.

That was how I worked.

I'd just never been able to manifest that through a computer screen.

A hitch in her breath was the first clue she gave me that she liked my brand of teasing so far.

The next was her desperate, "I need you, Hunter."

Her pussy melted onto the bulge of my shaft as she rode it, letting me feel her heat as she creamed all over the denim, hips rocking, clearly loving what I was doling out.

That was when I let go. It was also when I spanked her ass.

"Did I tell you that you could ride me?"

Her eyes flared wide in surprise and she froze on my lap. I had big hands, and my fingers were strong and callused from years of playing football. I tapped her again. And again. And again.

"Now you can," I crooned, watching her hips go back to rocking, and she was riding my jeans-covered cock as I spanked her. Over and over.

"You don't starve perfection, Aurora."

She sucked in a breath. "No, D—"

That particular slap to her ass had to sting because she whimpered as I informed her, "I'm not D. Who am I?"

Her head tipped back as I grabbed the ass cheek I'd been gracing with my attention, intending to leave marks behind. It prompted her to croak, "Hunter. You're Hunter."

"No more starving yourself—"

"It was only for the wedding!"

Another tap. "No more self-punishments." Tap. "You need to escape—" Tap. "—or you need to relax—" Tap. "—or you need to get out of your head—you come to me." Tap. *Tap.* "Do you understand?"

"I understand."

"We learn together." Tap. "Like always. Agreed?"

"Agreed."

Pleased by her easy capitulation, I twisted us around so that she was back on the bed. The movement surprised her but she didn't shriek, just watched me with those big brown eyes of hers that saw everything and registered nothing.

At least, that was how it *had* been.

Not anymore.

Looming over her now, her thighs higher up around my waist, I dragged one of her arms overhead, watching as she let it stay there, letting me join it with the twin a second later.

Gripping both her wrists with my fingers, I slipped my other hand around her thigh, and where my fingers touched, I pinched her.

She jolted the first time, but the second, she arched her back, pushing her hips into me.

The new angle didn't allow her to grind against me, though, but it let me see her pussy. The lips were parted, the clit ring gleamed, those fucking labia rings were as perfect as I'd known they'd be, and the slickness within told me exactly how she was doing even if her eyes were slowly growing dazed.

I'd half-feared there'd be a silent 'Why are you doing this to me?' hidden within those depths but there wasn't, and it eased me into this, gave me the confidence to rub my fingers along the mottled skin she'd left between her thighs. I had a feeling that she wasn't ashamed of this because D had seen them in a much worse state, but had I not been D, she might have tried to hide them away...

My Aurora: so perfectly complex.

I almost sighed at the thought even as I continued pinching her here and there, sharp bites of my fingers that would lead to quick stings that left pink flesh behind.

Shuffling the digits higher, I came to her breasts, did the same thing around the shape of those tits I'd been wanting to fuck since forever, purposely ignoring her nipples and the rings I really wanted to tug.

This time she angled high on her shoulders so that she could get closer, pressing her chest into me in a silent plea for attention, but the move had me scratching my short nails down her sides instead before I slapped her outer thigh.

I wasn't at home and she'd been my only playmate in the D/s life, so it wasn't like I carried around a flogger in my jeans. Improvisation was key.

"Please, Hunter," she whimpered, arms writhing against the mattress, not trying to break free of my simple restraint, more like luxuriating in it.

I bit my tongue at the sight then bowed my head and pressed kisses along the curve of her stomach.

Wherever I laid a kiss, I nipped her with my teeth shortly afterward, following that up with a quick lick around the indentations I left behind.

As I moved higher up again, I ignored her nipples, shifting to her throat where I sucked and bit and nipped, leaving so many marks I knew that she'd look like a Jackson Pollock painting by the time I was done with her. Her nose nuzzled my temple, her lips kissing me wherever she could reach.

My dick was aching like a fucker when I pulled back to look at the bright-pink skin on her neck, at the bites, the tinges of red from where I'd pinched her. All in all, there weren't enough marks. That much was clear.

Distracted by my study, I didn't realize she was wriggling around in an effort to kiss me until her lips were there. Below mine.

Before she could let them collide, I jerked back and with a sharp look, told her, "That kiss in the lobby was twenty years in the making, Aurora." My stern voice made her eyes widen and she fell against the mattress, her cheeks rosy from embarrassment. "From now on, you have to earn kisses, do you understand?"

The flush changed.

Morphing from embarrassment into something else entirely. "Like what? What do I have to do?"

"It depends on what I want that day."

"How do I earn your kiss today, Hunter?" she moaned, fulfilling at least three of my personal fantasies right there and then.

Teasing her by breathing against her lips, nuzzling my nose against hers, I let my other hand slide between her legs.

Ghosting my fingers over her slick flesh, I rumbled, "You're going to give me two orgasms. Then you earn a kiss. Do you think you can do that for me, baby girl?"

Her lashes fluttered. "I-I can try."

I nuzzled into her again, my nose drifting along the side of her jaw as my fingers finally found her clit ring. "You don't need to ask for permission to come."

She groaned and I closed my eyes at the surreal bliss of the moment.

Realizations plagued me like stray bullets. They didn't mar the moment, just rammed the reality home to me.

Fuck, she was sensitive.

Fuck, she was eager.

Fuck, she was needy.

Each one was a revelation that sank into my bones. Each one was a truth I'd never forget.

"I'm going to show you how perfect you are. How perfect we're going to be together."

"Yes," she begged. "Show me. Please!"

As I frigged her clit, teasing her by twisting the ring, I thought about the many times I'd seen her do this to herself and I transferred memory into action.

I rubbed it how she did.

I used to circle the flat of my fingers over and on top of a woman's clit, massaging the whole area as it were, but she didn't do that—she moved her fingers from side to side. It was awkward in my position but I wanted her pleasure more than I cared about carpal tunnel syndrome.

"Let's start with a nice simple orgasm to warm up," I breathed against her lips, watching her swallow as her eyes latched onto mine. "Just to get you nice and wet for the main event."

"I've wanted you for so long. Wanted this," she pleaded.

Had I ever heard sweeter words? I didn't think so.

"You'll get me, baby girl. You'll get me."

Her throat arched as she dug the back of her head into the mattress, the locket settling between her tits where I'd always wanted it to sit, the bright pink diamond gleaming against her olive skin.

Her toes dug into my hips before she spread her legs wider, triggering a memory of how she'd shuffle them apart so they were as wide as possible when she masturbated in front of me.

The memory encouraged me to let go of her arms.

"You move them, you lose my fingers," I warned her, feeling flushed when she gasped and tensed her biceps as if the threat alone worked better than any bindings.

With that edict set in stone, I grabbed her leg and positioned her knee so that it let me spread her thigh, pulling the inner muscles taut. The little divot at the side of her outer pussy lips made itself known and I promised myself later that I'd taste that spot. That I'd lick it. That I'd feast.

"I'm going to fuck you so hard you never forget the feel of my dick inside you, Aurora."

Watching as she dug her ankle into the mattress, obviously registering why I'd done what I had, I proceeded to scrape my nails along her inner thigh while I rubbed her clit, making sure to twist her piercing every couple strokes.

"I'm going to fill you so full of my cum that it's going to leak out of you at breakfast and you're going to sit there, eating your Nutella goddamn pancakes, dripping in my seed, Aurora."

"Please, please, please," she begged.

"I'm not going to stop until the only name on your lips is Hunter, Aurora. Hunter. Me."

"Yes, you," she sobbed, and as I started pinching her again, I let my fingers speed up and watched as she came.

It was short. It was sharp. It took her by surprise. And it was fucking glorious. *She* was fucking glorious. Everything I'd imagined, yet somehow more too.

As she climaxed, her arms stayed in place, and I growled, dropping my mouth to her throat to kiss her there, to tongue the sinews, to taste her pulse as it throbbed because of something *I'd* done to her.

Then, as the tension waned, I slid two fingers into her. She was hot silk, wicked sin personified. My downfall and my salvation in one swoop.

As those straining inner muscles clung to me, I shifted my other hand as I moved to rest my forehead atop hers, then I got to work.

She was wet enough for each thrust to make a noise that had my body reacting like she was deepthroating me, and I knew my cock was a fucking mess from the pre-cum she'd dragged out of me as a result.

When I found a rhythm, I stopped scissoring my digits wider, just pressed inside to the second knuckle. With my fingers atop her stomach, I gently palpated the area above her pubis while, on the inside, I used that as a guide to rake against them on the hunt for her G-spot. It took me a couple tries to manage it, but with our eyes locked on each other, I saw the exact moment I hit it.

A broken gasp escaped her and my wet dreams came true.

"H-Hunter!" she cried hoarsely as she exploded around me.

So that fucker Marcus hadn't bothered finding her G-spot.

That brokenly uttered whimper spoke of shock. Of surprise. Of newness.

Good.

It was mine.

That spot was fucking mine, and I was going to rail it every chance I could get until she knew who owned it. Until she knew who owned her pleasure.

I fucked her with my fingers, and despite her having come twice already, I didn't give her any slack. Grinding the butt of my wrist against her clit, moving faster and faster until her wetness wasn't just audible, it was as much a part of the performance as she and I were.

"You're going to burst, aren't you, Aurora? I wanna feel you explode. I'm going to tongue fuck your mouth the second you do. No respite. No rest. You're going to keep on coming. I'm not going to let you come down. I'm not stopping until you're addicted to my dick. Until you're addicted to what *I* can give you. Until you're addicted to *me*."

She let loose a hoarse grunt as she pushed her forehead into me, hips starting to rock, grinding back, not just accepting but actively taking part.

Maybe another Dom would have told her to lie there and not move, but I couldn't do that. It wasn't fucking in me.

I needed this.

I needed her to react because for the past fifteen years, that was all we'd had—inactivity.

Now, I needed the opposite.

Otherwise, how would I know if anything had changed?

I doubled down, refusing to stop until I found what I was looking for.

There.

Just. There.

When she came for the third time, I was grateful the floors below didn't have terraces apart from the corner units which were far away.

As for Stan, I hoped for his sake he was still passed out drunk.

I stemmed her sharp cry by thrusting my tongue into her mouth and stealing the sound for myself.

And as I tongue fucked her there, fulfilling my earlier promise, I carried on railing her with my hand until she was sobbing into my mouth. Sobbing *my name*. Mine. No one else's.

Triumph roared through me, and it made me greedy. The sound of my name on her lips, I knew, was going to become my personal heroin. But that was only right, wasn't it? A mutual addiction. To each other.

Sounded like paradise to me.

I carried on palpating her stomach, pushing down against my fingers, needing her to gift me something I knew from Sunny she'd never done before.

I wanted to own this memory.

It was mine.

I'd earned it.

After years of silence and years of patience.

This time, as she came, I swallowed the sound, but the sharp scream had dulled to be replaced with a panicked wail as, at long last, the release I'd been seeking exploded into being.

Hot, intense bursts of liquid drenched the front of my jeans as she twisted against me, writhing against the bed as she simultaneously sought to embrace and escape what I was giving her.

Tears sprang forth too, rolling down the sides of her cheeks as she wept as if she were breaking.

I wanted her to break.

How else could I repair what that fucker had done to her?

"Hunter," she choked out against my mouth, mangling my name with her plea, but I still recognized it and savored it.

I wanted to hear that version every day for the rest of my life.

"Hunter!" she screamed, body bucking until I finally, *finally*, stopped.

But even that wasn't enough. I pulled away, satisfied when she moved her arms for the first time to try to cling to me. That didn't mean I'd forgotten…

"Aurora," I barked, my tone gruffer than ever. She jerked at the sound, but something flashed in my eyes that had her swallowing. "Arms," I reminded her. They returned to their earlier position so quickly it was a wonder she didn't give herself goddamn whiplash.

Settling on my knees, I stared down at us both. The bites I'd left were starting to bruise, the pinches faded entirely.

As I wondered how to get them to stay, I reached down to unfasten my fly. Her cum made the fabric stick to my skin and the rawness of it almost made me shudder.

Dragging them down my ass, I pulled out my cock and slowly jacked off. Her eyes locked on it, mouth rounding in an O so perfect that I wanted to take her there first. I was like a starving man at an all-you-can-eat buffet in the Gallinaro. Wanting to glut on everything. Needing to sample every dish just in case it was the last time…

No.

I stopped that train of thought from forming fully.

I wasn't going to let her go.

Ever.

So, I shifted the narrative. There was only *one* first time. That was why I wanted to glut.

She didn't notice my hesitation. Instead, her gaze was focused on my hand which was slowly pumping my shaft.

I was wet from her juices and my pre-cum so it was an easy passage. When she licked her lips, I started to rock my hips, making a tunnel of my fist that was incomparable to the cunt I wanted inside of.

I'd stared at her so many times in this position, never imagining that she was Aurora. That I'd one day be here with the bullshit in the past and the truth between us.

"W-When did you get a piercing?"

Ah, that was what had caught her attention.

"February." Before shit had hit the fan with Dead To Me. "Like the look of it, Aurora?"

She groaned. "Yes, Hunter. Yes."

I fingered the Apadravya piercing, which ran vertically through my glans and had a slight lean to it. "This'll hit your G-Spot." If my grin was smug, then so be it. "You know where that is now." Appreciating her flush, I lowered my erection and showed her the ring at the pubis. "This'll stimulate your clit."

Aurora gifted me with another groan and the slightest, and I meant *slightest*, tremor rushed through her as if her entire body were prepping for the moment I'd enter her.

Her responsiveness took me aback. Seeing it one-sided through a camera was entirely different than real life, but this was more than I'd dared to hope.

"You want my dick, moonlight?"

The endearment tripped off my lips and I had no idea where it came from. It wasn't Sunlight, the second half of her handle, and it wasn't a standard pet name. But it fit her.

She wasn't sunlight.

She was darkness.

She was somber and moody and elegant and cool.

She was the night.

I was the day.

We were polar opposites.

But even the day and the night collided twice in a twenty-four-hour span.

"I do," she whispered. "Please, Hunter, can I have it?"

"Have you earned it?" I grated out.

"N-No."

"Why not?"

"I moved my arms when you told me not to."

Pleased by her honesty, I hummed and allowed my head to rock back on my neck.

"But I sent you my lines," she said hesitantly. Her admission prompted me to rock my head forward a half-inch this time. "And I sent you the pictures you wanted too." I gave her another half-inch. Sensing there was room for negotiation, she breathed, "I-I sent a text when I got home."

I rocked my neck from side to side as I mused, "But you didn't tell me you were coming to Vegas. You lied about your intentions in fact, *and* you didn't eat much of your breakfast. Which, to be frank, pisses me off more than any of those infractions."

My priorities were screwed—fucking sue me.

"I didn't touch my pussy," she countered, 'attorney' Aurora evidently coming in to parlay.

Fuck, I loved that.

I gave my cock another stroke. "Not once after I told you not to?"

"Well, in the shower." She bit her lip. "Does that count?"

"No," I drawled, amused. "It doesn't count. Unless, in the future, I want you wearing my cum for the day."

"Okay," she mewled, clearly more than fine with that.

Jesus, I needed in her.

"You wore those pasties." My head fell back, not only because I was controlling how much of my attention I was giving her, but also because I knew she'd see my furious expression. Aurora was incredibly bad at giving herself punishments. Reckless with what belonged to me. "I didn't permit you to wear those."

"I'm sorry, Hunter," she whispered, sounding miserable enough that it made me want to comfort her and that was not the point of this exercise.

"How else did you obey me today?"

"I didn't masturbate." Her tone was hopeful.

"You did this morning. So that's more of a technicality than anything seeing as you wouldn't be here if you *had* masturbated again," I said as I raised my head enough that I could look at her.

When she shot me a smile that was half-impish and half-rueful, I had to hide my grin.

"I made my living on technicalities," she pointed out. "Technicalities are my jam."

"They might be, but not between us," I reminded, the warning clear in my tone. "Beg for my cock, moonlight."

Her eyes drifted to my shaft again and she rocked her hips up and back in a way that told me she was imagining me sliding into her. "Hunter, I *need* your dick. I don't just want it."

I gave a slow stroke with my wrist.

She licked her lips. "I used to watch you before and I'd wonder if I could take all of you."

"Now that you can see it in the flesh, do you think you can?"

"I'll try."

"Good answer because, Aurora, you *are* going to take every fucking inch."

"Please?" she breathed, pupils gluttonously big.

"Well, wasn't that sweet?" I rumbled, my voice more of a growl than anything else. "Say it again."

"Please, Hunter, please. Pretty, pretty please."

Grunting at what that begging did to me, I released my hold on my dick and dragged my T-shirt over my head

The sight of my nipple rings had her mumbling, "They're new too."

"They are," I agreed as I snatched at her legs, hauling her to the edge of the bed and drawing her into me until the backs of her thighs pressed against my chest. I positioned one foot either side of my neck then leaned in so that I could trace the tip of my cock over her pussy.

She threw her head back the moment my piercing ran along her pierced clit. Those labia rings were going to be the death of me too. They spread her pussy lips apart, revealing the bright pink flesh beneath. When the barbell ran down that tender area, it quivered in response.

"Oh, God," she cried.

"Not God. Just me," I snarled, sliding through the tight channel I'd made with her thighs until she was arching into me, trying to get closer...

Who was I to argue when being inside her wouldn't be close enough?

I pushed the head into her slit. Just the very first inch. A guttural groan escaped me as her silken heat cosseted me. I sucked in a sharp breath, forcing myself back under control, and slowly thrust another inch in.

I was big, she was tight, and I didn't want her out of commission because I'd rushed this.

Even masochists didn't want to be sore *there*, surely? Didn't that defeat part of the purpose?

With that in mind, I reached for her clit and slowly stroked it with the edge of my thumb. For every inch she took, I continued to circle it, watching the flush on her cheeks spread to her throat, down to her chest.

She blossomed in front of me, her chocolate eyes turning panicked at the inexorable push of my cock into her.

Her head rocked from side to side, her chest started heaving, and it prompted me to say, "You're doing so well, baby girl. You take me so fucking prettily. Just look at that beautiful pussy, taking every inch like you said you would. Such a good girl for me. So fucking good."

Her panting breaths eased up, and when she stared at me again, that wildness was still prevalent in her gaze, but she'd calmed and I sensed her trying to relax, her muscles fluttering as she tried to let me move deeper.

When I was there, I angled downward, moving my hand away so that she could feel the pubic piercing, then I crossed her legs.

"FUCK!" I roared.

"Oh, my GOD," she screamed as I began to thrust into her, the impossibly tight clutch of her pussy transforming me into a fucking animal.

"*Chista è da me*," I growled at her, my fingers pinching her outer lips around my shaft, watching as she rocked her head in agreement. "This is mine."

She sobbed, "*Se! Chista è da te!* It's yours!"

Her admission drove me wild, and I fucked her. Harder than I meant to. But goddammit, she was perfect. Too fucking perfect. And I told her that. I gave her the praise she deserved because this pussy *was* mine. *She* was mine.

This was it.

No more running.

No more hiding.

She belonged to me.

"So fucking tight, baby girl, so fucking tight. What the hell are you doing to me? You're so goddamn beautiful, moonlight. So goddamn perfect. Mine. *Mine*," I snarled, turning my head to the side and taking a chunk of the fleshier part of her calf and biting down on it.

It was insane, but she'd made me insane. And when, at my bite, her cunt clamped down on me even more and she screamed through her orgasm, I didn't know if I'd survive. I swore to fuck I didn't.

I pumped into her, giving us both what we needed, forcing a path through the tight clasp of a cunt that would only ever know my cock, fingers, and tongue from this moment on, and then she slayed me by coming again.

Orgasming for the *fifth* time, she wept, "HUNTER, oh, God!"

And with that, the annihilation was complete. She burned every single synapse I possessed, setting fire to every nerve ending in my body.

Tunnel vision set in as finally, *finally,* I gave into the need that had been haunting me since I'd first known my cock had more than one use.

I came.

It was explosive. Implosive. Exhilarating and eviscerating.

She made it ten times hotter by screaming my name again, that single word a plea and a prayer, and I conceded defeat and just rolled with the best orgasm of my goddamn life.

36

AURORA
COLLIDE - HOWIE DAY

I GOT MY WISH.

A wish I hadn't really known I'd been making after every video call we'd shared together when I'd assumed that the aftercare was more for him than for me.

As he guided me from the terrace and into his suite, I wasn't sure what was happening, but when he took me into the bathroom, I figured it out quickly.

The biggest clue was the tub the size of a small pool, forged out of one solid piece of marble.

Hunter ran the water, testing it for the right heat, then he plopped in a ton of soap from the body wash I thought he showered in. After a couple moments, it perfumed the air, and I realized it was the same as his aftershave.

If I hadn't been exhausted, my body would have been primed from that alone as it associated that scent with the start of a scene.

Before I could get worked up, he put some music on, something soft that spoke about people colliding... (Metaphorically. At least, I hoped it was metaphorically.) The song played from invisible speakers, and he carefully scooped me up and placed me in the tub.

With the water smelling of him—much better than the bath bombs

—and though he didn't have candles, he just turned on the light in the mirror so it wasn't as bright as the overhead one, I let myself relax.

I wanted to invite him in as he bustled around, ordering our breakfast from a phone hooked up beside the toilet, but I stayed silent, not even teasing him about the phone and its location; instead I just watched him, eyes eagerly taking in every moment. Absorbing it because I'd never been able to do that before. To have *this*.

It felt good.

Right.

Perfect.

As I released a breath, he cast a look at me, then, thank God, he shuffled over and, without me having to ask, climbed into the water.

I leaped onto him, straddling him as his arms came up around my waist, and he held me close.

Fuck, I'd sold myself short all those years when I'd told myself the candles and the bath and the bath bombs were adequate aftercare.

Nothing could beat this.

He alternated between humming to the music and hushing me, stroking one hand over my hair and the other down my back while I clung to him.

Little kisses were dotted on my temple, the rub of his nose against my cheek—silent acts, each one imbued with a word I shouldn't label yet.

I sighed against him, finally relaxing, and we stayed that way for eons. It was strange because he didn't talk. We didn't need to here. Words weren't necessary to cross the distance. His arms did that for me, his solid embrace, and they were so much more impactful.

It was with regret that the water eventually cooled, and he encouraged me to climb out of the tub.

He toweled me dry, keeping it very clinical apart from a kiss that made my leg pop as he wrapped the bath sheet around my body, knotting it between my breasts.

Then he led me into the bedroom and dressed me in his football jersey from college and some boxer briefs.

After pulling on a pair of jeans and a tee, he guided me into a part of the suite that was clearly the dining area, where a trolley was sitting, waiting for us with the food he'd ordered.

Like a true gentleman, he guided me to the head of the table, held out the chair, and tucked me in before he placed the dish of pancakes in front of me.

Unfortunately for me, our peaceful moment was broken when, wearing nothing more than a pair of boxer briefs, Stan trundled in barely five minutes later, finding Hunter eating mozzarella sticks with marinara sauce and me with my pancakes.

He blinked at me, at him, then proving his brains weren't in his ball sac, declared, "You two fucked."

It wasn't a question.

But how the—

Oh.

My bottom lip was mottled where his teeth had bitten down and my throat was full of hickeys. There was no hiding from my outfit, either. I was wearing one of Hunter's tops, after all, and no bra. Not that I thought Stan would notice that part, but the Brown University jersey, sure. I was a silk robe kind of woman. Not a football jersey type of gal.

"So?" was Hunter's retort.

Stan scraped a hand over his bed head. "You get more of those mozzarella sticks?"

"Over on the sideboard."

My brother peered at me, frowning as he studied my mouth before dismissing me entirely as he retreated to the cloche-covered dishes.

Much as Hunter had predicted, the scent of food in the air had awoken the beast, which was why he'd ordered pancakes and mozzarella sticks for him too.

"You got a problem with this?" Hunter queried, not sounding particularly concerned either way.

My gaze drifted between the two of them. "What I do with my body and who I let inside it is my choice," I countered before he could reply.

Stan's nose scrunched at the bridge as he bit into the gooey cheese.

"I've spent almost as much time as you've been ignoring him trying to get you together. Why would I have a problem with this?"

Hunter's gaze dropped to his tablet which had lit up with a notification. "Just checking."

I arched a brow at my younger brother when I saw him stare at my throat. He smirked at me as he lumbered over to the table with the two dishes in his hands.

He was a heavyset man, all brawny muscles and brute strength, but that he was walking around like a Grizzly bear who'd knocked his head into a tree told me exactly how much he'd been drinking earlier.

As he demolished his breakfast, he asked, "Which guard did you bring with you?"

I shot him a narrow-eyed glance. "I didn't bring one with me."

"*Porca troia*, Aurora," he grumbled. "Why didn't you bring Giovi?"

"Because he was busy."

That made him splutter some more. "Busy doing what? Getting his fucking car washed? His job is to guard you."

While that was technically true, I tended to use him as an assistant more than anything. I was a ghost in the city so having a guard was superfluous in my opinion. Plus, Giovi was a tattletale. Everything ended up getting back to Luc.

Still, the best defense was offense. "He's busy clearing up *your* mess."

"My mess? Which mess?"

'*Which*' sounded about right.

I just sniffed. "How long are you staying in Vegas? Earlier, you said tonight. Has that plan changed?"

Still scowling, he shrugged. "Nah."

Relieved, I nodded. "Good. The city shouldn't be without one of us *in situ* for long. I can't be away for more than a few days—" I spoke the words to my brother, but mostly, that information was for Hunter. Not that I looked to see the effect my admission had on him. "—not after what happened yesterday."

Stan stared at me in confusion. "The wedding?"

"No. Before the wedding." I prodded the air in front of me with my finger. "That drug of yours is going to cause more trouble than it's worth."

"We're earning a fortune!"

"And that's enough for you after what I told you? You've forgotten, haven't you? Well, I haven't."

My anger must have triggered his memory—his shoulders hunched and he put down the mozzarella stick.

"What happened yesterday?" Hunter inquired, shifting my focus back to him.

"A client killed one of our girls. Strangled her then passed out in the bed because he had a weak heart."

Surprise flashed in Hunter's eyes. "Jesus."

I studied Stan's expression, read his guilt, and shook my head over it. He knew what he was getting into, and he undoubtedly knew the consequences better than most.

"I told the madams not to allow clients to hire girls if they're showing signs of being under Red's influence."

His mouth gaped. "You can't do that."

"Watch me," I seethed, feeling the fire of my temper starting to lick away at my control.

I prided myself on restraint, but nothing about yesterday had been a barrel of laughs. Nothing.

I felt Hunter's gaze on me, so I turned to him with raised brows. His smile was there. A smile I hadn't seen in years because we hadn't been face-to-face for that length of time. Somehow, now, I had different smiles to add to my memory banks. The one after he came. When I pleased him. When I displeased him…

God, I really didn't need to get horny now.

Stan broke into my lust-induced thoughts with: "The council will go crazy."

"They're crazy anyway. We're not running a charity, and we're not good guys, but I refuse to allow this to happen again.

"Carmela told me this is a growing problem, and the statistics don't lie. Around the board, all the madams have had to hire more security."

It pained me to say this, pained every last one of my feminist bones, but I had to embrace the bare truth of feminism—every woman had the right to do with her body what she willed. Including the selling thereof. "Each girl is a product, and these users are damaging the product."

"The council will argue that the profits are too high to risk."

"We're not the government, Stan. We don't sell out our people to make a quick buck, not when it's a stupid investment in the long term.

"A night with one hooker in some of our establishments is upwards of ten thousand dollars depending on the client's kinks. He beats the shit out of her—how many nights on the job is she going to have to pass on?"

"High-end hookers don't work every night," Hunter pointed out, making me glower at him.

"That's what you take from that comment?"

He hitched a shoulder. "I'm not disagreeing with you, just wanting to make sure you don't hit the council with that argument and they give you that as a rebuttal."

Huh.

Well, he did have a point.

I shifted the argument: "In one night alone, a cheaper priced hooker earns about a thousand—"

"Jesus. We're doing something wrong. They're averaging about five-hundred here."

Stan muttered, "Cost of living's higher in New York City." Pride filtered into his voice as he continued, "When Rory took over the stable, she upped the hookers' wages, doubling them. Not just for the high-end stuff, but for the regular working girls."

That same pride seeped into Hunter's expression. "So, a bad beating will take her out of work for at least four days, depending on the severity of the attack."

"Or, ya know, the permanency of it?" I sniped, agitated by this conversation even though I was the one who'd shifted us onto it.

Thinking of women as products pissed me off, but my only consolation was that for that grand they earned, we took a stipend of thirty percent. That meant they took home seven-hundred-bucks. I'd prefer that than working at a fast-food joint for fifteen bucks an hour and barely covering rent.

Hunter grimaced. "Poor girl."

My exhalation was shaky because my guilt was raw. "They only work at our establishments because we're supposed to provide safety. If Red nullifies that then we'll lose our stable."

"So it's true, then?"

Eying Hunter, I asked, "What's true?"

"That you freed all the trafficking victims from the Fieri brothels?"

I tipped my chin up. "That should not come as a surprise."

"It doesn't, but you've been managing to keep things nice and tight up there. Not much intel is flooding down this way."

"That's because I'm good at what I do." I sniffed at him, seeing the sparkle in his eye that... Wow. That meant something different now, didn't it?

In *Hunter*, it was his amusement at my cockiness.

In this version of Hunter, the one cross-sectioned with D, it probably meant something else.

Praise.

Or a potential punishment.

Oooh.

Immediately, I squirmed on my seat.

"If you're going to get turned on, I'm leaving," Stan threatened.

I didn't even blush. "Then get out."

"Fuck's sake," he grouched, but he gathered his dishes and headed out of the room, leaving me alone with the man who, at one point, I'd known better than I knew my brothers but who also came with new secrets. Secrets I wanted to uncover. "This suite better be fucking soundproofed. That's all I'm saying."

Neither of us watched him go. Our eyes were fixed on each other.

"Did you know I've been wanting to see you in my team jersey since college?"

"I didn't know that, but—" I cleared my throat. "—it didn't take much to figure it out when you dressed me in it."

His lips twitched. "I used to jack off to the thought of you in it."

"You did?" I whispered on a breath, the words hitting me harder than they should.

"I did." Then his satisfied hum of moments before disappeared and in its place, in a pleasant tone that had a bewildering concoction of dread and desire flooding my system, he said, "Don't think I've forgotten about you not bringing a guard with you, Rory. Stand up and show me what belongs to me. Show me the *tesoro* that I need to make sure is protected at all times."

That strange moment hit me again, the blurred lines of Hunter and D colliding as I got to my feet, feeling both embarrassed and needy as I lifted up the jersey.

"Higher."

I obeyed.

His jaw clenched. "Put your hand down the boxer briefs."

I complied.

His knuckles bled white as he clutched at the armrests of his chair as he saw my fingers through the white cotton.

His breathing turned heavy, loud in the silent room.

I knew D well enough to know that he'd have told me to touch my pussy if that was what he wanted so I kept my hand frozen in place.

He licked his lips. "Take off the jersey and the boxer briefs."

Tugging it overhead, I folded it and placed it on the table. "Hunter?"

"Yes?"

"Can I take the jersey back to New York with me?"

A guttural sound escaped him. "You want to sleep in it?"

I did.

But I also wanted to hear that noise again.

I peeped a look at him, noticed his knuckles were impossibly whiter than before, saw he seemed to be on the brink of losing his control. "I do."

"Fine," he choked out. "Take it with you. But I want pictures. That's the deal. Every night. Agreed? And when we video call, no more blue silk robe. You start off in that."

"Okay," I agreed shakily, oddly turned on by the idea too. He didn't want me in silks or laces. Peekaboo bras or corsets. Just his jersey.

How very *Hunter*, I thought as I dragged down the underwear so I was naked.

His gaze was fixed on the necklace he'd gifted me that sat between my breasts. "Now, eat your breakfast."

What?!

"Hunter!" I whined. "Is this because of the guard?"

He arched a brow at me.

That was a yes, then.

Fuck.

Cockblocked by past Aurora.

"I don't need a guard! No one knows me. I'm a ghost in the city."

Okay, so Robert Macmillan knew me...

"You're not a ghost here. This is a city belonging to another faction—"

"That you lead!"

"And you know we're having issues with the *Reyes Dorados!*" His tone turned silky. "Your safety is my priority even if it isn't yours. If losing out on what you should have had will ram that message home, so be it."

I sniffed.

"Eat your breakfast, Aurora, before I make it impossible for you to sit down," he bit off, patting his lips with a napkin. "Anyway, I only set out the jersey because Stan is a bloodhound for food. When we eat, no more clothes for you."

The notion was oddly arousing.

"Sit down."

With a pout, I obeyed.

A couple minutes later, he murmured, "We'll have to take the commute in turns. You can't leave New York and I can't leave Vegas, but we'll make it work. We can alternate with me flying up there and you flying down here—"

I should have known Hunter wouldn't put the load on me.

God, he was so *good*.

It was almost a tragedy that his grandfather had gotten him involved in this shady underworld.

"When I'm there, I'll pick the outfits I want you to bring down for your stay here and what I want you to wear that week—"

My brows rose because *that* was new.

He saw my surprise too. "Yes, Aurora, I want to control your wardrobe." His hands tightened around the armrest again. "I want to…" He gritted his teeth. "I'm going to have to work hard to not be totally overbearing."

"You don't have to." I took my seat again and calmly cut up some of the cold pancake. It wasn't as good as before, but somehow, with the AC hitting every inch of me, it was damn tasty regardless. "Green is go and red is stop, remember?"

His nostrils flared. "I don't punish like *him*."

No names were mentioned.

"I know."

"Is that going to be a problem?"

"Wasn't for the last couple years, was it?"

"You were still self-punishing. I won't allow that anymore, Aurora," he warned. "That *will* earn a punishment, and you won't like it."

"Maybe I don't like this," I grumbled. "Getting me riled up and then stopping."

"Your nipples tell me otherwise, and I know if I touched your cunt it would be drenched."

He had me there.

Bleugh.

"You come when I tell you to come. You eat when I tell you to eat. Got it?"

Well, there went my hunger for pancakes, switching with a thirst for his dick. Still…

"I do need—" I released a breath. "I need something, Hunter. Pain… the need for it won't go. I wish it would."

"And I'll give you that. Just in my own way. I've spent three years watching you, seeing how you function, Aurora. At this point, I know what gets you moaning more than you do."

My throat bobbed at his frank admission because he was undoubtedly correct.

I struggled with self-punishments. I craved the release but could never do it right. Never got the angle I needed. Never managed to scratch that itch so I was always heavy-handed to make up for it.

A couple spanks from him earlier and my ass was pinker than when I flogged myself. He had a *thuddy* spanking action that softened into a sharp sting. My butt was going to be sore when I flew out of here if he kept that up.

I almost purred at the thought.

"And I'll make sure that whatever we do, you'll feel throughout the rest of the week."

Now I did groan. "I brought the belt."

A twinkle appeared in his eye at my admission. "So, you justified this trip with the visit to Bert, but you came prepared to see me…"

It wasn't a question, but I answered it anyway, "I did."

He drummed his fingers against the armrest. "I like knowing that. And did you bring all the plugs?"

"I did. They're in my case in the car."

"Good. I think you need to get used to wearing that while we're apart, moonlight."

I swallowed but softly gave him a truth he was well aware of, "You know chastity isn't a punishment for me."

"I know. But the plugs are." He beamed at me as if that conversation had just resolved some thoughts and doubts that had come to him since that explosive sex out on the terrace, and he topped it off with a: "Finish your breakfast."

So, with me butt naked and remarkably comfortable despite the fact I'd never eaten naked at a table with a fully-dressed man before, conversation shifted and I rolled with it despite being beyond aware of my pussy and how wet I was and how there was going to be a stain on the seat below me.

We talked about the upcoming CONCACAF Gold Cup Final, which was taking place in Vegas, discussed last night's events with the branding iron, and I even shared news of 'Agatha' with him, to which he drawled:

"Trust Stan to besmirch a saint."

To which I'd slapped my hand against the table. "See? That's what I said! I told him to change the name."

"To what?"

"I didn't pick one for him. I'm not that much of a control freak. He could have picked *any* saint in the whole freakin' world. I'm not exactly a theist, but nooo, my baby brother had to call out Saint Agatha." I huffed. "Not on my watch."

He'd chuckled and we'd carried on talking, and once I'd finished my breakfast, I found myself sighing out a truth, "I missed you."

He'd just taken a sip of orange juice and my admission had him choking on it. I'd have smiled but I didn't want him to know that I liked having that power over him. He was still Hunter, after all. Still goofy. Even if he could paddle my ass better than I could when armed with a cat o'nine tails.

"You know I missed you," was his simple reply. "I won't let you run again, Aurora."

Swallowing at the intensity in his voice, I slowly nodded, accepting that truth at face value. "I need you to protect this, *us*, Hunter," I admitted. "Please?"

"You can trust me, Aurora."

"I know I can."

"No. You don't. It's been a day. A single day. That's not long enough to reverse back the hands of time, *but* you'll learn." He tilted his arm so he could look at his watch. "In your building, is there somewhere for my guard to stay?"

The change of topic had me frowning. "Of course."

His gaze turned distant. "If I'm still here, there's no problem with your security detail's living arrangements."

"It seems pretty damn pointless to have a guard when we'll be in our mutual apartments the whole time. They'll just be sitting on their asses."

"Who says we'll be in our apartments the whole time? Tonight, for example, I need to go to a meeting and then onto one of our clubs. I assume there'll be tasks you need to fulfill while I'm with you, no?"

"Yes. I suppose." I blinked. "You want me to come with you while you work?"

Scoffing, he told me, "You think I'm going to waste a single fucking moment that you're in Vegas, moonlight?"

A pleased blush graced my cheeks. "Oh."

He laughed because that had shut me up. "*Oh.*" Slyly, he asked, "Do you want to spend time with me? Or do you want to stay in this suite and wait for me to get back, hmm?"

"No," I blurted out. "I want to be with you, please, Hunter."

"And do you want me to spend the time we have together alone in your apartment while you're working?"

I blew out a breath. "No."

Did he have any idea what an admission that was?

From the gratified glint in his eye, I thought he might, but he only queried, "Then we need our guards with us, don't we?"

"Yes, Hunter. We do. I'm sorry."

A small smile curved his lips. "I like it when you say 'please' and 'thank you' and 'sorry.'"

I wasn't polite by nature. That meant I'd have to start saying them more, earning my way into his good graces with words when my actions fell short of his expectations.

I couldn't predict the future, but I knew my submissive side wasn't built for a 24/7 dynamic. I was too domineering, too ready to fight in my work.

Pissing him off was going to happen.

I thought he knew where my mind had taken me because a soft chuckle drifted from his lips. "Already planning a rebellion, Aurora? I have no problem dealing with mutiny. You'll learn that as we go."

Heat flashed in my veins like he'd replaced the blood with gas and had set it alight. "I look forward to the lessons, Hunter."

Something gleamed in his eye. Something that made the hairs at the back of my neck stand on end, but unfortunately, he changed the topic. "Before we go out, I have to check in at the casino floor, so I'll head into the stores downstairs and pick something for you to wear this evening."

"Thank you, Hunter. I'll need my case from my car, please."

He hummed his appreciation of my politeness. "Get me the key and I'll send someone to bring it up here."

Nodding, I made to stand, then I hesitated. "May I be excused, please?"

"You may," he said gruffly, without words telling me I'd pleased him once again by asking.

Shuffling back in the seat, hyperaware of my nudity and his focus on it, I headed to the door then paused when a thought occurred to me.

"Yes, Aurora?" he asked, noticing that I was hovering.

I turned back to look at him. "Stan might see."

He moved over to me, pressed a kiss to my temple, then opened the door and strode out.

Beckoning me forward, he shielded me as I walked down the hallway toward his room. Not once did either of us think to pick up his jersey or to cover me in it.

It was, somehow, the most exposed I'd ever been in my life, and I'd never felt more exhilarated or prouder.

I wanted his eyes on me. Nowhere else. *On* no one else. On me and only me.

I should have been too tired for the shiver that rushed down my spine, but I wasn't. It wasn't a horny shiver. It was like my body was telling my brain that it was in complete agreement.

My phone was atop the clothes I'd brought in from the foyer earlier, which was when I remembered I didn't have my car keys.

"The valet has my keys," I groaned. "I forgot. Sorry."

"No worries. I'll let reception know." He bowed his head and pressed his lips to the tip of my nose. I angled back to seek a deeper kiss but he tutted. "Those have to be earned. Remember?"

Hoping that rule was something that would change over time, I swallowed down my initial complaint and nodded.

He cupped my chin, squeezed it, then disappeared.

With him gone, it was like oxygen could flood the room again. I took a deep breath then reached for my phone, needing the equilibrium of work to soothe me.

I had lots of missed calls, hundreds of notifications, but I quickly whittled them down.

Commissioner Kingston had been discharged from the hospital, Giovi informed me.

Klara had been taken to a morgue where one of the techs owed us a couple hundred thousand at one of our gambling dens and he'd registered her as a Jane Doe.

Matri wanted to know why neither Stan nor I were picking up our cells and she was mad because I hadn't said good night last night.

After informing me he'd landed in Sicily, Luc wanted to know if everything was well because he'd 'heard'—Giovi was such a prick— about Klara.

Then there was Rachel.

Every single notification required my attention, but Rach deserved it more than most and I really needed to get that conversation over and done with or it would hang over my head like the sword of Damocles.

Though, to be honest, I'd have preferred being skewered with the sword than sharing the truth with her…

The thought had me pulling a face as I hit her number and waited for her to pick up.

"About damn time," she grouched in my ear as a greeting.

"I've been busy," I retorted with a huff. God, so busy. Deliciously so.

"Busy?" She fell silent. "Oh, my God, I know that voice."

My brow furrowed as I reached into my jeans' pocket where I knew there was a tube of Vaseline. "What?"

"I know that voice. That's your 'I've just had sex' voice."

My lips were sore at the corners so I rubbed the lip salve there, grumbling, "Don't be crass."

She hooted. "Don't be defensive. I heard enough of you and your dates in college to know that voice. The walls were far too thin."

"Jesus," I muttered, tossing the tube onto the bed once I was done.

"I remember because when you got off, it used to give me nightmares."

I wasn't sure if I was sad about that, offended, or just weirded out.

"I have no idea what to say to that."

She made a humming sound and I got the feeling she was eating. "You don't have to say anything. I'm just sharing a truth with you."

"Why?"

"To encourage you to share truths with me. I went to a Lamaze class and they were saying how you had to be honest with your birth partner."

"I'm not your birth partner," I pointed out.

"I'm glad you're not. You'd probably shout at me."

"I wish I could say I wouldn't."

"You get bossy when you're stressed. It's fine. Anyway, I recognized a couple things."

"Which are…?"

"The first was that I hate Lamaze classes."

Chuckling, I moved over to the window, feeling oddly liberated in standing there totally naked while looking over the Strip below. "I could have told you that. You don't like group settings. What are you eating?"

"Ice cream."

"Flavor?"

"*Dulce de leche*. It's delicious. So anyway, I got a doula. She's batshit, but she knows what she's talking about."

"What's a doula?"

"A kind of midwife who isn't trained in the conventional medical practices. Parker—" Her assistant. "—found her for me. She said she was crazy enough that she'd shut me up. I'm not sure if that's a compliment or not—"

"Why are you so chatty?" I butted in, wondering if I'd tumbled into the twilight zone without knowing it. I was, after all, fucking my best friend from when I was a child. A man who'd seen me at my worst. Throw in my ice queen BFF being *bubbly*? The universe was definitely messing with me. "I mean, I'm glad you're happy, babe, but Rex has really ruined you."

Her laugh sounded in my ear. "You say the sweetest things. Okay, but I was reaching the point if you'd let me get there… The doula also encouraged me to be truthful with Rex and I'm thinking we need that too."

"We're plenty truthful and I'm not going to be in the birthing room with you." I grimaced at the very thought.

"You've hidden the reason you and Hunter fell out from me for fifteen years, Aurora," she chided.

Okay, she had a point. Nose crinkling, I muttered, "Why couldn't you stick with a regular midwife?"

"Blame Parker."

"I will. Don't worry. Anyway, what truth did you share with Rex?"

"That after this kid, he'd better get a vasectomy or I'll never touch his penis again."

"When's he got one booked in?"

Her chuckle warmed my heart. "Last week."

That made me snort again. "Go, Rex."

"Yeah. He's… He makes me happy, Rory. I want that for you. So, come on. Please tell me Hunter is the one who fucked you because if he didn't, my heart might break for him, and you don't want to break the pregnant lady's heart, do you?"

"It was Hunter," I admitted then winced when she squealed in my ear. "Jesus, Rachel! You just busted my ear drum."

"I don't care. Oh, my God, he must be so happy. Is he walking around with a big grin? He's been waiting to tap you for so long that his balls are probably still blue."

"I doubt that," I denied. "It's not like either of us are inexperienced."

"Think about the last time you had sex. Think about the orgasm. Compare that to the orgasm you just had. It makes a world of difference when it's with the one you want to be with."

I cleared my throat. "The *five* orgasms I just had."

"Shut. Up! Hunter's got game! Woot!"

"You're irrationally excited about this," I complained. "It's weird."

"No, I've just been waiting for this moment since forever and I'm happy! My best friends are finally getting their act together and I no longer have to be referee."

"Don't resign just yet. I don't think we'll stop butting heads."

"Yeah, but you can fuck out the aggression. Yum! I used to wish you two would just screw each other's brains out so that you'd stop bickering all the time."

"We don't bicker."

"You do."

"We butt heads."

"Same difference."

"It isn't," I insisted. "Anyway, I don't have long. We're going out."

"You're not going to shortchange this moment, Aurora," she chided. "We can talk later—"

"It isn't that long of a story. But remember, it's bad. I warned you about that yesterday."

"You did, and I'm a defense attorney for an MC, the Sicilian mafia, and several other gangs in the city, Aurora. I can handle whatever you throw at me."

"I hope you're right," was my soft reply. Then, before I could talk myself out of it, I confessed, "I'm into BDSM."

"I can see that," she mused, her tone expressionless and free from judgment. It allowed me to breathe easier. "You're so uptight and controlled all the time that it probably feels good to hand over the reins. But… I wouldn't have said Hunter was like that."

I cleared my throat again—I figured that was going to happen a lot. "No, he is."

She whistled. "Hunter *does* have game. Okay, continue."

"This is very difficult for me, Rachel, and I'm only sharing this because I trust you implicitly. I hope you know that."

"I do, honey."

"Marcus was a—" I choked on the word 'my.' "—Master."

Her silence was telling. "Right?"

"I-I let Marcus do things to me, Rachel, that I've never allowed another man to do before *or* since. One day, we were alone in the house and he started working me over. I liked it at first, then he did something I didn't like and I safeworded but he didn't listen."

"The bastard."

Unable to argue, I sighed. "He was always testing my boundaries, though, and he got me through it and back into the scene."

"That was still a breach of trust."

"It was. Like I said, he started things up again, got me back into the frame of mind he wanted, and I now know that Hunter thought he was beating me. He walked into the room to save me."

"Hunter has the best timing, doesn't he?"

I rubbed the side of my neck. "I suppose he does."

"But I'm guessing you didn't feel appreciative at the time?"

That wasn't a simple yes or no question so I croaked out, "I've never been so humiliated in my entire life, and I don't know why, Rachel, I swear I don't, but when I looked at him, I climaxed. I came so hard.

"I was covered in sweat and Marcus's piss and cum and I was bruised and there were welts that were bleeding and…" I blew out a breath. "Hunter saw that. He saw me at my worst. He saw something I'd kept a secret my whole life."

"And that's why you pulled away from him?"

"Yes."

"It wasn't his fault, though," she pointed out gently.

"No. But I still had to run away. Mentally. Seeing as college wasn't going anywhere." I sucked in a breath this time as the cloying shame started to bite into my organs as if it were barbed with broken glass. It tore at the softest parts of my soul. "I didn't have a scene with Marcus again. We didn't have sex again. I-I'm probably why he attacked you," I confessed miserably, needing to get the words out.

Yes, Hunter had told me that my not putting out wasn't the reason for Marcus's behavior, but the worry was too ingrained to dismiss.

"He attacked me because he'd fetishized my pregnant body, Aurora," was her flat response. "He'd been making suggestive comments toward me for months. You did *not* control his actions. He abused you and he abused me. We were both his victims. Do you hear me?"

She didn't hate me.

I didn't realize, until that moment, how tense I'd been. I slumped against the window, twisting around so that my back collided with the glass and propped me upright.

"I hear you." God, I needed confirmation: "You don't hate me?"

"No. I don't hate you. I could never hate you. In a way, you're my Hunter—you've seen me at my worst, Aurora, and you never judged me for it."

"Never," I said passionately. "Ever."

But that made me feel bad about distancing myself from Hunter. Because she was right, yet she'd never pulled away from me.

I, on the other hand, had stacked a million miles between Hunter and me while we were still sharing the same roof, never mind after graduation.

"So why did you think I'd do the same with you?" she asked, drawing me out of my thoughts. "How many times did you stop me from hurting myself? Do you remember when you caught me when I was going to throw myself down the stairs to have a miscarriage?" Her voice had morphed, turned small.

Chirpy Rachel had been aggravating, but I realized that I liked that side of her better than this one. I was a bitch for giving her shit about being content.

"I remember. How could I forget?"

We were silent for a moment, but it wasn't as tense as I'd have expected. Fraught with the past, muddled with secrets, but not bitter or tense.

"We both wasted a lot of time on Marcus, didn't we?"

I released a soft exhalation. "I suppose we did."

"Yesterday, you asked me if I was keeping something from you." Her inhalation was audible. "Hunter told me earlier this year that it was 'your year'. That he was going to win you back.

"I hope you let him because I think you deserve a good guy like him, Aurora. You deserve to be loved. You deserve to have a life that isn't just work, work, work. Trust me, I know.

"We're such a pair, you and I. Both of us overworking overachievers. Coasting through life instead of experiencing it…

"But we're safe now. We've got men who'll fight past our obstinacy to see beneath the surface. We need that. Do you trust Hunter?"

I couldn't share the truth about Hunter being D and vice versa. That was too private, too personal right now, and it wasn't like she needed to know everything about our sex life, just like I didn't need to know everything about hers.

So, without that as proof that I was right to trust in him, I murmured, "I trust that he'll never hurt me. That if anyone hurts anyone, it'll be me doing the damage."

"You need to not let that happen, Aurora. No more running."

"He just told me that too."

"Listen to your best friends, then."

"He and I haven't been that for a long time, Rach, but maybe we can get that back. We've been texting more this year so maybe that's a start."

"I hope it is. Next time the three of us are in New York, we're going to meet up like old times, you hear me?"

"I hear you." Softly, I said, "Thanks for understanding, Rach."

"Was it really so difficult to share that with me?"

"You've no idea," was my raw reply. "But you deserved the truth. Thank you for not judging me."

"I love you, dingbat."

"Love you too, Rach." I heard the elevator ping. "I have to go but I'll call when I'm back in the city."

"Good. Have fun, Rory. You've earned it."

She cut the call so I didn't have to, and instead of heading to the door, I just stood there, staring at the room, letting the ghosts of the past fade away.

I'd shared that with her so I didn't have to share it again, and while I'd never be free of it, I determined that there'd be no more focusing on the past.

Just the present.
And, hopefully, the future.

37

HUNTER

I KNEW the extent of the outfit I'd chosen for her would have taken her by surprise.

She'd probably thought I'd just grab her a dress and that was it.

But, no.

I'd had decades to think about the moment she'd belong to me, and while that didn't look exactly as I'd imagined—with a ring on her finger and on mine—I was going to take every opportunity to bind her to me.

Hence the detail I'd gone to. Something she should get used to.

The Gallinaro had a luxury shopping mall in one of its many wings, and I'd had a personal shopper take up the full outfit as I dealt with business in the main hall of the casino where someone had been caught counting cards.

Small fry for the owner of the casino, but security knew to contact me with these situations because I was always intrigued by how they gamed the system.

The guy, unfortunately for me, had been a disappointment. No skills outside of a rudimentary understanding of how to count cards, nothing worthy enough to pick his brains over.

So when I headed upstairs, I was too late to watch her dress, but I got the punch to the gut instead of seeing her in her glory.

"Fuck," I growled, watching as she spun around in the process of putting on the earrings I'd chosen for her.

She shot me a smile that, for Aurora, was shy, then she did the cutest thing—she curtsied.

Well, there was next week's spank bank material.

"Thank you for the outfit."

Ah, she'd taken note of my earlier words that I appreciated it when she was polite...

"Do you like it?" I had a feeling she would but I wanted confirmation. Dressing her in things she didn't like wasn't my aim here.

"I love it. It's by one of my favorite designers." She bit her lip when she saw the single flower in my hand. "Is that for me?"

"It's for your buttonhole," I concurred, but I didn't move away from the doorjamb as, teasing, I drawled, "Give me a twirl."

A grin creased my jaw as I watched the woman of my dreams laugh like a little girl as she did as I asked.

Her dress was an oversized suit jacket that went down to midthigh, and it made me think of how she'd look if she wore *my* jacket but, of course, that would be scandalous for the circles in which we ran.

The sleeves were rolled up her forearms, and there were several buttons that made the sharp tailoring pull taut around her waistline, revealing the curves beneath the jacket to me.

In the deep V from the two lapels, I had the money shot of her tits. I'd pulled one of the De Laurentiis legacy necklaces from the vaults downstairs too, and the long rope of diamonds naturally fell between her cleavage. They matched the earring that she'd just slotted into her earlobe.

"You put everything on I had laid out for you?"

She slipped in the other earring. "Yes. And didn't put on what you missed."

That had my grin widening as it meant, beneath the jacket, she was bare apart from a garter belt and black stockings with a seam along the back. The dress was for her, but those, as well as the shoes, were for me.

On her feet, she wore strappy heels that were impractical as fuck but which did things to her legs that made me want them wrapped around my ears.

"Do you have a preference for my hair?"

"Down. Always wear it down when you're with me." Before I could kick myself for forgetting to specify that, she nodded and graced me with yet another shy smile that was going in my mental scrapbook. The urge to see what belonged to me now was too strong an impulse to ignore and it had me growling, "Open up the jacket, Aurora."

I heard her soft exhalation as she unfastened the buttons, and I could no more stop myself from moving toward her than I could stop my heart from taking its next beat.

Once I'd carefully placed the camellia onto the dresser, I reached for her, cupping one of her tits, tweaking the nipple hard enough that she moaned, tugging on it until she yelped and surged onto tiptoe, then I smoothed my fingers over the line of her stomach before reaching her pussy.

Allowing my fingers to ghost over the silky flesh, tips stroking over her piercings, I murmured, "No makeup. Good girl."

"You didn't leave any out."

"Such obedience," I teased then watched as she pressed her hands onto my chest, leaning into me as I ghosted my fingers over the outer labia then flipped her clit ring back and forth.

When her nails dug into my pecs, and her breath whispered over my lips, I knew how ready she was for my touch.

What I didn't realize was how ready *I* wasn't.

When I slid my fingers deeper, her slickness coated them.

"Is this pussy greedy for my cock, moonlight?"

She whimpered. "Y-Yes, Hunter."

I watched her face for any lingering signs of discomfort as I pressed my finger inside her. I hadn't been gentle with her earlier, but her eyelashes fluttered and she sagged into me as I used the lubrication of her juices to rub her clit.

Her forehead fell against my lips and I pressed a kiss there before I rumbled, "We're going to leave this suite with you drenched in my cum, Aurora." She tensed but didn't argue. "Wherever we go, you're going to feel me deep inside you, and you're going to know who you belong to."

A harsh breath soughed from her.

"Do you want that?"

"Please, Hunter. *Please*."

Satisfied she wanted that as much as I did, I continued, "I'm not going to close the door so if you make a sound, I'll stop. Do you understand me?"

Her cheeks pinkened. "Stan—"

"He's at the other end of the suite, but that doesn't matter. I don't want him to hear you so you'll obey or face the consequences."

Aurora leaned deeper into me. "Yes, Hunter."

I gave her temple another kiss then gently pushed her backward until we were near the windows. I had a choice—muss the jacket or muss her—but I wanted her dressed like this when we headed out so I ordered, "Give me the jacket." She shrugged it off her shoulders and passed it to me. "Hands on the glass, ass out."

With bloated pupils, she obeyed, hands moving to the window, her butt sticking out. She apparently had a sixth sense because she didn't move into an inverted 'L' position but pressed her tits to the glass and tipped up her ass for me. I gripped both cheeks, tugging them apart to reveal the rosette to my gaze.

The edge of my thumb brushed across it, making her shiver and urging me to change my plans.

"Stay here," I ordered before I retreated to the packages that I'd had sent up for myself earlier. "Where are the plugs, Aurora?"

"The top drawer of your dresser, Hunter."

My plans having shifted, I kept an eye on her as I moved to the door and gently pushed it to a close. Then, humming as I collected everything I needed, I placed the items on the armchair a few feet from where she was standing which was positioned to look out at the view that encompassed not only the Strip, but the city and the desert in the distance as well.

Once I'd undressed, I grabbed the drop-shaped plug first and rubbed the toy down her slit and back again. With my other hand, I parted her ass cheeks after I'd slipped my fingers inside her cunt. I used her juices to lube the rosette, gently thrusting a digit into her at first. I knew she could take my dick because of the plugs I'd made her use.

I prepped her until she was moaning, wriggling against me in a way that made my cock ache more than ever.

"Be still," I snarled at her, shaking my head when that only made her whimper—and not in distress, either.

Only when I could scissor three fingers inside her did I pull back. "I changed my mind. I want you to scream for me, Aurora." That was when I thrust the plug into her ass. She released a soft sob and surged onto her tiptoes.

Twisting the small shaft that ordinarily locked onto the chastity device, I watched as her pussy lips fluttered in response to the fullness in her ass. It was a siren song I couldn't ignore.

Unable to resist slipping my dick into her cunt first, I shuddered.

She felt like fucking heaven; everything I'd been dreaming of since puberty had hit me and I'd stopped seeing her as just a friend and as a girl. A girl who'd turned into a beautiful teen. A teen who'd morphed into a terrifyingly powerful woman who was willing to submit to me.

To *me*.

Goddammit, I wanted in that cunt more than I wanted her ass, enough that I tossed my plans away for a second time.

I guessed that was the problem when you had decades' worth of fantasies to work through.

"Oh, fuck," was her guttural response at being double stuffed as I slowly started to thrust deeper, her palms sliding against the glass as she struggled to take all of me with the thick plug in her ass too.

Sensing she was growing overwhelmed, I used my clean fingers to reach around us so I could rub her clit.

In the distance, the sky was beginning to change as twilight approached, but the entirety of the city was spread out beneath us.

When, finally, I bottomed out, I pressed my clean hand atop one of hers on the glass and, in her ear, whispered, "This city belongs to me but the only thing I want to be mine is you."

A mewl escaped her as I rocked my hips back and started a slow, easy pace, the smooth dildo in her ass making her impossibly tighter.

Bridging our fingers together, I gradually started to thrust into her faster. When her moans turned into grunts, I squeezed her digits before I unlocked them and grabbed her throat.

Gripping her there for a moment, I encouraged her to straighten up so her back and my front collided. With her in my chokehold, I let go of the reins on my control.

It wasn't enough.

Needing my other hand, I settled her throat in the V of my arm and held her to me. "You're fucking mine, aren't you?"

"Yes," she cried. "I'm yours. I'm yours."

"You belong to me, Aurora." With my clean fingers free now, I started spanking her pussy. "Don't you?"

"I do," she wept, juddering with every slap to her cunt. "I do."

"This cunt is mine, isn't it?"

"Yes," she shrieked when I gave her clit a quick rub before I patted the tender folds.

"You're doing so well, baby. Taking every inch of my cock like this," I snarled, aware that I sounded like a beast and not giving a damn about it because this was what she brought out in me. A side I hadn't even registered when I'd been D.

"I want every inch," she sobbed. "I need it!"

"Come for me, baby. Come for me," I growled, fucking her faster, spanking her harder, giving her what she needed until she exploded around me, everything clenching down until I was seeing stars.

She screamed and I groaned, my fingers tightening around her throat until she was whimpering, but her pussy milked me of every drop of cum I had.

As we both came down from the high, she drooped forward as I pumped my hips before I leaned over and awkwardly reached for the other plug that was waiting for me on the armchair. Only then did I pull out. I wanted to see my cum drip down her thighs but that was for later.

Tonight, I promised myself.

Thrusting the cold plug into her pussy sent her back onto her tiptoes, and I looked at her in satisfaction, stuffed full with toys I'd bought her.

Gently, though, I tugged on both until her hips were swaying, enticing me to come back home.

Knowing we had to leave, I stopped teasing us both. "Keep the plugs in until we go."

"Y-Yes, Hunter," she said shakily, letting me twist her around so I could rub my lips over her throat and the marks I'd left there. They were distinctive against her flesh, but they looked good.

People could misconstrue what had happened, but I didn't give a damn about anyone's opinion. My finger marks looked better on her than the rope of diamonds that had been in the family since the eighteen hundreds did.

Tenderly now, because I'd been so rough with her, I dropped a kiss on her lips. A loving one. She'd earned it.

Rory sagged into me, her trust, in that moment, so evident that it made me feel like I was on cloud nine.

As we deepened the caress, I smoothed my clean hand down her spine before I pulled back. Otherwise we'd never leave the Gallinaro and I had things I needed to take care of tonight.

"I just need to get changed then we can go."

She nodded and sank back against the glass as I retreated to the closet.

"I expect you to be ready to leave by the time I'm back," I warned her, amused when she yelped then scurried over to the bathroom to fix what, to me, was already perfection.

38

AURORA
DON'T WORRY, BABY - THE BEACH BOYS

THE 'RECENTLY FUCKED' look suited me.

After I'd made myself presentable and used the bathroom for the final time to remove the plugs, where I'd almost swooned at how much cum he'd pumped into me, I noticed the color in my cheeks, the gleam in my eyes, and the faintest spring to my step as I bustled around.

I'd been faithful to D so I hadn't had sex in ages, and I'd missed it. Missed the mess. The connection. The exhilaration.

Marcus hadn't destroyed sex for me, and I'd had my share of partners in the years since his death, but the submissive in me had definitely been too wary to try anything in real life.

There was an irony to the fact I'd thought I'd trust D enough for that, but it was only now that I was aware Hunter *was* D that I knew that to be a lie.

Hunter's unique position enabled me to open up to him. Enabled me to take a step on a path I'd been wary about traversing since my Master's death.

Checking myself out in the mirror, I had to admit—Hunter knew how to dress a woman.

In the masculine-cut jacket with the sexiest garter belt I'd ever seen beneath it—the straps weren't lacy, but were bands, so I looked like I was bound—and the most impractical shoes on my feet, I knew my wardrobe was in good hands if Hunter intended to choose my outfits as he'd said he wanted to over breakfast.

A small smile curved my lips once I was finished, but I was destined for disappointment because, rather than seeing Hunter's fine ass getting ready, Stan made an appearance at the bedroom door and was calling out, "Bro, Brunu's here."

Did that mean we were traveling with his Capo? Ugh. Fantasies of sucking him off on the journey to wherever we were going tonight disintegrated into dust.

Hunter called out in Sicilian, "Let him into the living room, will you?"

"Sure thing."

I opened the door and peered out, hissing, "Stan?"

My brother turned back to stare at me, his brows lifting as he took me in. "Well, look at you. Hate to say it, *soru*, but Hunter's clearly what you've been missing because your vibes are actually less Cruella De Vil and more Catherine Tramell right now."

"Is that supposed to be a compliment? I'm either channeling someone who'd steal and kill puppies for a fur coat or a psychopath who'll willingly flash her pussy to distract a bunch of men… You're really great for my ego."

He snickered. "How about Evita?"

"Have you been watching late night movies again?"

"They help me concentrate."

I didn't even bother rolling my eyes. "Are you leaving?"

"Yeah. Flight's in a couple hours. Good thing, too." His mouth pursed. "The council's pissed about the banning of Red in the brothels. They called a meeting."

Shit! I really needed to check my phone.

I'd forgotten how much of a distraction sex was.

No wonder I'd managed to reach the heights I had.

Chastity was good for career goals, apparently.

"When?"

"In two days."

I grimaced. "I'll be back by then."

"Why are you even here?"

"Hunter's grandfather wanted to see me."

"In prison?"

"Well, that's his new home, Stan, so yeah. I tried to go earlier but there was a lockdown."

Stan scratched his jaw—he'd only just shaved but stubble was peeping through already. "You have to be back for that council meeting or Luciu will end up breaking his—"

"I won't ruin his goddamn honeymoon," I interrupted with a glare. "I said I'll be there."

"Good. Without Luc, we'll both need to bring our A game to keep them in line."

I wafted a hand. "They'll be easy to control."

He sighed. "What do you have on them?"

"That would be telling." I smiled. "Don't worry about the council."

His grunt told me he was more worried about what I *wasn't* saying than their well-being. "What does De Laurentiis want to speak with you about? I didn't think you had a relationship."

"We don't."

"Must be business, then, but why not contact Luc? Don to Don?"

"He isn't the Don anymore. Hunter is."

Stan leaned against the wall. "He did good last night. Surprised me. Didn't think he had it in him."

I pondered what I knew about Hunter and hitched a shoulder. "Hunter's the kind of guy who has no problem buying his girl tampons and then killing her mugger." I didn't mention that he'd been dominating me for the last couple years. Didn't think that would be particularly prudent. "I'm not surprised by anything he does now."

Stan clucked his tongue. "A couple rounds in bed and he's tamed you already, *soru*? I'm disappointed."

"Hardly tamed, Custanzu, more like enlightened." I tipped my chin up. "I suppose I should thank you for playing the part of matchmaker."

He peered at his nails. "I think you should name your firstborn after me."

"As if," I scoffed, but I leaned up and pressed a kiss to his cheek. *"Grazii, frate."*

His smile was sheepish. "You and Hunter are like hotdogs and mustard, Rory. You match perfectly.

"Plus, you've been such a miserable bitch since you moved to New York that I had to do something. You got any sourer, you'd have been turning that wine you collect into vinegar."

"You're such a charmer," Hunter intoned, his words making an appearance before he moved out of the door, the camellia he'd bought for me earlier in his hand. Arching a brow at Stan, he demanded, "Who's the hotdog and who's the mustard in this setup of yours?"

Shooting a knowing look at the flower, Stan's retort was, "That's for me to know, and you to not find out."

Hunter settled his hand on the small of my back. My ovaries did the salsa at that unexpected touch which, somehow, reminded me of the courtly gesture down in the lobby when he'd kissed my wrist.

Rachel was right—Hunter did have game, and I'd been missing out on that my whole life.

I was a fucking moron.

"We have to go," Hunter said apologetically. "Council meeting."

"Rory's going with you?"

"Not officially." Hunter looked at me. "I'd like you to listen in."

I had no idea why that made me blush. "What for?"

"I've always valued your insight."

"You don't trust your council?" Stan queried.

"Do you trust yours?"

Stan chortled. "Fair, fair. Well, I'm going back to New York anyway. Before I leave, though…" He straightened up and slapped a hand on Hunter's shoulder. "Just know that if you hurt my sister, I'll have to chop you into pieces and throw you in the Hudson." He beamed a grin at him. "There, that's my brotherly duties sorted."

"Custanzu Valentini," I sniped, "we're not living in the eighteen hundreds."

He winked at me then started to saunter off. "Man's gotta do what a man's gotta do."

Hunter shrugged. "He has a point. I did the same for you with Marcus."

My mouth rounded. "What?"

"I didn't threaten him with the Hudson though. Just to dox him online and destroy his reputation." He grunted. "Not that that worked out in the end."

I turned into him, my hands settling on his pecs. "You didn't." I didn't mean to sound turned on, but I couldn't help it.

"Of course I did. Why wouldn't I?"

That had me swallowing. "I-I…" I leaned forward and pressed my forehead against his chest. "When will you stop surprising me? I literally just finished telling Stan that nothing you do surprises me then you go and prove me wrong."

I felt his laughter in my soul. "My life goal is to keep you on your toes, beautiful."

The compliment had me straightening up, and he took advantage by pressing a kiss to my temple and slotting the flower through the buttonhole. "As complex and intricate as you."

"What is?"

His lips twitched. "The camellia. Look at the patterns within the patterns." Before I could start gaping at him, he raised his arm and stared at his watch. "Damn, we have to move. We're running late. I hope the traffic isn't crazy," he grumbled under his breath as he hustled me down the hallway toward the main living area of the suite, completely unaware that he was blowing my mind.

Brunu reminded me of a Sicilian Peter Griffin but he was surprisingly charming as Hunter introduced us. The two of them immediately started talking business as we took the elevator down to the garage.

Content to listen to them discuss the troubles they'd been having with the *Reyes Dorados,* I remained quiet, watching the Strip as we drove by then peering with interest at the different neighborhoods we passed through.

Darkness hadn't fallen fully by the time we hit the Nine Hills area, so I got to see the reason *why* it was called that—nine peaks took up the entire distance, with the De Laurentiis *palazzo* overlooking all of them as well as the rest of the gated community that had congregated beneath the massive building.

Unsurprisingly, the interior of the house matched the Gallinaro.

Gold and marble were the major interior themes, bright red, the color of blood, thrown into the mix every now and then.

There were fountains in the main entrance, (yes, plural,) and the circular room reminded me of Luc's office in *Russu* because it, too, had several offshooting doors.

Brunu headed through one, and when I made to follow him, Hunter tugged on my hand. "This way."

"The Don has a special entrance to the council room?" I inquired curiously, the first words I'd spoken since we left the Gallinaro.

"No, but this is an alternative entrance and it means you can sit in and listen without anyone knowing."

"Brunu will know," I pointed out, curious about the subterfuge.

"I trust him implicitly. He was Bert's right-hand man for thirty years."

Even though I knew he was in a hurry, I forced him to stop moving.

When he whipped back to look at me, his brow furrowed with impatience, I asked him softly, "What in particular do you want me to listen out for?"

He studied me for so long that I didn't think he was going to answer, but, eventually, he admitted, "I'm not sure."

"You just have a bad feeling?"

"I do."

"You think there's a leak?"

"Yeah."

"To whom?"

"Either the DA's office *or* the *Reyes*. I'm not sure. Maybe both. To the outside eye, we've got a similar structure as the *Cosa Nostra*. But there are seven families on the council, not five." He reeled off the names. Then, he surprised me by saying, "They're not as powerful as they believe themselves to be."

"What's that supposed to mean?"

"Bert's actions, or as he'd say, *inactions*, after your grandfather's murder were down to his Consigliere advising him to stay out of East Coast business.

"Bert's never forgiven himself for that, and after he dealt with his Consigliere, he started to shift his power base."

I didn't let bitterness at those *inactions* of his grandfather distract me. "Explain."

"He has a kind of shadow council. The two never meet. Only Bert, and myself in recent months, ever attended both meetings."

"Why would he do that?"

"He had trust issues."

"Just like you."

He nodded. "I'll explain more if you're interested later, but I just... I've always trusted your input and, to be honest, this is the first council meeting I've ever headed and I like the idea of you being there."

Smiling, I stepped into him, my hand coming up to cup his chin. "You're so sweet sometimes."

He snorted. "That's not a compliment, is it?"

I didn't answer, just leaned up and pressed my lips to his cheek, careful to comply with his 'no kissing' rule.

I wasn't pleased about not being able to freely kiss him, but as I'd gotten ready earlier, I'd wondered if that was his way of protecting himself. Of keeping distance between us, distance he managed, until he was ready to trust me fully.

Subs weren't the only ones whose hearts could get broken.

He tilted his head to the side and slotted his hand to the small of my back again. "Was that for good luck?"

"I don't think you need it. I'll listen out for anything funky going on. I've got your back, Hunter."

Then, he proved my theory was right.

Light flickered in his eyes and, for whatever reason, that prompted him to gift me with something I really, *really* wanted.

His mouth.

He pressed a kiss to my lips. Soft, at first. More of gratitude. Then, out of nowhere, he blew up, shoving me against the wall, making the portraits nailed on either side of me flap with the force of our momentum.

His tongue thrust along mine, and one of his hands moved between my thighs. His fingertips sought and found my clit ring and he twisted it and teased it, grinding into my pubis bone as he fucked my mouth.

A soft cry escaped me in surprise, but I was *not* about to argue.

As he shifted his fingers down, thrusting one inside me, he rubbed my clit with the heel of his wrist and didn't stop kissing me until I was coming.

The explosive orgasm was as sharp as it was unexpected.

He left me a reeling, flustered mess as I used the wall to prop up my shaky legs when he pulled back. Dazed eyes stared at him in bewilderment, then I watched as he crouched down and, somehow, he was propping one of my legs on his shoulders, and his mouth was where his fingers had just been.

"I thought we were in a rush," I moaned.

He didn't answer. At least, not verbally.

His tongue swirled around my clit, sending sparks through the sensitive bundle of nerves. I cried out when he suckled it, his teeth tugging on the ring, moving down to slide into my gate where—

Fuck.

His groan told me what he felt about his cum in my cunt.

Shuddering, trying not to fall over, I pressed a hand to my mouth as I dealt with blow after blow as he ate me out as if I were a snack.

"Hunter!" I shrieked when his tongue returned to my clit. A couple sucks and I was a fucking goner.

As the explosions ricocheted through my system, he was rearranging me again. This time, his dick was out, my thighs were around his waist, and he was—

"Oh, Christ!" I screamed, fingers flaring against the wall for purchase.

"You take me so fucking beautifully, baby girl. Just look at us. Look at us, Aurora," he barked when I didn't immediately comply.

He pulled back so that I could see better, shifting the hem of my short dress away so that nothing hindered the view of his dick entering me, stretching my pussy lips wider apart than even the labia piercings parted them.

My head rolled on my neck as I watched us, my juices sliding out to make his shaft wet, streaks of white from his earlier attentions coating his length, his thick flesh so ruddy and mine so pink—it was *bewitching*. I almost wanted to recreate this in a sketch.

"You're so fucking beautiful, Aurora. Everything about you. Such a good girl for me. Look how right we are together. So goddamn right."

His words had me moaning, but that was nothing to the noises that escaped me when he started to thrust faster, uncaring that my shoulders were knocking into the wall, uncaring that it was making the portraits on either side of me bounce in response.

Hunter moved into me, his mouth settling around my earlobe before he tugged on it with his teeth—hard enough to sting. I cried out again, shrieking in pain while he growled in my ear, "This cunt is mine. Say it."

"It's yours."

"All of it," he spat.

"This cunt is yours," I whimpered.

"It belongs *only* to me."

"It belongs only to you. Only to you, Hunter, only to you," I sobbed.

His hips sped up, pistoning into me, jackhammering me, until I knew I'd feel him deep inside me for the rest of the week.

Then, his fingers were back on my clit. Just a couple gentle strokes, such a contrast to this rough fuck against the wall with millions of dollars of art surrounding us, and he detonated the explosion inside me again.

He razed me to the ground only to build me back up when he snarled his release in my ear, hissing and cursing through it as if it felt so good it was painful.

I knew how that worked—this was bittersweet delirious agony.

I continued sobbing through my orgasm, almost certain that I could feel his cum filling me, spurting inside, drenching my cunt with him.

When the pleasure waned, minutes or hours later, and reality returned, both of us were still breathing hard, and my face was nestled against his throat, and he was peppering kisses wherever he could reach.

"Mine, Aurora," he rumbled, the words and the timbre making me shiver as the small hairs on the back of my neck stood at attention.

"Yours, Hunter," I agreed softly, knowing that was his way of telling me he was going to pull back.

I shuddered as he did, his cock sliding out of me, cum with it.

"Clench your muscles. I want you to feel me inside you all night."

My skin heated at the order. Especially when, once I was back on my wobbly feet, he toyed with me further. His fingers delved between my thighs, touching what he'd just claimed before he lifted his hand to my mouth.

Without a word, I opened my lips and sucked the digit clean, tasting our mingled essences as I did so.

"Couldn't resist." *It wasn't an apology.* He sucked the finger I'd just licked clean, his eyes darkening as he stared into mine. "Later."

Well, that was a promise I intended to hold him to. Even if my body was buzzing from pleasure overload.

With a shaky inhalation, I staggered when he propped me against him and started walking me back down the hallway. It was long and the heels did interesting things to my stride, making me uber aware of how wet I was and how his cum was starting to slide down my inner thigh.

It should have been mortifying; instead I felt replete. *Complete.* Marked, and satisfied, and rested. My mind quiet.

It was heaven.

With my befuddled brain slow to return to full functionality, the first thing it noticed was that there was a line of portraits on the walls, not just a few staggered here and there.

It was an interior corridor, but the windows were arched with marble surrounds, and benches were lined between the arches so a visitor could appreciate the art, not the incredible view of the Nine Hills beyond.

As I glanced at each portrait, I came to recognize a piece by Mary

Cassatt—not unlike the one in the Met, it depicted a mother with her child. A boy this time, though. Dressed in a sailor suit.

My heart stopped at the sight, and the urge to draw it, to try to recreate such a simple display of a mother's love was all-encompassing.

I sucked in a breath and Hunter, proving how in tune he was with me even if his mind was on work, especially as we were beyond late for this meeting, asked, "Are you okay?"

"*Se.*" I didn't realize I'd answered in Sicilian until he arched a brow at me. I rarely spoke my mother tongue, something that hadn't changed in our years apart. "I just recognize that artist."

He cast a look at the painting and smiled slightly, his fingers squeezing mine before he said, "The council room is just over here."

Guiding us through a door a couple paintings away from the one I wanted to look at in more detail, I found myself in a small sitting room. There was an open arched doorway that led into a hall where I could hear men's voices but couldn't see a table where they were seated.

He guided me over to the back wall where I wouldn't be seen and raised my hand to his mouth.

When he kissed my inner wrist like he'd done earlier, I shivered which made him grin. It was light in nature, happy, but something was gleaming in his eyes…

I'd seen it in Luc.

The moment the man became the Don.

God, if that wasn't hot too.

Winking at me in farewell, he strolled over to the arch. I watched him go, dressed in his three-piece suit that was tailored to perfection, lovingly cut to his every inch.

My tongue about cleaved to the roof of my mouth.

Unaware of what he'd done to me and, voice gruffer than usual, he declared in Sicilian, "Gentleman, take a seat," as he passed through it.

I'd have fanned myself if my business brain didn't kick in and overtake the Neanderthal instincts that made me want to tackle him to the ground and have him fuck me again at the idea of him holding that meeting with my pussy juices on his mouth.

God help me.

Three times we'd had sex today. *Three*. I was sore and I didn't even give a damn.

A chorus of 'Don' from seven different voices jarred my thoughts before the proceedings commenced in earnest.

The entire meeting was in Sicilian. I didn't know why that surprised me, but it did.

That Hunter was trusting my opinion, my *instinct*, made me want to be of use to him. Hell, it made it *imperative* that I was of use especially when my own council gave me so much shit because of my chromosomes.

Thanks to years of pulling apart testimonies and witness statements, I quickly figured out who was who. Something that was facilitated by the fact that, much like with my council, only the heads talked unless they were Hunter's Capo, Brunu, or his Consigliere, a guy named Paulu.

Lombardo had a lisp. Marina rolled his 'r's. Abellardo had the worst accent in the history of the world, where Papparlardo spoke perfectly, using the Catanian vernacular much as my family and Hunter did. Amato's line hailed from Palermo, and La Rosa sounded like he'd deepthroated a tin can at some point in his life.

"We heard about last night," was Lombardo's 'greeting.' "Why didn't you kill him?"

"Are you going to be bringing out the brand more often, Don?" Papparlardo queried, the notion seemed to excite him. "I remember the good old days when Alberto used it. We had everyone pissing themselves in fear."

Hunter grunted. "The *Reyes* want to fight dirty. I'm willing to play their game. And, Lombardo, I didn't kill him because killing him wouldn't do anything. His boss doesn't give a shit about him.

"Would you care if one of your foot soldiers ended up dead? Of course not. You'd pay for the funeral and make sure the widow was cared for, but that's it.

"I set a new precedent last night—any *Reyes* who are found on our territory are to be treated to the brand. Understood?"

Murmurs started up at that, and Brunu stated, "The Don asked me to get them replicated. Should take a week but every head of house will get one."

"They get branded just for trespassing?" Amato asked.

"Yeah. Then we know what we're dealing with. Did you do the sweep like I asked, Brunu?"

"I delegated that to the La Rosas. They know that area better than me."

"What did you find, La Rosa?"

"More bodies than we initially thought. They've been using that area as a dumping ground for a while."

"Jesus," Hunter snapped. "How did you only discover this now?"

"It's the desert, Don," Paulu muttered. "How do we sweep an area that big?"

"You find a fucking way, that's how." I heard fingers drumming against the table. "Nobody knew about their graveyard?"

La Rosa cleared his throat. "Graveyards, Don. Plural."

"How many?"

"At least four. Some are bigger than others, and some are better tended than others."

"Meaning?"

"Meaning that some, they dug deep. Others have been ravaged by the wildlife."

I pulled a face at that. *Lovely imagery.*

"Why did they just dump the bodies out there yesterday if their practice is to bury the dead?" Hunter questioned.

Paulu spoke up, "They must have been in a hurry."

La Rosa argued, "I don't think so, Paulu."

"The reason we knew about the bodies in the first place was because the LVPD told us," Paulu argued. "They must have been disturbed by the cops."

"No," La Rosa countered. "They'd been there too long."

"They weren't dumped there yesterday?"

"No."

"What did you do with the corpses?" Hunter asked.

"Burned 'em." La Rosa grunted. "I can still fucking smell it too."

"Has anyone heard this news about *Las Alphas* joining forces with the *Reyes*?" Lombardo queried which, unsurprisingly, triggered outrage around the council table.

Las Alphas were the Mexican street gang that strung up their enemies on the sides of bridges. They ran Baja California and Sonora, the two states that bordered this part of the US.

Uneasy now, I straightened up in my seat, curious as to what the others were going to have to say to that.

I'd heard nothing about a potential business deal between one of the largest street gangs in Mexico and a small fry gang in L.A., and that was the kind of shit I listened out for.

Lombardo, fighting to be heard over the loud voices, declared, "I'll tell you what I know if you'd just fucking listen!"

The murmurs faded but not altogether. They stopped entirely, however, when Hunter barked, "Let the man talk!"

Christ. That was D talking right there. And this was not the moment to remember him getting all 'D-like' in the hallway ten minutes ago.

"Thanks, Don," Lombardo said, his pouting audible because his word hadn't been enough to command the room's silence. "I got a man down in San Diego—"

"Why?" Hunter questioned.

"His wife's family lives there and she's pregnant. They're staying in the city until after she gives birth. My man, his name's Marco, said there's talk about some product drifting into the city that's pure as hell.

"Don't know how they're getting it, but it's starting to trickle in. Don't think it will be long before it's in L.A. The *Reyes* were getting their product from the Guadalajara Cartel, but they had that falling out back in May."

"When the *Reyes'* leader stole the head of the Cartel's daughter, no?"

"Yes, Don. They're living up here now."

Christ, I remembered hearing about that. The *Reyes'* gangbanger was in his early thirties, and she was only seventeen.

"They're a regular Romeo and Juliet," Hunter mocked before asking, "What's L.A.'s poison of choice?"

"Meth and weed," Abellardo answered. "But since the opioid epidemic, heroin's making a strong comeback. It overtook meth last month for the first time."

Hunter hummed. "Lombardo, what product are they trickling into San Diego?"

"Heroin," he confirmed.

"The cartel must be getting it from the Middle East then. That's the best supply of poppy, no? We might need to reestablish ties over there."

"The Sheikh wanted to meet with Bert back in June, Don," Brunu admitted. "But it wasn't possible with the court case."

"Damn. I wonder if that was why he wanted to meet." Hunter heaved a sigh. "Okay, that's a priority that lands on my desk. I need to know if he's diversifying his portfolio or if we're still his only clients.

"As for this shit with *Las Alphas,* if they get their foot in the door in L.A., we can kiss that territory goodbye. We'll meet in two days and I want to brainstorm ways to stop L.A. from turning into a war zone again.

"Did anyone manage to get through to Alberto?"

"No," Brunu replied. "Lockdown until tomorrow at 9am. No calls in or out and we haven't managed to get a phone to him yet."

I didn't have to see Hunter's scowl to know that he was pissed. "Shit. I was hoping to find out why he wants to speak with Aurora."

"That's why the Valentini girl is down here?" Abellardo queried. "Bert sent for her?"

'Valentini girl.'

I huffed.

"Apparently." Hunter grunted his annoyance. "Okay, before we end this, is there anything else?"

The sound of something dropping on the table made itself known to me. Something made me think it was a stack of papers.

My ears pricked as Hunter demanded, "What the fuck is this?"

"We got them in the mail this evening," Paulu muttered, and something in his tone… I had no idea why, but I knew he'd just lied.

Only, what was there to lie about?

When he'd received whatever it was Hunter was looking at?

"They're surveilling me?"

I straightened up.

"It's not the cops or the Feds. The local bureau is friendly to us. You know that, Don." Brunu grunted and then I heard the sound of knocking. It took me a minute to realize he was tapping the table. "See this one? Dumbass got his arm in the shot as well as most of your bedroom furniture rather than the stars of his fucked-up show. Look at that ink."

"The *Reyes* are tailing me?" Hunter repeated, his voice darker than ever.

"Looks like it, Don," Brunu said uneasily.

Papparlardo, around a chuckle, inquired, "Does Luciu Valentini know you're messing around with his sister?"

Mortification flooded me. Horror came next. Shame and then distress followed swiftly on their heels.

I was in the photos too?

"This is a threat," Hunter rumbled. "Some of these pictures go back weeks, but they send them today? When Aurora's here?"

"Maybe they're trying to cause bad blood between the Camorra and the *Cosa Nostra*?" Amato asked. "Stir up trouble there, divide our attention?"

"I'm friendly with the Valentinis—"

Papparlardo snorted. "We can see that for ourselves."

"Friendlier with some more than others," Abellardo agreed around a chuckle.

I was going to be sick.

Oh, God. I—

They were looking at pictures of me having sex with Hunter.

This afternoon… the beautiful—

What we'd experienced…

It was being weaponized.

I staggered to my feet and rushed out of the room as fast as I could.

Once again, my sex life was being held against me. *Used* against me.

Was it any wonder my sexuality was entangled with shame? With disgust?

I didn't care if the council had heard my departure. I rushed down the hall, but it took too long in my heels, so I ripped them off, flung them as hard as I could at the floor, and I started running.

Ignoring Hunter's shout, I didn't stop until I found the door we'd come through. When I was back in the entranceway, I knew I must have been turning green with the need to vomit, and that was when he caught up to me.

He cast me a single look, seemed to read between the lines that I wasn't just running away, then picked me up as if I weighed nothing. I struggled at first, but when it agitated my stomach even more, I stopped and gasped, "Bathroom."

"On my way," he said gruffly.

A couple seconds later, I was in a restroom that looked as if it belonged in a bordello, and Hunter was supporting me as I threw up everything I'd eaten that day.

He didn't move away. He stayed there, holding my hair back as I sobbed over the toilet. His other hand shifted to my back and he ran it up and down, soothing me—it didn't work.

A part of me wanted to see the pictures, wanted to know how graphic they were, but I knew it'd make me want to vomit again if I did.

After a couple minutes where nothing came up, with my stomach settling somewhat, I shifted back, closed the lid, flushed it, and woodenly asked, "How bad?"

"Bad." He pressed a kiss to my temple which was both sweet and gross considering how close I was to the toilet. "I'll deal with this."

Turning my head to the side, I stared at him, saw the resolve on his face, and my mouth trembled. "I—"

"Hush," he rumbled before repeating, "I will deal with this."

"How can you? They saw us together—your council, and the *Reyes*." Bile curdled in my stomach again. "They—Oh, God—"

My gender was consistently used against me in New York. That the same was happening here made me want to scream.

This afternoon, when he'd asked me to go onto the terrace, I'd hesitated. *For good reason.* I should have said no. I should have fought back. God damn me for being a fool. I'd been led around by my clitoris, letting my pussy think for me rather than my brain. My brain that had *never* failed me. Ever.

Submission made me dumb.

It made me—

One of his hands cupped my chin, and another gripped me by the nape. I started to struggle free, not in the mood for this, until he snarled, "Aurora, nothing we did together is shameful. As much as they saw of you, they saw of me, and I'm not puking my guts out or crying about it.

"I understand it's different for you, and I'm sorry this has happened, but my biggest concern is the fact they sent the photos *today* of all days.

"You. Are. Mine. I will make whoever breached our privacy pay and I will get back every copy of those images and I'll burn them. And any enemy who looked at them will regret it because I'll scoop out their fucking eyes with a spoon. But you do *not* retreat from me, do you understand? No running away."

My mouth quivered as I sobbed, "They saw us—"

"Keyword there is *us*. And we're in this together."

Gaze bleak, I sagged against the toilet. His hand curled in my hair again and he gently tugged on it, drawing my head back. When his lips returned to my temple, I shuddered.

"I'm sorry, moonlight," he breathed against the tender skin. "I'm sorry that they took our private moments together and tainted them. I'm sorry that your privacy was breached and that something you hopefully enjoyed was marred by this. I'm sorry that your sexuality is being used against you—"

He got it.

He. Got. It.

I almost started sobbing again at his sensitivity. His ability to empathize even though the fallout from these situations almost always fell more on the woman than on the man, as his council had proved with their remarks.

The old boys' club would paint me as the whore, but he was the one boning a Valentini and getting kudos for it.

"We're not heading to the club anymore," he continued. "We'll return to the Gallinaro—"

"No!" I shrieked. "I'm not going back there. They clearly know how to surveil you there."

"We'll stay at the *palazzo* then. I'll take you to the rooms I use when I sleep here." He hesitated and I knew it took a lot for him to ask me: "Do you want me to use a different room?"

Did I?

This wasn't his fault.

But… "No. But I don't want to—"

He hushed me. "We don't have to do anything you don't want, moonlight. Plus, there's more to what we have than just sex, Aurora." Straightening up, he held out his hand and helped me onto my feet. "I'll get you settled in, but then I have to work. Will you be okay? Do you need some warm milk to sleep?"

When I didn't reply, just wavered between my options, he hummed and answered for me: "It'll help. Just a small glass."

When he picked me up again, like I was some delicate flower not the mastermind behind the *Cosa Nostra's* downfall and rebirth, I didn't argue.

I burrowed my face into his throat, trying not to exhale too heavily so he wouldn't scent vomit on my breath, and I let him do what I allowed no one in my life to do—I let him take care of me.

He held me like I was precious.

He murmured soft words to me as he carried me down hallways and past a myriad of rooms, explaining the layout of the place as we went. Only stopping to hit the intercom and to mutter something I didn't bother trying to understand before, eventually, we reached a room that was actually bearable, which told me Hunter had been behind the decoration in this suite, and he placed me on the floor beside the bed.

I took in the mishmash of themes with muted interest as he unbuttoned my jacket/dress and stripped me out of it. Next came the garter belt and stockings.

Something that should have been a distinctly sexual act of disrobing me morphed into one of a caretaker.

I permitted him that, not knowing if he was aware how special that made him, how rare an occasion this was, and when he tucked me beneath the sheets, I turned on my side and stared at some art across the way.

The place was cool and calm, dotted with trinkets that reminded me of Luc's apartment in the city.

He and Hunter always had been packrats, but Hunter had traveled more and that was evident in the different styles in the suite.

He had African carvings and a big amethyst geode on a dresser above which was the line drawing that caught my eye. Large, about six feet in height, it depicted a woman, the lines of her back straight, arms overhead like she was reaching for the sun.

As I studied it, Hunter moved around, retreating at one point when a soft knock sounded at the door then returning with something in his hand.

When I saw it was a glass of water and a tumbler of milk, I rasped, "I don't need that. The water, yes, but not the milk."

He placed the glasses beside me on the nightstand. "It's there if you change your mind." He surprised me by grabbing a thin bottle of mouthwash and a second small tumbler from his jacket pocket. I blinked, wondering what else he'd retrieve from his Mary Poppins pockets, but apparently that was it for the moment because he ordered, "Wash out your mouth."

It was more practical to use the restroom.

Though exhaustion hit me like a Mack truck, I knew I'd regret not using the bathroom later. So, grabbing the bottle and clambering out of the covers, I headed over to his connecting bath and used the facilities then gargled the mouthwash.

Upon my return, he was standing there, watching me, his gaze concerned as he helped me into bed like I was frail, and he settled the sheets around me again.

It was comforting, enough so that, within minutes, I was out.

Distress might have triggered this nap, but that didn't mean my brain went to sleep too.

And deep in the night, late enough for the moon to be heavy in the sky, I woke up in Hunter's arms. He had one leg hooked over mine, his forearm clamped over my stomach with his face burrowed in my throat.

Any other man, I'd have probably tried to get out of his hold. Though I really needed to use the bathroom again, I stayed there, relaxing in his embrace as I ironed out the particulars in my mind whilst staring at the camellia he'd dropped into a glass on the nightstand.

The *Reyes Dorados* thought they could invade our privacy and get away with it?

They thought they could weaponize a tender moment between us?

They thought they could leave threats at our door to make us cower into submission?

Never.

Aurora Valentini bowed for only one man and he was currently wrapped around her like a glove.

As if he knew I was getting angry, a soft mumble sounded in my ear, "You okay, moonlight?"

I didn't know where the made-up nickname came from, but I loved it. Loved the intonation on his lips. Loved how it felt like a verbal caress.

Instead of demurring, instead of talking about what had happened, I queried, "Have you heard of a man called Martinez?"

"Pretty common name," he muttered drowsily, his nose moving along the curve of my ear.

"Not when it's the only one he goes by." I knew that from Luciu. Jennifer had once been Martinez's accountant. She'd had to falsify his birth certificate earlier this year to open up an offshore bank account for him. "His partner's Eva Kingston."

Oh, the irony, considering I'd only met her father, the commissioner, yesterday morning.

Her name got his attention. "Wasn't there gossip about her decapitating a fellow cop while undercover?"

"There was."

"And didn't it come out that the decapitation rumor was a New World Sparrows' conspiracy against her? Savannah Daniels reported it and it went viral?"

"It did. Martinez is her husband. He used to lead *Los Lobos Rojos* in New York." I could feel the cogs in Hunter's brain stirring to life but he didn't butt in, so I continued, "Martinez started that street gang when he was a teenager and he turned it into a private army. *Los Lobos* are the largest providers of guns in the tristate area."

"Where are you going with this, Aurora?"

"A wolf doesn't recognize a king," I mused softly, using the literal translation of both gangs' names. With the *Reyes*, supposedly, being the golden kings, and the *lobos* being the red wolves. "All a wolf sees is prey. We've had dealings with Martinez. He'll meet with me—"

"You want him to deal with the *Reyes*? Why would he get involved in a gang war on the West Coast?"

I loved that that was his first question and not one about why I was getting involved in Camorra business.

Last night's despair hadn't weakened me in his eyes.

There was no fury like a woman scorned; and after all these years apart, he still knew that among the Valentini siblings, I was the one who was quicker to embrace a vendetta.

"Because he's been out of the game for a long time, Hunter. I bet he and his wife are bored shitless. Plus, his brother started the Guadalajara Cartel. There's bound to be bad blood when a gangbanger steals a seventeen-year-old from her family... A seventeen-year-old who just happens to be Martinez's niece..."

Hunter was quiet a moment. "He'll need to accept Camorran dominion over Vegas and our L.A. territories."

My smile was bloodthirsty. "Leave the negotiations to me."

39

AURORA
ETERNITY - ROBBIE WILLIAMS

THE FOLLOWING DAY

WITH MY FLIGHT to Aspen chartered on a Camorra jet, and an initial meeting arranged with Martinez and his wife, Eva Kingston, I'd been in the gallery staring at the Cassatt portrait since before dawn, using a ballpoint pen and a sheet of printer paper to try and self-soothe.

Keyword being 'try' because it hadn't worked.

With everything that had been going on, it was no surprise that I'd found it impossible to calm down. It just took me a while to figure that out. Sure, I was pissed about the breach of privacy, but mostly, I was resentful about having to leave Hunter.

That resentment made the lines of the drawing harsh, revealing an anger to the world that was probably impossible to note by my expression.

When Hunter tracked me down and made me drink the coffee he brought me, he said, "The prison's open for visits today."

My pen skewed off course, scraping over the little boy's cheek. "Okay."

He took a seat beside me. "Are you going to go see Bert?"

"I guess I'd better."

"I doctored a flight log so that it looks as if you left Vegas this morning."

Impressed, I stared at him. "You can do that?"

He shot me a grin. "I just did. Had one of my men return your rental car, too, so you can drive to the prison in one of my rides.

"Behind you, there'll be two guards following in an SUV. They won't be allowed onto the facility, but they'll escort you to the private airfield after the visit, okay?"

"Seems like a lot of effort—"

"Seems like the perfect amount of effort from where I'm standing," he said with a scowl.

"You're not standing. You're sitting." I took the cup from him and sipped at it. "This is good stuff."

"Only the best in my grandfather's *palazzo*," he teased, making my lips twitch.

I turned to look at him, saw the fatigue in the shadows beneath his eyes. "You didn't get much sleep last night, did you?"

"No. I was tracking down the places where the photographer was positioned."

"Did you find them all?"

He yawned. "No. But I'll get back to it in a little while."

I bumped my shoulder with his. "You should nap."

"I want to finish that up first." He stared down at the sketch. "I'm glad you still do this."

"It usually clears my mind and helps me problem-solve so it's not as relaxing as it looks."

"We need to get you some hobbies."

I thought about the conversation Stan and I had had at the wedding reception, and I hummed noncommittally.

"How about collecting furniture for you to bend over?"

I darted a look at him, saw his blank expression, and chuckled to myself. "Sounds like the kind of hobby a man would pick."

"True, true." He raised his arm, then, and almost as if he expected me to reject him, cautiously slipped it around my shoulder.

It was a sharp cry from D's dominance, but I found that I liked that. If he'd have shoved it in my face, I'd probably have slapped him.

Everything in its proper place.

And reminding me that I liked to be flogged and whipped and be bossed around and have my wardrobe selected for me wasn't the way to go this morning.

I didn't sink into him, but neither did I push him away. We just sat like that as I continued sketching, pretending that I hadn't destroyed the little boy's face with that jarring line of ink on his cheek, taking intermittent sips of coffee from the cup he held for me.

When his watch beeped, I saw the notification on the screen. "It's okay. You can go."

He grunted. "I don't want to."

"I should leave early anyway. If I'm going to see your grandfather before my flight."

"I figured we'd have more time."

My throat felt tight with emotions I didn't know how to express. "Me too." I peeped a look at him. "Will you come to New York like you said?"

He leaned forward, cupped my cheek, and pressed a kiss to my nose. "Try and stop me."

I released a shaky breath, grateful that he hadn't asked if that was okay with me. If he had, I might have said no, and that was the last thing I wanted—distance between us—but my brain controlled my vocal cords and my brain had recently learned that Aurora was a pushover for this combination of D/Hunter.

We parted ways there.

With every step that separated us, I wanted to call him back. Wanted a deeper kiss. A better hug. I wanted to tell him that I was confused and scared but that none of this was his fault.

Instead, I just watched him go, feeling, God help me, like he was taking my heart with him.

An hour later, I headed off the estate in one of Hunter's rides.

Behind me, two guards were in an SUV as he'd promised.

Just like yesterday, the ride to the prison was uneventful, but this time, I was allowed onto the compound for my visit.

On my way to the entrance doors of the visitation room, the sounds of locks clicking and irritating buzzers echoing in the distance, a woman bumped into me as she turned toward her car.

Hell, she more than 'bumped.'

Both of us nearly went crashing to the ground, and had I been wearing my usual heels and not a pair of Vans, we probably would have.

She picked up her shit, dark hair flopping around her face as she scurried to collect the random objects that had dropped from her purse, and because I wasn't rude, I reached for some of the stuff and helped her gather her things together.

Dark eyes captured mine. "Thank you."

Shrugging, I started to get to my feet, but though I could have taken off, I stared at her instead.

"Do I know you?"

She blinked at me, her voice hesitant. "No, I don't think so."

Something about her words, *her tone*, didn't gel with what her expression was telling me.

She didn't evade eye contact, though.

Her lashes fluttered a second too late, and while her shoulders had been hunched before we went down, with her crouching on the ground now, her natural posture was more evident in how she held herself— straight back, weight balanced.

Through her thin shirt, I could also see the muscles in her torso. You didn't get whippet lean without working out hard.

It was, however, the sustained eye contact that sealed the deal— what was with the fake submissive act?

I didn't have an eidetic memory, but I had a thing for people. Nothing like that woman in Rachel's MC who had the unfortunate ability of remembering every single face she'd ever seen, but if they went on my stand, then I remembered them.

But that was what was weird about her—she was distinctly unmemorable aside from how much makeup she was wearing.

I wasn't being dismissive; it was simply that I wondered if she was covering up bruises or something.

Lips pursing, I hitched a shoulder before I nodded at her in farewell. Before I stepped into the facility, I turned to look back at her and found that her eyes, oddly enough, were still on me.

We shared another polite smile before I put her out of my mind and headed over to the entryway where, upon registering, I went through the regular song and dance of showing my ID, getting patted down, and signing the myriad consent forms that were required for visitations.

That was when a guard appeared at my side and I followed her lead.

As she motioned to the controller to open the doors for me, and as more buzzers went off and locks clicked, call it a sixth sense, but my suspicions amped up all the more when I headed into the visitation room and there was no one inside but Hunter's grandfather.

The setup was different than usual.

The guards didn't wait inside, no one hovered, and… the cameras were aimed at the walls.

Call me crazy but I got the feeling the woman I'd bumped into had been here to visit him too.

Going with my gut when I saw him standing behind a table, I mused, "Busy morning, Mr. De Laurentiis?"

To anyone else, that greeting would have been respectful. For me, it wasn't.

I should have greeted him as Don. Ex or not, it was only a matter of days since his incarceration. Don would have been polite.

Except, after last night, I wasn't feeling polite.

Not only was I on edge after that collision with the woman, but I was also bitterly angry and I was sick of men thinking they could bend me to their will when I did *not* give them my consent to do so.

Alberto De Laurentiis, seeming to sense my anger, wisely held out a hand and, tone polite, greeted, "Aurora Valentini, it's a pleasure."

This was my thousandth time in a correctional facility such as this one because my work had taken me here more often than I'd like.

Peering around the visitor's room which was similar to all the others I'd been in—industry-standard moss-green walls, linoleum-lined floors, vending machines with prices that were practically racketeering —I sniped, "Not exactly fancy for a first meeting." But I moved over to take his hand and shake it, taking note of how he looked like an older, more tired Hunter, in a jumpsuit that had been pressed to within an inch of its life.

"The best I can do right now, unfortunately."

Humming, I walked over to the vending machine as he took a seat. I pulled out the coins that I'd brought with me for this purpose, asking, "Preference?"

"Never was that much into candy."

"Gotten a taste for it since you were brought in?"

"Not particularly, but I'd appreciate a selection."

I went through the vending machine, getting one of almost everything with the forty dollars I'd brought with me, then I returned to the table and stacked it all in front of me.

"You clearly have the facility under your thumb already," I stated, pointedly glancing at the cameras on the walls and the lack of guards standing in the corners. "But are they taking care of you? Medically, I mean?"

After reading my *prozio's* medical notes, I knew how the prison system fell short with geriatric patients, and Alberto wasn't a young man.

"I'm not making waves about it. I have to die of something, and I don't intend on living until I'm a hundred under these conditions."

Something about his words had me pausing. "You're not being treated at all?"

"The bare minimum so far." His eyes twinkled. "I'm not concerned. You and I both know I won't make it past Labor Day."

Frowning, I argued, "You can be placed in protective custody—"

"Gussied up solitary confinement?" He snorted. "I'll go out how I came into this world—kicking and screaming. I'm fine with dying, Aurora Valentini, but before I go, I want things settled."

With a stern stare, I asked, "Who was the woman before me?"

"You think she was a girlfriend?" He laughed. "The heart might be willing, but the body isn't anymore. Not that Star would appreciate the inference."

"Star?"

That twinkle made another reappearance. "Hmm. Star."

I angled up my chin. "I know her from somewhere."

"I'm sure you do. She has one of those faces."

"A changeable one?" I scoffed.

Another hum.

"Is she an Enforcer of yours?"

"Did you know that, officially, there are females working for the Camorra, much as, *officially*, there are none working for the *Cosa Nostra*?"

"That's not an answer," I disregarded, ignoring his pointed remark about my status within the *Cosa Nostra*.

"I think you'll find it is. Women are an underestimated tool in our arsenal. They manage to slip through cracks where men's egos won't permit them entry." He reached for a can of soda, pulled the tab, and took a deep sip. "Before I was incarcerated, I never drank soda. Diabetes. Doctors told me I'd go blind if I didn't regulate my blood sugar."

"You wouldn't want to go blind in here," I said uneasily.

"It won't come to that."

The words set me on edge. If he were anyone other than Hunter's grandfather, I wouldn't give a damn. But this *was* Hunter's grandfather, and family mattered.

"Why am I here? Hunter didn't know why you'd want to visit with me either."

He reached for a bag of chips. "You're here to make a deal with me —" Business? Okay, I could handle that. "Just not as the *Cosa Nostra's* Consigliere." He smirked. "Official or not."

Stiff with tension, I grated out, "What kind of deal?"

"I've been watching you, Aurora Valentini, almost your whole life. Not just because of my boy, either, though I've had eyes on him since the day he was born.

"I saw you defend his honor from kids who tried to bully him, watched him fall for you even though you didn't think of him like that—"

"Why am I here?" I interrupted.

"You're here because I love my grandson. But, more than that, you're here because I let your grandfather down."

"Excuse me?"

He waggled the bag of chips at me. "Would you like one?"

"No, thank you," I choked out.

"At the time of your…" He heaved a sigh and, for a scant second, sorrow flashed onto his features. "When your family was murdered, my Consigliere was a fool, and when the Fieris overran the *Cosa Nostra*, he advised me to stay out of it. Not to get involved." He inhaled noisily through his mouth. "I trusted him like Luciu trusts you. That'll explain, I'm sure, why I listened to him."

"How do you know what I do?" was my wary retort.

"I made sure that I know what you're up to. You're cunning. I like that in a woman. Never know what game you're playing, always four steps ahead. Keeps an old man on his toes." More crunching ensued as he ate another mouthful of chips. "First, the only way to make amends was to make sure your grandmother got out of the state—"

"She did that on her own," I sneered. "Don't lie—"

He waggled a finger at me. "You think a woman like her could do that? She was mafia royalty, Aurora Valentini. Much like you, but far less able. Used to having everything done for her. Plus, she was pregnant, and afterward, she was isolated. It wasn't an easy pregnancy, let me tell you.

"Who do you think got her and your father onto that damn boat to Sicily? Who do you think kept her safe? Who do you think arranged for her to marry that farmer?" He pshawed. "She had help. Me."

"How do I know that?"

"You just have to trust me because I don't have any money in this game. If anything, I've spent a fortune trying to make things right." I stiffened at that, on the cusp of telling him his amends came too late for my family, but he shook his head. "You need to calm down. Eat some candy. You could do with the sugar. Might sweeten you up."

"It doesn't seem to be working on you," I groused, but, annoyed, I snagged a roll of Smarties and tore into the wrapper.

Satisfied, he continued, "I'm not telling you this to gain points. There's no need. I can die knowing that I fucked up and I can die knowing that I tried to fix the situation as best I could.

"You and your family wouldn't be reigning over Manhattan again if it weren't for my intervention, and when I get to St. Peter's gates, and if your grandfather is there waiting, he can break my nose a couple times, take me down, but I know, in the end, he'll thank me.

"*You* aren't the Valentini I need forgiveness from."

While his point was bizarre, I conceded to it with a dip of my chin.

"Anyways, I've kept the Camorra unaligned from the Fieris. Never liked how they were the Sparrows' front. Didn't agree with the shit they were doing. Done stuff my way for as long as I've been Don, and this is going to be my final act as that.

"Hunter might wear the ring, but we both know he isn't the Don yet. His place needs cementing, and to be honest, I'm not sure he can do it.

"I love that boy, love him more than my own son, to be honest. He's made these last ten years on this planet a joy to experience, and if I'm disappointed about anything, it's losing time with *him*. But I know his weaknesses and his strengths…

"He's gotten up to stuff over the years," he mused, shaking his head. "Case in point, your husband." I swallowed at his easy mention of Marcus's murder. "Runs the books for a consortium of hitmen—"

"What?!" I sputtered.

He grinned, his pride beaming at me with all the force of a fog light. "Yeah, I was proud of that when he set it up. Kept shit nice and tight too. His Ledger makes the Camorra a tidy sum—"

"Hunter's behind the—" I almost screeched the name, but I remembered where we were and whispered, "He's behind the Ledger?!"

"Sure is. But that's him all round. He's admin. He ain't fists. He needs a wife who'll bring something more to the table than just a pretty face. He needs a wife who'll keep him alive." His gaze was measured as he stared at me. "He needs *you*."

I stilled. "My role is administrative."

"You forget what I've seen over the years." He tapped his nose. "That boy who blackmailed you into being with him… Nice way of dealing with the issue—getting the father arrested for embezzlement. How did you figure that one out?"

My throat bobbed. But… for some crazy reason, I admitted, "He'd pass out from drinking too much vodka. I'd head into his father's office and read things that weren't meant for my eyes."

"That was just the start, wasn't it?"

"I don't know what you're talking about." I did, of course.

"I'm talking about revenge, Aurora Valentini. I'm talking about sixty-five percent of the prisoners you got convicted dying before they served a full year inside." He whistled. "Smart. Real smart. Pulling your own deals. Dangerous, too, of course."

"Worth it," was all I had to say.

"Sure was seeing as most of that sixty-five percent were rapists. Fitting considering your past." He wafted a hand when I jerked upright. "We digress. You're my kind of administrator. You're the kind of administrator that Hunter needs by his side.

"Plus, it helps that the boy's been in love with you since he knew his cock had more use than just aiming at the toilet bowl."

My mouth snagged up in a sneer at the vulgar words. "As you yourself pointed out, I already have a job."

"Where you're hiding in the shadows. A woman like you deserves more than that. A woman like you isn't a Consigliere—she's a queen." He arched a brow at me. "Check your pockets."

"Why?"

"Just check them," he said, tone calm as he continued eating his chips.

The sound made me want to headbutt him.

With a huff, I checked my jacket pockets. They'd been empty earlier—they weren't anymore.

That twinkle made another appearance in his eyes as I pulled out the pieces of paper and placed them on the table between us.

"The one on the left is Star's contact number. She's ex-CIA, ex-a lot of things."

"What about her? Why are you giving me her details?"

"Because she wants Hunter at the top of the Camorra as much as we do."

Drumming my fingers against the table, I mused, "Star… Is her handle Lodestar?"

"Like a door handle?"

My smile was mirthless. "If you expect me to believe the 'old man' act when your grandson is a hacker, then you must think I'm a moron."

A laugh escaped him, and for the first time, sadness penetrated his gaze. *Grief.* "I'd kill to see the children you and Hunter will make."

That made me feel like he had my throat in a chokehold. "What?!"

"Now's not the time for being coy, Aurora Valentini—"

"You can say things about me carrying your great-grandchildren but can't call me by my full name?"

"You won't be a Valentini for long."

Outrage washed through me. "You can't arrange my life for me. You sure as hell can't arrange a marriage—"

"Can't I? It's funny how things have a habit of turning out right. You two would always have been contracted to each other if your childhoods had been spent here, where they *should* have been spent. But fate always catches up with you." He dropped the bag of chips and pointed to another slip of paper. "Read it."

I didn't bother looking at the note. "*Was* that woman Lodestar?"

"She was."

"How do you know her?"

"You don't know Lodestar. She knows you. There's a difference, and I can say that despite being there for her baptism."

"She works for us," I said gruffly.

"I know she does. You can trust her. She won't rat, and she's wicked smart. You just can't trust what she'll do with what she learns."

"What the hell is that supposed to mean?"

"It means she has bigger fish to fry than the mafia." When my brow furrowed, he clarified, "The New World Sparrows. She wants to take them down. She's had my blessing for a long time. Knew her father back in the day. Gerry was a good man," he mused. "His band, *noxxious,* always played at the Gallinaro when he was in town.

"That wife of his though… Never did trust her. Gerry wasn't the same after she got herself killed."

"Doubt she asked to die," I mocked.

"Liars tend to end up six feet under faster than most. Look at the next note."

If we had a short staring match, I'd admit that I didn't back down until he rolled his eyes and conceded defeat.

When I peered at the note, he murmured, "Go there. The contracts are all laid out. My signature's on them, and they just need yours."

"What contracts?"

"For your marriage to Hunter."

I had to laugh. "You know, in these circumstances, it's usually the bride who's in the dark about her upcoming nuptials."

"You're not a regular bride, and it's not as if Hunter's going to complain about who his wife will be. Not when he's been pining after you since he was a kid.

"It'd be embarrassing if it didn't remind me of how my own *patri* was with my *matri.*" He reached for a tube of soft mints. "Like I said, everything is laid out in the contracts—"

"Why did you invite me here and not Luciu?" I demanded, well aware that he was deadly serious, and well aware that this meeting had not taken the turn I expected it would.

Jesus, I doubted even Hunter knew about this, because if he did, he'd be fucking furious.

Somehow, that soothed my temper more than anything else.

"Luciu isn't the one walking down the aisle."

"Wouldn't have thought that'd bother you. Not like most women in the mafia want to marry their husbands."

"Aren't you lucky, then?"

"Maybe I don't want to marry anyone," I snapped.

"I know your council wants you wed. Know that they want to fob a mediocre middleman from one of the families onto you in the hopes of gaining some influence in the inner circle.

"What's the plan? He'll be your beard?" De Laurentiis pshawed. "Woman like you? That'll never work. Dipshit middleman will think he's the power broker in the marriage and you'll end up killing him when he tries to rape you to get you pregnant to make you stay at home and tie you to the stove. That'll cause infighting in the council.

"Pretty soon, a war'll start up and your chokehold on the leadership will come under threat thanks to the mutiny it'll cause—"

"What are you? Zoltar?" I sniped, but I'd admit to feeling shaken because that was something I'd envisaged too.

Mafiosos were proud men. Stubborn. Fool-headed, for the most part.

They wouldn't appreciate me not putting out on our wedding night. They'd think a baby would slow me down. They'd force the issue when I refused to stop working.

It didn't matter that everyone knew *why* I was getting married. The reasons would be inexplicably lost and all of a sudden, I'd be the bad guy for blowing out my husband's brains when he tried to forcibly impregnate me.

Of course, that was just one of the many ways in which things could go wrong.

I had a fertile imagination and a decade in prosecution—I knew how bad things could get behind closed doors.

"My brothers need me," I rasped. I wasn't sure why that was my initial reply, but it was.

He shrugged. "You're not going anywhere, are you?"

My palms felt sweaty as I stared at him. For his part, his calm composure agitated me even more. After the last couple days I'd had, this was the last thing I needed.

"I don't want my grandson to die, Aurora Valentini. I want him to live as long as I have. I want him to have the woman he loves. I want him to have a family."

"You meant it when you said you love him," I choked out.

"I do. My son denied me access to Hunter so it hits deeper knowing that Hunt chose to have a relationship with me despite what I am. Despite why his father picked up and ran."

"Why did he?"

"Never had the balls for it. Hunter's got *some* potential, but he's too diplomatic for his own good. Diplomacy will get his head blown off. I want to stop that. I want you to be his Consigliere."

That had me sucking in a sharp breath. "Out in the open?"

"Out in the open," he confirmed.

"I'm a woman."

"Figured that out without you telling me."

"You already have a Consigliere."

He hitched a shoulder. "Paulu is mediocre at best."

I thought about last night's jibes. "The Camorra is just as anti-quated as the *Cosa Nostra*."

"It is, but we do things differently. We have women in white-collar positions all over the establishment and my men are used to that.

"Most of the casinos are run by women, in fact. The men tend to do the grunt work. Not that I tell them that." His smirk reminded me of Hunter, and it made me wonder if that was what Hunter had meant when he'd said there was a Camorran shadow council. "If you work it smart, you won't have to hide your role in the organization. We've got a turf war going down in L.A.—" No shit. "—and if you two make those fuckers bend the knee to our rule, you'll get the others on side. Fast."

"My life is in New York. My family—"

"We got things called airplanes. They're brilliant inventions. See, the thing is, Aurora Valentini, I worked hard to make sure that I'm the one in here and not my grandson—"

We shared a look.

"Marcus's brother told me once that he wouldn't stop until the person behind his 'disappearance' was behind bars."

"Exactly." He held out his hands. "I sit here so Hunter can be free. I don't begrudge that. In fact, I'm glad it worked out. I'm old, I'm gonna die anyway, but he's still got plenty of years left."

"If you believe in him, why are you making these maneuvers behind his back?"

"Because Brunu, that's my man—"

"Met him."

His lips quirked up. "Brunu and I have figured out a way to keep in touch but we didn't account for lockdown. That messed with things." I'd hazard a guess and say he hadn't heard about the *Reyes* tailing his grandson, as he didn't comment on their audacity just groused, "So I know Hunter's been slow to act.

"He should have called a council meeting the night I was sent up. Instead, he flies to New York to attend a wedding." De Laurentiis huffed around his candy. "Now, we're lucky that it's the Valentini wedding, and we're luckier that you're going to be his bride, because him looking like he's running out of Vegas ain't good optics, wouldn't you agree?"

"I'd agree," I rumbled, flushing.

His bride.

How was this happening?

And why wasn't I telling him to stick his notes and his contracts where the sun didn't shine?

He dipped his chin. "Brunu tells me the second Hunter's away and my ass is in a jumpsuit, our territory gets tainted by those *Reyes*." His cheeks gusted as he sighed. "Slippery slope, *capisci*?"

I nodded.

"Doesn't take much for a house of cards to fall, and the West Coast, though it might not realize it, requires a strong Camorra. We keep the balance. Without us, those penny-ante gangs will make L.A. implode."

"Does Hunter know about this master plan of yours?"

"No."

"Why not?"

"It was only at this moment that I knew you'd agree to it."

Annoyed, I got to my feet. "I haven't agreed to anything."

Alberto just smiled at me. It was a silent, 'Haven't you?' and it pissed me off like nothing else could.

He stood too, carefully weeded through the candy, picked up a box of Mike & Ikes and tossed a couple into his mouth once he'd opened the pack. "You'll make a fantastic wife, a wonderful mother, and an even better Camorran Consigliere, *if* you allow yourself to have it all.

"I can lead a horse to water, but I can't make it drink."

"Charming," I sniped as he moved around the table toward me.

I didn't tense up as he approached, but when he placed a hand on my shoulder as he stared down at me, I scowled at him, severely resenting the height difference because I wasn't wearing heels.

"Your name is fitting."

I blinked. "What?" Why did he never say what I thought he would? Just like his grandson.

"Aurora—a new dawn. Look after my grandson when I'm gone. When I'm not around to keep his ass alive, you're not ready for the level of mischief he can trigger."

"You can't mean—"

"You knew him as a young man. He's not a young man anymore." That twinkle was back in his eyes. "Tell him about the arrangement or don't. Tell him what my plans are or don't. It's up to you.

"Just know that the good of the Camorra is linked intrinsically to the De Laurentiises, and just know that I think he'll get himself killed if he doesn't have someone watching his back.

"I stacked the odds in his favor before I left, but there's a power vacuum if Hunt doesn't step up, and I don't want him swallowed up in it. Only you can stop that, Aurora. *You.*"

He bowed his head then reached for my hand and pressed a kiss to my knuckles.

The move was old world, making me realize Hunter had learned this from him, and when he released his hold on me, I gently ran my thumb over the place where his lips had landed.

"You should ask him about Reilly Green."

"Who?"

He winked by way of an answer.

As he started to walk toward the doors that would lead him back to his cell, I called out, "I won't drop the Valentini."

He didn't even look over his shoulder. "Then my poor great-grand-children will have a severely long name, won't they?"

A guard appeared and he greeted Alberto with a dipped chin that oozed respect. As the door closed behind them both, I watched until I couldn't see the back of either man's heads. Not once did he turn to look at me.

For some reason, that had the breath whooshing from my lungs.

Picking up a can of soda from the mixed snacks he'd left behind, I plunked my ass down on the stool and took a deep sip as I stared at the notes Lodestar had gone to the effort of planting on me.

Brain whirring, I processed the morning's bizarre interactions as best I could before I got to my feet and retreated to the outer limits of the prison where I collected my personal items again.

Once my cell was in my hand, I called the number we used for Lodestar.

"The number you have dialed is not in service. Please check the number and dial again."

Mouth tightening, I picked up the piece of paper I'd been slipped and tapped that one in.

No answer.

That was when I saw I had a couple text messages from an unknown number and some from Luc too.

Luciu: *Where the fuck is the jet?*

Me: *New York? In its hangar?*

Luciu: *It isn't. I tried to make arrangements to fly back for the council meeting, and it isn't there. Have you taken it somewhere?*

Me: *No. I flew to Vegas last night (I'll explain later) but I used a commercial flight.*

Luciu: *Then where the hell is it?*

My brow puckered in thought.

Had Stan used the private jet to fly home? But if he had, he'd have arrived late last night New York time, wouldn't he? The plane would be back in its hangar, just waiting for my neurotic twin to call it to Sicily after only twenty-four-hours on his honeymoon.

Me: *I'll make discreet inquiries.*

Luciu: *I leave for a day and everything goes to shit.*

Me: *Hardly. There's no need to come to the council meeting, culu. I can handle it. Now, fuck off and let me figure out what's going on.*

Switching conversations, I opened up the text chat with the unknown number.

There was a video in the window. Of Stan? In the private jet?

Frowning, I hit play but it didn't immediately load. Squinting against the sun, I shielded the screen, but it was still impossible to see the thumbnail.

Mostly, I could see a tiny Stan sitting on a plane. Well, at least I could tell Luc that Stan was using the jet.

Trying Lodestar's number again, I waited to see if there'd be a response this time.

"Why, hello there."

She sounded so chipper that it immediately pissed me off. Enough that I snapped, "What the hell is going on?"

"I'm afraid that's above your pay grade. I won't be responding to calls from you on the regular, but Bert inferred that you'd be phoning me soon after your visit so I made sure to be available.

"You've caught me just before I'm boarding a flight so we have enough time for me to inform you of the new terms of service.

"I'm not your friendly neighborhood hacker. However, because of my agreement with Bert, I will help whenever you need me, and once I'm out of the country, I have people who can help me if you require them. I just request that you don't send me things that a child could decode, hmm?"

We didn't use her that often, so I wasn't worried about that. But...

"What kind of people?"

"People that even folks like you should be afraid of," she drawled. "You're welcome, by the way."

Dazed, I asked, "What? Why?"

"I'm the reason your brother's wearing the family heirlooms again." She clucked her tongue at my silence. "The amber ring? The cuff links?"

I swallowed. "You're behind that?"

Earlier this year, Luc and Stan had gone to Fieri's grave to rob him of the jewelry the bastard had stolen from my grandfather. Someone had been waiting. Someone who'd done the grave robbing for them.

"Well, Bert and I. It's not like he could visit New York City without triggering an international incident. Consider it a 'welcome back' present from 'Secret Friends of the Valentinis.' There are three of us at the moment. It's a small club."

God, she was annoying.

"How are you tangled up with Alberto De Laurentiis?"

"He called in a favor. Make sure to let me know when his funeral is. I want to send flowers— Ah," she said smugly as alarms blared behind me. "Right on time."

I'd started my short walk over to the car but the alarms had me jumping in shock.

Twisting around to stare at the prison, I saw that guards were running out of nowhere, armed to the nines.

One of them shouted at me, "Ma'am, please vacate the area." Then, when I hovered in place, frozen to the floor, he snarled, "*NOW!*"

That was when I heard a scream of, "Prisoner down!" over a radio, which made my heart start racing and stirred me into action.

Running to my vehicle, I jumped inside. "Was that you?"

She chuckled in my ear. "I'm about to board a plane. Remember?"

"What's going on?"

"I told you—Bert called in a favor."

When the line went dead in my ear, I switched to the 'unknown number' text thread to see what kind of prank Stan was pulling.

Alberto's certainty that he wouldn't make it past Labor Day echoed around my head, tugging at my attention.

"No. It *must* be a coincidence," I mumbled to myself as I hit play on the video.

The only problem was I didn't expect anyone to reply to me.

"Coincidences don't exist." Which was when I felt the tip of a gun digging into my spine through the soft leather cushion of the driver's seat and I heard the click of the safety being removed. "Start driving, Ms. Valentini, and don't stop until I say so."

And as luck would goddamn have it, the video finally began rolling.

Stan's voice declared to the car:

"Aurora, don't you fucking dare come after me." I heard the sound of a smack, of a grunt, but through that groan, my baby brother snarled, "*Para bellum, soru.*"

The family motto.

'Prepare for war.'

TO BE CONTINUED IN 'THE ORACLE'
www.books2read.com/ValentiniFour

AUTHOR NOTE

You may have learned that there has been a delay on THE ORACLE. (You can preorder that here www.books2read.com/ValentiniFour)

Covid as well as the death of my beloved Yorkie, Trever, is to blame for this.

Grief has hit me hard, and Covid has laid waste to me.

But, there was joy in Rory and Hunter's developing love story, and I hope you felt the stirrings of hope too. I'm just slower than my usual self. THE ORACLE has so much heat in it, it'll boil your kindle, so prepare for that.

And, of course, *prepare for war*. ;)

Don't forget the second THE CONSIGLIERE hits 500 reviews, I'll be dropping a bonus scene in my Diva reader group and on my Discord server!!

You can join here to read it when it happens: www.facebook.com/groups/SerenaAkeroydsDivas or here : https://discord.gg/TJp9Pz7MNJ

If after reading Hunter and Rory's story you are interested in finding out how we reached this point, start with Filthy and follow the reading order you can find here:

https://serenaakeroyd.com/my-books/the-five-points-mob-collection-universe/

Much love to you all,
Serena
xoxo

THE CROSSOVER READING ORDER
WITH THE SINNERS & VALENTINIS

FILTHY
FILTHY SINNER
NYX
LINK
FILTHY RICH
SIN
STEEL
FILTHY DARK
CRUZ
MAVERICK
FILTHY SEX
HAWK
FILTHY HOT
STORM
THE DON
THE LADY
FILTHY SECRET
REX
RACHEL
FILTHY KING

REVELATION BOOK ONE
REVELATION BOOK TWO
FILTHY LIES
FILTHY TRUTH

RUSSIAN MAFIA
Adjacent to the universe, but can be read as a standalone
SILENCED

FREE BOOK!

Don't forget to grab your free e-Book!
Secrets & Lies is now free!

Meg's love life was missing a spark until she discovered her need to be dominated. When her fiancé shared the same kink, she thought all her birthdays had come at once, and then she came to learn their relationship was one big fat lie.

Gabe has loved Meg for years, watching her from afar, and always wishing he'd been the one to date her first and not his brother. When he has the chance to have Meg in his bed—even better, tied to it—it's an opportunity he can't refuse.

With disastrous consequences.

Can Gabe make Meg realize she's the one woman he's always wanted? But once secrets and lies have wormed their way into a relationship, is it impossible to establish the firm base of trust needed between lovers, and more importantly, between sub and Sir…?

This story features orgasm control in a BDSM setting.
Secrets & Lies is now free!

CONNECT WITH SERENA

For the latest updates, be sure to check out my website!
But if you'd like to hang out with me and get to know me better, then I'd love to see you in my Diva reader's group where you can find out all the gossip on new releases as and when they happen. You can join here: www.facebook.com/groups/SerenaAkeroydsDivas. Or you can always PM or email me. I love to hear from you guys: serenaakeroyd@gmail.com.

ABOUT THE AUTHOR

I'm a romance novelaholic and I won't touch a book unless I know there's a happy ending. This addiction is what made me craft stories that suit my voracious need for raunchy romance. I love twists and unexpected turns, and my novels all contain sexy guys, dark humor, and hot AF love scenes.

I write MF, menage, and reverse harem (also known as why choose romance,) in both contemporary and paranormal. Some of my stories are darker than others, but I can promise you one thing, you will always get the happy ending your heart needs!

NAMES & CHARACTERS OF INTEREST

MAIN CHARACTERS:

HUNTER LACHLAN -

Grandson of Alberto 'Bert' De Laurentiis, new Don of the Camorra.

AURORA VALENTINI -

Consigliere of the *Cosa Nostra*, twin sister and sibling of Luciu (Luc) Valentini, the Don, and Custanzu (Stan) Valentini, the Capo. Legal surname is Fitzwilliam. (Maternal grandparents' family name.)

SIDE CHARACTERS:

RACHEL LAKER - Best friend of Hunter and Aurora, lawyer to the *Cosa Nostra,* Old Lady of Rex, Prez of the Satan's Sinners' MC.
Jennifer Valentini, née MacNeill - Wife of Luciu Valentini,

friends with Aoife O'Grady (wife of the Irish Mob) and Savannah O'Donnelly (wife of the Irish Mob.)

Lodestar - Lone wolf who found refuge with the Satan's Sinners.

Alberto 'Bert' De Laurentiis - previous Don of the Camorra.

Lauren Valentini - Mother of Luciu, Aurora, and Custanzu. British.

Custantinu Valentini - Father of Luciu, Aurora, and Custanzu. Sicilian.

Currau Valentini - Great-Uncle of Luciu, Aurora, and Custanzu.

Brunu - Capo of the Camorra.

Paulu - Consigliere of the Camorra.

Giovi - Foot soldier of the *Cosa Nostra,* works with Aurora.

Grainne Ledger - High-profile Madam, affiliated with the Five Point Mob (Irish.)

'Fieri' family - Arch-nemesis of the Valentini family. The previous leaders of the *Cosa Nostra* until their eradication. They worked with the New World Sparrows.

ORGANIZATIONS:

CAMORRA - SICILIAN MAFIA on the West Coast. Ruled by the De Laurentiis family.

Not to be confused with the *Cosa Nostra,* who are ruled by the Valentinis and which governs the East Coast.

Five Points' Mob - Irish Mob, allied to the Valentinis, ruled by the O'Donnelly family.

Satan's Sinners' MC - a motorcycle club in West Orange, New Jersey. Allied to the Five Points. Led by Rex, the Prez.

Russian Bratva - Allied to the Five Points and the Valentinis. Led by Maxim Lyanov, the Pakhan.

New World Sparrows - often abbreviated to NWS. The members are known as Sparrows.

One of three global secret societies of criminals hidden in plain sight, mostly known for sex trafficking. Having infiltrated every aspect of US society, from the government to the courts to law enforcement agencies, they've escaped justice for their heinous crimes for decades.

Éire le chéile go deo - often abbreviated to ECD. The members are known as *cheiles*. An Irish organization dedicated to uniting Northern Ireland with the Republic and removing the British from their land.